FANNY HERSELF

"She loved luxury. She smiled and flashed at the handsome old priest opposite her."

—*Page 198*

# FANNY
# HERSELF

## Edna Ferber

*Illustrated by*
J. Henry

*Introduction by*
Lawrence R. Rodgers

University of Illinois Press
Urbana and Chicago

Reprinted from the 1917 edition published by
Frederick A. Stokes Company.

Library of Congress Cataloging-in-Publication Data
Ferber, Edna, 1887–1968.
Fanny herself / Edna Ferber ; illustrated by J. Henry ;
introduction by Lawrence R. Rodgers.
p.   cm.
Includes bibliographical references.
ISBN 0-252-02689-6 (cloth : acid-free paper)
ISBN 0-252-06946-3 (pbk. : acid-free paper)
1. Jewish families—Fiction. 2. Mothers and
daughters—Fiction. 3. Jewish girls—Fiction.
4. Wisconsin—Fiction. I. Title.
PS3511.E46F47    2001
813'.52—dc21    00-51229

TO

WILLIAM ALLEN WHITE

# ILLUSTRATIONS

# INTRODUCTION

## Lawrence R. Rodgers

At thirty-one, Edna Ferber had already published
five books when she finished *Fanny Herself* in February 1917. But her career as a writer was just getting started. She had debuted to modest success six
years earlier with a novel about a Milwaukee news-
paperwoman, *Dawn O'Hara,* and followed with a story collection the next year, *Buttered Side Down.*
Generally kind reviews had christened her a clever
new voice and likened her to O. Henry. Thereafter,
she published three volumes of short stories in
quick succession about Emma McChesney, a dauntless traveling saleswoman and divorced single mother, whose ability to outwit, outsell, and outmaneuver
her male competitors and suitors made her one of
the country's favorite fictional personalities. Emma
counted Theodore Roosevelt among her fans. She
was popular enough to become the subject of a
Broadway show and put Ferber on the path to becoming a major American writer. But despite a loyal
stable of readers, Ferber grew weary of writing
about her saleswoman and decided to retire her to
focus on fresher and deeper artistic challenges.

*Fanny Herself* was the novel that followed. As "the
most serious, extended and dignified of Miss Ferber's
books," in the words of one reviewer, and her only
work of fiction with a strong autobiographical ele-
ment, it represents a fascinating opportunity for
contemporary readers to engage an unfamiliar side

of Ferber.[1] The novel is an intensely personal chronicle of a young girl growing up Jewish in a small midwestern town. It showcases the author's enduring interest in the capacity of strong women to transcend the limitations of their environment and control their own circumstances. Like Ferber, Fanny Brandeis is the daughter of a sadly inept father who years earlier had arrived with his family in Winnebago, Wisconsin, to open a general store called Brandeis' Bazaar. His wife, Molly, learns "the things one should not do in business, from watching Ferdinand Brandeis do them all" (4). His rapid exit early on sets the stage for the novel's real subject, which is to chart Fanny's emotional growth through her relationship with the shrewd, sympathetic Molly. Even after her unexpected death, Molly remains the standard by which Fanny measures her intellectual and spiritual progress. The hardships Fanny faces as she alternately confirms and denies her Jewish identity further complicate her development. Ferber substantiates her connection to Fanny's story in the first of her two real autobiographies, *A Peculiar Treasure,* when she writes that "certainly my mother, idealized, went to make up Molly Brandeis. Bits and pieces of myself crept into the character of Fanny Brandeis. Appleton undoubtedly was the book's background, and little Rabbi Gerechter and Arthur Howe and Father Fitzmaurice and a dozen others formed the real basis of the book's people."[2]

The novel adds an underrepresented perspective on gender, geography, and theme to Jewish-American literature of the period. Published the same year as a very different coming-of-age story, Abraham Cahan's *The Rise of David Levinsky, Fanny Herself,* with its celebration of a Jewish daughter's journey away from her mother and then back to the values she represents, could hardly be more distant from

Cahan's grim naturalistic tale set in New York's Lower East Side. Ferber's and Cahan's novels coincided with the waning days of the largest wave of Jewish immigration to the United States. Between 1880 and 1920, more than 2.5 million Jews arrived in this country. Among these was Jacob Charles Ferber, Edna's father, who at the age of seventeen left the "hard dull routine of farm life" in a small village called Oylso in Hungary to strike out for the "dream world across the ocean."[3] Jacob was one of nearly .5 million immigrants from the Austro-Hungarian empire who joined a much larger group of 1.5 million Jews arriving mostly from the Pale of Settlement in czarist Russia. The causes of this mass exodus were tied into a complex climate of diminishing labor opportunities and increasingly harsh persecution that paralleled a large rise in the Jewish population during a time of an "open-door" immigration policy in the United States. Mirroring Cahan's disappointment with the working and living conditions that greeted the recent arrivals, Mike Gold (nee Irwin Granich) christened these new immigrants "Jews without money" in his semi-autobiographical 1930 novel of the same name. But despite rampant poverty, sweatshops, and unbearable housing, a vibrant American Jewish cultural life, whose dominant language was Yiddish and whose headquarters was New York's Lower East Side, quickly began to thrive. Estimates suggest that about 90 percent of the current Jewish population residing in the United States is made up of the American-born descendants of these migrants.

The numbers and influence of this wave dwarfed the earlier contributions of several hundred thousand Ashkenazic Jews who had begun arriving in the 1820s from German-speaking central Europe. Among these was Ferber's maternal grandfather,

Louis Naumann, who hailed from a distinguished Jewish clan of businessmen. He met and married Ferber's grandmother after arriving in Chicago, where the two of them established a household filled with mirth and culture that, years later, Ferber would remember in the most glowing terms. Her grandfather's path typified that of many mid-nineteenth-century immigrants who had been pushed out of Germany by anti-Jewish legislation and a hostile peasant economy, yet transformed themselves, far more quickly than the following generation, into a generally prosperous class of American merchants, manufacturers, and bankers ably capitalizing on American industrial opportunity and westward expansion.

The cultural and economic chasm separating German-American, middle-class Jews from the struggles of Eastern European immigrants manifested itself in Ferber's rendition of her own family tree. One branch upheld the glamorous lineage of her mother, with all its "vivacity and bounce"; the other supported her father's more humble origins, which seemed so inconsequential to her that she never bothered to ask him to fill in the few spare details she knew.[4] Her father was a quiet, genial shopowner from "good middle-class people of no outstanding quality of mind or achievement."[5] After marrying Ferber's mother, Julia, he opened his first dry-goods store in Kalamazoo, Michigan, where Ferber was born the second of two daughters on August 15, 1885. She writes damningly in her autobiography that "Jacob Ferber was not then, and never was, a shrewd or even fairly capable businessman. He was well meaning and possessed of singularly bad judgment. Like most people of unsound judgment, he called this bad luck."[6] Indeed, he would eventually fail at business in Kalamazoo, Chicago, and Ottumwa, Iowa, before settling in 1897 in the more progressive town of Appleton, the Winnebago of *Fanny Herself.* He died there in 1909 after eye problems and deteriorating health rendered him a nearly helpless invalid.

The work of minding the store was left to Ferber's mother, who, like Molly Brandeis, was easily up to the task, despite a hostile local climate all too willing to cast judgment on a woman who not only ran a business and supported her family but also had the audacity to do it quite well. Betraying the aristocratic roots of her ancestors, Julia Ferber was as strong, energetic, and lively as Jacob was weak. In spite of a complex ambivalence about her mother's strong personality, Julia was Edna's exemplar for her career-making strong female heroines. "Every Ferber heroine," writes Ferber's biographer, "had young Julia's qualities. Almost every Ferber fictional male owned Jacob's deficiencies."[7]

\* \* \*

Edna Ferber is not especially well known today, which might disappoint her contemporary audience as much as it would surprise her. In her time, few American writers were as prolific or well loved. She was a celebrity in an era when writers could genuinely lay claim to that title. Following her death in 1968 after an extended bout with cancer, her front page *New York Times* obituary proclaimed her "among the best-read novelists in the nation, and critics of the nineteen-twenties and thirties did not hesitate to call her the greatest American woman novelist of the day."[8] In all, she would publish thirty-four books, the majority of them best-sellers, as well as produce several dozen plays and film treatments. But even these sizable numbers understate the breadth of her vision. She was, like so many notable American novelists, a writer of region.

But unlike William Faulkner, Flannery O'Connor, or Sarah Orne Jewett, she had little interest either in generating material by turning inward to her own experience or limiting her writing to one locality that she could claim as her own. If Faulkner turned his own "little postage stamp of native soil" in northern Mississippi into a universal examination of all aspects of human experience, Ferber turned the national experience of being an American into a series of local narratives.

Her trademark was an uncanny ability to enter a world far afield from her own, and through a combination of extensive research and inventive storytelling, carve a vivid slice of an American historical place and moment. She claimed the ability to "project myself into any age, environment, condition, situation, character or emotion that interests me deeply. I need never have experienced it or seen it or, to my knowledge, heard or read about it."[9] However vainly stated was her gift, it produced results. Her 1924 Pulitzer Prize–winning *So Big,* which many regard as her best work, portrayed Chicago at the turn of the twentieth century. *Cimarron* turned the era of Oklahoma land runs into a western epic (whose film version won the 1930 Academy Award for best picture). *American Beauty* moved back east to Connecticut. *Come and Get It* featured Michigan and Wisconsin. And *Giant,* her most famous and controversial novel, pared the vast Texas prairies down to a manageable size.

Despite (or perhaps because of) her success as a regionalist, however, Ferber has remained mostly a footnote in contemporary accounts of Jewish-American literature (a hyphenate category that itself is surrounded by unending debate). The basis of her obscurity lies both in how critics have set forth the terms by which Jewish-American writing has con-

ventionally been apprehended and in Ferber's con-
ception of herself as a writer and a Jew. For much
of its history, Jewish-American fiction has been represented as a mostly male enterprise dominated by
narratives that explore, in general terms, "the process of assimilation and its concomitant crisis of
identity."[10] Writers time and again have depicted the
immigrant Jew as a transitional figure, precariously
perched between irreconcilable impulses that pit in-
grained traditions of the "old world" against the se-
ductions of an inviting, though hostile "new world."
This figure is bound by a shared cultural experience
that Irving Howe has labeled "tradition as disconti-
nuity."[11] Recognizing this tradition goes far in helping to comprehend the achievements, say, of Cahan,
Gold, Ludwig Lewisohn, Meyer Levin, Saul Bellow,
and the two Roths, Henry and Philip (while admit-
tedly charting a linear course that overlooks a range
of interesting reversions). It is less serviceable for
comprehending the unabashed patriotism of Mary
Antin, the anarchic spirit of Emma Goldman, or, especially, the literary personality of Ferber, which
reflects hardly a trace of a crisis of identity.[12] As a
tale of a Jew in a non-Jewish world, a speciality of
Bernard Malamud, Philip Roth, and especially Bellow, *Fanny Herself* lets us rethink Jewish connec-
tions to dominant culture from a small-town, female,
adolescent point of view. As a story about knowledge
as the basis for cultural emancipation, its heroine
allows for some interesting parallels with the later
generation of Jewish academics known as the New
York Intellectuals. As the story of a young girl's attempt to come to terms with the powerful legacy of
her mother—a "daughter's drama of disconnection,"
by one critic's label—it has no male precedent at
all.[13]

Apart from *Fanny Herself* and a 1948 play about

refugees called *Bravo!* she wrote with George S. Kaufman (which flopped), Ferber depicted few Jewish characters and tended to eschew Jewish subject matter in favor of more broadly American themes surrounding regional distinctiveness. She herself grew up around only a handful of other Jewish families. She was neither observant—a woman of religious conviction—nor felt any strong attachment to a synagogue or to Jewish holidays (though she recalled devouring pounds of matzos at Passover). She viewed herself more as an American woman who happened to be Jewish than as a Jew who lived in America. Her willingness to celebrate a range of experiences and settings well beyond her own circumstances helped solidify her claim, as the daughter of an immigrant, to native citizenship.[14] She "resolved the tension between her American and her Jewish identities by insisting they were complementary."[15] With her "melting pot" ideal she showed minimal interest in appraising individual cultures on their own terms (in contrast to much contemporary multiculturalism, which tends to celebrate the distinctive qualities of individual groups). She favored, instead, not cultural preservation, but an exploration of the means by which different groups, including Jews, helped create a common American fabric.

Nonetheless, even as Ferber inscribed herself into numerous American locales, she took extraordinary pride in her Jewish identity—as her sympathetic rendering of the many cultural obstacles facing Fanny Brandeis attests. Fanny's Jewishness made her feel "different" (121) and "set apart" (190) in ways that appealed to her need to be special. Fanny's great challenge is coming to learn that being Jewish is an "asset." As a Catholic priest tells her, "You can't take a people and persecute them for thousands of years, hounding them from place to place... without leaving some sort of brand on them—a mark that differentiates.... You've suffered, you Jews, for centuries and centuries, until you're all artists" (121–22). It is hardly surprising that Ferber would underscore the redemptive capacity of suffering, which, Fanny is told, "breeds genius" (190). If her fiction generally lacks a certain Jewish resonance, it was not because she was exempt from the persecution that came from being cast in the role of the "other." In *A Peculiar Treasure,* she recounts facing such brutal anti-Semitism in Ottumwa that she would register its effects the rest of her life. She also describes, with no little satisfaction, several occasions as an adult when she would hear an anti-Semitic remark and confront the speaker by pointedly announcing herself as a Jew. Ferber grapples with similar instances of insensitivity in *Fanny Herself.* Coming to terms with anti-Semitism proved more crucial to forming the basis of both the author's and her character's Jewish identities than any abiding sense of religious devotion. In this way, Ferber foregrounds her and Fanny's Jewish affiliations less through a rich heritage of Jewish "assets" than through representations negatively imposed by non-Jews. Such a focus helps account for Ferber's continued absence from a Jewish-American literary canon that favors writers who exhibit a more pronounced commitment to uncovering the full richness of Jewish life.

In the end, nonetheless, it is the personal connection between the author and her subject that makes *Fanny Herself* unique among Ferber's many books. She was a writer of such vast scope and so invested in showcasing the diverse range of American character that her fiction rarely provided occasions for a glimpse into the person behind the prose. *Fanny Herself* offers that opportunity. It is Ferber's effort to create a character who, though a young woman still coming of age, a Jew, and a midwesterner from a small town, is not alienated from the world she inhabits, but active in establishing the terms of her own identity, full of self-agency. The difference, by these terms, between Edna and Fanny is indistinguishable.

## NOTES

1. "Fanny Herself," *Dial*, Nov. 8, 1917: 463.

2. Edna Ferber, *A Peculiar Treasure* (New York: Doubleday, Doran, 1939), 223. Ferber's second autobiography, *A Kind of Magic* (New York: Doubleday, 1963), was also her final book. Her grandniece, Julie Goldsmith Gilbert, has published the only extended biography to date: *Ferber: A Biography* (Garden City, N.Y.: Doubleday, 1978). For additional biographical sources, see Steven P. Horowitz and Miriam J. Landsman, "Edna Ferber," in *Dictionary of Literary Biography: Twentieth-Century American Jewish Fiction Writers,* ed. Daniel Walden (Detroit: Gale Research, 1984), 28:58–64; and Ellen Serlen Uffen, "Edna Ferber," in *Dictionary of Literary Biography: American Short-Story Writers, 1910–1945,* ed. Bobby Ellen Kimbel (Detroit: Gale Research, 1992), 86:91–98.

3. Ferber, *A Peculiar Treasure,* 15.

4. Ibid., 29.

5. Ibid., 15.

6. Ibid., 18.

7. Gilbert, *Ferber,* 424.

8. *New York Times,* Apr. 17, 1968, 1.

9. Ferber, *A Peculiar Treasure,* 277.

10. Allen Guttman, *The Jewish Writer in America: Assimilation and the Crisis of Identity* (New York: Oxford University Press, 1971), 19.

11. Irving Howe, ed. *Jewish-American Stories* (New York: New American Library, 1977), 13.

12. The need to recognize the contribution of Jewish-American women writers apart from their male counterparts has been a fruitful area of recent literary scholarship. A range of critical works and anthologies have been

instrumental in both charting out the distinct literary topographies of Jewish women and reintroducing out-of-print primary texts to present readers. Among the many recent works are Mary Dearborn's *Pocahontas's Daughters: Gender and Ethnicity in American Culture* (New York: Oxford University Press, 1986); Joyce Antler's *America and I: Short Stories by American Jewish Women Writers* (New York: Beacon, 1991); Diana Lichtenstein's *Writing Their Nations: The Tradition of Nineteenth-Century American Jewish Women Writers* (Bloomington: Indiana University Press, 1992); Ellen Surlen Uffen's *Strands of the Cable: The Place of the Past in Jewish American Women's Writing* (New York: Peter Lang, 1992); Anne Shapiro's edited collection *Jewish American Women Writers* (Westport, Conn.: Greenwood Press, 1994); Janet Handler Burstein's *Writing Mothers, Writing Daughters: Tracing the Maternal in Stories by American Jewish Women* (Urbana: University of Illinois Press, 1996); Ben Siegel and Jay L. Hailio's edited collection *Daughters of Valor: Contemporary Jewish American Women Writers* (Newark: University of Delaware Press, 1997); Sylvia Barack Fishman's *Follow My Footprints: Changing Images of Women in American Jewish Fiction* (Waltham, Mass.: Brandeis University Press, 1992); and Lillian Kremer's *Women's Holocaust Writing: Memory and Imagination* (Lincoln: University of Nebraska Press, 1999).

13. Burstein, *Writing Mothers,* 50.

14. Diana Lichtenstein has persuasively argued that Ferber's non-Jewish, nonreligious women characters often embody the characteristics of a nineteenth-century ideal Jewish woman (*Writing Their Nations,* 129–41). Ferber thus may not have moved as far afield from a representative "Mother of Israel" as her various non-Jewish settings and subjects would otherwise suggest.

15. Burstein, *Writing Mothers,* 51.

# PREFACE

It has become the fashion among novelists to introduce their hero in knee pants, their heroine in pinafore and pigtails. Time was when we were rushed up to a stalwart young man of twenty-four, who was presented as the pivot about whom the plot would revolve. Now we are led, protesting, up to a grubby urchin of five and are invited to watch him through twenty years of intimate minutiæ. In extreme cases we have been obliged to witness his evolution from swaddling clothes to dresses, from dresses to shorts (he is so often English), from shorts to Etons.

The thrill we get for our pains is when, at twenty-five, he jumps over the traces and marries the young lady we met in her cradle on page two. The process is known as a psychological study. A publisher's note on page five hundred and seventy-three assures us that the author is now at work on Volume Two, dealing with the hero's adult life. A third volume will present his pleasing senility. The whole is known as a trilogy. If the chief character is of the other sex we are dragged through her dreamy girlhood, or hoydenish. We see her in her graduation white, in her bridal finery. By the time she is twenty we know her better than her mother ever will, and are infinitely more bored by her.

Yet who would exchange one page in the life of the boy, David Copperfield, for whole chapters dealing with Trotwood Copperfield, the man? Who would relinquish the button-bursting Peggotty for the saintly Agnes? And that other David—he of the sling-shot; one could not love him so well in his psalm-singing days had one not known him first as the gallant, dauntless vanquisher of giants. As for Becky Sharp, with her treachery, her cruelty, her vindicativeness, perhaps we could better have understood and forgiven her had we known her lonely and neglected childhood, with the drunken artist father and her mother, the French opera girl.

With which modest preamble you are asked to be patient with Miss Fanny Brandeis, aged thirteen. Not only must you suffer Fanny, but Fanny's mother as well, without whom there could be no understanding Fanny. For that matter, we shouldn't wonder if Mrs. Brandeis were to turn out the heroine in the end. She is that kind of person.

FANNY HERSELF

# FANNY HERSELF

## CHAPTER ONE

YOU could not have lived a week in Winnebago without being aware of Mrs. Brandeis. In a town of ten thousand, where every one was a personality, from Hen Cody, the drayman, in blue overalls (magically transformed on Sunday mornings into a suave black-broadcloth usher at the Congregational Church), to A. J. Dawes, who owned the waterworks before the city bought it. Mrs. Brandeis was a super-personality. Winnebago did not know it. Winnebago, buying its dolls, and china, and Battenberg braid and tinware and toys of Mrs. Brandeis, of Brandeis' Bazaar, realized vaguely that here was some one different.

When you entered the long, cool, narrow store on Elm Street, Mrs. Brandeis herself came forward to serve you, unless she already was busy with two customers. There were two clerks—three, if you count Aloysius, the boy—but to Mrs. Brandeis belonged the privilege of docketing you first. If you happened in during a moment of business lull, you were likely to find her reading in the left-hand corner at the front of the store, near the shelf where were ranged the dolls' heads, the pens, the pencils, and school supplies.

You saw a sturdy, well-set-up, alert woman, of the kind that looks taller than she really is; a woman with a long, straight, clever nose that indexed her character, as did everything about her, from her crisp, vigorous, abundant hair to the way she came down hard

on her heels in walking. She was what might be called
a very definite person. But first you remarked her
eyes. Will you concede that eyes can be piercing, yet
velvety? Their piercingness was a mental quality, I
suppose, and the velvety softness a physical one. One
could only think, somehow, of wild pansies—the brown
kind. If Winnebago had taken the trouble to glance
at the title of the book she laid face down on the pencil
boxes as you entered, it would have learned that the
book was one of Balzac's, or, perhaps, Zangwill's, or
Zola's. She never could overcome that habit of snatching a chapter here and there during dull moments. She
was too tired to read when night came.

There were many times when the little Wisconsin
town lay broiling in the August sun, or locked in the
January drifts, and the main business street was as
silent as that of a deserted village. But more often
she came forward to you from the rear of the store,
with bits of excelsior clinging to her black sateen apron.
You knew that she had been helping Aloysius as he
unpacked a consignment of chamber sets or a hogshead
of china or glassware, chalking each piece with the
price mark as it was dug from its nest of straw and
paper.

"How do you do!" she would say. "What can I do
for you?" And in that moment she had you listed,
indexed, and filed, were you a farmer woman in a black
shawl and rusty bonnet with a faded rose bobbing
grotesquely atop it, or one of the patronizing East
End set who came to Brandeis' Bazaar because Mrs.
Brandeis' party favors, for one thing, were of a variety that could be got nowhere else this side of Chicago. If, after greeting you, Mrs. Brandeis called,
"Sadie! Stockings!" (supposing stockings were your
quest), you might know that Mrs. Brandeis had
weighed you and found you wanting.

There had always been a store—at least, ever since

Fanny could remember. She often thought how queer it would seem to have to buy pins, or needles, or dishes, or soap, or thread. The store held all these things, and many more. Just to glance at the bewildering display outside gave you promise of the variety within. Winnebago was rather ashamed of that display. It was before the day of repression in decoration, and the two benches in front of the windows overflowed with lamps, and water sets, and brooms, and boilers and tinware and hampers. Once the *Winnebago Courier* had had a sarcastic editorial about what they called the Oriental bazaar (that was after the editor, Lem Davis, had bumped his shin against a toy cart that protruded unduly), but Mrs. Brandeis changed nothing. She knew that the farmer women who stood outside with their husbands on busy Saturdays would not have understood repression in display, but they did understand the tickets that marked the wares in plain figures—this berry set, $1.59; that lamp, $1.23. They talked it over, outside, and drifted away, and came back, and entered, and bought.

She knew when to be old-fashioned, did Mrs. Brandeis, and when to be modern. She had worn the first short walking skirt in Winnebago. It cleared the ground in a day before germs were discovered, when women's skirts trailed and flounced behind them in a cloud of dust. One of her scandalized neighbors (Mrs. Nathan Pereles, it was) had taken her aside to tell her that no decent woman would dress that way.

"Next year," said Mrs. Brandeis, "when you are wearing one, I'll remind you of that." And she did, too. She had worn shirtwaists with a broad "Gibson" shoulder tuck, when other Winnebago women were still encased in linings and bodices. Do not get the impression that she stood for emancipation, or feminism, or any of those advanced things. They had scarcely been touched on in those days. She was just an extraordinarily alert woman, mentally and physically, with a shrewd sense of values. Molly Brandeis never could set a table without forgetting the spoons, or the salt, or something, but she could add a double column of figures in her head as fast as her eye could travel.

There she goes, running off with the story, as we were afraid she would. Not only that, she is using up whole pages of description when she should be giving us dialogue. Prospective readers, running their eyes over a printed page, object to the solid block formation of the descriptive passage. And yet it is fascinating to weave words about her, as it is fascinating to turn a fine diamond this way and that in the sunlight, to catch its prismatic hues. Besides, you want to know— do you not?—how this woman who reads Balzac should be waiting upon you in a little general store in Winnebago, Wisconsin?

In the first place, Ferdinand Brandeis had been a dreamer, and a potential poet, which is bad equipment for success in the business of general merchandise. Four times, since her marriage, Molly Brandeis had packed her household goods, bade her friends good-by, and with her two children, Fanny and Theodore, had followed her husband to pastures new. A heart-breaking business, that, but broadening. She knew nothing of the art of buying and selling at the time of her marriage, but as the years went by she learned unconsciously the things one should not do in business, from watching Ferdinand Brandeis do them all. She even suggested this change and that, but to no avail. Ferdinand Brandeis was a gentle and lovable man at home; a testy, quick-tempered one in business.

That was because he had been miscast from the first, and yet had played one part too long, even though unsuccessfully, ever to learn another. He did not make friends with the genial traveling salesmen who breezed in, slapped him on the back, offered him a cigar, inquired after his health, opened their sample cases and flirted with the girl clerks, all in a breath. He was a man who talked little, listened little, learned little. He had never got the trick of turning his money over quickly—that trick so necessary to the success of the small-town business.

So it was that, in the year preceding Ferdinand Brandeis' death, there came often to the store a certain grim visitor. Herman Walthers, cashier of the First National Bank of Winnebago, was a kindly-enough, shrewd, small-town banker, but to Ferdinand Brandeis and his wife his visits, growing more and more frequent, typified all that was frightful, presaged misery and despair. He would drop in on a bright summer morning, perhaps, with a cheerful greeting. He would stand for a moment at the front of the store, balancing airily from toe to heel, and glancing about from shelf to bin and back again in a large, speculative way. Then he would begin to walk slowly and ruminatively about, his shrewd little German eyes appraising the stock. He would hum a little absent-minded tune as he walked, up one aisle and down the next (there were only two), picking up a piece of china there, turning it over to look at its stamp, holding it up to the light, tapping it a bit with his knuckles, and putting it down carefully before going musically on down the aisle to the water sets, the lamps, the stockings, the hardware, the toys. And so, his hands behind his back, still humming, out the swinging screen door and into the sunshine of Elm Street, leaving gloom and fear behind him.

One year after Molly Brandeis took hold, Herman Walthers' visits ceased, and in two years he used to rise to greet her from his little cubbyhole when she came into the bank.

Which brings us to the plush photograph album. The

plush photograph album is a concrete example of what makes business failure and success. More than that, its brief history presents a complete characterization of Ferdinand and Molly Brandeis.

Ten years before, Ferdinand Brandeis had bought a large bill of Christmas fancy-goods—celluloid toilette sets, leather collar boxes, velvet glove cases. Among the lot was a photograph album in the shape of a huge acorn done in lightning-struck plush. It was a hideous thing, and expensive. It stood on a brass stand, and its leaves were edged in gilt, and its color was a nauseous green and blue, and it was altogether the sort of thing to grace the chill and funereal best room in a Wisconsin farmhouse. Ferdinand Brandeis marked it at six dollars and stood it up for the Christmas trade. That had been ten years before. It was too expensive, or too pretentious, or perhaps even too horrible for the bucolic purse. At any rate, it had been taken out, brushed, dusted, and placed on its stand every holiday season for ten years. On the day after Christmas it was always there, its lightning-struck plush face staring wildly out upon the ravaged fancy-goods counter. It would be packed in its box again and consigned to its long summer's sleep. It had seen three towns, and many changes. The four dollars that Ferdinand Brandeis had invested in it still remained unturned.

One snowy day in November (Ferdinand Brandeis died a fortnight later) Mrs. Brandeis, entering the store, saw two women standing at the fancy-goods counter, laughing in a stifled sort of way. One of them was bowing elaborately to a person unseen. Mrs. Brandeis was puzzled. She watched them for a moment, interested. One of the women was known to her. She came up to them and put her question, bluntly, though her quick wits had already given her a suspicion of the truth.

"What are you bowing to?"

The one who had done the bowing blushed a little, but giggled too, as she said, "I'm greeting my old friend, the plush album. I've seen it here every Christmas for five years."

Ferdinand Brandeis died suddenly a little more than a week later. It was a terrible period, and one that might have prostrated a less resolute and balanced woman. There were long-standing debts, not to speak of the entire stock of holiday goods to be paid for. The day after the funeral Winnebago got a shock. The Brandeis house was besieged by condoling callers. Every member of the little Jewish congregation of Winnebago came, of course, as they had come before the funeral. Those who had not brought cakes, and salads, and meats, and pies, brought them now, as was the invariable custom in time of mourning.

Others of the townspeople called, too; men and women who had known and respected Ferdinand Brandeis. And the shock they got was this: Mrs. Brandeis was out. Any one could have told you that she should have been sitting at home in a darkened room, wearing a black gown, clasping Fanny and Theodore to her, and holding a black-bordered handkerchief at intervals to her reddened eyes. And that is what she really wanted to do, for she had loved her husband, and she respected the conventions. What she did was to put on a white shirtwaist and a black skirt at seven o'clock the morning after the funeral.

The store had been closed the day before. She entered it at seven forty-five, as Aloysius was sweeping out with wet sawdust and a languid broom. The extra force of holiday clerks straggled in, uncertainly, at eight or after, expecting an hour or two of undisciplined gossip. At eight-ten Molly Brandeis walked briskly up to the plush photograph album, whisked

off its six-dollar price mark, and stuck in its place a
neatly printed card bearing these figures: "To-day—
79c!" The plush album went home in a farmer's
wagon that afternoon.

## CHAPTER TWO

RIGHT here there should be something said about Fanny Brandeis. And yet, each time I turn to her I find her mother plucking at my sleeve. There comes to my mind the picture of Mrs. Brandeis turning down Norris Street at quarter to eight every morning, her walk almost a march, so firm and measured it was, her head high, her chin thrust forward a little, as a fighter walks, but not pugnaciously; her short gray skirt clearing the ground, her shoulders almost consciously squared. Other Winnebago women were just tying up their daughters' pigtails for school, or sweeping the front porch, or watering the hanging baskets. Norris Street residents got into the habit of timing themselves by Mrs. Brandeis. When she marched by at seven forty-five they hurried a little with the tying of the hair bow, as they glanced out of the window. When she came by again, a little before twelve, for her hasty dinner, they turned up the fire under the potatoes and stirred the flour thickening for the gravy.

Mrs. Brandeis had soon learned that Fanny and Theodore could manage their own school toilettes, with, perhaps, some speeding up on the part of Mattie, the servant girl. But it needed her keen brown eye to detect corners that Aloysius had neglected to sweep out with wet sawdust, and her presence to make sure that the counter covers were taken off and folded, the outside show dusted and arranged, the windows washed, the whole store shining and ready for business by eight o'clock. So Fanny had even learned to do her own tight, shiny, black, shoulder-length curls, which she

9

tied back with a black bow. They were wet, meek, and tractable curls at eight in the morning. By the time school was out at four they were as wildly unruly as if charged with electric currents—which they really were, when you consider the little dynamo that wore them.

Mrs. Brandeis took a scant half hour to walk the six blocks between the store and the house, to snatch a hurried dinner, and traverse the distance to the store again. It was a program that would have killed a woman less magnificently healthy and determined. She seemed to thrive on it, and she kept her figure and her wit when other women of her age grew dull, and heavy, and ineffectual. On summer days the little town often lay shimmering in the heat, the yellow road glaring in it, the red bricks of the high school reflecting it in waves, the very pine knots in the sidewalks gummy and resinous with heat, and sending up a pungent smell that was of the woods, and yet stifling. She must have felt an almost irresistible temptation to sit for a moment on the cool, shady front porch, with its green-painted flower boxes, its hanging fern baskets and the catalpa tree looking boskily down upon it.

But she never did. She had an almost savage energy and determination. The unpaid debts were ever ahead of her; there were the children to be dressed and sent to school; there was the household to be kept up; there were Theodore's violin lessons that must not be neglected—not after what Professor Bauer had said about him.

You may think that undue stress is being laid upon this driving force in her, upon this business ability. But remember that this was fifteen years or more ago, before women had invaded the world of business by the thousands, to take their place, side by side, salary for salary, with men. Oh, there were plenty of women wage earners in Winnebago, as elsewhere; clerks, stenographers, school teachers, bookkeepers. The paper mills were full of girls, and the canning factory too. But here was a woman gently bred, untrained in business, left widowed with two children at thirty-eight, and worse than penniless—in debt.

And that was not all. As Ferdinand Brandeis' wife she had occupied a certain social position in the little Jewish community of Winnebago. True, they had never been moneyed, while the others of her own faith in the little town were wealthy, and somewhat purse-proud. They had carriages, most of them, with two handsome horses, and their houses were spacious and veranda-encircled, and set in shady lawns. When the Brandeis family came to Winnebago five years before, these people had waited, cautiously, and investigated, and then had called. They were of a type to be found in every small town; prosperous, conservative, constructive citizens, clannish, but not so much so as their city cousins, mingling socially with their Gentile neighbors, living well, spending their money freely, taking a vast pride in the education of their children. But here was Molly Brandeis, a Jewess, setting out to earn her living in business, like a man. It was a thing to stir Congregation Emanu-el to its depths. Jewish women, they would tell you, did not work thus. Their husbands worked for them, or their sons, or their brothers.

"Oh, I don't know," said Mrs. Brandeis, when she heard of it. "I seem to remember a Jewess named Ruth who was left widowed, and who gleaned in the fields for her living, and yet the neighbors didn't talk. For that matter, she seems to be pretty well thought of, to this day."

But there is no denying that she lost caste among her own people. Custom and training are difficult to overcome. But Molly Brandeis was too deep in her own affairs to care. That Christmas season following her husband's death was a ghastly time, and yet a grimly wonderful one, for it applied the acid test to Molly Brandeis and showed her up pure gold.

The first week in January she, with Sadie and Pearl, the two clerks, and Aloysius, the boy, took inventory. It was a terrifying thing, that process of casting up accounts. It showed with such starkness how hideously the Brandeis ledger sagged on the wrong side. The three women and the boy worked with a sort of dogged cheerfulness at it, counting, marking, dusting, washing. They found shelves full of forgotten stock, dust-covered and profitless. They found many articles of what is known as hard stock, akin to the plush album; glass and plated condiment casters for the dining table, in a day when individual salts and separate vinegar cruets were already the thing; lamps with straight wicks when round wicks were in demand.

They scoured shelves, removed the grime of years from boxes, washed whole battalions of chamber sets, bathed piles of plates, and bins of cups and saucers. It was a dirty, back-breaking job, that ruined the finger nails, tried the disposition, and caked the throat with dust. Besides, the store was stove-heated and, near the front door, uncomfortably cold. The women wore little shoulder shawls pinned over their waists, for warmth, and all four, including Aloysius, sniffled for weeks afterward.

That inventory developed a new, grim line around Mrs. Brandeis' mouth, and carved another at the corner of each eye. After it was over she washed her hair, steamed her face over a bowl of hot water, packed two valises, left minute and masterful instructions with Mattie as to the household, and with Sadie and Pearl as to the store, and was off to Chicago on her first buying trip. She took Fanny with her, as ballast. It was a trial at which many men would have quailed. On the shrewdness and judgment of that buying trip depended the future of Brandeis' Bazaar, and Mrs. Brandeis, and Fanny, and Theodore.

Mrs. Brandeis had accompanied her husband on many of his trips to Chicago. She had even gone with him occasionally to the wholesale houses around La Salle Street, and Madison, and Fifth Avenue, but she had never bought a dollar's worth herself. She saw that he bought slowly, cautiously, and without imagination. She made up her mind that she would buy quickly, intuitively. She knew slightly some of the salesmen in the wholesale houses. They had often made presents to her of a vase, a pocketbook, a handkerchief, or some such trifle, which she accepted reluctantly, when at all. She was thankful now for these visits. She found herself remembering many details of them. She made up her mind, with a canny knowingness, that there should be no presents this time, no theater invitations, no lunches or dinners. This was business, she told herself; more than business—it was grim war.

They still tell of that trip, sometimes, when buyers and jobbers and wholesale men get together. Don't imagine that she came to be a woman captain of finance. Don't think that we are to see her at the head of a magnificent business establishment, with buyers and department heads below her, and a private office done up in mahogany, and stenographers and secretaries. No, she was Mrs. Brandeis, of Brandeis' Bazaar, to the end. The bills she bought were ridiculously small, I suppose, and the tricks she turned on that first trip were pitiful, perhaps. But they were magnificent too, in their way. I am even bold enough to think that she might have made business history, that plucky woman, if she had had an earlier start, and if she had not, to the very end, had a pack of unmanageable handicaps yelping at her heels, pulling at her skirts.

It was only a six-hour trip to Chicago. Fanny Brandeis' eyes, big enough at any time, were surely twice their size during the entire journey of two hundred miles or more. They were to have lunch on the train! They were to stop at an hotel! They were to go to the theater! She would have lain back against the red plush seat of the car, in a swoon of joy, if there had not been so much to see in the car itself, and through the car window.

"We'll have something for lunch," said Mrs. Brandeis when they were seated in the dining car, "that we never have at home, shall we?"

"Oh, yes!" replied Fanny in a whisper of excitement. "Something—something queer, and different, and not so very healthy!"

They had oysters (a New Yorker would have sniffed at them), and chicken potpie, and asparagus, and ice cream. If that doesn't prove Mrs. Brandeis was game, I should like to know what could! They stopped at the Windsor-Clifton, because it was quieter and less expensive than the Palmer House, though quite as full of red plush and walnut. Besides, she had stopped at the Palmer House with her husband, and she knew how buyers were likely to be besieged by eager salesmen with cards, and with tempting lines of goods spread knowingly in the various sample-rooms.

Fanny Brandeis was thirteen, and emotional, and incredibly receptive and alive. It is impossible to tell what she learned during that Chicago trip, it was so crowded, so wonderful. She went with her mother to the wholesale houses and heard and saw and, unconsciously, remembered. When she became fatigued with the close air of the dim showrooms, with their endless aisles piled with every sort of ware, she would sit on a chair in some obscure corner, watching those sleek, over-lunched, genial-looking salesmen who were chewing their cigars somewhat wildly when Mrs. Brandeis finished with them. Sometimes she did not accompany her mother, but lay in bed, deliciously, until the middle of the morning, then dressed, and chatted with the obliging Irish chamber maid, and read until her mother came for her at noon.

Everything she did was a delightful adventure; everything she saw had the tang of novelty. Fanny Brandeis was to see much that was beautiful and rare in her full lifetime, but she never again, perhaps, got quite the thrill that those ugly, dim, red-carpeted, gas-lighted hotel corridors gave her, or the grim bedroom, with its walnut furniture and its Nottingham curtains. As for the Chicago streets themselves, with their perilous corners (there were no czars in blue to regulate traffic in those days), older and more sophisticated pedestrians experienced various emotions while negotiating the corner of State and Madison.

That buying trip lasted ten days. It was a racking business, physically and mentally. There were the hours of tramping up one aisle and down the other in the big wholesale lofts. But that brought bodily fatigue only. It was the mental strain that left Mrs. Brandeis spent and limp at the end of the day. Was she buying wisely? Was she over-buying? What did she know about buying, anyway? She would come back to her hotel at six, sometimes so exhausted that the dining-room and dinner were unthinkable. At such times they would have dinner in their room—another delicious adventure for Fanny. She would try to tempt the fagged woman on the bed with bits of this or that from one of the many dishes that dotted the dinner tray. But Molly Brandeis, harrowed in spirit and numbed in body, was too spent to eat.

But that was not always the case. There was that unforgettable night when they went to see Bernhardt the divine. Fanny spent the entire morning following standing before the bedroom mirror, with her hair pulled out in a wild fluff in front, her mother's old marten-fur scarf high and choky around her neck, trying to smile that slow, sad, poignant, tear-compelling smile; but she had to give it up, clever mimic though she was. She only succeeded in looking as though a pin were sticking her somewhere. Besides, Fanny's own smile was a quick, broad, flashing grin, with a generous glint of white teeth in it, and she always forgot about being exquisitely wistful over it until it was too late.

I wonder if the story of the china religious figures will give a wrong impression of Mrs. Brandeis. Perhaps not, if you will only remember this woman's white-lipped determination to wrest a livelihood from the world, for her children and herself. They had been in Chicago a week, and she was buying at Bauder & Peck's. Now, Bauder & Peck, importers, are known the world over. It is doubtful if there is one of you who has not been supplied, indirectly, with some imported bit of china or glassware, with French opera glasses or cunning toys and dolls, from the great New York and Chicago showrooms of that company.

Young Bauder himself was waiting on Mrs. Brandeis, and he was frowning because he hated to sell women. Young Bauder was being broken into the Chicago end of the business, and he was not taking gracefully to the process.

At the end of a long aisle, on an obscure shelf in a dim corner, Molly Brandeis' sharp eyes espied a motley collection of dusty, grimy china figures of the kind one sees on the mantel in the parlor of the small-town Catholic home. Winnebago's population was two-thirds Catholic, German and Irish, and very devout.

Mrs. Brandeis stopped short. "How much for that lot?" She pointed to the shelf. Young Bauder's gaze followed hers, puzzled. The figures were from five inches to a foot high, in crude, effective blues, and gold, and crimson, and white. All the saints were there in assorted sizes, the Pietà, the cradle in the manger. There were probably two hundred or more of the little figures.

"Oh, those!" said young Bauder vaguely. "You don't want that stuff. Now, about that Limoges china. As I said, I can make you a special price on it if you carry it as an open-stock pattern. You'll find——"

"How much for that lot?" repeated Mrs. Brandeis.

"Those are left-over samples, Mrs. Brandeis. Last year's stuff. They're all dirty. I'd forgotten they were there."

"How much for the lot?" said Mrs. Brandeis, pleasantly, for the third time.

"I really don't know. Three hundred, I should say. But——"

"I'll give you two hundred," ventured Mrs. Brandeis, her heart in her mouth and her mouth very firm.

"Oh, come now, Mrs. Brandeis! Bauder & Peck don't do business that way, you know. We'd really rather not sell them at all. The things aren't worth much to us, or to you, for that matter. But three hundred——"

"Two hundred," repeated Mrs. Brandeis, "or I cancel my order, including the Limoges. I want those figures."

And she got them. Which isn't the point of the story. The holy figures were fine examples of foreign workmanship, their colors, beneath the coating of dust, as brilliant and fadeless as those found in the churches of Europe. They reached Winnebago duly, packed in straw and paper, still dusty and shelf-worn. Mrs. Brandeis and Sadie and Pearl sat on up-ended boxes at the rear of the store, in the big barn-like room in which newly arrived goods were unpacked. As Aloysius dived deep into the crate and brought up figure after figure, the three women plunged them into warm and soapy water and proceeded to bathe and scour the entire school of saints, angels, and cherubim. They came out brilliantly fresh and rosy.

All the Irish ingenuity and artistry in Aloysius came to the surface as he dived again and again into the great barrel and brought up the glittering pieces.

"It'll make an elegant window," he gasped from the depths of the hay, his lean, lengthy frame jack-knifed over the edge. "And cheap." His shrewd wit had long ago divined the store's price mark. "If Father Fitzpatrick steps by in the forenoon I'll bet they'll be gone before nighttime to-morrow. You'll be letting me do the trim, Mrs. Brandeis?"

He came back that evening to do it, and he threw his whole soul into it, which, considering his ancestry and temperament, was very high voltage for one small-town store window. He covered the floor of the window with black crêpe paper, and hung it in long folds, like a curtain, against the rear wall. The gilt of the scepters, and halos, and capes showed up dazzlingly against this background. The scarlets, and pinks, and blues, and whites of the robes appeared doubly bright. The whole made a picture that struck and held you by its vividness and contrast.

Father Fitzpatrick, very tall and straight, and handsome, with his iron-gray hair and his cheeks pink as a girl's, did step by next morning on his way to the post-office. It was whispered that in his youth Father Fitzpatrick had been an actor, and that he had deserted the footlights for the altar lights because of a disappointment. The drama's loss was the Church's gain. You should have heard him on Sunday morning, now flaying them, now swaying them! He still had the actor's flexible voice, vibrant, tremulous, or strident, at will. And no amount of fasting or praying had ever dimmed that certain something in his eye—the something which makes the matinée idol.

Not only did he step by now; he turned, came back; stopped before the window. Then he entered.

"Madam," he said to Mrs. Brandeis, "you'll probably save more souls with your window display than I could in a month of hell-fire sermons." He raised his hand. "You have the sanction of the Church." Which was the beginning of a queer friendship between the Roman Catholic priest and the Jewess shopkeeper that lasted as long as Molly Brandeis lived.

By noon it seemed that the entire population of Winnebago had turned devout. The figures, a tremendous bargain, though sold at a high profit, seemed to melt away from the counter that held them.

By three o'clock, "Only one to a customer!" announced Mrs. Brandeis. By the middle of the week the window itself was ravished of its show. By the end of the week there remained only a handful of the duller and less desirable pieces—the minor saints, so to speak. Saturday night Mrs. Brandeis did a little figuring on paper. The lot had cost her two hundred dollars. She had sold for six hundred. Two from six leaves four. Four hundred dollars! She repeated it to herself, quietly. Her mind leaped back to the plush photograph album, then to young Bauder and his cool contempt. And there stole over her that warm, comfortable glow born of reassurance and triumph. Four hundred dollars. Not much in these days of big business. We said, you will remember, that it was a pitiful enough little trick she turned to make it, though an honest one. And—in the face of disapproval—a rather magnificent one too. For it gave to Molly Brandeis that precious quality, self-confidence, out of which is born success.

## CHAPTER THREE

B<sup>Y</sup> spring Mrs. Brandeis had the farmer women coming to her for their threshing dishes and kitchenware, and the West End Culture Club for their whist prizes. She seemed to realize that the days of the general store were numbered, and she set about making hers a novelty store. There was something terrible about the earnestness with which she stuck to business. She was not more than thirty-eight at this time, intelligent, healthy, fun-loving. But she stayed at it all day. She listened and chatted to every one, and learned much. There was about her that human quality that invites confidence.

She made friends by the hundreds, and friends are a business asset. Those blithe, dressy, and smooth-spoken gentlemen known as traveling men used to tell her their troubles, perched on a stool near the stove, and show her the picture of their girl in the back of their watch, and asked her to dinner at the Haley House. She listened to their tale of woe, and advised them; she admired the picture of the girl, and gave some wholesome counsel on the subject of traveling men's lonely wives; but she never went to dinner at the Haley House.

It had not taken these debonair young men long to learn that there was a woman buyer who bought quickly, decisively, and intelligently, and that she always demanded a duplicate slip. Even the most unscrupulous could not stuff an order of hers, and when it came to dating she gave no quarter. Though they wore clothes that were two leaps ahead of the styles

worn by the Winnebago young men—their straw sailors
were likely to be saw-edged when the local edges were
smooth, and their coats were more flaring, or their
trousers wider than the coats and trousers of the Winnebago boys—they were not, for the most part, the
gay dogs that Winnebago's fancy painted them. Many
of them were very lonely married men who missed their
wives and babies, and loathed the cuspidored discomfort of the small-town hotel lobby. They appreciated
Mrs. Brandeis' good-natured sympathy, and gave her
the long end of a deal when they could. It was Sam
Kiser who had begged her to listen to his advice to put
in Battenberg patterns and braid, long before the Battenberg epidemic had become widespread and virulent.

"Now listen to me, Mrs. Brandeis," he begged, almost tearfully. "You're a smart woman. Don't let
this get by you. You know that I know that a salesman would have as much chance to sell you a gold
brick as to sell old John D. Rockefeller a gallon of
oil."

Mrs. Brandeis eyed his samples coldly. "But it looks
so unattractive. And the average person has no imagination. A bolt of white braid and a handful of
buttons—they wouldn't get a mental picture of the
completed piece. Now, embroidery silk——"

"Then give 'em a real picture!" interrupted Sam.
"Work up one of these water-lily pattern table covers.
Use No. 100 braid and the smallest buttons. Stick it
in the window and they'll tear their hair to get patterns."

She did it, taking turns with Pearl and Sadie at
weaving the great, lacy square during dull moments.
When it was finished they placed it in the window,
where it lay like frosted lace, exquisitely graceful and
delicate, with its tracery of curling petals and feathery
fern sprays. Winnebago gazed and was bitten by the
Battenberg bug. It wound itself up in a network of

Battenberg braid, in all the numbers. It bought buttons of every size; it stitched away at Battenberg covers, doilies, bedspreads, blouses, curtains. Battenberg tumbled, foamed, cascaded over Winnebago's front porches all that summer. Listening to Sam Kiser had done it.

She listened to the farmer women too, and to the mill girls, and to the scant and precious pearls that dropped from the lips of the East End society section. There was something about her brown eyes and her straight, sensible nose that reassured them so that few suspected the mischievous in her. For she was mischievous. If she had not been I think she could not have stood the drudgery, and the heartbreaks, and the struggle, and the terrific manual labor.

She used to guy people, gently, and they never guessed it. Mrs. G. Manville Smith, for example, never dreamed of the joy that her patronage brought Molly Brandeis, who waited on her so demurely. Mrs. G. Manville Smith (née Finnegan) scorned the Winnebago shops, and was said to send to Chicago for her hairpins. It was known that her household was run on the most niggardly basis, however, and she short-rationed her two maids outrageously. It was said that she could serve less real food on more real lace doilies than any other housekeeper in Winnebago. Now, Mrs. Brandeis sold Scourine two cents cheaper than the grocery stores, using it as an advertisement to attract housewives, and making no profit on the article itself. Mrs. G. Manville Smith always patronized Brandeis' Bazaar for Scourine alone, and thus represented pure loss. Also she my-good-womaned Mrs. Brandeis. That lady, seeing her enter one day with her comic, undulating gait, double-actioned like a giraffe's, and her plumes that would have shamed a Knight of Pythias, decided to put a stop to these unprofitable visits.

She waited on Mrs. G. Manville Smith, a dangerous gleam in her eye.

"Scourine," spake Mrs. G. Manville Smith.

"How many?"

"A dozen."

"Anything else?"

"No. Send them."

Mrs. Brandeis, scribbling in her sales book, stopped, pencil poised. "We cannot send Scourine unless with a purchase of other goods amounting to a dollar or more."

Mrs. G. Manville Smith's plumes tossed and soared agitatedly. "But my good woman, I don't want anything else!"

"Then you'll have to carry the Scourine."

"Certainly not! I'll send for it."

"The sale closes at five." It was then 4:57.

"I never heard of such a thing! You can't expect me to carry them."

Now, Mrs. G. Manville Smith had been a dining-room girl at the old Haley House before she married George Smith, and long before he made his money in lumber.

"You won't find them so heavy," Molly Brandeis said smoothly.

"I certainly would! Perhaps you would not. You're used to that sort of thing. Rough work, and all that."

Aloysius, doubled up behind the lamps, knew what was coming, from the gleam in his boss's eye.

"There may be something in that," Molly Brandeis returned sweetly. "That's why I thought you might not mind taking them. They're really not much heavier than a laden tray."

"Oh!" exclaimed the outraged Mrs. G. Manville Smith. And took her plumes and her patronage out of Brandeis' Bazaar forever.

That was as malicious as Molly Brandeis ever could be. And it was forgivable malice.

Most families must be described against the background of their homes, but the Brandeis family life was bounded and controlled by the store. Their meals and sleeping hours and amusements were regulated by it. It taught them much, and brought them much, and lost them much. Fanny Brandeis always said she hated it, but it made her wise, and tolerant and, in the end, famous. I don't know what more one could ask of any institution. It brought her in contact with men and women, taught her how to deal with them. After school she used often to run down to the store to see her mother, while Theodore went home to practice. Perched on a high stool in some corner she heard, and saw, and absorbed. It was a great school for the sensitive, highly-organized, dramatic little Jewish girl, for, to paraphrase a well-known stage line, there are just as many kinds of people in Winnebago as there are in Washington.

It was about this time that Fanny Brandeis began to realize, actively, that she was different. Of course, other little Winnebago girls' mothers did not work like a man, in a store. And she and Bella Weinberg were the only two in her room at school who stayed out on the Day of Atonement, and on New Year, and the lesser Jewish holidays. Also, she went to temple on Friday night and Saturday morning, when the other girls she knew went to church on Sunday. These things set her apart in the little Middle Western town; but it was not these that constituted the real difference. She played, and slept, and ate, and studied like the other healthy little animals of her age. The real difference was temperamental, or emotional, or dramatic, or historic, or all four. They would be playing tag, perhaps, in one of the cool, green ravines that were the beauty spots of the little Wisconsin town.

They nestled like exquisite emeralds in the embrace of the hills, those ravines, and Winnebago's civic surge had not yet swept them away in a deluge of old tin cans, ashes, dirt and refuse, to be sold later for building lots. The Indians had camped and hunted in them. The one under the Court Street bridge, near the Catholic church and monastery, was the favorite for play. It lay, a lovely, gracious thing, below the hot little town, all green, and lush, and cool, a tiny stream dimpling through it. The plump Capuchin Fathers, in their coarse brown robes, knotted about the waist with a cord, their bare feet thrust into sandals, would come out and sun themselves on the stone bench at the side of the monastery on the hill, or would potter about the garden. And suddenly Fanny would stop quite still in the midst of her tag game, struck with the beauty of the picture it called from the past.

Little Oriental that she was, she was able to combine the dry text of her history book with the green of the trees, the gray of the church, and the brown of the monk's robes, and evolve a thrilling mental picture therefrom. The tag game and her noisy little companions vanished. She was peopling the place with stealthy Indians. Stealthy, cunning, yet savagely brave. They bore no relation to the abject, contemptible, and rather smelly Oneidas who came to the back door on summer mornings, in calico, and ragged overalls, with baskets of huckleberries on their arm, their pride gone, a broken and conquered people. She saw them wild, free, sovereign, and there were no greasy, berry-peddling Oneidas among them. They were Sioux, and Pottawatomies (that last had the real Indian sound), and Winnebagos, and Menomonees, and Outagamis. She made them taciturn, and beady-eyed, and lithe, and fleet, and every other adjectival thing her imagination and history book could supply. The fat and placid Capuchin Fathers on the hill became Jes-

uits, sinister, silent, powerful, with France and the
Church of Rome behind them. From the shelter of that
big oak would step Nicolet, the brave, first among
Wisconsin explorers, and last to receive the credit for
his hardihood. Jean Nicolet! She loved the sound of
it. And with him was La Salle, straight, and slim, and
elegant, and surely wearing ruffles and plumes and
sword even in a canoe. And Tonty, his Italian friend
and fellow adventurer—Tonty of the satins and vel-
vets, graceful, tactful, poised, a shadowy figure; his
menacing iron hand, so feared by the ignorant savages,
encased always in a glove. Surely a perfumed g——
Slap! A rude shove that jerked her head back sharply
and sent her forward, stumbling, and jarred her like
a fall.

"Ya-a-a! Tag! You're it! Fanny's it!"

Indians, priests, cavaliers, *coureurs de bois*, all vanished. Fanny would stand a moment, blinking stu-
pidly. The next moment she was running as fleetly as
the best of the boys in savage pursuit of one of her
companions in the tag game.

She was a strange mixture of tomboy and book-
worm, which was a mercifully kind arrangement for
both body and mind. The spiritual side of her was
groping and staggering and feeling its way about as
does that of any little girl whose mind is exceptionally
active, and whose mother is unusually busy. It was on
the Day of Atonement, known in the Hebrew as Yom
Kippur, in the year following her father's death that
that side of her performed a rather interesting hand-
spring.

Fanny Brandeis had never been allowed to fast on
this, the greatest and most solemn of Jewish holy days.
Molly Brandeis' modern side refused to countenance
the practice of withholding food from any child for
twenty-four hours. So it was in the face of disapproval that Fanny, making deep inroads into the steak

and fried sweet potatoes at supper on the eve of the
Day of Atonement, announced her intention of fasting
from that meal to supper on the following evening.
She had just passed her plate for a third helping of
potatoes. Theodore, one lap behind her in the race,
had entered his objection.

"Well, for the land's sakes!" he protested. "I guess
you're not the only one who likes sweet potatoes."

Fanny applied a generous dab of butter to an already buttery morsel, and chewed it with an air of
conscious virtue.

"I've got to eat a lot. This is the last bite I'll have
until to-morrow night."

"What's that?" exclaimed Mrs. Brandeis, sharply.

"Yes, it is!" hooted Theodore.

Fanny went on conscientiously eating as she explained.

"Bella Weinberg and I are going to fast all day.
We just want to see if we can."

"Betcha can't," Theodore said.

Mrs. Brandeis regarded her small daughter with a
thoughtful gaze. "But that isn't the object in fasting, Fanny—just to see if you can. If you're going
to think of food all through the Yom Kippur ser-
vices——"

"I sha'n't?" protested Fanny passionately. "Theodore would, but I won't."

"Wouldn't any such thing," denied Theodore. "But
if I'm going to play a violin solo during the memorial
service I guess I've got to eat my regular meals."

Theodore sometimes played at temple, on special
occasions. The little congregation, listening to the
throbbing rise and fall of this fifteen-year-old boy's
violin playing, realized, vaguely, that here was something disturbingly, harrowingly beautiful. They did
not know that they were listening to genius.

Molly Brandeis, in her second best dress, walked to

temple Yom Kippur eve, her son at her right side, her daughter at her left. She had made up her mind that she would not let this next day, with its poignantly beautiful service, move her too deeply. It was the first since her husband's death, and Rabbi Thalmann rather prided himself on his rendition of the memorial service that came at three in the afternoon.

A man of learning, of sweetness, and of gentle wit was Rabbi Thalmann, and unappreciated by his congregation. He stuck to the Scriptures for his texts, finding Moses a greater leader than Roosevelt, and the miracle of the Burning Bush more wonderful than the marvels of twentieth-century wizardy in electricity. A little man, Rabbi Thalmann, with hands and feet as small and delicate as those of a woman. Fanny found him fascinating to look on, in his rabbinical black broadcloth and his two pairs of glasses perched, in reading, upon his small hooked nose. He stood very straight in the pulpit, but on the street you saw that his back was bent just the least bit in the world—or perhaps it was only his student stoop, as he walked along with his eyes on the ground, smoking those slender, dapper, pale brown cigars that looked as if they had been expressly cut and rolled to fit him.

The evening service was at seven. The congregation, rustling in silks, was approaching the little temple from all directions. Inside, there was a low-toned buzz of conversation. The Brandeis' seat was well toward the rear, as befitted a less prosperous member of the rich little congregation. This enabled them to get a complete picture of the room in its holiday splendor. Fanny drank it in eagerly, her dark eyes soft and luminous. The bare, yellow-varnished wooden pews glowed with the reflection from the chandeliers. The seven-branched candlesticks on either side of the pulpit were entwined with smilax. The red plush curtain that hung in front of the Ark on ordinary days, and the red plush pulpit cover too, were replaced by gleaming white satin edged with gold fringe and finished at the corners with heavy gold tassels. How the rich white satin glistened in the light of the electric candles! Fanny Brandeis loved the lights, and the gleam, and the music, so majestic, and solemn, and the sight of the little rabbi, sitting so straight and serious in his high-backed chair, or standing to read from the great Bible. There came to this emotional little Jewess a thrill that was not born of religious fervor at all, I am afraid.

The sheer drama of the thing got her. In fact, the thing she had set herself to do to-day had in it very little of religion. Mrs. Brandeis had been right about that. It was a test of endurance, as planned. Fanny had never fasted in all her healthy life. She would come home from school to eat formidable stacks of bread and butter, enhanced by brown sugar or grape jelly, and topped off with three or four apples from the barrel in the cellar. Two hours later she would attack a supper of fried potatoes, and liver, and tea, and peach preserve, and more stacks of bread and butter. Then there were the cherry trees in the back yard, and the berry bushes, not to speak of sundry bags of small, hard candies of the jelly-bean variety, fitted for quick and secret munching during school. She liked good things to eat, this sturdy little girl, as did her friend, that blonde and creamy person, Bella Weinberg.

The two girls exchanged meaningful glances during the evening service. The Weinbergs, as befitted their station, sat in the third row at the right, and Bella had to turn around to convey her silent messages to Fanny. The evening service was brief, even to the sermon. Rabbi Thalmann and his congregation would need their strength for to-morrow's trial.

The Brandeises walked home through the soft September night, and the children had to use all their Yom Kippur dignity to keep from scuffling through the piled-up drifts of crackling autumn leaves. Theodore went to the cellar and got an apple, which he ate with what Fanny considered an unnecessary amount of scrunching. It was a firm, juicy apple, and it gave forth a cracking sound when his teeth met in its white meat. Fanny, after regarding him with gloomy superiority, went to bed.

She had willed to sleep late, for gastronomic reasons, but the mental command disobeyed itself, and she woke early, with a heavy feeling. Early as it was, Molly Brandeis had tiptoed in still earlier to look at her strange little daughter. She sometimes did that on Saturday mornings when she left early for the store and Fanny slept late. This morning Fanny's black hair was spread over the pillow as she lay on her back, one arm outflung, the other at her breast. She made a rather startlingly black and white and scarlet picture as she lay there asleep. Fanny did things very much in that way, too, with broad, vivid, unmistakable splashes of color. Mrs. Brandeis, looking at the black-haired, red-lipped child sleeping there, wondered just how much determination lay back of the broad white brow. She had said little to Fanny about this feat of fasting, and she told herself that she disapproved of it. But in her heart she wanted the girl to see it through, once attempted.

Fanny awoke at half past seven, and her nostrils dilated to that most exquisite, tantalizing and fragrant of smells—the aroma of simmering coffee. It permeated the house. It tickled the senses. It carried with it visions of hot, brown breakfast rolls, and eggs, and butter. Fanny loved her breakfast. She turned over now, and decided to go to sleep again. But she could not. She got up and dressed slowly and carefully. There was no one to hurry her this morning with the call from the foot of the stairs of, "Fanny! Your egg'll get cold!"

She put on clean, crisp underwear, and did her hair expertly. She slipped an all-enveloping pinafore over her head, that the new silk dress might not be crushed before church time. She thought that Theodore would surely have finished his breakfast by this time. But when she came down-stairs he was at the table. Not only that, he had just begun his breakfast. An egg, all golden, and white, and crisply brown at the frilly edges, lay on his plate. Theodore always ate his egg in a mathematical sort of way. He swallowed the white hastily first, because he disliked it, and Mrs. Brandeis insisted that he eat it. Then he would brood a moment over the yolk that lay, unmarred and complete, like an amber jewel in the center of his plate. Then he would suddenly plunge his fork into the very heart of the jewel, and it would flow over his plate, mingling with the butter, and he would catch it deftly with little mops of warm, crisp, buttery roll.

Fanny passed the breakfast table just as Theodore plunged his fork into the egg yolk. She caught her breath sharply, and closed her eyes. Then she turned and fled to the front porch and breathed deeply and windily of the heady September Wisconsin morning air. As she stood there, with her stiff, short black curls still damp and glistening, in her best shoes and stockings, with the all-enveloping apron covering her sturdy little figure, the light of struggle and renunciation in her face, she typified something at once fine and earthy.

But the real struggle was to come later. They went to temple at ten, Theodore with his beloved violin tucked carefully under his arm. Bella Weinberg was waiting at the steps.

"Did you?" she asked eagerly.

"Of course not," replied Fanny disdainfully. "Do

you think I'd eat old breakfast when I said I was going to fast all day?" Then, with sudden suspicion, "Did you?"

"No!" stoutly.

And they entered, and took their seats. It was fascinating to watch the other members of the congregation come in, the women rustling, the men subdued in the unaccustomed dignity of black on a week day. One glance at the yellow pews was like reading a complete social and financial register. The seating arrangement of the temple was the Almanach de Gotha of Congregation Emanu-el. Old Ben Reitman, patriarch among the Jewish settlers of Winnebago, who had come over an immigrant youth, and who now owned hundreds of rich farm acres, besides houses, mills and banks, kinged it from the front seat of the center section. He was a magnificent old man, with a ruddy face, and a fine head with a shock of heavy iron-gray hair, keen eyes, undimmed by years, and a startling and unexpected dimple in one cheek that gave him a mischievous and boyish look.

Behind this dignitary sat his sons, and their wives, and his daughters and their husbands, and their children, and so on, back to the Brandeis pew, third from the last, behind which sat only a few obscure families branded as Russians, as only the German-born Jew can brand those whose misfortune it is to be born in that region known as hinter-Berlin.

The morning flew by, with its music, its responses, its sermon in German, full of four- and five-syllable German words like *Barmherzigkeit* and *Eigentümlichkeit*. All during the sermon Fanny sat and dreamed and watched the shadow on the window of the pine tree that stood close to the temple, and was vastly amused at the jaundiced look that the square of yellow window glass cast upon the face of the vain and overdressed Mrs. Nathan Pereles. From time to time Bella would turn to bestow upon her a look intended to convey intense suffering and a resolute though dying condition. Fanny stonily ignored these mute messages. They offended something in her, though she could not tell what.

At the noon intermission she did not go home to the tempting dinner smells, but wandered off through the little city park and down to the river, where she sat on the bank and felt very virtuous, and spiritual, and hollow. She was back in her seat when the afternoon service was begun. Some of the more devout members had remained to pray all through the midday. The congregation came straggling in by twos and threes. Many of the women had exchanged the severely corseted discomfort of the morning's splendor for the comparative ease of second-best silks. Mrs. Brandeis, absent from her business throughout this holy day, came hurrying in at two, to look with a rather anxious eye upon her pale and resolute little daughter.

The memorial service was to begin shortly after three, and lasted almost two hours. At quarter to three Bella slipped out through the side aisle, beckoning mysteriously and alluringly to Fanny as she went. Fanny looked at her mother.

"Run along," said Mrs. Brandeis. "The air will be good for you. Come back before the memorial service begins."

Fanny and Bella met, giggling, in the vestibule.

"Come on over to my house for a minute," Bella suggested. "I want to show you something." The Weinberg house, a great, comfortable, well-built home, with encircling veranda, and a well-cared-for lawn, was just a scant block away. They skipped across the street, down the block, and in at the back door. The big sunny kitchen was deserted. The house seemed very quiet and hushed. Over it hung the delicious fragrance of freshly-baked pastry. Bella, a rather baleful look in her eyes, led the way to the butler's pantry that was as large as the average kitchen. And there, ranged on platters, and baking boards, and on snowy-white napkins, was that which made Tantalus's feast seem a dry and barren snack. The Weinberg's had baked.

It is the custom in the household of Atonement Day fasters of the old school to begin the evening meal, after the twenty-four hours of abstainment, with coffee and freshly-baked coffee cake of every variety. It was a lead-pipe blow at one's digestion, but delicious beyond imagining. Bella's mother was a famous cook, and her two maids followed in the ways of their mistress. There were to be sisters and brothers and out-of-town relations as guests at the evening meal, and Mrs. Weinberg had outdone herself.

"Oh!" exclaimed Fanny in a sort of agony and delight.

"Take some," said Bella, the temptress.

The pantry was fragrant as a garden with spices, and fruit scents, and the melting, delectable perfume of brown, freshly-baked dough, sugar-coated. There was one giant platter devoted wholly to round, plump cakes, with puffy edges, in the center of each a sunken pool that was all plum, bearing on its bosom a snowy sifting of powdered sugar. There were others whose centers were apricot, pure molten gold in the sunlight. There were speckled expanses of cheese *kuchen,* the golden-brown surface showing rich cracks through which one caught glimpses of the lemon-yellow cheese beneath—cottage cheese that had been beaten up with eggs, and spices, and sugar, and lemon. Flaky crust rose, jaggedly, above this plateau. There were cakes with jelly, and cinnamon *kuchen,* and cunning cakes with almond slices nestling side by side. And there was freshly-baked bread—twisted loaf, with poppy seed freckling its braid, and its sides glistening with the

butter that had been liberally swabbed on it before it
had been thrust into the oven.

Fanny Brandeis gazed, hypnotized. As she gazed
Bella selected a plum tart and bit into it—bit generously, so that her white little teeth met in the very middle of the oozing red-brown juice and one heard a little
squirt as they closed on the luscious fruit. At the
sound Fanny quivered all through her plump and
starved little body.

"Have one," said Bella generously. "Go on. Nobody'll ever know. Anyway, we've fasted long enough
for our age. I could fast till supper time if I wanted
to, but I don't want to." She swallowed the last morsel of the plum tart, and selected another—apricot,
this time, and opened her moist red lips. But just
before she bit into it (the Inquisition could have used
Bella's talents) she selected its counterpart and held it
out to Fanny. Fanny shook her head slightly. Her
hand came up involuntarily. Her eyes were fastened
on Bella's face.

"Go on," urged Bella. "Take it. They're grand!
M-m-m-m!" The first bite of apricot vanished between her rows of sharp white teeth. Fanny shut her
eyes as if in pain. She was fighting the great fight of
her life. She was to meet other temptations, and perhaps more glittering ones, in her lifetime, but to her
dying day she never forgot that first battle between the
flesh and the spirit, there in the sugar-scented pantry
—and the spirit won. As Bella's lips closed upon the
second bite of apricot tart, the while her eye roved
over the almond cakes and her hand still held the sweet
out to Fanny, that young lady turned sharply, like a
soldier, and marched blindly out of the house, down the
back steps, across the street, and so into the temple.

The evening lights had just been turned on. The
little congregation, relaxed, weary, weak from hunger,
many of them, sat rapt and still except at those times

when the prayer book demanded spoken responses. The voice of the little rabbi, rather weak now, had in it a timbre that made it startlingly sweet and clear and resonant. Fanny slid very quietly into the seat beside Mrs. Brandeis, and slipped her moist and cold little hand into her mother's warm, work-roughened palm. The mother's brown eyes, very bright with unshed tears, left their perusal of the prayer book to dwell upon the white little face that was smiling rather wanly up at her. The pages of the prayer book lay two-thirds or more to the left. Just as Fanny remarked this, there was a little moment of hush in the march of the day's long service. The memorial hour had begun.

Little Doctor Thalmann cleared his throat. The congregation stirred a bit, changed its cramped position. Bella, the guilty, came stealing in, a pink-and-gold picture of angelic virtue. Fanny, looking at her, felt very aloof, and clean, and remote.

Molly Brandeis seemed to sense what had happened. "But you didn't, did you?" she whispered softly.

Fanny shook her head.

Rabbi Thalmann was seated in his great carved chair. His eyes were closed. The wheezy little organ in the choir loft at the rear of the temple began the opening bars of Schumann's Traümerei. And then, above the cracked voice of the organ, rose the clear, poignant wail of a violin. Theodore Brandeis had begun to play. You know the playing of the average boy of fifteen—that nerve-destroying, uninspired scraping. There was nothing of this in the sounds that this boy called forth from the little wooden box and the stick with its taut lines of catgut. Whatever it was—the length of the thin, sensitive fingers, the turn of the wrist, the articulation of the forearm, the something in the brain, or all these combined—Theodore Brandeis possessed that which makes for greatness. You realized that as he crouched over his violin to get his cello tones. As he played to-day the little congregation sat very still, and each was thinking of his ambitions and his failures; of the lover lost, of the duty left undone, of the hope deferred; of the wrong that was never righted; of the lost one whose memory spells remorse. It felt the salt taste on its lips. It put up a furtive, shamed hand to dab at its cheeks, and saw that the one who sat in the pew just ahead was doing likewise. This is what happened when this boy of fifteen wedded his bow to his violin. And he who makes us feel all this has that indefinable, magic, glorious thing known as Genius.

When it was over, there swept through the room that sigh following tension relieved. Rabbi Thalmann passed a hand over his tired eyes, like one returning from a far mental journey; then rose, and came forward to the pulpit. He began, in Hebrew, the opening words of the memorial service, and so on to the prayers in English, with their words of infinite humility and wisdom.

"Thou hast implanted in us the capacity for sin, but not sin itself!"

Fanny stirred. She had learned that a brief half hour ago. The service marched on, a moving and harrowing thing. The amens rolled out with a new fervor from the listeners. There seemed nothing comic now in the way old Ben Reitman, with his slower eyes, always came out five words behind the rest who tumbled upon the responses and scurried briskly through them, so that his fine old voice, somewhat hoarse and quavering now, rolled out its "Amen!" in solitary majesty. They came to that gem of humility, the mourners' prayer; the ancient and ever-solemn Kaddish prayer. There is nothing in the written language that, for sheer drama and magnificence, can equal it as it is chanted in the Hebrew.

As Rabbi Thalmann began to intone it in its monot-
onous repetition of praise, there arose certain black-
robed figures from their places and stood with heads
bowed over their prayer books. These were members
of the congregation from whom death had taken a toll
during the past year. Fanny rose with her mother and
Theodore, who had left the choir loft to join them.
The little wheezy organ played very softly. The black-
robed figures swayed. Here and there a half-stifled
sob rose, and was crushed. Fanny felt a hot haze that
blurred her vision. She winked it away, and another
burned in its place. Her shoulders shook with a sob.
She felt her mother's hand close over her own that held
one side of the book. The prayer, that was not of
mourning but of praise, ended with a final crescendo
from the organ. The silent black-robed figures were
seated.

Over the little, spent congregation hung a glorious
atmosphere of detachment. These Jews, listening to
the words that had come from the lips of the prophets
in Israel, had been, on this day, thrown back thousands
of years, to the time when the destruction of the temple was as real as the shattered spires and dome of the
cathedral at Rheims. Old Ben Reitman, faint with
fasting, was far removed from his everyday thoughts
of his horses, his lumber mills, his farms, his mortgages.
Even Mrs. Nathan Pereles, in her black satin and
bugles and jets, her cold, hard face usually unlighted
by sympathy or love, seemed to feel something of this
emotional wave. Fanny Brandeis was shaken by it.
Her head ached (that was hunger) and her hands were
icy. The little Russian girl in the seat just behind them
had ceased to wriggle and squirm, and slept against her
mother's side. Rabbi Thalmann, there on the platform, seemed somehow very far away and vague. The
scent of clove apples and ammonia salts filled the air.
The atmosphere seemed strangely wavering and lu-

minous. The white satin of the Ark curtain gleamed and shifted.

The long service swept on to its close. Suddenly organ and choir burst into a pæon. Little Doctor Thalmann raised his arms. The congregation swept to its feet with a mighty surge. Fanny rose with them, her face very white in its frame of black curls, her eyes luminous. She raised her face for the words of the ancient benediction that rolled, in its simplicity and grandeur, from the lips of the rabbi:

"May the blessing of the Lord our God rest upon you all. God bless thee and keep thee. May God cause His countenance to shine upon thee and be gracious unto thee. May God lift up His countenance unto thee, and grant thee peace."

The Day of Atonement had come to an end. It was a very quiet, subdued and spent little flock that dispersed to their homes. Fanny walked out with scarcely a thought of Bella. She felt, vaguely, that she and this school friend were formed of different stuff. She knew that the bond between them had been the grubby, physical one of childhood, and that they never would come together in the finer relation of the spirit, though she could not have put this new knowledge into words.

Molly Brandeis put a hand on her daughter's shoulder.

"Tired, Fanchen?"

"A little."

"Bet you're hungry!" from Theodore.

"I was, but I'm not now."

"M-m-m—wait! Noodle soup. And chicken!"

She had intended to tell of the trial in the Weinberg's pantry. But now something within her—something fine, born of this day—kept her from it. But Molly Brandeis, to whom two and two often made five, guessed something of what had happened. She had felt a great surge of pride, had Molly Brandeis, when her

son had swayed the congregation with the magic of
his music. She had kissed him good night with infinite
tenderness and love. But she came into her daughter's
tiny room after Fanny had gone to bed, and leaned
over, and put a cool hand on the hot forehead.

"Do you feel all right, my darling?"

"Umhmph," replied Fanny drowsily.

"Fanchen, doesn't it make you feel happy and clean
to know that you were able to do the thing you started
out to do?"

"Umhmph."

"Only," Molly Brandeis was thinking aloud now,
quite forgetting that she was talking to a very little
girl, "only, life seems to take such special delight in
offering temptation to those who are able to withstand
it. I don't know why that's true, but it is. I hope—oh,
my little girl, my baby—I hope——"

But Fanny never knew whether her mother finished
that sentence or not. She remembered waiting for
the end of it, to learn what it was her mother hoped.
And she had felt a sudden, scalding drop on her hand
where her mother bent over her. And the next thing
she knew it was morning, with mellow September sunshine.

# CHAPTER FOUR

I T was the week following this feat of fasting that two things happened to Fanny Brandeis—two seemingly unimportant and childish things—that were to affect the whole tenor of her life. It is pleasant to predict thus. It gives a certain weight to a story and a sense of inevitableness. It should insure, too, the readers's support to the point, at least, where the prediction is fulfilled. Sometimes a careless author loses sight altogether of his promise, and then the tricked reader is likely to go on to the very final page, teased by the expectation that that which was hinted at will be revealed.

Fanny Brandeis had a way of going to the public library on Saturday afternoons (with a bag of very sticky peanut candy in her pocket, the little sensualist!) and there, huddled in a chair, dreamily and almost automatically munching peanut brittle, her cheeks growing redder and redder in the close air of the ill-ventilated room, she would read, and read, and read. There was no one to censor her reading, so she read promiscuously, wading gloriously through trash and classic and historical and hysterical alike, and finding something of interest in them all.

She read the sprightly "Duchess" novels, where mad offers of marriage were always made in flower-scented conservatories; she read Dickens, and Thelma, and old bound *Cosmopolitans*, and Zola, and de Maupassant, and the "Wide, Wide World," and "Hans Brinker, or The Silver Skates," and "Jane Eyre." All of which are merely mentioned as examples of her

41

catholicism in literature.  As she read she was unaware of the giggling boys and girls who came in noisily, and made dates, and were coldly frowned on by the austere Miss Perkins, the librarian.  She would read until the fading light would remind her that the short fall or winter day was drawing to a close.

She would come, shivering a little after the fetid atmosphere of the overheated library, into the crisp, cold snap of the astringent Wisconsin air.  Sometimes she would stop at the store for her mother.  Sometimes she would run home alone through the twilight, her heels scrunching the snow, her whole being filled with a vague and unchildish sadness and disquiet as she faced the tender rose, and orange, and mauve, and pale lemon of the winter sunset.  There were times when her very heart ached with the beauty of that color-flooded sky; there were times, later, when it ached in much the same way at the look in the eyes of a pushcart peddler; there were times when it ached, seemingly, for no reason at all—as is sometimes the case when one is a little Jew girl, with whole centuries of suffering behind one.

On this day she had taken a book from the library. Miss Perkins, at sight of the title, had glared disapprovingly, and had hesitated a moment before stamping the card.

"Is this for yourself?" she had asked.

"Yes'm."

"It isn't a book for little girls," snapped Miss Perkins.

"I've read half of it already," Fanny informed her sweetly.  And went out with it under her arm.  It was Zola's "The Ladies' Paradise" (*Au Bonheur des Dames*).  The story of the shop girl, and the crushing of the little dealer by the great and moneyed company had thrilled and fascinated her.

Her mind was full of it as she turned the corner on

Norris Street and ran full-tilt, into a yowling, taunting, torturing little pack of boys. They were gathered in close formation about some object which they were teasing, and knocking about in the mud, and otherwise abusing with the savagery of their years. Fanny, the fiery, stopped short. She pushed into the ring. The object of their efforts was a weak-kneed and hollow-chested little boy who could not fight because he was cowardly as well as weak, and his name (oh, pity!) was Clarence—Clarence Heyl. There are few things that a mischievous group of small boys cannot do with a name like Clarence. They whined it, they catcalled it, they shrieked it in falsetto imitation of Clarence's mother. He was a wide-mouthed, sallow and pindling little boy, whose pipe-stemmed legs looked all the thinner for being contrasted with his feet, which were long and narrow. At that time he wore spectacles, too, to correct a muscular weakness, so that his one good feature—great soft, liquid eyes—passed unnoticed. He was the kind of little boy whose mother insists on dressing him in cloth-top, buttoned, patent-leather shoes for school. His blue serge suit was never patched or shiny. His stockings were virgin at the knee. He wore an overcoat on cool autumn days. Fanny despised and pitied him. We ask you not to, because in this puny, shy and ugly little boy of fifteen you behold Our Hero.

He staggered to his feet now, as Fanny came up. His school reefer was mud-bespattered. His stockings were torn. His cap was gone and his hair was wild. There was a cut or scratch on one cheek, from which the blood flowed.

"I'll tell my mother on you!" he screamed impotently, and shook with rage and terror. "You'll see, you will! You let me alone, now!"

Fanny felt a sick sensation at the pit of her stomach, and in her throat. Then:

"He'll tell his ma!" sneered the boys in chorus. "Oh, mamma!" And called him the Name. And at that a she wildcat broke loose among them. She pounced on them without warning, a little fury of blazing eyes and flying hair, and white teeth showing in a snarl. If she had fought fair, or if she had not taken them so by surprise, she would have been powerless among them. But she had sprung at them with the suddenness of rage. She kicked, and scratched, and bit, and clawed and spat. She seemed not to feel the defensive blows that were showered upon her in turn. Her own hard little fists were now doubled for a thump or opened, like a claw, for scratching.

"Go on home!" she yelled to Clarence, even while she fought. And Clarence, gathering up his tattered school books, went, and stood not on the order of his going. Whereupon Fanny darted nimbly to one side, out of the way of boyish brown fists. In that moment she was transformed from a raging fury into a very meek and trembling little girl, who looked shyly and pleadingly out from a tangle of curls. The boys were for rushing at her again.

"Cowardy-cats! Five of you fighting one girl," cried Fanny, her lower lip trembling ever so little. "Come on! Hit me! Afraid to fight anything but girls! Cowardy-cats!" A tear, pearly, pathetic, coursed down her cheek.

The drive was broken. Five sullen little boys stood and glared at her, impotently.

"You hit us first," declared one boy. "What business d' you have scratching around like that, I'd like to know! You old scratch cat!"

"He's sickly," said Fanny. "He can't fight. There's something the matter with his lungs, or something, and they're going to make him quit school. Besides, he's a billion times better than any of you, anyway."

At once, "Fanny's stuck on Clar-ence! Fanny's stuck on Clar-ence!"

Fanny picked up her somewhat battered Zola from where it had flown at her first onslaught. "It's a lie!" she shouted. And fled, followed by the hateful chant.

She came in at the back door, trying to look casual. But Mattie's keen eye detected the marks of battle, even while her knife turned the frying potatoes.

"Fanny Brandeis! Look at your sweater! And your hair!"

Fanny glanced down at the torn pocket dangling untidily. "Oh, that!" she said airily. And, passing the kitchen table, deftly filched a slice of cold veal from the platter, and mounted the back stairs to her room. It was a hungry business, this fighting. When Mrs. Brandeis came in at six her small daughter was demurely reading. At supper time Mrs. Brandeis looked up at her daughter with a sharp exclamation.

"Fanny! There's a scratch on your cheek from your eye to your chin."

Fanny put up her hand. "Is there?"

"Why, you must have felt it. How did you get it?"

Fanny said nothing. "I'll bet she was fighting," said Theodore with the intuitive knowledge that one child has of another's ways.

"Fanny!" The keen brown eyes were upon her.

"Some boys were picking on Clarence Heyl, and it made me mad. They called him names."

"What names?"

"Oh, names."

"Fanny dear, if you're going to fight every time you hear that name——"

Fanny thought of the torn sweater, the battered Zola, the scratched cheek. "It is pretty expensive," she said reflectively.

After supper she settled down at once to her book. Theodore would labor over his algebra after the dining-room table was cleared. He stuck his cap on his head now, and slammed out of the door for a half-hour's play under the corner arc-light. Fanny rarely brought books from school, and yet she seemed to get on rather brilliantly, especially in the studies she liked. During that winter following her husband's death Mrs. Brandeis had a way of playing solitaire after supper; one of the simpler forms of the game. It seemed to help her to think out the day's problems, and to soothe her at the same time. She would turn down the front of the writing desk, and draw up the piano stool.

All through that winter Fanny seemed to remember reading to the slap-slap of cards, and the whir of their shuffling. In after years she was never able to pick up a volume of Dickens without having her mind hark back to those long, quiet evenings. She read a great deal of Dickens at that time. She had a fine contempt for his sentiment, and his great ladies bored her. She did not know that this was because they were badly drawn. The humor she loved, and she read and reread the passages dealing with Samuel Weller, and Mr. Micawber, and Sairey Gamp, and Fanny Squeers. It was rather trying to read Dickens before supper, she had discovered. Pickwick Papers was fatal, she had found. It sent one to the pantry in a sort of trance, to ransack for food—cookies, apples, cold meat, anything. But whatever one found, it always fell short of the succulent sounding beefsteak pies, and saddles of mutton, and hot pineapple toddy of the printed page.

To-night Mrs. Brandeis, coming in from the kitchen after a conference with Mattie, found her daughter in conversational mood, though book in hand.

"Mother, did you ever read this?" She held up "The Ladies' Paradise."

"Yes; but child alive, what ever made you get it? That isn't the kind of thing for you to read. Oh, I wish I had more time to give——"

Fanny leaned forward eagerly. "It made me think a lot of you. You know—the way the big store was crushing the little one, and everything. Like the thing you were talking to that man about the other day. You said it was killing the small-town dealer, and he said some day it would be illegal, and you said you'd never live to see it."

"Oh, that! We were talking about the mail-order business, and how hard it was to compete with it, when the farmers bought everything from a catalogue, and had whole boxes of household goods expressed to them. I didn't know you were listening, Fanchen."

"I was. I almost always do when you and some traveling man or somebody like that are talking. It—it's interesting."

Fanny went back to her book then. But Molly Brandeis sat a moment, eyeing her queer little daughter thoughtfully. Then she sighed, and laid out her cards for solitaire. By eight o'clock she was usually so sleepy that she would fall, dead-tired, asleep on the worn leather couch in the sitting-room. She must have been fearfully exhausted, mind and body. The house would be very quiet, except for Mattie, perhaps, moving about in the kitchen or in her corner room upstairs. Sometimes the weary woman on the couch would start suddenly from her sleep and cry out, choked and gasping, "No! No! No!" The children would jump, terrified, and come running to her at first, but later they got used to it, and only looked up to say, when she asked them, bewildered, what it was that wakened her, "You had the no-no-nos."

She had never told of the thing that made her start out of her sleep and cry out like that. Perhaps it was just the protest of the exhausted body and the over-wrought nerves. Usually, after that, she would sit up, haggardly, and take the hairpins out of her short thick hair, and announce her intention of going to bed. She always insisted that the children go too, though they often won an extra half hour by protesting and teasing. It was a good thing for them, these nine o'clock bed hours, for it gave them the tonic sleep that their young, high-strung natures demanded.

"Come, children," she would say, yawning.

"Oh, mother, please just let me finish this chapter!"

"How much?"

"Just this little bit. See? Just this."

"Well, just that, then," for Mrs. Brandeis was a reasonable woman, and she had the book-lover's knowledge of the fascination of the unfinished chapter.

Fanny and Theodore were not always honest about the bargain. They would gallop, hot-cheeked, through the allotted chapter. Mrs. Brandeis would have fallen into a doze, perhaps. And the two conspirators would read on, turning the leaves softly and swiftly, gulping the pages, cramming them down in an orgy of mental bolting, like naughty children stuffing cake when their mother's back is turned. But the very concentration of their dread of waking her often brought about the feared result. Mrs. Brandeis would start up rather wildly, look about her, and see the two buried, red-cheeked and eager, in their books.

"Fanny! Theodore! Come now! Not another minute!"

Fanny, shameless little glutton, would try it again. "Just to the end of this chapter! Just this weenty bit!"

"Fiddlesticks! You've read four chapters since I spoke to you the last time. Come now!"

Molly Brandeis would see to the doors, and the windows, and the clock, and then, waiting for the weary little figures to climb the stairs, would turn out the light, and, hairpins in one hand, corset in the other, perhaps, mount to bed.

By nine o'clock the little household would be sleeping, the children sweetly and dreamlessly, the tired woman restlessly and fitfully, her overwrought brain still surging with the day's problems. It was not like a household at rest, somehow. It was like a spirited thing standing, quivering for a moment, its nerves tense, its muscles twitching.

Perhaps you have quite forgotten that here were to be retailed two epochal events in Fanny Brandeis's life. If you have remembered, you will have guessed that the one was the reading of that book of social protest, though its writer has fallen into disfavor in these fickle days. The other was the wild and unladylike street brawl in which she took part so that a terrified and tortured little boy might escape his tormentors.

## CHAPTER FIVE

THERE was no hard stock in Brandeis' Bazaar now. The packing-room was always littered with straw and excelsior dug from hogsheads and great crates. Aloysius lorded it over a small red-headed satellite who disappeared inside barrels and dived head first into huge boxes, coming up again with a lamp, or a doll, or a piece of glassware, like a magician. Fanny, perched on an overturned box, used to watch him, fascinated, while he laboriously completed a water set, or a tea set. A preliminary dive would bring up the first of a half dozen related pieces, each swathed in tissue paper. A deft twist on the part of the attendant Aloysius would strip the paper wrappings and disclose a ruby-tinted tumbler, perhaps. Another dive, and another, until six gleaming glasses stood revealed, like chicks without a hen mother. A final dip, much scratching and burrowing, during which armfuls of hay and excelsior were thrown out, and then the red-headed genie of the barrel would emerge, flushed and triumphant, with the water pitcher itself, thus completing the happy family.

Aloysius, meanwhile, would regale her with one of those choice bits of gossip he had always about him, like a jewel concealed, and only to be brought out for the appreciative. Mrs. Brandeis disapproved of store gossip, and frowned on Sadie and Pearl whenever she found them, their heads close together, their stifled shrieks testifying to his wit. There were times when Molly Brandeis herself could not resist the spell of his tongue. No one knew where Aloysius got his in-

formation. He had news that Winnebago's two daily
papers never could get, and wouldn't have dared to
print if they had.

"Did you hear about Myrtle Krieger," he would begin, "that's marryin' the Hempel boy next month?
The one in the bank. She's exhibiting her trewsow at
the Outagamie County Fair this week, for the handwork and embroid'ry prize. Ain't it brazen? They
say the crowd's so thick around the table that they
had to take down the more pers'nal pieces. The first
day of the fair the grand-stand was, you might say,
empty, even when they was pullin' off the trottin' races
and the balloon ascension. It's funny—ain't it?—how
them garmints that you wouldn't turn for a second
look at on the clothesline or in a store winda' becomes
kind of wicked and interestin' the minute they get what
they call the human note. There it lays, that virgin
lawnjerie, for all the county to look at, with pink rib-
bons run through everything, and the poor Krieger girl
never dreamin' she's doin' somethin' indelicate. She
says yesterday if she wins the prize she's going to put
it toward one of these kitchen cabinets."

I wish we could stop a while with Aloysius. He is
well worth it. Aloysius, who looked a pass between
Ichabod Crane and Smike; Aloysius, with his bit of
scandal burnished with wit; who, after a long, hard
Saturday, would go home to scrub the floor of the
dingy lodgings where he lived with his invalid mother,
and who rose in the cold dawn of Sunday morning to
go to early mass, so that he might return to cook the
dinner and wait upon the sick woman. Aloysius, whose
trousers flapped grotesquely about his bony legs, and
whose thin red wrists hung awkwardly from his too-
short sleeves, had in him that tender, faithful and
courageous stuff of which unsung heroes are made.
And he adored his clever, resourceful boss to the point
of imitation. You should have seen him trying to sell

a sled or a doll's go-cart in her best style. But we cannot stop for Aloysius. He is irrelevant, and irrelevant matter halts the progress of a story. Any one, from Barrie to Harold Bell Wright, will tell you that a story, to be successful, must march.

We'll keep step, then, with Molly Brandeis until she drops out of the ranks. There is no detouring with Mrs. Brandeis for a leader. She is the sort that, once her face is set toward her goal, looks neither to right nor left until she has reached it.

When Fanny Brandeis was fourteen, and Theodore was not quite sixteen, a tremendous thing happened. Schabelitz, the famous violinist, came to Winnebago to give a concert under the auspices of the Young Men's Sunday Evening Club.

The Young Men's Sunday Evening Club of the Congregational Church prided itself (and justifiably) on what the papers called its "auspices." It scorned to present to Winnebago the usual lyceum attractions— Swiss bell ringers, negro glee clubs, and Family Fours. Instead, Schumann-Heink sang her *lieder* for them; McCutcheon talked and cartooned for them; Madame Bloomfield-Zeisler played. Winnebago was one of those wealthy little Mid-Western towns whose people appreciate the best and set out to acquire it for themselves.

To the Easterner, Winnebago, and Oshkosh, and Kalamazoo, and Emporia are names invented to get a laugh from a vaudeville audience. Yet it is the people from Winnebago and Emporia and the like whom you meet in Egypt, and the Catalina Islands, and at Honolulu, and St. Moritz. It is in the Winnebago living-room that you are likely to find a prayer rug got in Persia, a bit of gorgeous glaze from China, a scarf from some temple in India, and on it a book, hand-tooled and rare. The Winnebagoans seem to know what is being served and worn, from salad to veilings,

surprisingly soon after New York has informed itself
on those subjects.   The 7:52 Northwestern morning
train out of Winnebago was always pretty comfortably
crowded with shoppers who were taking a five-hour
run down to Chicago to get a hat and see the new
musical show at the Illinois.

So Schabelitz's coming was an event, but not an un-
precedented one.   Except to Theodore.   Theodore had
a ticket for the concert (his mother had seen to that),
and he talked of nothing else.   He was going with his
violin teacher, Emil Bauer.   There were strange stories
as to why Emil Bauer, with his gift of teaching, should
choose to bury himself in this obscure little Wisconsin
town.   It was known that he had acquaintance with
the great and famous of the musical world.   The East
End set fawned upon him, and his studio suppers were
the exclusive social events in Winnebago.

Schabelitz was to play in the evening.   At half past
three that afternoon there entered Brandeis' Bazaar
a white-faced, wide-eyed boy who was Theodore Brandeis; a plump, voluble, and excited person who was
Emil Bauer; and a short, stocky man who looked
rather like a foreign-born artisan—plumber or steam-
fitter—in his Sunday clothes.   This was Levine Schabelitz.

Molly Brandeis was selling a wash boiler to a fussy
housewife who, in her anxiety to assure herself of the
flawlessness of her purchase, had done everything but
climb inside it.   It had early been instilled in the minds
of Mrs. Brandeis's children that she was never to be
approached when busy with a customer.   There were
times when they rushed into the store bursting with
news or plans, but they had learned to control their
eagerness.   This, though, was no ordinary news that
had blanched Theodore's face.   At sight of the three,
Mrs. Brandeis quietly turned her boiler purchaser over
to Pearl and came forward from the rear of the store.

"Oh, Mother!" cried Theodore, an hysterical note in his voice. "Oh, Mother!"

And in that moment Molly Brandeis knew. Emil Bauer introduced them, floridly. Molly Brandeis held out her hand, and her keen brown eyes looked straight and long into the gifted Russian's pale blue ones. According to all rules he should have started a dramatic speech, beginning with "Madame!" hand on heart. But Schabelitz the great had sprung from Schabelitz the peasant boy, and in the process he had managed, somehow, to retain the simplicity which was his charm. Still, there was something queer and foreign in the way he bent over Mrs. Brandeis's hand. We do not bow like that in Winnebago.

"Mrs. Brandeis, I am honored to meet you."

"And I to meet you," replied the shopkeeper in the black sateen apron.

"I have just had the pleasure of hearing your son play," began Schabelitz.

"Mr. Bauer called me out of my economics class at school, Mother, and said that——"

"Theodore!" Theodore subsided.

"He is only a boy," went on Schabelitz, and put one hand on Theodore's shoulder. "A very gifted boy. I hear hundreds. Oh, how I suffer, sometimes, to listen to their devilish scraping! To-day, my friend Bauer met me with that old plea, 'You must hear this pupil play. He has genius.' 'Bah! Genius!' I said, and I swore at him a little, for he is my friend, Bauer. But I went with him to his studio—Bauer, that is a remarkably fine place you have there, above that drug store; a room of exceptional proportions. And those rugs, let me tell you——"

"Never mind the rugs, Schabelitz. Mrs. Brandeis here——"

"Oh, yes, yes! Well, dear lady, this boy of yours will be a great violinist if he is willing to work, and work, and work. He has what you in America call the spark. To make it a flame he must work, always work. You must send him to Dresden, under Auer."

"Dresden!" echoed Molly Brandeis faintly, and put one hand on the table that held the fancy cups and saucers, and they jingled a little.

"A year, perhaps, first, in New York with Wolf-sohn."

Wolfsohn! New York! Dresden! It was too much even for Molly Brandeis' well-balanced brain. She was conscious of feeling a little dizzy. At that moment Pearl approached apologetically. "Pardon *me*, Mis' Brandeis, but Mrs. Trost wants to know if you'll send the boiler special this afternoon. She wants it for the washing early to-morrow morning."

That served to steady her.

"Tell Mrs. Trost I'll send it before six to-night." Her eyes rested on Theodore's face, flushed now, and glowing. Then she turned and faced Schabelitz squarely. "Perhaps you do not know that this store is our support. I earn a living here for myself and my two children. You see what it is—just a novelty and notion store in a country town. I speak of this because it is the important thing. I have known for a long time that Theodore's playing was not the playing of the average boy, musically gifted. So what you tell me does not altogether surprise me. But when you say Dresden—well, from Brandeis' Bazaar in Winnebago, Wisconsin, to Auer, in Dresden, Germany, is a long journey for one afternoon."

"But of course you must have time to think it over. It must be brought about, somehow."

"Somehow——" Mrs. Brandeis stared straight ahead, and you could almost hear that indomitable will of hers working, crashing over obstacles, plowing through difficulties. Theodore watched her, breathless, as though expecting an immediate solution. His

mother's eyes met his own intent ones, and at that her
mobile mouth quirked in a sudden smile. "You look as
if you expected pearls to pop out of my mouth, son.
And, by the way, if you're going to a concert this evening don't you think it would be a good idea to squan-
der an hour on study this afternoon? You may be
a musical prodigy, but geometry's geometry."

"Oh, Mother! Please!"

"I want to talk to Mr. Schabelitz and Mr. Bauer,
alone." She patted his shoulder, and the last pat ended
in a gentle push. "Run along."

"I'll work, Mother. You know perfectly well I'll
work." But he looked so startlingly like his father as
he said it that Mrs. Brandeis felt a clutching at her
heart.

Theodore out of the way, they seemed to find very
little to discuss, after all. Schabelitz was so quietly
certain, Bauer so triumphantly proud.

Said Schabelitz, "Wolfsohn, of course, receives ten
dollars a lesson ordinarily."

"Ten dollars!"

"But a pupil like Theodore is in the nature of an
investment," Bauer hastened to explain. "An advertisement. After hearing him play, and after what
Schabelitz here will have to say for him, Wolfsohn
will certainly give Theodore lessons for nothing, or
next to nothing. You remember"—proudly—"I offered to teach him without charge, but you would not
have it."

Schabelitz smote his friend sharply on the shoulder.
"The true musician! Oh, Bauer, Bauer! That you
should bury yourself in this——"

But Bauer stopped him with a gesture. "Mrs. Brandeis is a busy woman. And as she says, this thing needs
thinking over."

"After all," said Mrs. Brandeis, "there isn't much
to think about. I know just where I stand. It's

a case of mathematics, that's all. This business of mine is just beginning to pay. From now on I shall be able to save something every year. It might be enough to cover his musical education. It would mean that Fanny—my daughter—and I would have to give up everything. For myself, I should be only too happy, too proud. But it doesn't seem fair to her. After all, a girl——"

"It isn't fair," broke in Schabelitz. "It isn't fair. But that is the way of genius. It never is fair. It takes, and takes, and takes. I know. My mother could tell you, if she were alive. She sold the little farm, and my sisters gave up their dowries, and with them their hopes of marriage, and they lived on bread and cabbage. That was not to pay for my lessons. They never could have done that. It was only to send me to Moscow. We were very poor. They must have starved. I have come to know, since, that it was not worth it. That nothing could be worth it."

"But it was worth it. Your mother would do it all over again, if she had the chance. That's what we're for."

Bauer pulled out his watch and uttered a horrified exclamation. "Himmel! Four o'clock! And I have a pupil at four." He turned hastily to Mrs. Brandeis. "I am giving a little supper in my studio after the concert to-night."

"Oh, Gott!" groaned Schabelitz.

"It is in honor of Schabelitz here. You see how overcome he is. Will you let me bring Theodore back with me after the concert? There will be some music, and perhaps he will play for us."

Schabelitz bent again in his queer little foreign bow. "And you, of course, will honor us, Mrs. Brandeis." He had never lived in Winnebago.

"Oh, certainly," Bauer hastened to say. He had.

"I!" Molly Brandeis looked down at her apron,

and stroked it with her fingers. Then she looked up with a little smile that was not so pleasant as her smile usually was. There had flashed across her quick mind a picture of Mrs. G. Manville Smith. Mrs. G. Manville Smith, in an evening gown whose décolletage was discussed from the Haley House to Gerretson's department store next morning, was always a guest at Bauer's studio affairs. "Thank you, but it is impossible. And Theodore is only a schoolboy. Just now he needs, more than anything else in the world, nine hours of sleep every night. There will be plenty of time for studio suppers later. When a boy's voice is changing, and he doesn't know what to do with his hands and feet, he is better off at home."

"God! These mothers!" exclaimed Schabelitz. "What do they not know!"

"I suppose you are right." Bauer was both rueful and relieved. It would have been fine to show off Theodore as his pupil and Schabelitz's protégé. But Mrs. Brandeis? No, that would never do. "Well, I must go. We will talk about this again, Mrs. Brandeis. In two weeks Schabelitz will pass through Winnebago again on his way back to Chicago. Meanwhile he will write Wolfsohn. I also. So! Come, Schabelitz!"

He turned to see that gentleman strolling off in the direction of the notion counter behind which his expert eye had caught a glimpse of Sadie in her white shirt-waist and her trim skirt. Sadie always knew what they were wearing on State Street, Chicago, half an hour after Mrs. Brandeis returned from one of her buying trips. Shirtwaists had just come in, and with them those neat leather belts with a buckle, and about the throat they were wearing folds of white satin ribbon, smooth and high and tight, the two ends tied pertly at the back. Sadie would never be the saleswoman that Pearl was, but her unfailing good nature and her cheery self-confidence made her an asset in the store.

Besides, she was pretty. Mrs. Brandeis knew the value of a pretty clerk.

At the approach of this stranger Sadie leaned coyly against the stocking rack and patted her paper sleevelets that were secured at wrist and elbow with elastic bands. Her method was sure death to traveling men. She prepared now to try it on the world-famous virtuoso. The ease with which she succeeded surprised even Sadie, accustomed though she was to conquest.

"Come, come, Schabelitz!" said Bauer again. "I must get along."

"Then go, my friend. Go along and make your preparations for that studio supper. The only interesting woman in Winnebago—" he bowed to Mrs. Brandeis—"will not be there. I know them, these small-town society women, with their imitation city ways. And bony! Always! I am enjoying myself. I shall stay here."

And he did stay. Sadie, talking it over afterward with Pearl and Aloysius, put it thus:

"They say he's the grandest violin player in the world. Not that I care much for the violin, myself. Kind of squeaky, I always think. But it just goes to show they're all alike. Ain't it the truth? I jollied him just like I did Sam Bloom, of Ganz & Pick, Novelties, an hour before. He laughed just where Sam did. And they both handed me a line of talk about my hair and eyes, only Sam said I was a doll, and this Schabelitz, or whatever his name is, said I was as alluring as a Lorelei. I guess he thought he had me there, but I didn't go through the seventh reader for nothing. 'If you think I'm flattered,' I said to him, 'you're mistaken. She was the mess who used to sit out on a rock with her back hair down, combing away and singing like mad, and keeping an eye out for sailors up and down the river. If I had to work that hard to get some attention,' I said, 'I'd give up the struggle, and

settle down with a cat and a teakettle.' At that he just
threw back his head and roared. And when Mrs. Brandeis came up he said something about the wit of these
American women. 'Work is a great sharpener of wit
—and wits,' Mrs. Brandeis said to him. 'Pearl, did
Aloysius send Eddie out with that boiler, special?'
And she didn't pay any more attention to him, or make
any more fuss over him, than she would to a traveler
with a line of samples she wasn't interested in. I guess
that's why he had such a good time."

Sadie was right. That was the reason. Fanny, coming into the store half an hour later, saw this man who
had swayed thousands with his music, down on his hands
and knees in the toy section at the rear of Brandeis'
Bazaar. He and Sadie and Aloysius were winding up
toy bears, and clowns, and engines, and carriages, and
sending them madly racing across the floor. Sometimes their careening career was threatened with dis-
aster in the form of a clump of brooms or a stack of
galvanized pails. But Schabelitz would scramble forward with a shout and rescue them just before the crash
came, and set them deftly off again in the opposite
direction.

"This I must have for my boy in New York." He
held up a miniature hook and ladder. "And this wind-
mill that whirls so busily. My Leo is seven, and his
head is full of engines, and motors, and things that run
on wheels. He cares no more for music, the little
savage, than the son of a bricklayer."

"Who is that man?" Fanny whispered, staring at
him.

"Levine Schabelitz."

"Schabelitz! Not the—"

"Yes."

"But he's playing on the floor like—like a little boy!
And laughing! Why, Mother, he's just like anybody
else, only nicer."

If Fanny had been more than fourteen her mother might have told her that all really great people are like that, finding joy in simple things. I think that is the secret of their genius—the child in them that keeps their viewpoint fresh, and that makes us children again when we listen to them. It is the Schabelitzes of this world who can shout over a toy engine that would bore a Bauer to death.

Fanny stood looking at him thoughtfully. She knew all about him. Theodore's talk of the past week had accomplished that. Fanny knew that here was a man who did one thing better than any one else in the world. She thrilled to that thought. She adored the quality in people that caused them to excel. Schabelitz had got hold of a jack-in-the-box, and each time the absurd head popped out, with its grin and its squawk, he laughed like a boy. Fanny, standing behind the wrapping counter, and leaning on it with her elbows the better to see this great man, smiled too, as her flexible spirit and her mobile mind caught his mood. She did not know she was smiling. Neither did she know why she suddenly frowned in the intensity of her concentration, reached up for one of the pencils on the desk next the wrapping counter, and bent over the topmost sheet of yellow wrapping paper that lay spread out before her. Her tongue-tip curled excitedly at one corner of her mouth. Her head was cocked to one side.

She was rapidly sketching a crude and startling likeness of Levine Schabelitz as he stood there with the ridiculous toy in his hand. It was a trick she often amused herself with at school. She had drawn her school-teacher one day as she had looked when gazing up into the eyes of the visiting superintendent, who was a married man. Quite innocently and unconsciously she had caught the adoring look in the eyes of Miss McCook, the teacher, and that lady, happening upon the sketch later, had dealt with Fanny in a manner seemingly unwarranted. In the same way it was not only the exterior likeness of the man which she was catching now—the pompadour that stood stiffly perpendicular like a brush; the square, yellow peasant teeth; the strong, slender hands and wrists; the stocky figure; the high cheek bones; the square-toed, foreign-looking shoes and the trousers too wide at the instep to have been cut by an American tailor. She caught and transmitted to paper, in some uncanny way, the simplicity of the man who was grinning at the jack-in-the-box that smirked back at him. Behind the veneer of poise and polish born of success and adulation she had caught a glimpse of the Russian peasant boy delighted with the crude toy in his hand. And she put it down eagerly, wetting her pencil between her lips, shading here, erasing there.

Mrs. Brandeis, bustling up to the desk for a customer's change, and with a fancy dish to be wrapped, in her hand, glanced over Fanny's shoulder. She leaned closer. "Why, Fanny, you witch!"

Fanny gave a little crow of delight and tossed her head in a way that switched her short curls back from where they had fallen over her shoulders. "It's like him, isn't it?"

"It looks more like him than he does himself." With which Molly Brandeis unconsciously defined the art of cartooning.

Fanny looked down at it, a smile curving her lips. Mrs. Brandeis, dish in hand, counted her change expertly from the till below the desk, and reached for the sheet of wrapping paper just beneath that on which Fanny had made her drawing. At that moment Schabelitz, glancing up, saw her, and came forward, smiling, the jack-in-the-box still in his hand.

"Dear lady, I hope I have not entirely disorganized your shop. I have had a most glorious time. Would you believe it, this jack-in-the-box looks exactly—but exactly—like my manager, Weber, when the box-office receipts are good. He grins just—"

And then his eye fell on the drawing that Fanny was trying to cover with one brown paw. "Hello! What's this?" Then he looked at Fanny. Then he grasped her wrist in his fingers of steel and looked at the sketch that grinned back at him impishly. "Well, I'm damned!" exploded Schabelitz in amusement, and surprise, and appreciation. And did not apologize. "And who is this young lady with the sense of humor?"

"This is my little girl, Fanny."

He looked down at the rough sketch again, with its clean-cut satire, and up again at the little girl in the school coat and the faded red tam o' shanter, who was looking at him shyly, and defiantly, and provokingly, all at once.

"Your little girl Fanny, h'm? The one who is to give up everything that the boy Theodore may become a great violinist." He bent again over the crude, effective cartoon, then put a forefinger gently under the child's chin and tipped her glowing face up to the light. "I am not so sure now that it will work. As for its being fair! Why, no! No!"

Fanny waited for her mother that evening, and they walked home together. Their step and swing were very much alike, now that Fanny's legs were growing longer. She was at the *báckfisch* age.

"What did he mean, Mother, when he said that about Theodore being a great violinist, and its not being fair? What isn't fair? And how did he happen to be in the store, anyway? He bought a heap of toys, didn't he? I suppose he's awfully rich."

"To-night, when Theodore's at the concert, I'll tell you what he meant, and all about it."

"I'd love to hear him play, wouldn't you? I'd just love to."

Over Molly Brandeis's face there came a curious

look. "You could hear him, Fanny, in Theodore's place. Theodore would have to stay home if I told him to."

Fanny's eyes and mouth grew round with horror. "Theodore stay home! Why Mrs.—Molly—Brandeis!" Then she broke into a little relieved laugh. "But you're just fooling, of course."

"No, I'm not. If you really want to go I'll tell Theodore to give up his ticket to his sister."

"Well, my goodness! I guess I'm not a pig. I wouldn't have Theodore stay home, not for a million dollars."

"I knew you wouldn't," said Molly Brandeis as they swung down Norris Street. And she told Fanny briefly of what Schabelitz had said about Theodore.

It was typical of Theodore that he ate his usual supper that night. He may have got his excitement vicariously from Fanny. She was thrilled enough for two. Her food lay almost untouched on her plate. She chattered incessantly. When Theodore began to eat his second baked apple with cream, her outraged feelings voiced their protest.

"But, Theodore, I don't see how you can!"

"Can what?"

"Eat like that. When you're going to hear him play. And after what he said, and everything."

"Well, is that any reason why I should starve to death?"

"But I don't see how you *can*," repeated Fanny helplessly, and looked at her mother. Mrs. Brandeis reached for the cream pitcher and poured a little more cream over Theodore's baked apple. Even as she did it her eyes met Fanny's, and in them was a certain sly amusement, a little gleam of fun, a look that said, "Neither do I." Fanny sat back, satisfied. Here, at least, was some one who understood.

At half past seven Theodore, looking very brushed

and sleek, went off to meet Emil Bauer. Mrs. Brandeis had looked him over, and had said, "Your nails!" and sent him back to the bathroom, and she had resisted the desire to kiss him because Theodore disliked demonstration. "He hated to be pawed over," was the way he put it. After he had gone, Mrs. Brandeis went into the dining-room where Fanny was sitting. Mattie had cleared the table, and Fanny was busy over a book and a tablet, by the light of the lamp that they always used for studying. It was one of the rare occasions when she had brought home a school lesson. It was arithmetic, and Fanny loathed arithmetic. She had no head for mathematics. The set of problems were eighth-grade horrors, in which A is digging a well 20 feet deep and 9 feet wide; or in which A and B are papering two rooms, or building two fences, or plastering a wall. If A does his room in $9\frac{1}{2}$ days, the room being 12 feet high, 20 feet long, and $15\frac{1}{2}$ feet wide, how long will it take B to do a room 14 feet high, $11\frac{3}{4}$ feet, etc.

Fanny hated the indefatigable A and B with a bitter personal hatred. And as for that occasional person named C, who complicated matters still more—!

Sometimes Mrs. Brandeis helped to disentangle Fanny from the mazes of her wall paper problems, or dragged her up from the bottom of the well when it seemed that she was down there for eternity unless a friendly hand rescued her. As a rule she insisted that Fanny crack her own mathematical nuts. She said it was good mental training, not to speak of the moral side of it. But to-night she bent her quick mind upon the problems that were puzzling her little daughter, and cleared them up in no time.

When Fanny had folded her arithmetic papers neatly inside her book and leaned back with a relieved sigh Molly Brandeis bent forward in the lamplight and began to talk very soberly. Fanny, red-cheeked and

bright-eyed from her recent mental struggles, listened
interestedly, then intently, then absorbedly. She attempted to interrupt, sometimes, with an occasional,
"But, Mother, how——" but Mrs. Brandeis shook her
head and went on. She told Fanny a few things about
her early married life—things that made Fanny look
at her with new eyes. She had always thought of her
mother as her mother, in the way a fourteen-year-old
girl does. It never occurred to her that this mother
person, who was so capable, so confident, so worldly-
wise, had once been a very young bride, with her life
before her, and her hopes stepping high, and her love
keeping time with her hopes. Fanny heard, fascinated,
the story of this girl who had married against the
advice of her family and her friends.

Molly Brandeis talked curtly and briefly, and her
very brevity and lack of embroidering details made the
story stand out with stark realism. It was such a
story of courage, and pride, and indomitable will, and
sheer pluck as can only be found among the seemingly
commonplace.

"And so," she finished, "I used to wonder, sometimes, whether it was worth while to keep on, and what
it was all for. And now I know. Theodore is going to
make up for everything. Only we'll have to help him,
first. It's going to be hard on you, Fanchen. I'm
talking to you as if you were eighteen, instead of fourteen. But I want you to understand. That isn't fair
to you either—my expecting you to understand. Only
I don't want you to hate me too much when you're a
woman, and I'm gone, and you'll remember——"

"Why, Mother, what in the world are you talking
about? Hate you!"

"For what I took from you to give to him, Fanny.
You don't understand now. Things must be made easy
for Theodore. It will mean that you and I will have
to scrimp and save. Not now and then, but all the

time. It will mean that we can't go to the theater, even occasionally, or to lectures, or concerts. It will mean that your clothes won't be as pretty or as new as the other girls' clothes. You'll sit on the front porch evenings, and watch them go by, and you'll want to go too."

"As if I cared."

"But you will care. I know. I know. It's easy enough to talk about sacrifice in a burst of feeling; but it's the everyday, shriveling grind that's hard. You'll want clothes, and books, and beaux, and education, and you ought to have them. They're your right. You ought to have them!" Suddenly Molly Brandeis' arms were folded on the table, and her head came down on her arms and she was crying, quietly, horribly, as a man cries. Fanny stared at her a moment in unbelief. She had not seen her mother cry since the day of Ferdinand Brandeis' death. She scrambled out of her chair and thrust her head down next her mother's, so that her hot, smooth cheek touched the wet, cold one. "Mother, don't! Don't Molly dearie. I can't bear it. I'm going to cry too. Do you think I care for old dresses and things? I should say not. It's going to be fun going without things. It'll be like having a secret or something. Now stop, and let's talk about it."

Molly Brandeis wiped her eyes, and sat up, and smiled. It was a watery and wavering smile, but it showed that she was mistress of herself again.

"No," she said, "we just won't talk about it any more. I'm tired, that's what's the matter with me, and I haven't sense enough to know it. I'll tell you what. I'm going to put on my kimono, and you'll make some fudge. Will you? We'll have a party, all by ourselves, and if Mattie scolds about the milk to-morrow you just tell her I said you could. And I think there are some walnut meats in the third cocoa can on the shelf in the pantry. Use 'em all."

## CHAPTER SIX

THEODORE came home at twelve o'clock that
night. He had gone to Bauer's studio party after
all. It was the first time he had deliberately disobeyed
his mother in a really big thing. Mrs. Brandeis and
Fanny had nibbled fudge all evening (it had turned out
deliciously velvety) and had gone to bed at their usual
time. At half past ten Mrs. Brandeis had wakened
with the instinctive feeling that Theodore was not in
the house. She lay there, wide awake, staring into the
darkness until eleven. Then she got up and went into
his room, though she knew he was not there. She was
not worried as to his whereabouts or his well-being.
That same instinctive feeling told her where he was. She
was very angry, and a little terrified at the significance
of his act. She went back to bed again, and she felt
the blood pounding in her head. Molly Brandeis had
a temper, and it was surging now, and beating against
the barriers of her self-control.

She told herself, as she lay there, that she must deal
with him coolly and firmly, though she wanted to spank
him. The time for spankings was past. Some one was
coming down the street with a quick, light step. She
sat up in bed, listening. The steps passed the house,
went on. A half hour passed. Some one turned the
corner, whistling blithely. But, no, he would not be
whistling, she told herself. He would sneak in, quietly.
It was a little after twelve when she heard the front
door open (Winnebago rarely locked its doors). She
was surprised to feel her heart beating rapidly. He
was trying to be quiet, and was making a great deal
of noise about it. His shoes and the squeaky fifth stair

alone would have convicted him. The imp of perversity in Molly Brandeis made her smile, angry as she was, at the thought of how furious he must be at that stair.

"Theodore!" she called quietly, just as he was tiptoeing past her room.

"Yeh."

"Come in here. And turn on the light."

He switched on the light and stood there in the doorway. Molly Brandeis, sitting up in bed in the chilly room, with her covers about her, was conscious of a little sick feeling, not at what he had done, but that a son of hers should ever wear the sullen, defiant, hang-dog look that disfigured Theodore's face now.

"Bauer's?"

A pause. "Yes."

"Why?"

"I just stopped in there for a minute after the concert. I didn't mean to stay. And then Bauer introduced me around to everybody. And then they asked me to play, and—"

"And you played badly."

"Well, I didn't have my own violin."

"No football game Saturday. And no pocket money this week. Go to bed."

He went, breathing hard, and muttering a little under his breath. At breakfast next morning Fanny plied him with questions and was furious at his cool uncommunicativeness.

"Was it wonderful, Theodore? Did he play—oh— like an angel?"

"Played all right. Except the 'Swan' thing. Maybe he thought it was too easy, or something, but I thought he murdered it. Pass the toast, unless you want it all."

It was not until the following autumn that Theodore went to New York. The thing that had seemed so impossible was arranged. He was to live in Brooklyn with a distant cousin of Ferdinand Brandeis, on a business basis, and he was to come into New York three times a week for his lessons. Mrs. Brandeis took him as far as Chicago, treated him to an extravagant dinner, put him on the train and with difficulty stifled the impulse to tell all the other passengers in the car to look after her Theodore. He looked incredibly grown up and at ease in his new suit and the hat that they had wisely bought in Chicago. She did not cry at all (in the train), and she kissed him only twice, and no man can ask more than that of any mother.

Molly Brandeis went back to Winnebago and the store with her shoulders a little more consciously squared, her jaw a little more firmly set. There was something almost terrible about her concentrativeness. Together she and Fanny began a life of self-denial of which only a woman could be capable. They saved in ways that only a woman's mind could devise; petty ways, that included cream and ice, and clothes, and candy. It was rather fun at first. When that wore off it had become a habit. Mrs. Brandeis made two resolutions regarding Fanny. One was that she should have at least a high school education, and graduate. The other that she should help in the business of the store as little as possible. To the first Fanny acceded gladly. To the second she objected.

"But why? If you can work, why can't I? I could help you a lot on Saturdays and at Christmas time, and after school."

"I don't want you to," Mrs. Brandeis had replied, almost fiercely. "I'm giving my life to it. That's enough. I don't want you to know about buying and selling. I don't want you to know a bill of lading from a sales slip when you see it. I don't want you to know whether f. o. b. is a wireless signal or a branch of the

Masons." At which Fanny grinned. No one appreciated her mother's humor more than she.

"But I do know already. The other day when that fat man was selling you those go-carts I heard him say, 'F. o. b. Buffalo,' and I asked Aloysius what it meant, and he told me."

It was inevitable that Fanny Brandeis should come to know these things, for the little household revolved about the store on Elm Street. By the time she was eighteen and had graduated from the Winnebago high school, she knew so many things that the average girl of eighteen did not know, and was ignorant of so many things that the average girl of eighteen did know, that Winnebago was almost justified in thinking her queer. She had had a joyous time at school, in spite of algebra and geometry and physics. She took the part of the heroine in the senior class play given at the Winnebago opera house, and at the last rehearsal electrified those present by announcing that if Albert Finkbein (who played the dashing Southern hero) didn't kiss her properly when the curtain went down on the first act, just as he was going into battle, she'd rather he didn't kiss her at all.

"He just makes it ridiculous," she protested. "He sort of gives a peck two inches from my nose, and then giggles. Everybody will laugh, and it'll spoil everything."

With the rather startled elocution teacher backing her she rehearsed the bashful Albert in that kiss until she had achieved the effect of realism that she thought the scene demanded. But when, on the school sleighing parties and hay rides the boy next her slipped a wooden and uncertain arm about her waist while they all were singing "Jingle Bells, Jingle Bells," and "Good Night Ladies," and "Merrily We Roll Along," she sat up stiffly and unyieldingly until the arm, discouraged, withdrew to its normal position. Which two instances are quoted as being of a piece with what Winnebago termed her queerness.

Not that Fanny Brandeis went beauless through school. On the contrary, she always had some one to carry her books, and to take her to the school parties and home from the Friday night debating society meetings. Her first love affair turned out disastrously. She was twelve, and she chose as the object of her affections a bullet-headed boy named Simpson. One morning, as the last bell rang and they were taking their seats, Fanny passed his desk and gave his coarse and stubbly hair a tweak. It was really a love tweak, and intended to be playful, but she probably put more fervor into it than she knew. It brought the tears of pain to his eyes, and he turned and called her the name at which she shrank back, horrified. Her shock and unbelief must have been stamped on her face, for the boy, still smarting, had snarled, "Ya-as, I mean it, too!"

It was strange how she remembered that incident years after she had forgotten important happenings in her life. Clarence Heyl, whose very existence you will have failed to remember, used to hover about her uncertainly, always looking as if he would like to walk home with her, but never summoning the courage to do it. They were graduated from the grammar school together, and Clarence solemnly read a graduation essay entitled "Where is the Horse?" Automobiles were just beginning to flash plentifully up and down Elm Street. Clarence had always been what Winnebago termed sickly, in spite of his mother's noodle soup, and coddling. He was sent West, to Colorado, or to a ranch in Wyoming, Fanny was not quite sure which, perhaps because she was not interested. He had come over one afternoon to bid her good-by, and had dangled about the front porch until she went into the house and shut the door.

When she was sixteen there was a blond German boy whose taciturnity attracted her volubility and vivacity. She mistook his stolidness for depth, and it was a long time before she realized that his silence was not due to the weight of his thoughts but to the fact that he had nothing to say. In her last year at high school she found herself singled out for the attentions of Harmon Kent, who was the Beau Nash of the Winnebago high school. His clothes were made by Schwartze, the tailor, when all the other boys of his age got theirs at the spring and fall sales of the Golden Eagle Clothing Store. It was always nip and tuck between his semester standings and his track team and football possibilities. The faculty refused to allow flunkers to take part in athletics.

He was one of those boys who have definite charm, and manner, and poise at seventeen, and who crib their exams off their cuffs. He was always at the head of any social plans in the school, and at the dances he rushed about wearing in his coat lapel a ribbon marked Floor Committee. The teachers all knew he was a bluff, but his engaging manner carried him through. When he went away to the state university he made Fanny solemnly promise to write; to come down to Madison for the football games; to be sure to remember about the Junior prom. He wrote once—a badly spelled scrawl—and she answered. But he was the sort of person who must be present to be felt. He could not project his personality. When he came home for the Christmas holidays Fanny was helping in the store. He dropped in one afternoon when she was selling whisky glasses to Mike Hearn of the Farmers' Rest Hotel.

They did not write at all during the following semester, and when he came back for the long summer vacation they met on the street one day and exchanged a few rather forced pleasantries. It suddenly dawned

on Fanny that he was patronizing her much as the scion
of an aristocratic line banters the housemaid whom he
meets on the stairs. She bit an imaginary apron corner, and bobbed a curtsy right there on Elm Street,
in front of the *Courier* office and walked off, leaving
him staring. It was shortly after this that she began
a queer line of reading for a girl—lives of Disraeli,
Spinoza, Mendelssohn, Mozart—distinguished Jews
who had found their religion a handicap.

The year of her graduation she did a thing for
which Winnebago felt itself justified in calling her different. Each member of the graduating class was
allowed to choose a theme for a thesis. Fanny Brandeis called hers "A Piece of Paper." On Winnebago's
Fox River were located a number of the largest and
most important paper mills in the country. There
were mills in which paper was made of wood fiber, and
others in which paper was made of rags. You could
smell the sulphur as soon as you crossed the bridge
that led to the Flats. Sometimes, when the wind was
right, the pungent odor of it spread all over the town.
Strangers sniffed it and made a wry face, but the
natives liked it.

The mills themselves were great ugly brick buildings,
their windows festooned with dust webs. Some of them
boasted high detached tower-like structures where a
secret acid process went on. In the early days the
mills had employed many workers, but newly invented
machinery had come to take the place of hand labor.
The rag-rooms alone still employed hundreds of girls
who picked, sorted, dusted over the great suction bins.
The rooms in which they worked were gray with dust.
They wore caps over their hair to protect it from the
motes that you could see spinning and swirling in the
watery sunlight that occasionally found its way through
the gray-filmed window panes. It never seemed to occur
to them that the dust cap so carefully pulled down

about their heads did not afford protection for their lungs. They were pale girls, the rag-room girls, with a peculiarly gray-white pallor.

Fanny Brandeis had once been through the Winnebago Paper Company's mill and she had watched, fascinated, while a pair of soiled and greasy old blue overalls were dusted and cleaned, and put through this acid vat, and that acid tub, growing whiter and more pulpy with each process until it was fed into a great crushing roller that pressed the moisture out of it, flattened it to the proper thinness and spewed it out at last, miraculously, in the form of rolls of crisp, white paper.

On the first day of the Easter vacation Fanny Brandeis walked down to the office of the Winnebago Paper Company's mill and applied at the superintendent's office for a job. She got it. They were generally short-handed in the rag-room. When Mrs. Brandeis heard of it there followed one of the few stormy scenes between mother and daughter.

"Why did you do it?" demanded Mrs. Brandeis.

"I had to, to get it right."

"Oh, don't be silly. You could have visited the mill a dozen times."

Fanny twisted the fingers of her left hand in the fingers of her right as was her way when she was terribly in earnest, and rather excited.

"But I don't want to write about the paper business as a process."

"Well, then, what do you want?"

"I want to write about the overalls on some railroad engineer, perhaps; or the blue calico wrapper that belonged, maybe, to a scrub woman. And how they came to be spotted, or faded, or torn, and finally all worn out. And how the rag man got them, and the mill, and how the girls sorted them. And the room in which they do it. And the bins. And the machinery. Oh, it's the most fascinating, and—and sort of relentless

machinery. And the acid burns on the hands of the
men at the vats. And their shoes. And then the paper,
so white. And the way we tear it up, or crumple it,
and throw it in the waste basket. Just a piece of
paper, don't you see what I mean? Just a piece of
paper, and yet all that—" she stopped and frowned a
little, and grew inarticulate, and gave it up with a
final, "Don't you see what I mean, Mother? Don't
you see what I mean?"

Molly Brandeis looked at her daughter in a startled
way, like one who, walking tranquilly along an accustomed path, finds himself confronting a new and hith-
erto unsuspected vista, formed by a peculiar arrangement of clouds, perhaps, or light, or foliage, or all
three blended. "I see what you mean," she said. "But
I wish you wouldn't do it. I—I wish you didn't feel
that you wanted to do it."

"But how can I make it real if I don't?"

"You can't," said Molly Brandeis. "That's just it.
You can't, ever."

Fanny got up before six every morning of that
Easter vacation, and went to the mill, lunch box in
hand. She came home at night dead-tired. She did
not take the street car to and from the mill, as she
might have, because she said the other girls in the rag-
room walked, some of them from the very edge of town.
Mrs. Brandeis said that she was carrying things too
far, but Fanny stuck it out for the two weeks, at the
end of which period she spent an entire Sunday in a
hair-washing, face-steaming, and manicuring bee. She
wrote her paper from notes she had taken, and turned
it in at the office of the high school principal with the
feeling that it was not at all what she had meant it to
be. A week later Professor Henning called her into
his office. The essay lay on his desk.

"I've read your thesis," he began, and stopped, and
cleared his throat. He was not an eloquent man.

"Where did you get your information, Miss Brandeis?"

"I got it at the mill."

"From one of the employees?"

"Oh, no. I worked there, in the rag-room."

Professor Henning gave a little startled exclamation that he turned hastily into a cough. "I thought that perhaps the editor of the *Courier* might like to see it—it being local. And interesting."

He brought it down to the office of the little paper himself, and promised to call for it again in an hour or two, when Lem Davis should have read it. Lem Davis did read it, and snorted, and scuffled with his feet in the drift of papers under his desk, which was a way he had when enraged.

"Read it!" he echoed, at Professor Henning's question. "Read it! Yes, I read it. And let me tell you it's socialism of the rankest kind, that's what! It's anarchism, that's what! Who's this girl? Mrs. Brandeis's daughter—of the Bazaar? Let me tell you I'd go over there and tell her what I think of the way she's bringing up that girl—if she wasn't an advertiser. 'A Piece of Paper'! Hell!" And to show his contempt for what he had read he wadded together a great mass of exchanges that littered his desk and hurled them, a crumpled heap, to the floor, and then spat tobacco juice upon them.

"I'm sorry," said Professor Henning, and rose; but at the door he turned and said something highly unprofessorial. "It's a darn fine piece of writing." And slammed the door. At supper that night he told Mrs. Henning about it. Mrs. Henning was a practical woman, as the wife of a small-town high school principal must needs be. "But don't you know," she said, "that Roscoe Moore, who is president of the Outagamie Pulp Mill and the Winnebago Paper Company, practically owns the *Courier?*"

Professor Henning passed a hand over his hair, ruefully, like a school boy. "No, Martha, I didn't know. If I knew those things, dear, I suppose we wouldn't be eating sausage for supper to-night." There was a little silence between them. Then he looked up. "Some day I'm going to brag about having been that Brandeis girl's teacher."

Fanny was in the store a great deal now. After she finished high school they sent Mattie away and Fanny took over the housekeeping duties, but it was not her *milieu*. Not that she didn't do it well. She put a perfect fury of energy and care into the preparation of a pot roast. After she had iced a cake she enhanced it with cunning arabesques of jelly. The house shone as it never had, even under Mattie's honest régime. But it was like hitching a high-power engine to a butter churn. There were periods of maddening restlessness. At such times she would set about cleaning the cellar, perhaps. It was a three-roomed cellar, brick-floored, cool, and having about it that indefinable cellar smell which is of mold, and coal, and potatoes, and onions, and kindling wood, and dill pickles and ashes.

Other girls of Fanny's age, at such times, cleaned out their bureau drawers and read forbidden novels. Fanny armed herself with the third best broom, the dust-pan, and an old bushel basket. She swept up chips, scraped up ashes, scoured the preserve shelves, washed the windows, cleaned the vegetable bins, and got gritty, and scarlet-cheeked and streaked with soot. It was a wonderful safety valve, that cellar. A pity it was that the house had no attic.

Then there were long, lazy summer afternoons when there was nothing to do but read. And dream. And watch the town go by to supper. I think that is why our great men and women so often have sprung from small towns, or villages. They have had time to dream in their adolescence. No cars to catch, no matinées, no city streets, none of the teeming, empty, energy-consuming occupations of the city child. Little that is competitive, much that is unconsciously absorbed at the most impressionable period, long evenings for reading, long afternoons in the fields or woods. With the cloth laid, and the bread cut and covered with a napkin, and the sauce in the glass bowl, and the cookies on a blue plate, and the potatoes doing very, very slowly, and the kettle steaming with a Peerybingle cheerfulness, Fanny would stroll out to the front porch again to watch for the familiar figure to appear around the corner of Norris Street. She would wear her blue-and-white checked gingham apron deftly twisted over one hip, and tucked in, in deference to the passers-by. And the town would go by—Hen Cody's drays, rattling and thundering; the high school boys thudding down the road, dog-tired and sweaty in their football suits, or their track pants and jersies, on their way from the athletic field to the school shower baths; Mrs. Mosher flying home, her skirts billowing behind her, after a protracted afternoon at whist; little Ernie Trost with a napkin-covered peach basket carefully balanced in his hand, waiting for the six-fifteen interurban to round the corner near the switch, so that he could hand up his father's supper; Rudie Maas, the butcher, with a moist little packet of meat in his hand, and lurching ever so slightly, and looking about defiantly. Oh, Fanny probably never realized how much she saw and absorbed, sitting there on Brandeis' front porch, watching Winnebago go by to supper.

At Christmas time she helped in the store, afternoons and evenings. Then, one Christmas, Mrs. Brandeis was ill for three weeks with grippe. They had to have a helper in the house. When Mrs. Brandeis was able to come back to the store Sadie left to marry, not one of her traveling-men victims, but a steady person, in the paper-hanging way, whose suit had long been considered hopeless. After that Fanny took her place.

She developed a surprising knack at selling. Yet it was not so surprising, perhaps, when one considered her teacher. She learned as only a woman can learn who is brought into daily contact with the outside world. It was not only contact: it was the relation of buyer and seller. She learned to judge people because she had to. How else could one gauge their tastes, temperaments, and pocketbooks? They passed in and out of Brandeis' Bazaar, day after day, in an endless and varied procession—traveling men, school children, housewives, farmers, worried hostesses, newly married couples bent on house furnishing, business men.

She learned that it was the girls from the paper mills who bought the expensive plates—the ones with the red roses and green leaves hand-painted in great smears and costing two dollars and a half, while the golf club crowd selected for a gift or prize one of the little white plates with the faded-looking blue sprig pattern, costing thirty-nine cents. One day, after she had spent endless time and patience over the sale of a nondescript little plate to one of Winnebago's socially elect, she stared wrathfully after the retreating back of the trying customer.

"Did you see that? I spent an hour with her. One hour! I showed her everything from the imported Limoges bowls to the Sèvres cups and saucers, and all she bought was that miserable little bonbon dish with the cornflower pattern. Cat!"

Mrs. Brandeis spoke from the depths of her wisdom.

"Fanny, I didn't miss much that went on during that hour, and I was dying to come over and take her away from you, but I didn't because I knew you needed the lesson, and I knew that that McNulty woman never spends more than twenty-five cents, anyway. But I want to tell you now that it isn't only a matter of plates. It's a matter of understanding folks. When you've learned whom to show the expensive hand-painted things to, and when to suggest quietly the little, vague things, with what you call the faded look, why, you've learned just about all there is to know of human nature. Don't expect it, at your age."

Molly Brandeis had never lost her trick of chatting with customers, or listening to them, whenever she had a moment's time. People used to drop in, and perch themselves on one of the stools near the big glowing base burner and talk to Mrs. Brandeis. It was incredible, the secrets they revealed of business, and love and disgrace; of hopes and aspirations, and troubles, and happiness. The farmer women used to fascinate Fanny by their very drabness. Mrs. Brandeis had a long and loyal following of these women. It was before the day when every farmhouse boasted an automobile, a telephone, and a phonograph.

A worn and dreary lot, these farmer women, living a skimmed milk existence, putting their youth, and health, and looks into the soil. They used often to sit back near the stove in winter, or in a cool corner near the front of the store in summer, and reveal, bit by bit, the sordid, tragic details of their starved existence. Fanny was often shocked when they told their age— twenty-five, twenty-eight, thirty, but old and withered from drudgery, and child-bearing, and coarse, unwholesome food. Ignorant women, and terribly lonely, with the dumb, lack-luster eyes that bespeak monotony. When they smiled they showed blue-white, glassily perfect false teeth that flashed incongruously in the ruin of their wrinkled, sallow, weather-beaten faces. Mrs. Brandeis would question them gently.

Children? Ten. Living? Four. Doctor? Never had one in the house. Why? He didn't believe in them. No proper kitchen utensils, none of the devices that lighten the deadeningly montonous drudgery of housework. Everything went to make his work easier—new harrows, plows, tractors, wind mills, reapers, barns, silos. The story would come out, bit by bit, as the woman sat there, a worn, unlovely figure, her hands—toil-blackened, seamed, calloused, unlovelier than any woman's hands were ever meant to be—lying in unaccustomed idleness in her lap.

Fanny learned, too, that the woman with the shawl, and with her money tied in a corner of her handkerchief, was more likely to buy the six-dollar doll, with the blue satin dress, and the real hair and eye-lashes, while the Winnebago East End society woman haggled over the forty-nine cent kind, which she dressed herself.

I think their loyalty to Mrs. Brandeis might be explained by her honesty and her sympathy. She was so square with them. When Minnie Mahler, out Centerville way, got married, she knew there would be no redundancy of water sets, hanging lamps, or pickle dishes.

"I thought like I'd get her a chamber set," Minnie's aunt would confide to Mrs. Brandeis.

"Is this for Minnie Mahler, of Centerville?"

"Yes; she gets married Sunday."

"I sold a chamber set for that wedding yesterday. And a set of dishes. But I don't think she's got a parlor lamp. At least I haven't sold one. Why don't you get her that? If she doesn't like it she can change it. Now there's that blue one with the pink roses."

And Minnie's aunt would end by buying the lamp.

Fanny learned that the mill girls liked the bright-colored and expensive wares, and why; she learned that the woman with the "fascinator" (tragic misnomer!) over her head wanted the finest sled for her boy. She learned to keep her temper. She learned to suggest without seeming to suggest. She learned to do surprisingly well all those things that her mother did so surprisingly well—surprisingly because both the women secretly hated the business of buying

and selling. Once, on the Fourth of July, when there
was a stand outside the store laden with all sorts of
fireworks, Fanny came down to find Aloysius and the
boy Eddie absent on other work, and Mrs. Brandeis
momentarily in charge. The sight sickened her, then
infuriated her.

"Come in," she said, between her teeth. "That isn't
your work."

"Somebody had to be there. Pearl's at dinner. And
Aloysius and Eddie were—"

"Then leave it alone. We're not starving—yet. I
won't have you selling fireworks like that—on the
street. I won't have it! I won't have it!"

The store was paying, now. Not magnificently, but
well enough. Most of the money went to Theodore, in
Dresden. He was progressing, though not so meteoric-
ally as Bauer and Schabelitz had predicted. But that
sort of thing took time, Mrs. Brandeis argued. Fanny
often found her mother looking at her these days with
a questioning sadness in her eyes. Once she suggested
that Fanny join the class in drawing at the Winnebago university—a small fresh-water college. Fanny
did try it for a few months, but the work was not what
she wanted; they did fruit pictures and vases, with a
book, on a table; or a clump of very pink and very
white flowers. Fanny quit in disgust and boredom.
Besides, they were busy at the store, and needed her.

There came often to Winnebago a woman whom
Fanny Brandeis admired intensely. She was a traveling saleswoman, successful, magnetic, and very much
alive. Her name was Mrs. Emma McChesney, and
between her and Mrs. Brandeis there existed a warm
friendship. She always took dinner with Mrs. Brandeis and Fanny, and they made a special effort to give
her all those delectable home-cooked dishes denied her
in her endless round of hotels.

"Noodle soup!" she used to say, almost lyrically.

"With real hand-made, egg noodles! You don't know what it means. You haven't been eating vermicelli soup all through Illinois and Wisconsin."

"We've made a dessert, though, that—"

"Molly Brandeis, don't you dare to tell me what you've got for dessert. I couldn't stand it. But, oh, suppose, *suppose* it's homemade strawberry shortcake!"

Which it more than likely was.

Fanny Brandeis used to think that she would dress exactly as Mrs. McChesney dressed, if she too were a successful business woman earning a man-size salary. Mrs. McChesney was a blue serge sort of woman—and her blue serge never was shiny in the back. Her collar, or jabot, or tie, or cuffs, or whatever relieving bit of white she wore, was always of the freshest and crispest. Her hats were apt to be small and full of what is known as "line." She usually would try to arrange her schedule so as to spend a Sunday in Winnebago, and the three alert, humor-loving women, grown wise and tolerant from much contact with human beings, would have a delightful day together.

"Molly," Mrs. McChesney would say, when they were comfortably settled in the living-room, or on the front porch, "with your shrewdness, and experience, and brains, you ought to be one of those five or ten thousand a year buyers. You know how to sell goods and handle people. And you know values. That's all there is to the whole game of business. I don't advise you to go on the road. Heaven knows I wouldn't advise my dearest enemy to do that, much less a friend. But you could do bigger things, and get bigger results. You know most of the big wholesalers, and retailers too. Why don't you speak to them about a department position? Or let me nose around a bit for you."

Molly Brandeis shook her head, though her expressive eyes were eager and interested. "Don't you think I've thought of that, Emma? A thousand times? But

I'm—I'm afraid. There's too much at stake. Suppose I couldn't succeed? There's Theodore. His whole future is dependent on me for the next few years. And there's Fanny here. No, I guess I'm too old. And I'm sure of the business here, small as it is."

Emma McChesney glanced at the girl. "I'm thinking that Fanny has the making of a pretty capable business woman herself."

Fanny drew in her breath sharply, and her face sparkled into sudden life, as always when she was tremendously interested.

"Do you know what I'd do if I were in Mother's place? I'd take a great, big running jump for it—and land! I'd take a chance. What is there for her in this town? Nothing! She's been giving things up all her life, and what has it brought her?"

"It has brought me a comfortable living, and the love of my two children, and the respect of my townspeople."

"Respect? Why shouldn't they respect you? You're the smartest woman in Winnebago, and the hardest working."

Emma McChesney frowned a little, in thought. "What do you two girls do for recreation?"

"I'm afraid we have too little of that, Emma. I know Fanny has. I'm so dog-tired at the end of the day. All I want is to take my hairpins out and go to bed."

"And Fanny?"

"Oh, I read. I'm free to pick my book friends, at least."

"Now, just what do you mean by that, child? It sounds a little bitter."

"I was thinking of what Chesterfield said in one of his Letters to His Son. 'Choose always to be in the society of those above you,' he wrote. I guess he never lived in Winnebago, Wisconsin. I'm a working woman, and a Jew, and we haven't any money or social position. And unless she's a Becky Sharp any small town girl with all those handicaps might as well choose a certain constellation of stars in the sky to wear as a breastpin, as try to choose the friends she really wants."

From Molly Brandeis to Emma McChesney there flashed a look that said, "You see?" And from Emma McChesney to Molly Brandeis another that said, "Yes; and it's your fault."

"Look here, Fanny, don't you see any boys—men?"

"No. There aren't any. Those who have any sense and initiative leave to go to Milwaukee, or Chicago, or New York. Those that stay marry the banker's lovely daughter."

Emma McChesney laughed at that, and Molly Brandeis too, and Fanny joined them a bit ruefully. Then quite suddenly, there came into her face a melting, softening look that made it almost lovely. She crossed swiftly over to where her mother sat, and put a hand on either cheek (grown thinner of late) and kissed the tip of her nose. "We don't care—really. Do we Mother? We're poor wurkin' girruls. But gosh! Ain't we proud? Mother, your mistake was in not doing as Ruth did."

"Ruth?"

"In the Bible. Remember when What's-his-name, her husband, died? Did she go back to her home town? No, she didn't. She'd lived there all her life, and she knew better. She said to Naomi, her mother-in-law, 'Whither thou goest I will go.' And she went. And when they got to Bethlehem, Ruth looked around, knowingly, until she saw Boaz, the catch of the town. So she went to work in his fields, gleaning, and she gleaned away, trying to look just as girlish, and dreamy, and unconscious, but watching him out of the corner of her eye all the time. Presently Boaz came along, looking

over the crops, and he saw her. 'Who's the new damsel?' he asked. 'The peach?' "

"Fanny Brandeis, aren't you ashamed?"

"But, Mother, that's what it says in the Bible, actually. 'Whose damsel is this?' They told him it was
Ruth, the dashing widow. After that it was all off
with the Bethlehem girls. Boaz paid no more attention to them than if they had never existed. He married
Ruth, and she led society. Just a little careful schem-
ing, that's all."

"I should say you have been reading, Fanny Brandeis," said Emma McChesney. She was smiling, but
her eyes were serious. "Now listen to me, child. The
very next time a traveling man in a brown suit and a
red necktie asks you to take dinner with him at the
Haley House—even one of those roast pork, queen-
fritter-with-rum-sauce, Roman punch Sunday dinners
—I want you to accept."

"Even if he wears an Elks' pin, and a Masonic
charm, and a diamond ring and a brown derby?"

"Even if he shows you the letters from his girl in
Manistee," said Mrs. McChesney solemnly. "You've
been seeing too much of Fanny Brandeis."

## CHAPTER SEVEN

THEODORE had been gone six years. His letters, all too brief, were events in the lives of the two women. They read and reread them. Fanny unconsciously embellished them with fascinating details made up out of her own imagination.

"They're really triumphs of stupidity and dullness," she said one day in disgust, after one of Theodore's long-awaited letters had proved particularly dry and sparse. "Just think of it! Dresden, Munich, Leipsic, Vienna, Berlin, Frankfurt! And from his letters you would never know he had left Winnebago. I don't believe he actually sees anything of these cities—their people, and the queer houses, and the streets. I suppose a new city means nothing to him but another platform, another audience, another piano, all intended as a background for his violin. He could travel all over the world and it wouldn't touch him once. He's got his mental fingers crossed all the time."

Theodore had begun to play in concert with some success, but he wrote that there was no real money in it yet. He was not well enough known. It took time. He would have to get a name in Europe before he could attempt an American tour. Just now every one was mad over Greinert. He was drawing immense audiences. He sent them a photograph at which they gasped, and then laughed, surprisedly. He looked so awfully German, so different, somehow.

"It's the way his hair is clipped, I suppose," said Fanny. "High, like that, on the temples. And look at his clothes! That tie! And his pants! And that

awful collar! Why, his very features look German,
don't they? I suppose it's the effect of that haber-
dashery."

A month after the photograph, came a letter announcing his marriage. Fanny's quick eye, leaping
ahead from line to line, took in the facts that her mind
seemed unable to grasp. Her name was Olga Stumpf.
(In the midst of her horror some imp in Fanny's brain
said that her hands would be red, and thick, with a
name like that.) An orphan. She sang. One of the
Vienna concert halls, but so different from the other
girls. And he was so happy. And he hated to ask
them for it, but if they could cable a hundred or so.
That would help. And here was her picture.

And there was her picture. One of the so-called
vivacious type of Viennese of the lower class, smiling a
conscious smile, her hair elaborately waved and dressed,
her figure high-busted, narrow-waisted; earrings,
chains, bracelets. You knew that she used a heavy
scent. She was older than Theodore. Or perhaps it
was the earrings.

They cabled the hundred.

After the first shock of it Molly Brandeis found
excuses for him. "He must have been awfully lonely,
Fanny. Often. And perhaps it will steady him, and
make him more ambitious. He'll probably work all the
harder now."

"No, he won't. But you will. And I will. I didn't
mind working for Theodore, and scrimping, and never
having any of the things I wanted, from blouses to
music. But I won't work and deny myself to keep a
great, thick, cheap, German barmaid, or whatever she
is in comfort. I won't!"

But she did. And quite suddenly Molly Brandeis, of
the straight, firm figure and the bright, alert eye, and
the buoyant humor, seemed to lose some of those electric qualities. It was an almost imperceptible letting

down. You have seen a fine race horse suddenly break
and lose his stride in the midst of the field, and pull
up and try to gain it again, and go bravely on, his
stride and form still there, but his spirit broken? That
was Molly Brandeis.

Fanny did much of the buying now. She bought
quickly and shrewdly, like her mother. She even went
to the Haley House to buy, when necessary, and Winnebagoans, passing the hotel, would see her slim, erect
figure in one of the sample-rooms with its white-covered
tables laden with china, or glassware, or Christmas
goods, or whatever that particular salesman happened
to carry. They lifted their eye-brows at first, but,
somehow, it was impossible to associate this girl with
the blithe, shirt-sleeved, cigar-smoking traveling men
who followed her about the sample-room, order book
in hand.

As time went on she introduced some new features
into the business, and did away with various old ones.
The overflowing benches outside the store were curbed,
and finally disappeared altogether. Fanny took charge
of the window displays, and often came back to the
store at night to spend the evening at work with
Aloysius. They would tack a piece of muslin around
the window to keep off the gaze of passers-by, and
together evolve a window that more than made up for
the absent show benches.

This, I suppose, is no time to stop for a description
of Fanny Brandeis. And yet the impulse to do so is
irresistible. Personally, I like to know about the hair,
and eyes, and mouth of the person whose life I am following. How did she look when she said that? What
sort of expression did she wear when this happened?
Perhaps the thing that Fanny Brandeis said about herself one day, when she was having one of her talks with
Emma McChesney, who was on her fall trip for the
Featherbloom Petticoat Company, might help.

"No ballroom would ever be hushed into admiring awe when I entered," she said. "No waiter would ever drop his tray, dazzled, and no diners in a restaurant would stop to gaze at me, their forks poised halfway, their eyes blinded by my beauty. I could tramp up and down between the tables for hours, and no one would know I was there. I'm one of a million women who look their best in a tailor suit and a hat with a line. Not that I ever had either. But I have my points, only they're blunted just now."

Still, that bit of description doesn't do, after all. Because she had distinct charm, and some beauty. She was not what is known as the Jewish type, in spite of her coloring. The hair that used to curl, waved now. In a day when coiffures were a bird's-nest of puffs and curls and pompadour, she wore her hair straight back from her forehead and wound in a coil at the neck. Her face in repose was apt to be rather lifeless, and almost heavy. But when she talked, it flashed into sudden life, and you found yourself watching her mouth, fascinated. It was the key to her whole character, that mouth. Mobile, humorous, sensitive, the sensuousness of the lower lip corrected by the firmness of the upper. She had large, square teeth, very regular, and of the yellow-white tone that bespeaks health. She used to make many of her own clothes, and she always trimmed her hats. Mrs. Brandeis used to bring home material and styles from her Chicago buying trips, and Fanny's quick mind adapted them. She managed, somehow, to look miraculously well dressed.

The Christmas following Theodore's marriage was the most successful one in the history of Brandeis' Bazaar. And it bred in Fanny Brandeis a lifelong hatred of the holiday season. In years after she always tried to get away from the city at Christmas time. The two women did the work of four men. They had a big stock on hand. Mrs. Brandeis was everywhere at once.

She got an enormous amount of work out of her clerks,
and they did not resent it. It is a gift that all born leaders have. She herself never sat down, and the clerks unconsciously followed her example.    She never com-
plained of weariness, she never lost her temper, she
never lost patience with a customer, even the tight-
fisted farmer type who doled their money out with that
reluctance found only in those who have wrung it from
the soil.

In the midst of the rush she managed, somehow,
never to fail to grasp the humor of a situation.    A
farmer woman came in for a doll's head, which she chose
with incredible deliberation and pains.  As it was being
wrapped she explained that it was for her little girl,
Minnie.  She had promised the head this year.  Next
Christmas they would buy a body for it.  Molly Brandeis's quick sympathy went out to the little girl who
was to lavish her mother-love on a doll's head for a
whole year.  She saw the head, in ghastly decapitation,
staring stiffly out from the cushions of the chill
and funereal parlor sofa, and the small Minnie peering in to feast her eyes upon its blond and waxen
beauty.

"Here," she had said, "take this, and sew it on the
head, so Minnie'll have something she can hold, at
least."    And she had wrapped a pink cambric, saw-
dust-stuffed body in with the head.

It was a snowy and picturesque Christmas, and intensely cold, with the hard, dry, cutting cold of Wisconsin.  Near the door the little store was freezing.
Every time the door opened it let in a blast.  Near the
big glowing stove it was very hot.

The aisles were packed so that sometimes it was
almost impossible to wedge one's way through.   The
china plates, stacked high, fairly melted away, as did
the dolls piled on the counters.  Mrs. Brandeis imported her china and dolls, and no store in Winnebago,

not even Gerretson's big department store, could touch them for value.

The two women scarcely stopped to eat in the last ten days of the holiday rush. Often Annie, the girl who had taken Mattie's place in the household, would bring down their supper, hot and hot, and they would eat it quickly up in the little gallery where they kept the sleds, and doll buggies, and drums. At night (the store was open until ten or eleven at Christmas time) they would trudge home through the snow, so numb with weariness that they hardly minded the cold. The icy wind cut their foreheads like a knife, and made the temples ache. The snow, hard and resilient, squeaked beneath their heels. They would open the front door and stagger in, blinking. The house seemed so weirdly quiet and peaceful after the rush and clamor of the store.

"Don't you want a sandwich, Mother, with a glass of beer?"

"I'm too tired to eat it, Fanny. I just want to get to bed."

Fanny grew to hate the stock phrases that met her with each customer. "I want something for a little boy about ten. He's really got everything." Or, "I'm looking for a present for a lady friend. Do you think a plate would be nice?" She began to loathe them—these satiated little boys, these unknown friends, for whom she must rack her brains.

They cleared a snug little fortune that Christmas. On Christmas Eve they smiled wanly at each other, like two comrades who have fought and bled together, and won. When they left the store it was nearly midnight. Belated shoppers, bundle-laden, carrying holly wreaths, with strange handles, and painted heads, and sticks protruding from lumpy brown paper burdens, were hurrying home.

They stumbled home, too spent to talk. Fanny,

groping for the keyhole, stubbed her toe against a wooden box between the storm door and the inner door. It had evidently been left there by the expressman or a delivery boy. It was a very heavy box.

"A Christmas present!" Fanny exclaimed. "Do you think it is? But it must be." She looked at the address, "Miss Fanny Brandeis." She went to the kitchen for a crowbar, and came back, still in her hat and coat. She pried open the box expertly, tore away the wrappings, and disclosed a gleaming leather-bound set of Balzac, and beneath that, incongruously enough, Mark Twain.

"Why!" exclaimed Fanny, sitting down on the floor rather heavily. Then her eye fell upon a card tossed aside in the hurry of unpacking. She picked it up, read it hastily. "Merry Christmas to the best daughter in the world. From her Mother."

Mrs. Brandeis had taken off her wraps and was standing over the sitting-room register, rubbing her numbed hands and smiling a little.

"Why, Mother!" Fanny scrambled to her feet. "You darling! In all that rush and work, to take time to think of me! Why!—" Her arms were around her mother's shoulders. She was pressing her glowing cheek against the pale, cold one. And they both wept a little, from emotion, and weariness, and relief, and enjoyed it, as women sometimes do.

Fanny made her mother stay in bed next morning, a thing that Mrs. Brandeis took to most ungracefully. After the holiday rush and strain she invariably had a severe cold, the protest of the body she had over-driven and under-nourished for two or three weeks. As a patient she was as trying and fractious as a man, tossing about, threatening to get up, demanding hot-water bags, cold compresses, alcohol rubs. She fretted about the business, and imagined that things were at a standstill during her absence.

Fanny herself rose early. Her healthy young body, after a night's sleep, was already recuperating from the month's strain. She had planned a real Christmas dinner, to banish the memory of the hasty and unpalatable lunches they had had to gulp during the rush. There was to be a turkey, and Fanny had warned Annie not to touch it. She wanted to stuff it and roast it herself. She spent the morning in the kitchen, aside from an occasional tip-toeing visit to her mother's room. At eleven she found her mother up, and no amount of coaxing would induce her to go back to bed. She had read the papers and she said she felt rested already.

The turkey came out a delicate golden-brown, and deliciously crackly. Fanny, looking up over a drumstick, noticed, with a shock, that her mother's eyes looked strangely sunken, and her skin, around the jaws and just under the chin, where her loose wrapper revealed her throat, was queerly yellow and shriveled. She had eaten almost nothing.

"Mother, you're not eating a thing! You really must eat a little."

Mrs. Brandeis began a pretense of using knife and fork, but gave it up finally and sat back, smiling rather wanly. "I guess I'm tireder than I thought I was, dear. I think I've got a cold coming on, too. I'll lie down again after dinner, and by to-morrow I'll be as chipper as a sparrow. The turkey's wonderful, isn't it? I'll have some, cold, for supper."

After dinner the house felt very warm and stuffy. It was crisply cold and sunny outdoors. The snow was piled high except on the sidewalks, where it had been neatly shoveled away by the mufflered Winnebago sons and fathers. There was no man in the Brandeis household, and Aloysius had been too busy to perform the chores usually considered his work about the house. The snow lay in drifts upon the sidewalk in front of the Brandeis house, except where passing feet had trampled it a bit.

"I'm going to shovel the walk," Fanny announced suddenly. "Way around to the woodshed. Where are those old mittens of mine? Annie, where's the snow shovel? Sure I am. Why not?"

She shoveled and scraped and pounded, bending rhythmically to the work, lifting each heaping shovelful with her strong young arms, tossing it to the side, digging in again, and under. An occasional neighbor passed by, or a friend, and she waved at them, gayly, and tossed back their badinage. "Merry Christmas!" she called, again and again, in reply to a passing acquaintance. "Same to you!"

At two o'clock Bella Weinberg telephoned to say that a little party of them were going to the river to skate. The ice was wonderful. Oh, come on! Fanny skated very well. But she hesitated. Mrs. Brandeis, dozing on the couch, sensed what was going on in her daughter's mind, and roused herself with something of her old asperity.

"Don't be foolish, child. Run along! You don't intend to sit here and gaze upon your sleeping beauty of a mother all afternoon, do you? Well, then!"

So Fanny changed her clothes, got her skates, and ran out into the snap and sparkle of the day. The winter darkness had settled down before she returned, all glowing and rosy, and bright-eyed. Her blood was racing through her body. Her lips were parted. The drudgery of the past three weeks seemed to have been blotted out by this one radiant afternoon.

The house was dark when she entered. It seemed very quiet, and close, and depressing after the sparkle and rush of the afternoon on the river. "Mother! Mother dear! Still sleeping?"

Mrs. Brandeis stirred, sighed, awoke. Fanny flicked on the light. Her mother was huddled in a kimono on the sofa. She sat up rather dazedly now, and stared at Fanny.

"Why—what time is it? What? Have I been sleeping all afternoon? Your mother's getting old."

She yawned, and in the midst of it caught her breath with a little cry of pain.

"What is it? What's the matter?"

Molly Brandeis pressed a hand to her breast. "A stitch, I guess. It's this miserable cold coming on. Is there any asperin in the house? I'll dose myself after supper, and take a hot foot bath and go to bed. I'm dead."

She ate less for supper than she had for dinner. She hardly tasted the cup of tea that Fanny insisted on making for her. She swayed a little as she sat, and her lids came down over her eyes, flutteringly, as if the weight of them was too great to keep up. At seven she was up-stairs, in bed, sleeping, and breathing heavily.

At eleven, or thereabouts, Fanny woke up with a a start. She sat up in bed, wide-eyed, peering into the darkness and listening. Some one was talking in a high, queer voice, a voice like her mother's, and yet unlike. She ran, shivering with the cold, into her mother's bedroom. She switched on the light. Mrs. Brandeis was lying on the pillow, her eyes almost closed, except for a terrifying slit of white that showed between the lids. Her head was tossing to and fro on the pillow. She was talking, sometimes clearly, and sometimes mumblingly.

"One gross cups and saucers . . . and now what do you think you'd like for a second prize . . . in the basement, Aloysius . . . the trains . . . I'll see that they get there to-day . . . yours of the tenth at hand . . ."

"Mother! Mother! Molly dear!" She shook her gently, then almost roughly. The voice ceased. The eyes remained the same. "Oh, God!" She ran to the back of the house. "Annie! Annie, get up! Mother's sick. She's out of her head. I'm going to 'phone for the doctor. Go in with her."

She got the doctor at last. She tried to keep her voice under control, and thought, with a certain pride, that she was succeeding. She ran up-stairs again. The voice had begun again, but it seemed thicker now. She got into her clothes, shaking with cold and terror, and yet thinking very clearly, as she always did in a crisis. She put clean towels in the bathroom, pushed the table up to the bed, got a glass of water, straightened the covers, put away the clothes that the tired woman had left about the room. Doctor Hertz came. He went through the usual preliminaries, listened, tapped, counted, straightened up at last.

"Fresh air," he said. "Cold air. All the windows open." They rigged up a device of screens and sheets to protect the bed from the drafts. Fanny obeyed orders silently, like a soldier. But her eyes went from the face on the pillow to that of the man bent over the bed. Something vague, cold, clammy, seemed to be closing itself around her heart. It was like an icy hand, squeezing there. There had suddenly sprung up that indefinable atmosphere of the sick-room—a sick-room in which a fight is being waged. Bottles on the table, glasses, a spoon, a paper shade over the electric light globe.

"What is it?" said Fanny, at last. "Grip?—grip?"

Doctor Hertz hesitated a moment. "Pneumonia."

Fanny's hands grasped the footboard tightly. "Do you think we'd better have a nurse?"

"Yes."

The nurse seemed to be there, somehow, miraculously. And the morning came. And in the kitchen Annie went about her work, a little more quietly than usual. And yesterday seemed far away. It was afternoon; it was twilight. Doctor Hertz had been there for hours. The

last time he brought another doctor with him—Thorn.
Mrs. Brandeis was not talking now. But she was
breathing. It filled the room, that breathing; it filled
the house. Fanny took her mother's hand, that hand
with the work-hardened palm and the broken nails. It
was very cold. She looked down at it. The nails were
blue. She began to rub it. She looked up into the
faces of the two men. She picked up the other hand—
snatched at it. "Look here!" she said. "Look here!"
And then she stood up. The vague, clammy thing that
had been wound about her heart suddenly relaxed. And
at that something icy hot rushed all over her body and
shook her. She came around to the foot of the bed,
and gripped it with her two hands. Her chin was
thrust forward, and her eyes were bright and staring.
She looked very much like her mother, just then. It
was a fighting face. A desperate face.

"Look here," she began, and was surprised to find
that she was only whispering. She wet her lips and
smiled, and tried again, forming the words carefully
with her lips. "Look here. She's dying—isn't she?
Isn't she! She's dying, isn't she?"

Doctor Hertz pursed his lips. The nurse came over
to her, and put a hand on her shoulder. Fanny shook
her off.

"Answer me. I've got a right to know. Look at
this!" She reached forward and picked up that inert,
cold, strangely shriveled blue hand again.

"My dear child—I'm afraid so."

There came from Fanny's throat a moan that began
high, and poignant, and quavering, and ended in a
shiver that seemed to die in her heart. The room was
still again, except for the breathing, and even that was
less raucous.

Fanny stared at the woman on the bed—at the long,
finely-shaped head, with the black hair wadded up so
carelessly now; at the long, straight, clever nose; the

full, generous mouth. There flooded her whole being a great, blinding rage. What had she had of life? she demanded fiercely. What? What? Her teeth came together grindingly. She breathed heavily through her nostrils, as if she had been running. And suddenly she began to pray, not with the sounding, unctious thees and thous of the Church and Bible; not elegantly or eloquently, with well-rounded phrases, as the righteous pray, but threateningly, hoarsely, as a desperate woman prays. It was not a prayer so much as a cry of defiance—a challenge.

"Look here, God!" and there was nothing profane as she said it. "Look here, God! She's done her part. It's up to You now. Don't You let her die! Look at her. Look at her!" She choked and shook herself angrily, and went on. "Is that fair? That's a rotten trick to play on a woman that gave what she gave! What did she ever have of life? Nothing! That little miserable, dirty store, and those little miserable, dirty people. You give her a chance, d'You hear? You give her a chance, God, or I'll——"

Her voice broke in a thin, cracked quaver. The nurse turned her around, suddenly and sharply, and led her from the room.

## CHAPTER EIGHT

Y OU can come down now. They're all here, I guess.
Doctor Thalmann's going to begin." Fanny,
huddled in a chair in her bedroom, looked up into the
plump, kindly face of the woman who was bending over
her. Then she stood up, docilely, and walked toward
the stairs with a heavy, stumbling step.

"I'd put down my veil if I were you," said the
neighbor woman. And reached up for the black folds
that draped Fanny's hat. Fanny's fingers reached for
them too, fumblingly. "I'd forgotten about it," she
said. The heavy crape fell about her shoulders, mercifully hiding the swollen, discolored face. She went
down the stairs. There was a little stir, a swaying
toward her, a sibilant murmur of sympathy from the
crowded sitting-room as she passed through to the
parlor where Rabbi Thalmann stood waiting, prayer
book in hand, in front of that which was covered with
flowers. Fanny sat down. A feeling of unreality was
strong upon her. Doctor Thalmann cleared his throat
and opened the book.

After all, it was not Rabbi Thalmann's funeral sermon that testified to Mrs. Brandeis's standing in the
community. It was the character of the gathering
that listened to what he had to say. Each had his own
opinion of Molly Brandeis, and needed no final eulogy
to confirm it. Father Fitzpatrick was there, tall, handsome, ruddy, the two wings of white showing at the temples making him look more than ever like a leading man.
He had been of those who had sat in what he called
Mrs. Brandeis's confessional, there in the quiet little

store. The two had talked of things theological and things earthy. His wit, quick though it was, was no match for hers, but they both had a humor sense and a drama sense, and one day they discovered, queerly enough, that they worshiped the same God. Any one of these things is basis enough for a friendship. Besides, Molly Brandeis could tell an Irish story inimitably. And you should have heard Father Fitzpatrick do the one about Ikey and the nickel. No, I think the Catholic priest, seeming to listen with such respectful attention, really heard very little of what Rabbi Thalmann had to say.

Herman Walthers was there, he of the First National Bank of Winnebago, whose visits had once brought such terror to Molly Brandeis. Augustus G. Gerretson was there, and three of his department heads. Emil Bauer sat just behind him. In a corner was Sadie, the erstwhile coquette, very subdued now, and months behind the fashions in everything but baby clothes. Hen Cody, who had done all of Molly Brandeis's draying, sat, in unaccustomed black, next to Mayor A. J. Dawes. Temple Emmanu-el was there, almost a unit. The officers of Temple Emanu-el Ladies' Aid Society sat in a row. They had never honored Molly Brandeis with office in the society—she who could have managed its business, politics and social activities with one hand tied behind her, and both her bright eyes shut. In the kitchen and on the porch and in the hallway stood certain obscure people—women whose finger tips stuck out of their cotton gloves, and whose skirts dipped ludicrously in the back. Only Molly Brandeis could have identified them for you. Mrs. Brosch, the butter and egg woman, hovered in the dining-room doorway. She had brought a pound of butter. It was her contribution to the funeral baked meats. She had deposited it furtively on the kitchen table. Birdie Callahan, head waitress at the Haley House, found a seat just next to the elegant Mrs. Morehouse, who led the Golf Club crowd. A haughty young lady in the dining-room, Birdie Callahan, in her stiffly starched white, but beneath the icy crust of her hauteur was a molten mass of good humor and friendliness. She and Molly Brandeis had had much in common.

But no one—not even Fanny Brandeis—ever knew who sent the great cluster of American Beauty roses that had come all the way from Milwaukee. There had been no card, so who could have guessed that they came from Blanche Devine. Blanche Devine, of the white powder, and the minks, and the diamonds, and the high-heeled shoes, and the plumes, lived in the house with the closed shutters, near the freight depot. She often came into Brandeis' Bazaar. Molly Brandeis had never allowed Sadie, or Pearl, or Fanny or Aloysius to wait on her. She had attended to her herself. And one day, for some reason, Blanche Devine found herself telling Molly Brandeis how she had come to be Blanche Devine, and it was a moving and terrible story. And now her cardless flowers, a great, scarlet sheaf of them, lay next the chaste white roses that had been sent by the Temple Emanu-el Ladies' Aid. Truly, death is a great leveler.

In a vague way Fanny seemed to realize that all these people were there. I think she must even have found a certain grim comfort in their presence. Hers had not been the dry-eyed grief of the strong, such as you read about. She had wept, night and day, hopelessly, inconsolably, torturing herself with remorseful questions. If she had not gone skating, might she not have seen how ill her mother was? Why hadn't she insisted on the doctor when her mother refused to eat the Christmas dinner? Blind and selfish, she told herself; blind and selfish. Her face was swollen and distorted now, and she was thankful for the black veil that shielded her. Winnebago was scandalized to see that she wore no other black. Mrs. Brandeis had never wanted Fanny to wear it; she hadn't enough color, she said. So now she was dressed in her winter suit of blue, and her hat with the pert blue quill. And the little rabbi's voice went on and on, and Fanny knew that it could not be true. What had all this dust-to-dust talk to do with any one as vital, and electric, and constructive as Molly Brandeis. In the midst of the service there was a sharp cry, and a little stir, and the sound of stifled sobbing. It was Aloysius the merry, Aloysius the faithful, whose Irish heart was quite broken. Fanny ground her teeth together in an effort at self-control.

And so to the end, and out past the little hushed, respectful group on the porch, to the Jewish cemetery on the state road. The snow of Christmas week was quite virgin there, except for that one spot where the sexton and his men had been at work. Then back at a smart jog trot through the early dusk of the winter afternoon, the carriage wheels creaking upon the hard, dry snow. And Fanny Brandeis said to herself (she must have been a little light-headed from hunger and weeping):

"Now I'll know whether it's true or not. When I go into the house. If she's there she'll say, 'Well Fanchen! Hungry? Oh, but my little girl's hands are cold! Come here to the register and warm them.' O God, let her be there! Let her be there!"

But she wasn't. The house had been set to rights by brisk and unaccustomed hands. There was a bustle and stir in the dining-room, and from the kitchen came the appetizing odors of cooking food. Fanny went up to a chair that was out of its place, and shoved it back against the wall where it belonged. She straightened a rug, carried the waste basket from the desk to the spot near the living-room table where it had always

served to hide the shabby, worn place in the rug.
Fanny went up-stairs, past The Room that was once
more just a comfortable, old fashioned bedroom, instead of a mysterious and awful chamber; bathed her
face, tidied her hair, came down-stairs again, ate and
drank things hot and revivifying. The house was full
of kindly women.

Fanny found herself clinging to them—clinging desperately to these ample, broad-bosomed, soothing
women whom she had scarcely known before. They
were always there, those women, and their husbands
too; kindly, awkward men, who patted her shoulder,
and who spoke of Molly Brandeis with that sincerity of
admiration such as men usually give only to men. People were constantly popping in at the back door with
napkin-covered trays, and dishes and baskets. A wonderful and beautiful thing, that homely small-town sympathy that knows the value of physical comfort in time
of spiritual anguish.

Two days after the funeral Fanny Brandeis went
back to the store, much as her mother had done many
years before, after her husband's death. She looked
about at the bright, well-stocked shelves and tables
with a new eye—a speculative eye. The Christmas season was over. January was the time for inventory and
for replenishment. Mrs. Brandeis had always gone to
Chicago the second week in January for the spring
stock. But something was forming in Fanny Brandeis's mind—a resolve that grew so rapidly as to take
her breath away. Her brain felt strangely clear and
keen after the crashing storm of grief that had shaken
her during the past week.

"What are you going to do now?" people had asked
her, curious and interested. "Is Theodore coming
back?"

"I don't know—yet." In answer to the first. And,
"No. Why should he? He has his work."

"But he could be of such help to you."

"I'll help myself," said Fanny Brandeis, and smiled a curious smile that had in it more of bitterness and less of mirth than any smile has a right to have.

Mrs. Brandeis had left a will, far-sighted business woman that she was. It was a terse, clear-headed document, that gave "to Fanny Brandeis, my daughter," the six-thousand-dollar insurance, the stock, good-will and fixtures of Brandeis' Bazaar, the house furnishings, the few pieces of jewelry in their old-fashioned setting. To Theodore was left the sum of fifteen hundred dollars. He had received his share in the years of his musical education.

Fanny Brandeis did not go to Chicago that January. She took inventory of Brandeis' Bazaar, carefully and minutely. And then, just as carefully and minutely she took stock of Fanny Brandeis. There was something relentless and terrible in the way she went about this self-analysis. She walked a great deal that winter, often out through the drifts to the little cemetery. As she walked her mind was working, working. She held long mental conversations with herself during these walks, and once she was rather frightened to find herself talking aloud. She wondered if she had done that before. And a plan was maturing in her brain, while the fight went on within herself, thus:

"You'll never do it, Fanny. You're not built that way."

"Oh, won't I! Watch me! Give me time."

"You'll think of what your mother would have done under the same conditions, and you'll do that thing."

"I won't. Not unless it's the long-headed thing to do. I'm through being sentimental and unselfish. What did it bring her? Nothing!"

The weeks went by. Fanny worked hard in the store, and bought little. February came, and with

the spring her months of private thinking bore fruit.
There came to Fanny Brandeis a great resolve. She
would put herself in a high place. Every talent she
possessed, every advantage, every scrap of knowledge,
every bit of experience, would be used toward that end.
She would make something of herself. It was a worldly,
selfish resolve, born of a bitter sorrow, and ambition,
and resentment. She made up her mind that she would
admit no handicaps. Race, religion, training, natural
impulses—she would discard them all if they stood
in her way. She would leave Winnebago behind. At
best, if she stayed there, she could never accomplish
more than to make her business a more than ordinarily
successful small-town store. And she would be—nobody. No, she had had enough of that. She would
crush and destroy the little girl who had fasted on
that Day of Atonement; the more mature girl who
had written the thesis about the paper mill rag-room;
the young woman who had drudged in the store on
Elm Street. In her place she would mold a hard, keen-
eyed, resolute woman, whose godhead was to be success, and to whom success would mean money and position. She had not a head for mathematics, but out of
the puzzling problems and syllogisms in geometry she
had retained in her memory this one immovable truth:

A straight line is the shortest distance between two
points.

With her mental eye she marked her two points,
and then, starting from the first, made directly for
the second. But she forgot to reckon with the law of
tangents. She forgot, too, how paradoxical a creature
was this Fanny Brandeis whose eyes filled with tears
at sight of a parade—just the sheer drama of it—
were the marchers G. A. R. veterans, school children
in white, soldiers, Foresters, political marching clubs;
and whose eyes burned dry and bright as she stood
over the white mound in the cemetery on the state

road.   Generous, spontaneous, impulsive, warm-
hearted, she would be cold, calculating, deliberate, she
told herself.

Thousands of years of persecution behind her made
her quick to appreciate suffering in others, and gave
her an innate sense of fellowship with the downtrodden.
She resolved to use that sense as a searchlight aiding
her to see and overcome obstacles.   She told herself
that she was done with maudlin sentimentality.   On the
rare occasions when she had accompanied her mother
to Chicago, the two women had found delight in wan-
dering about the city's foreign quarters.   When other
small-town women buyers snatched occasional moments
of leisure for the theater or personal shopping, these
two had spent hours in the ghetto around Jefferson
and Taylor, and Fourteenth Streets.   Something in
the sight of these people—alien, hopeful, emotional,
often grotesque—thrilled and interested both the
women.   And at sight of an ill-clad Italian, with his
slovenly, wrinkled old-young wife, turning the handle
of his grind organ whilst both pairs of eyes searched
windows and porches and doorsteps with a hopeless
sort of hopefulness, she lost her head entirely and
emptied her limp pocketbook of dimes, and nickels,
and pennies.   Incidentally it might be stated that she
loved the cheap and florid music of the hand organ
itself.

It was rumored that Brandeis' Bazaar was for sale.
In the spring Gerretson's offered Fanny the position
of buyer and head of the china, glassware, and kitchenware sections.   Gerretson's showed an imposing block
of gleaming plate-glass front now, and drew custom
from a dozen thrifty little towns throughout the Fox
River Valley.   Fanny refused the offer.   In March she
sold outright the stock, good-will, and fixtures of
Brandeis' Bazaar.   The purchaser was a thrifty, far-
sighted traveling man who had wearied of the road

and wanted to settle down. She sold the household goods too—those intimate, personal pieces of wood and cloth that had become, somehow, part of her life. She had grown up with them. She knew the history of every nick, every scratch and worn spot. Her mother lived again in every piece. The old couch went off in a farmer's wagon. Fanny turned away when they joggled it down the front steps and into the rude vehicle. It was like another funeral. She was furious to find herself weeping again. She promised herself punishment for that.

Up in her bedroom she opened the bottom drawer of her bureau. That bureau and its history and the history of every piece of furniture in the room bore mute testimony to the character of its occupant; to her protest against things as she found them, and her determination to make them over to suit her. She had spent innumerable Sunday mornings wielding the magic paint brush that had transformed the bedroom from dingy oak to gleaming cream enamel. She sat down on the floor now, before the bureau, and opened the bottom drawer.

In a corner at the back, under the neat pile of garments, was a tightly-rolled bundle of cloth. Fanny reached for it, took it out, and held it in her hands a moment. Then she unrolled it slowly, and the bundle revealed itself to be a faded, stained, voluminous gingham apron, blue and white. It was the kind of apron women don when they perform some very special household ritual—baking, preserving, house cleaning. It crossed over the shoulders with straps, and its generous fullness ran all the way around the waist. It was discolored in many places with the brown and reddish stains of fruit juices. It had been Molly Brandeis' canning apron. Fanny had come upon it hanging on a hook behind the kitchen door, after that week in December. And at sight of it all her fortitude and forced calm had fled. She had spread her arms over the limp, mute, yet speaking thing dangling there, and had wept so wildly and uncontrollably as to alarm even herself.

Nothing in connection with her mother's death had power to call up such poignant memories as did this homely, intimate garment. She saw again the steamy kitchen, deliciously scented with the perfume of cooking fruit, or the tantalizing, mouth-watering spiciness of vinegar and pickles. On the stove the big dishpan, in which the jelly glasses and fruit jars, with their tops and rubbers, bobbed about in hot water. In the great granite kettle simmered the cooking fruit. Molly Brandeis, enveloped in the familiar blue-and-white apron, stood over it, like a priestess, stirring, stirring, slowly, rhythmically. Her face would be hot and moist with the steam, and very tired too, for she often came home from the store utterly weary, to stand over the kettle until ten or eleven o'clock. But the pride in it as she counted the golden or ruby tinted tumblers gleaming in orderly rows as they cooled on the kitchen table!

"Fifteen glasses of grape jell, Fan! And I didn't mix a bit of apple with it. I didn't think I'd get more than ten. And nine of the quince preserve. That makes—let me see—eighty-three, ninety-eight—one hundred and seven altogether."

"We'll never eat it, Mother."

"You said that last year, and by April my preserve cupboard looked like Old Mother Hubbard's."

But then, Mrs. Brandeis was famous for her preserves, as Father Fitzpatrick, and Aloysius, and Doctor Thalmann, and a dozen others could testify. After the strain and flurry of a busy day at the store there was something about this homely household rite that brought a certain sense of rest and peace to Molly Brandeis.

All this moved through Fanny Brandeis's mind as she sat with the crumpled apron in her lap, her eyes swimming with hot tears. The very stains that discolored it, the faded blue of the front breadth, the frayed buttonhole, the little scorched place where she had burned a hole when trying unwisely to lift a steaming kettle from the stove with the apron's corner, spoke to her with eloquent lips. That apron had become a vice with Fanny. She brooded over it as a mother broods over the shapeless, scuffled bit of leather that was a baby's shoe; as a woman, widowed, clings to a shabby, frayed old smoking jacket. More than once she had cried herself to sleep with the apron clasped tightly in her arms.

She got up from the floor now, with the apron in her hands, and went down the stairs, opened the door that led to the cellar, walked heavily down those steps and over to the furnace. She flung open the furnace door. Red and purple the coal bed gleamed, with little white flame sprites dancing over it. Fanny stared at it a moment, fascinated. Her face was set, her eyes brilliant. Suddenly she flung the tightly-rolled apron into the heart of the gleaming mass. She shut her eyes then. The fire seemed to hold its breath for a moment. Then, with a gasp, it sprang upon its food. The bundle stiffened, writhed, crumpled, sank, lay a blackened heap, was dissolved. The fire bed glowed red and purple as before, except for a dark spot in its heart. Fanny shivered a little. She shut the furnace door and went up-stairs again.

"Smells like something burning—cloth, or something," called Annie, from the kitchen.

"It's only an old apron that was cluttering up my —my bureau drawer."

Thus she successfully demonstrated the first lesson in the cruel and rigid course of mental training she had mapped out for herself.

Leaving Winnebago was not easy. There is something about a small town that holds you. Your life is so intimately interwoven with that of your neighbor. Existence is so safe, so sane, so sure. Fanny knew that when she turned the corner of Elm Street every third person she met would speak to her. Life was made up of minute details, too trivial for the notice of the hurrying city crowds. You knew when Milly Glaenzer changed the baby buggy for a go-cart. The youngest Hupp boy—Sammy—who was graduated from High School in June, is driving A. J. Dawes's automobile now. My goodness, how time flies! Doeppler's grocery has put in plate-glass windows, and they're getting out-of-season vegetables every day now from Milwaukee. As you pass you get the coral glow of tomatoes, and the tender green of lettuces. And that vivid green? Fresh young peas! And in February. Well! They've torn down the old yellow brick National Bank, and in its place a chaste Greek Temple of a building looks rather contemptuously down its classic columns upon the farmer's wagons drawn up along the curb. If Fanny Brandeis' sense of proportion had not been out of plumb she might have realized that, to Winnebago, the new First National Bank building was as significant and epochal as had been the Woolworth Building to New York.

The very intimacy of these details, Fanny argued, was another reason for leaving Winnebago. They were like detaining fingers that grasped at your skirts, impeding your progress.

She had early set about pulling every wire within her reach that might lead, directly or indirectly, to the furtherance of her ambition. She got two offers from Milwaukee retail stores. She did not consider them for a moment. Even a Chicago department store of the second grade (one of those on the wrong side of State Street) did not tempt her. She knew her value. She could afford to wait. There was money enough on which to live comfortably until the right chance presented itself. She knew every item of her equipment, and she conned them to herself greedily: Definite charm of manner; the thing that is called magnetism; brains; imagination; driving force; health; youth; and, most precious of all, that which money could not buy, nor education provide—experience. Experience, a priceless weapon, that is beaten into shape only by much contact with men and women, and that is sharpened by much rubbing against the rough edges of this world.

In April her chance came to her; came in that accidental, haphazard way that momentous happenings have. She met on Elm Street a traveling man from whom Molly Brandeis had bought for years. He dropped both sample cases and shook hands with Fanny, eying her expertly and approvingly, and yet without insolence. He was a wise, road-weary, skillful member of his fraternity, grown gray in years of service, and a little bitter. Though perhaps that was due partly to traveling man's dyspepsia, brought on by years of small-town hotel food.

"So you've sold out."

"Yes. Over a month ago."

"H'm. That was a nice little business you had there. Your ma built it up herself. There was a woman! Gosh! Discounted her bills, even during the panic."

Fanny smiled a reflective little smile. "That line is a complete characterization of my mother. Her life was a series of panics. But she never lost her head. And she always discounted."

He held out his hand. "Well, glad I met you." He picked up his sample cases. "You leaving Winnebago?"

"Yes."

"Going to the city, I suppose. Well you're a smart girl. And your mother's daughter. I guess you'll get along all right. What house are you going with?"

"I don't know. I'm waiting for the right chance. It's all in starting right. I'm not going to hurry."

He put down his cases again, and his eyes grew keen and kindly. He gesticulated with one broad forefinger. "Listen, m' girl. I'm what they call an old-timer. They want these high-power, eight-cylinder kids on the road these days, and it's all we can do to keep up. But I've got something they haven't got —yet. I never read anybody on the Psychology of Business, but I know human nature all the way from Elm Street, Winnebago, to Fifth Avenue, New York."

"I'm sure you do," said Fanny politely, and took a little step forward, as though to end the conversation.

"Now wait a minute. They say the way to learn is to make mistakes. If that's true, I'm at the head of the class. I've made 'em all. Now get this. You start out and specialize. Specialize! Tie to one thing, and make yourself an expert in it. But first be sure it's the right thing."

"But how is one to be sure?"

"By squinting up your eyes so you can see ten years ahead. If it looks good to you at that distance —better, in fact, than it does close by—then it's right. I suppose that's what they call having imagination. I never had any. That's why I'm still selling goods on the road. To look at you I'd say you had too much. Maybe I'm wrong. But I never yet saw a woman with a mouth like yours who was cut out for business—unless it was your mother—And her eyes were different. Let's see, what was I saying?"

"Specialize."

"Oh, yes. And that reminds me. Bunch of fellows in the smoker last night talking about Haynes-Cooper. Your mother hated 'em like poison, the way every

small-town merchant hates the mail-order houses. But,
I hear they've got an infants' wear department that's
just going to grass for lack of a proper head. You're
only a kid. And they have done you dirt all these
years, of course. But if you could sort of horn in
there—why, say, there's no limit to the distance you
could go. No limit! With your brains and experience."

That had been the beginning. From then on the
thing had moved forward with a certain inevitableness.
There was something about the vastness of the thing
that appealed to Fanny. Here was an organization
whose great arms embraced the world. Haynes-Cooper, giant among mail-order houses, was said to
eat a small-town merchant every morning for breakfast.

"There's a Haynes-Cooper catalogue in every farmer's kitchen," Molly Brandeis used to say. "The Bible's
in the parlor, but they keep the H. C. book in the
room where they live."

That she was about to affiliate herself with this
house appealed to Fanny Brandeis's sense of comedy.
She had heard her mother presenting her arguments
to the stubborn farmer folk who insisted on ordering
their stove, or dinner set, or plow, or kitchen goods
from the fascinating catalogue. "I honestly think
it's just the craving for excitement that makes them
do it," she often said. "They want the thrill they
get when they receive a box from Chicago, and open
it, and take off the wrappings, and dig out the thing
they ordered from a picture, not knowing whether it
will be right or wrong."

Her arguments usually left the farmer unmoved.
He would drive into town, mail his painfully written
letter and order at the post-office, dispose of his load
of apples, or butter, or cheese, or vegetables, and
drive cheerfully back again, his empty wagon bump-

ing and rattling down the old corduroy road. Express, breakage, risk, loyalty to his own region—all these arguments left him cold.

In May, after much manipulation, correspondence, two interviews, came a definite offer from the Haynes-Cooper Company. It was much less than the State Street store had offered, and there was something tentative about the whole agreement. Haynes-Cooper proffered little and demanded much, as is the way of the rich and mighty. But Fanny remembered the ten-year viewpoint that the weary-wise old traveling man had spoken about. She took their offer. She was to go to Chicago almost at once, to begin work June first.

Two conversations that took place before she left are perhaps worth recording. One was with Father Fitzpatrick of St. Ignatius Catholic Church. The other with Rabbi Emil Thalmann of Temple Emanu-el.

An impulse brought her into Father Fitzpatrick's study. It was a week before her departure. She was tired. There had been much last signing of papers, nailing of boxes, strapping of trunks. When things began to come too thick and fast for her she put on her hat and went for a walk at the close of the May day. May, in Wisconsin, is a thing all fragrant, and gold, and blue; and white with cherry blossoms; and pink with apple blossoms; and tremulous with budding things.

Fanny struck out westward through the neat streets of the little town, and found herself on the bridge over the ravine in which she had played when a little girl —the ravine that her childish imagination had peopled with such pageantry of redskin, and priests, and voyageurs, and cavaliers. She leaned over the iron railing and looked down. Where grass, and brook, and wild flower had been there now oozed great eruptions of ash heaps, tin cans, broken bottles, mounds of dirt. Win-

nebago's growing pains had begun. Fanny turned
away with a little sick feeling. She went on across
the bridge past the Catholic church. Just next
the church was the parish house where Father Fitzpatrick lived. It always looked as if it had been
scrubbed, inside and out, with a scouring brick. Its
windows were a reproach and a challenge to every
housekeeper in Winnebago.

Fanny wanted to talk to somebody about that ravine.
She was full of it. Father Fitzpatrick's study overlooked it. Besides, she wanted to see him before she
left Winnebago. A picture came to her mind of his
handsome, ruddy face, twinkling with humor as she
had last seen it when he had dropped in at Brandeis'
Bazaar for a chat with her mother. She turned in at
the gate and ran up the immaculate, gray-painted
steps, that always gleamed as though still wet with the
paint brush.

"I shouldn't wonder if that housekeeper of his comes
out with a pail of paint and does 'em every morning
before breakfast," Fanny said to herself as she rang
the bell.

Usually it was that sparse and spectacled person
herself who opened the parish house door, but to-day
Fanny's ring was answered by Father Casey, parish
assistant. A sour-faced and suspicious young man,
Father Casey, thick-spectacled, and pointed of nose.
Nothing of the jolly priest about him. He was new
to the town, but he recognized Fanny and surveyed
her darkly.

"Father Fitzpatrick in? I'm Fanny Brandeis."

"The reverend father is busy," and the glass door
began to close.

"Who is it?" boomed a voice from within. "Who're
you turning away, Casey?"

"A woman, not a parishioner." The door was almost shut now.

Footsteps down the hall. "Good! Let her in." The door opened ever so reluctantly. Father Fitzpatrick loomed up beside his puny assistant, dwarfing him. He looked sharply at the figure on the porch. "For the love of—! Casey, you're a fool! How you ever got beyond being an altar-boy is more than I can see. Come in, child. Come in! The man's cut out for a jailor, not a priest."

Fanny's two hands were caught in one of his big ones, and she was led down the hall to the study. It was the room of a scholar and a man, and the one spot in the house that defied the housekeeper's weapons of broom and duster. A comfortable and disreputable room, full of books, and fishing tackle, and chairs with sagging springs, and a sofa that was dented with friendly hollows. Pipes on the disorderly desk. A copy of "Mr. Dooley" spread face down on what appeared to be next Sunday's sermon, rough-drafted.

"I just wanted to talk to you." Fanny drifted to the shelves, book-lover that she was, and ran a finger over a half-dozen titles. "Your assistant was justified, really, in closing the door on me. But I'm glad you rescued me." She came over to him and stood looking up at him. He seemed to loom up endlessly, though hers was a medium height. "I think I really wanted to talk to you about that ravine, though I came to say good-by."

"Sit down, child, sit down!" He creaked into his great leather-upholstered desk chair, himself. "If you had left without seeing me I'd have excommunicated Casey. Between you and me the man's mad. His job ought to be duenna to a Spanish maiden, not assistant to a priest with a leaning toward the flesh."

Now, Father Fitzpatrick talked with a—no, you couldn't call it a brogue. It was nothing so gross as that. One does not speak of the flavor of a rare wine; one calls attention to its bouquet. A subtle, teasing, elusive something that just tickles the senses instead of punching them in the ribs. So his speech was permeated with a will-o'-the-wisp, a tingling richness that evaded definition. You will have to imagine it. There shall be no vain attempt to set it down. Besides, you always skip dialect.

"So you're going away. I'd heard. Where to?"

"Chicago, Haynes-Cooper. It's a wonderful chance. I don't see yet how I got it. There's only one other woman on their business staff—I mean working actually in an executive way in the buying and selling end of the business. Of course there are thousands doing clerical work, and that kind of thing. Have you ever been through the plant? It's—it's incredible."

Father Fitzpatrick drummed with his fingers on the arm of his chair, and looked at Fanny, his handsome eyes half shut.

"So it's going to be business, h'm? Well, I suppose it's only natural. Your mother and I used to talk about you often. I don't know if you and she ever spoke seriously of this little trick of drawing, or cartooning, or whatever it is you have. She used to think about it. She said once to me, that it looked to her more than just a knack. An authentic gift of caricature, she called it—if it could only be developed. But of course Theodore took everything. That worried her."

"Oh, nonsense! That! I just amuse myself with it."

"Yes. But what amuses you might amuse other people. There's all too few amusing things in the world. Your mother was a smart woman, Fanny. The smartest I ever knew."

"There's no money in it, even if I were to get on with it. What could I do with it? Who ever heard of a woman cartoonist! And I couldn't illustrate.

Those pink cheesecloth pictures the magazines use. I want to earn money. Lots of it. And now."

She got up and went to the window, and stood looking down the steep green slope of the ravine that lay, a natural amphitheater, just below.

"Money, h'm?" mused Father Fitzpatrick. "Well, it's popular and handy. And you look to me like the kind of girl who'd get it, once you started out for it. I've never had much myself. They say it has a way of turning to dust and ashes in the mouth, once you get a good, satisfying bite of it. But that's only talk, I suppose."

Fanny laughed a little, still looking down at the ravine. "I'm fairly accustomed to dust and ashes by this time. It won't be a new taste to me." She whirled around suddenly. "And speaking of dust and ashes, isn't this a shame? A crime? Why doesn't somebody stop it? Why don't you stop it?" She pointed to the desecrated ravine below. Her eyes were blazing, her face all animation.

Father Fitzpatrick came over and stood beside her. His face was sad. "It's a—" He stopped abruptly, and looked down into her glowing face. He cleared his throat. "It's a perfectly natural state of affairs," he said smoothly. "Winnebago's growing. Especially over there on the west side, since the new mill went up, and they've extended the street car line. They need the land to build on. It's business. And money."

"Business! It's a crime! It's wanton! Those ravines are the most beautiful natural spots in Wisconsin. Why, they're history, and romance, and beauty!"

"So that's the way you feel about it?"

"Of course. Don't you? Can't you stop it? Petitions—"

"Certainly I feel it's an outrage. But I'm just a poor fool of a priest, and sentimental, with no head

for business. Now you're a business woman, and different."

"I! You're joking."

"Say, listen, m' girl. The world's made up of just
two things: ravines and dump heaps. And the dump-
ers are forever edging up, and squeedging up, and trying to grab the ravines and spoil 'em, when nobody's
looking. You've made your choice, and allied yourself
with the dump heaps. What right have you to cry
out against the desecration of the ravines?"

"The right that every one has that loves them."

"Child, you're going to get so used to seeing your
ravines choked up at Haynes-Cooper that after a while
you'll prefer 'em that way."

Fanny turned on him passionately. "I won't! And
if I do, perhaps it's just as well. There's such a
thing as too much ravine. What do you want me to
do? Stay here, and grub away, and become a crabbed
old maid like Irma Klein, thankful to be taken around
by the married crowd, joining the Aid Society and
going to the card parties on Sunday nights? Or I
could marry a traveling man, perhaps, or Lee Kohn
of the Golden Eagle. I'm just like any other ambitious
woman with brains—"

"No you're not. You're different. And I'll tell
you why. You're a Jew."

"Yes, I've got that handicap."

"That isn't a handicap, Fanny. It's an asset.
Outwardly you're like any other girl of your age.
Inwardly you've been molded by occupation, training,
religion, history, temperament, race, into something—"

"Ethnologists have proved that there is no such
thing as a Jewish race," she interrupted pertly.

"H'm. Maybe. I don't know what you'd call it,
then. You can't take a people and persecute them
for thousands of years, hounding them from place to
place, herding them in dark and filthy streets, with-

out leaving some sort of brand on them—a mark that differentiates. Sometimes it doesn't show outwardly. But it's there, inside. You know, Fanny, how it's always been said that no artist can became a genius until he has suffered. You've suffered, you Jews, for centuries and centuries, until you're all artists—quick to see drama because you've lived in it, emotional, oversensitive, cringing, or swaggering, high-strung, demonstrative, affectionate, generous.

"Maybe they're right. Perhaps it isn't a race. But what do you call the thing, then, that made you draw me as you did that morning when you came to ten o'clock mass and did a caricature of me in the pulpit. You showed up something that I've been trying to hide for twenty years, till I'd fooled everybody, including myself. My church is always packed. Nobody else there ever saw it. I'll tell you, Fanny, what I've always said: the Irish would be the greatest people in the world—it it weren't for the Jews."

They laughed together at that, and the tension was relieved.

"Well, anyway," said Fanny, and patted his great arm, "I'd rather talk to you than to any man in the world."

"I hope you won't be able to say that a year from now, dear girl."

And so they parted. He took her to the door himself, and watched her slim figure down the street and across the ravine bridge, and thought she walked very much like her mother, shoulders squared, chin high, hips firm. He went back into the house, after surveying the sunset largely, and encountered the dour Casey in the hall.

"I'll type your sermon now, sir—if it's done."

"It isn't done, Casey. And you know it. Oh, Casey,"—(I wish your imagination would supply that brogue, because it was such a deliciously soft and racy thing)—"Oh, Casey, Casey! you're a better priest than I am—but a poorer man."

Fanny was to leave Winnebago the following Saturday. She had sold the last of the household furniture, and had taken a room at the Haley House. She felt very old and experienced—and sad. That, she told herself, was only natural. Leaving things to which one is accustomed is always hard. Queerly enough, it was her good-by to Aloysius that most unnerved her. Aloysius had been taken on at Gerretson's, and the dignity of his new position sat heavily upon him. You should have seen his ties. Fanny sought him out at Gerretson's.

"It's flure-manager of the basement I am," he said, and struck an elegant attitude against the case of misses'-ready-to-wear coats. "And when you come back to Winnebago, Miss Fanny,—and the saints send it be soon—I'll bet ye'll see me on th' first flure, keepin' a stern but kindly eye on the swellest trade in town Ev'ry last thing I know I learned off yur poor ma."

"I hope it will serve you here, Aloysius."

"Sarve me!" He bent closer. "Meanin' no offense, Miss Fanny; but say, listen: Oncet ye get a Yiddish business education into an Irish head, and there's no limit to the length ye can go. If I ain't a dry-goods king be th' time I'm thirty I hope a packin' case'll fall on me."

The sight of Aloysius seemed to recall so vividly all that was happy and all that was hateful about Brandeis' Bazaar; all the bravery and pluck, and resourcefulness of the bright-eyed woman he had admiringly called his boss, that Fanny found her self-control slipping. She put out her hand rather blindly to meet his great red paw (a dressy striped cuff seemed to make it all the redder), murmured a word of thanks in return for his fervent good wishes, and fled up the basement stairs.

On Friday night (she was to leave next day) she went to the temple. The evening service began at seven. At half past six Fanny had finished her early supper. She would drop in at Doctor Thalmann's house and walk with him to temple, if he had not already gone.

"*Nein, der Herr Rabbi ist noch hier*—sure," the maid said in answer to Fanny's question. The Thalmann's had a German maid—one Minna—who bullied the invalid Mrs. Thalmann, was famous for her cookies with walnuts on the top, and who made life exceedingly difficult for unlinguistic callers.

Rabbi Thalmann was up in his study. Fanny ran lightly up the stairs.

"Who is it, Emil? That Minna! Next Monday her week is up. She goes."

"It's I, Mrs. Thalmann. Fanny Brandeis."

"Na, Fanny! Now what do you think!"

In the brightly-lighted doorway of his little study appeared Rabbi Thalmann, on one foot a comfortable old romeo, on the other a street shoe. He held out both hands. "Only at supper we talked about you. Isn't that so, Harriet?" He called into the darkened room.

"I came to say good-by. And I thought we might walk to temple together. How's Mrs. Thalmann tonight?"

The little rabbi shook his head darkly, and waved a dismal hand. But that was for Fanny alone. What he said was: "She's really splendid to-day. A little tired, perhaps; but what is that?"

"Emil!" from the darkened bedroom. "How can you say that? But how! What I have suffered to-day, only! Torture! And because I say nothing I'm not sick."

"Go in," said Rabbi Thalmann.

So Fanny went in to the woman lying, yellow-faced,

on the pillows of the dim old-fashioned bedroom with
its walnut furniture, and its red plush mantel drape.
Mrs. Thalmann held out a hand. Fanny took it in
hers, and perched herself on the edge of the bed. She
patted the dry, devitalized hand, and pressed it in her
own strong, electric grip. Mrs. Thalmann raised her
head from the pillow.

"Tell me, did she have her white apron on?"

"White apron?"

"Minna, the girl."

"Oh!" Fanny's mind jerked back to the gingham-
covered figure that had opened the door for her.
"Yes," she lied, "a white one—with crochet around the
bottom. Quite grand."

Mrs. Thalmann sank back on the pillow with a satisfied sigh. "A wonder." She shook her head. "What
that girl wastes alone, when I am helpless here."

Rabbi Thalmann came into the room, both feet
booted now, and placed his slippers neatly, toes out,
under the bed. "Ach, Harriet, the girl is all right.
You imagine. Come, Fanny." He took a great, fat
watch out of his pocket. "It is time to go."

Mrs. Thalmann laid a detaining hand on Fanny's
arm. "You will come often back here to Winnebago?"

"I'm afraid not. Once a year, perhaps, to visit
my graves."

The sick eyes regarded the fresh young face. "Your
mother, Fanny, we didn't understand her so well, here
in Winnebago, among us Jewish ladies. She was different."

Fanny's face hardened. She stood up. "Yes, she
was different."

"She comes often into my mind now, when I am
here alone, with only the four walls. We were *aber
dumm*, we women—but how *dumm!* She was too smart
for us, your mother. Too smart. *Und eine sehr brave
frau.*"

And suddenly Fanny, she who had resolved to set her face against all emotion, and all sentiment, found herself with her glowing cheek pressed against the withered one, and it was the weak old hand that patted her now. So she lay for a moment, silent. Then she got up, straightened her hat, smiled.

"*Auf Wiedersehen,*" she said in her best German. "*Und gute Besserung.*"

But the rabbi's wife shook her head. "Good-by."

From the hall below Doctor Thalmann called to her. "Come, child, come!" Then, "Ach, the light in my study! I forgot to turn it out, Fanny, be so good, yes?"

Fanny entered the bright little room, reached up to turn off the light, and paused a moment to glance about her. It was an ugly, comfortable, old-fashioned room that had never progressed beyond the what-not period. Fanny's eye was caught by certain framed pictures on the walls. They were photographs of Rabbi Thalmann's confirmation classes. Spindling-legged little boys in the splendor of patent-leather buttoned shoes, stiff white shirts, black broadcloth suits with satin lapels; self-conscious and awkward little girls—these in the minority—in white dresses and stiff white hair bows. In the center of each group sat the little rabbi, very proud and alert. Fanny was not among these. She had never formally taken the vows of her creed. As she turned down the light now, and found her way down the stairs, she told herself that she was glad this was so.

It was a matter of only four blocks to the temple. But they were late, and so they hurried, and there was little conversation. Fanny's arm was tucked comfortably in his. It felt, somehow, startlingly thin, that arm. And as they hurried along there was a jerky feebleness about his gait. It was with difficulty that Fanny restrained herself from supporting him when

they came to a rough bit of walk or a sudden step.
Something fine in her prompted her not to. But the
alert mind in that old frame sensed what was going
on in her thoughts.

"He's getting feeble, the old rabbi, h'm?"

"Not a bit of it. I've got all I can do to keep up
with you. You set such a pace."

"I know. I know. They are not all so kind, Fanny.
They are too prosperous, this congregation of mine.
And some day, 'Off with his head!' And in my place
there will step a young man, with eye-glasses instead of
spectacles. They are tired of hearing about the
prophets. Texts from the Bible have gone out of
fashion. You think I do not see them giggling, h'm?
The young people. And the whispering in the choir
loft. And the buzz when I get up from my chair after
the second hymn. 'Is he going to have a sermon?
Is he? Sure enough!' Na, he will make them sit up,
my successor. Sex sermons! Political lectures. That's
it. Lectures." They were turning in at the temple
now. "The race is to the young, Fanny. To the
young. And I am old."

She squeezed the frail old arm in hers. "My dear!"
she said. "My dear!" A second breaking of her new
resolutions.

One by one, two by two, they straggled in for the
Friday evening service, these placid, prosperous people, not unkind, but careless, perhaps, in their prosperity.

"He's worth any ten of them," Fanny said hotly
to herself, as she sat in her pew that, after to-morrow,
would no longer be hers. "The dear old thing. 'Sex
sermons.' And the race is to the young. How right
he is. Well, no one can say I'm not getting an early
start."

The choir had begun the first hymn when there came
down the aisle a stranger. There was a little stir

among the congregation. Visitors were rare. He was
dark and very slim—with the slimness of steel wire.
He passed down the aisle rather uncertainly. A traveling man, Fanny thought, dropped in, as sometimes
they did, to say Kaddish for a departed father or
mother. Then she changed her mind. Her quick eye
noted his walk; a peculiar walk, with a spring in it.
Only one unfamiliar with cement pavements could walk
like that. The Indians must have had that same light,
muscular step. He chose an empty pew halfway down
the aisle and stumbled into it rather awkwardly. Fanny
thought he was unnecessarily ugly, even for a man.
Then he looked up, and nodded and smiled at Lee Kohn,
across the aisle. His teeth were very white, and the
smile was singularly sweet. Fanny changed her mind
again. Not so bad-looking, after all. Different, anyway. And then—why, of course! Little Clarence
Heyl, come back from the West. Clarence Heyl, the
cowardy-cat.

Her mind went back to that day of the street fight.
She smiled. At that moment Clarence Heyl, who
had been screwing about most shockingly, as though
searching for some one, turned and met her smile, intended for no one, with a startlingly radiant one of
his own, intended most plainly for her. He half
started forward in his pew, and then remembered, and
sat back again, but with an effect of impermanence
that was ludicrous. It had been years since he had
left Winnebago. At the time of his mother's death
they had tried to reach him, and had been unable to
get in touch with him for weeks. He had been off
on some mountain expedition, hundreds of miles from
railroad or telegraph. Fanny remembered having read
about him in the Winnebago *Courier*. He seemed to
be climbing mountains a great deal—rather difficult
mountains, evidently, from the fuss they made over it.
A queer enough occupation for a cowardy-cat. There

had been a book, too. About the Rockies. She had
not read it. She rather disliked these nature books,
as do most nature lovers. She told herself that when
she came upon a flaming golden maple in October she
was content to know it was a maple, and to warm her
soul at its blaze.

There had been something in the Chicago *Herald*,
though—oh, yes; it had spoken of him as the brilliant
young naturalist, Clarence Heyl. He was to have
gone on an expedition with Roosevelt. A sprained
ankle, or some such thing, had prevented. Fanny
smiled again, to herself. His mother, the fussy person who had been responsible for his boyhood reefers
and too-shiny shoes, and his cowardice too, no doubt,
had dreamed of seeing her Clarence a rabbi.

From that point Fanny's thoughts wandered to the
brave old man in the pulpit. She had heard almost
nothing of the service. She looked at him now—at
him, and then at his congregation, inattentive and
palpably bored. As always with her, the thing stamped
itself on her mind as a picture. She was forever seeing a situation in terms of its human value. How
small he looked, how frail, against the background of
the massive Ark with its red velvet curtain. And how
bravely he glared over his blue glasses at the two
Aarons girls who were whispering and giggling together, eyes on the newcomer.

So this was what life did to you, was it? Squeezed
you dry, and then cast you aside in your old age, a
pulp, a bit of discard. Well, they'd never catch her
that way.

Unchurchly thoughts, these. The little place was
very peaceful and quiet, lulling one like a narcotic.
The rabbi's voice had in it that soothing monotony
bred of years in the pulpit. Fanny found her thoughts
straying back to the busy, bright little store on Elm
Street, then forward, to the Haynes-Cooper plant and

the fight that was before her.  There settled about her
mouth a certain grim line that sat strangely on so
young a face.  The service marched on.  There came
the organ prelude that announced the mourners'
prayer.  Then Rabbi Thalmann began to intone the
Kaddish.  Fanny rose, prayer book in hand.  At that
Clarence Heyl rose too, hurriedly, as one unaccustomed to the service, and stood with unbowed head,
looking at the rabbi interestedly, thoughtfully, rev-
erently.  The two stood alone.  Death had been kind
to Congregation Emanu-el this year.  The prayer
ended.  Fanny winked the tears from her eyes, almost wrathfully.  She sat down, and there swept over
her a feeling of finality.  It was like the closing of
Book One in a volume made up of three parts.

She said to herself: "Winnebago is ended, and my
life here.  How interesting that I should know that,
and feel it.  It is like the first movement in one of the
concertos Theodore was forever playing.  Now for the
second movement!  It's got to be lively.  Fortissimo!
Presto!"

For so clever a girl as Fanny Brandeis, that was a
stupid conclusion at which to arrive.  How could she
think it possible to shed her past life, like a garment?
Those impressionable years, between fourteen and
twenty-four, could never be cast off.  She might don
a new cloak to cover the old dress beneath, but the
old would always be there, its folds peeping out here
and there, its outlines plainly to be seen.  She might
eat of things rare, and drink of things costly, but the
sturdy, stocky little girl in the made-over silk dress,
who had resisted the Devil in Weinberg's pantry on
that long-ago Day of Atonement, would always be there
at the feast.  Myself, I confess I am tired of these
stories of young women who go to the big city, there
to do battle with failure, to grapple with temptation,
sin and discouragement.  So it may as well be ad-

mitted that Fanny Brandeis' story was not that of a painful hand-over-hand climb. She was made for success. What she attempted, she accomplished. That which she strove for, she won. She was too sure, too vital, too electric, for failure. No, Fanny Brandeis' struggle went on inside. And in trying to stifle it she came near making the blackest failure that a woman can make. In grubbing for the pot of gold she almost missed the rainbow.

Rabbi Thalmann raised his arms for the benediction. Fanny looked straight up at him as though stamping a picture on her mind. His eyes were resting gently on her—or perhaps she just fancied that he spoke to her alone as he began the words of the ancient closing prayer:

"May the blessings of the Lord Our God rest upon you. God bless thee and keep thee. May He cause His countenance to shine upon thee and be gracious unto thee. May God lift up His countenance unto thee . . ."

At the last word she hurried up the aisle, and down the stairs, into the soft beauty of the May night. She felt she could stand no good-bys. In her hotel room she busied herself with the half-packed trunks and bags. So it was she altogether failed to see the dark young man who hurried after her eagerly, and who was stopped by a dozen welcoming hands there in the temple vestibule. He swore a deep inward "Damn!" as he saw her straight, slim figure disappear down the steps and around the corner, even while he found himself saying, politely, "Why, thanks! It's good to *be* back." And, "Yes, things have changed. All but the temple, and Rabbi Thalmann."

Fanny left Winnebago at eight next morning.

## CHAPTER NINE

"M R. FENGER will see you now." Mr. Fenger, general manager, had been a long time about it. This heel-cooling experience was new to Fanny Brandeis. It had always been her privilege to keep others waiting. Still, she felt no resentment as she sat in Michael Fenger's outer office. For as she sat there, waiting, she was getting a distinct impression of this unseen man whose voice she could just hear as he talked over the telephone in his inner office. It was characteristic of Michael Fenger that his personality reached out and touched you before you came into actual contact with the man. Fanny had heard of him long before she came to Haynes-Cooper. He was the genie of that glittering lamp. All through the gigantic plant (she had already met department heads, buyers, merchandise managers) one heard his name, and felt the impress of his mind:

"You'll have to see Mr. Fenger about that."

"Yes,"—pointing to a new conveyor, perhaps,— "that has just been installed. It's a great help to us. Doubles our shipping-room efficiency. We used to use baskets, pulled by a rope. It's Mr. Fenger's idea."

Efficiency, efficiency, efficiency. Fenger had made it a slogan in the Haynes-Cooper plant long before the German nation forced it into our everyday vocabulary. Michael Fenger was System. He could take a muddle of orders, a jungle of unfilled contracts, a horde of incompetent workers, and of them make a smooth-running and effective unit. Untangling snarls was his pastime. *Esprit de corps* was his shibboleth.

Order and management his idols. And his war-cry
was "Results!"

It was eleven o'clock when Fanny came into his
outer office. The very atmosphere was vibrant with
his personality. There hung about the place an air
of repressed expectancy. The room was electrically
charged with the high-voltage of the man in the inner
office. His secretary was a spare, middle-aged, anxious-looking woman in snuff-brown and spectacles; his
stenographer a blond young man, also spectacled
and anxious; his office boy a stern youth in knickers,
who bore no relation to the slangy, gum-chewing, red-
headed office boy of the comic sections.

The low-pitched, high-powered voice went on inside,
talking over the long-distance telephone. Fenger was
the kind of man who is always talking to New York
when he is in Chicago, and to Chicago when he is in
New York. Trains with the word Limited after them
were invented for him and his type. A buzzer sounded.
It galvanized the office boy into instant action. It
brought the anxious-looking stenographer to the doorway, notebook in hand, ready. It sent the lean secretary out, and up to Fanny.

"Temper," said Fanny, to herself, "or horribly
nervous and high-keyed. They jump like a set of pup-
pets on a string."

It was then that the lean secretary had said, "Mr.
Fenger will see you now."

Fanny was aware of a pleasant little tingle of excitement. She entered the inner office.

It was characteristic of Michael Fenger that he employed no cheap tricks. He was not writing as Fanny
Brandeis came in. He was not telephoning. He was
not doing anything but standing at his desk, waiting
for Fanny Brandeis. As she came in he looked at her,
through her, and she seemed to feel her mental processes
laid open to him as a skilled surgeon cuts through

skin and flesh and fat, to lay bare the muscles and
nerves and vital organs beneath. He put out his hand.
Fanny extended hers. They met in a silent grip. It
was like a meeting between two men. Even as he indexed her, Fanny's alert mind was busy docketing,
numbering, cataloguing him. They had in common
a certain force, a driving power. Fanny seated herself opposite him, in obedience to a gesture. He crossed
his legs comfortably and sat back in his big desk
chair. A great-bodied man, with powerful square
shoulders, a long head, a rugged crest of a nose—
the kind you see on the type of Englishman who has
the imagination and initiative to go to Canada, or
Australia, or America. He wore spectacles, not the
fashionable horn-rimmed sort, but the kind with gold
ear pieces. They were becoming, and gave a certain
humanness to a face that otherwise would have
been too rugged, too strong. A man of forty-five, perhaps.

He spoke first. "You're younger than I thought."

"So are you."

"Old inside."

"So am I."

He uncrossed his legs, leaned forward, folded his
arms on the desk.

"You've been through the plant, Miss Brandeis?"

"Yes. Twice. Once with a regular tourist party.
And once with the special guide."

"Good. Go through the plant whenever you can.
Don't stick to your own department. It narrows one."
He paused a moment. "Did you think that this opportunity to come to Haynes-Cooper, as assistant to
the infants' wear department buyer was just a piece
of luck, augmented by a little pulling on your part?"

"Yes."

"It wasn't. You were carefully picked by me, and
I don't expect to find I've made a mistake. I sup-

pose you know very little about buying and selling infants' wear?"

"Less than about almost any other article in the world—at least, in the department store, or mail order world."

"I thought so. And it doesn't matter. I pretty well know your history, which means that I know your training. You're young; you're ambitious; you're experienced; you're imaginative. There's no length you can't go, with these. It just depends on how farsighted your mental vision is. Now listen, Miss Brandeis: I'm not going to talk to you in millions. The guides do enough of that. But you know we do buy and sell in terms of millions, don't you? Well, our infants' wear department isn't helping to roll up the millions; and it ought to, because there are millions of babies born every year, and the golden-spoon kind are in the minority. I've decided that that department needs a woman, your kind of woman. Now, as a rule, I never employ a woman when I can use a man. There's only one other woman filling a really important position in the merchandise end of this business. That's Ella Monahan, head of the glove department, and she's a genius. She is a woman who is limited in every other respect—just average; but she knows glove materials in a way that's uncanny. I'd rather have a man in her place; but I don't happen to know any men glove-geniuses. Tell me, what do you think of that etching?"

Fanny tried—and successfully—not to show the jolt her mind had received as she turned to look at the picture to which his finger pointed. She got up and strolled over to it, and she was glad her suit fitted and hung as it did in the back.

"I don't like it particularly. I like it less than any other etching you have here." The walls were hung with them. "Of course you understand I know nothing about them. But it's too flowery, isn't it, to be good? Too many lines. Like a writer who spoils his effect by using too many words."

Fenger came over and stood beside her, staring at the black and white and gray thing in its frame. "I felt that way, too." He stared down at her, then. "Jew?" he asked.

A breathless instant. "No," said Fanny Brandeis.

Michael Fenger smiled for the first time. Fanny Brandeis would have given everything she had, everything she hoped to be, to be able to take back that monosyllable. She was gripped with horror at what she had done. She had spoken almost mechanically. And yet that monosyllable must have been the fruit of all these months of inward struggle and thought. "Now I begin to understand you," Fenger went on. "You've decided to lop off all the excrescences, eh? Well, I can't say that I blame you. A woman in business is handicapped enough by the very fact of her sex." He stared at her again. "Too bad you're so pretty."

"I'm not!" said Fanny hotly, like a school-girl.

"That's a thing that can't be argued, child. Beauty's subjective, you know.'

"I don't see what difference it makes, anyway."

"Oh, yes, you do." He stopped. "Or perhaps you don't, after all. I forget how young you are. Well, now, Miss Brandeis, you and your woman's mind, and your masculine business experience and sense are to be turned loose on our infants' wear department. The buyer, Mr. Slosson, is going to resent you. Naturally. I don't know whether we'll get results from you in a month, or six months or a year. Or ever. But something tells me we're going to get them. You've lived in a small town most of your life. And we want that small-town viewpoint. D'you think you've got it?"

Fanny was on her own ground here. "If knowing

the Wisconsin small-town woman, and the Wisconsin farmer woman—and man too, for that matter—means knowing the Oregon, and Wyoming, and Pennsylvania, and Iowa people of the same class, then I've got it."

"Good!" Michael Fenger stood up. "I'm not going to load you down with instructions, or advice. I think I'll let you grope your own way around, and bump your head a few times. Then you'll learn where the low places are. And, Miss Brandeis, remember that suggestions are welcome in this plant. We take suggestions all the way from the elevator starter to the president." His tone was kindly, but not hopeful.

Fanny was standing too, her mental eye on the door. But now she turned to face him squarely.

"Do you mean that?"

"Absolutely."

"Well, then, I've one to make. Your stock boys and stock girls walk miles and miles every day, on every floor of this fifteen-story building. I watched them yesterday, filling up the bins, carrying orders, covering those enormous distances from one bin to another, up one aisle and down the next, to the office, back again. Your floors are concrete, or cement, or some such mixture, aren't they? I just happened to think of the boy who used to deliver our paper on Norris Street, in Winnebago, Wisconsin. He covered his route on roller skates. It saved him an hour. Why don't you put roller skates on your stock boys and girls?"

Fenger stared at her. You could almost hear that mind of his working, like a thing on ball bearings. "Roller skates." It wasn't an exclamation. It was a decision. He pressed a buzzer—the snuff-brown secretary buzzer. "Tell Clancy I want him. Now." He had not glanced up, or taken his eyes from Fanny. She was aware of feeling a little uncomfortable, but elated, too. She moved toward the door. Fenger stood at his desk. "Wait a minute." Fanny waited. Still Fenger did not speak. Finally, "I suppose you know you've earned six months' salary in the last five minutes."

Fanny eyed him coolly. "Considering the number of your stock force, the time, energy, and labor saved, including wear and tear on department heads and their assistants, I should say that was a conservative statement." And she nodded pleasantly, and left him.

Two days later every stock clerk in the vast plant was equipped with light-weight roller skates. They made a sort of carnival of it at first. There were some spills, too, going around corners, and a little too much hilarity. That wore off in a week. In two weeks their roller skates were part of them; just shop labor-savers. The report presented to Fenger was this: Time and energy saved, fifty-five per cent; stock staff decreased by one third. The picturesqueness of it, the almost ludicrous simplicity of the idea appealed to the entire plant. It tickled the humor sense in every one of the ten thousand employees in that vast organization. In the first week of her association with Haynes-Cooper Fanny Brandeis was actually more widely known than men who had worked there for years. The president, Nathan Haynes himself, sent for her, chuckling.

Nathan Haynes—but then, why stop for him? Nathan Haynes had been swallowed, long ago, by this monster plant that he himself had innocently created. You must have visited it, this Gargantuan thing that sprawls its length in the very center of Chicago, the giant son of a surprised father. It is one of the city's show places, like the stockyards, the Art Institute, and Field's. Fifteen years before, a building had been erected to accommodate a prosperous mail order business. It had been built large and roomy, with plenty of seams, planned amply, it was thought, to allow the

boy to grow. It would do for twenty-five years, surely.
In ten years Haynes-Cooper was bursting its seams.
In twelve it was shamelessly naked, its arms and legs
sticking out of its inadequate garments. New red
brick buildings—another—another. Five stories added
to this one, six stories to that, a new fifteen story
merchandise building.

The firm began to talk in tens of millions. Its stock
became gilt-edged, unattainable. Lucky ones who had
bought of it diffidently, discreetly, with modest visions
of four and a half per cent in their unimaginative
minds, saw their dividends doubling, trebling, quad-
rupling, finally soaring gymnastically beyond all reason. Listen to the old guide who (at fifteen a week)
takes groups of awed visitors through the great plant.
How he juggles figures; how grandly they roll off his
tongue. How glib he is with Nathan Haynes's millions.

"This, ladies and gentlemen, is our mail department.
From two thousand to twenty-five hundred pounds of
mail, comprising over one hundred thousand letters,
are received here every day. Yes, madam, I said every
day. About half of these letters are orders. Last
year the banking department counted one hundred and
thirty millions of dollars. One hundred and thirty
millions!" He stands there in his ill-fitting coat, and
his star, and rubs one bony hand over the other.

"Dear me!" says a lady tourist from Idaho, rather
inadequately. And yet, not so inadequately. What
exclamation is there, please, that fits a sum like one
hundred and thirty millions of anything?

Fanny Brandeis, fresh from Winnebago, Wisconsin,
slipped into the great scheme of things at the Haynes-
Cooper plant like part of a perfectly planned blue
print. It was as though she had been thought out
and shaped for this particular corner. And the reason
for it was, primarily, Winnebago, Wisconsin. For

Haynes-Cooper grew and thrived on just such towns, with their surrounding farms and villages. Haynes-Cooper had their fingers on the pulse and heart of the country as did no other industry. They were close, close. When rugs began to take the place of ingrain carpets it was Haynes-Cooper who first sensed the change. Oh, they had had them in New York years before, certainly. But after all, it isn't New York's artistic progress that shows the development of this nation. It is the thing they are thinking, and doing, and learning in Backwash, Nebraska, that marks time for these United States. There may be a certain significance in the announcement that New York has dropped the Russian craze and has gone in for that quaint Chinese stuff. My dear, it makes the loveliest hangings and decorations. When Fifth Avenue takes down its filet lace and eyelet embroidered curtains, and substitutes severe shantung and chaste net, there is little in the act to revolutionize industry, or stir the art-world. But when the Haynes-Cooper company, by referring to its inventory ledgers, learns that it is selling more Alma Gluck than Harry Lauder records; when its statistics show that Tchaikowsky is going better than Irving Berlin, something epochal is happening in the musical progress of a nation. And when the orders from Noose Gulch, Nevada, are for those plain dimity curtains instead of the cheap and gaudy Nottingham atrocities, there is conveyed to the mind a fact of immense, of overwhelming significance. The country has taken a step toward civilization and good taste.

So. You have a skeleton sketch of Haynes-Cooper, whose feelers reach the remotest dugout in the Yukon, the most isolated cabin in the Rockies, the loneliest ranch-house in Wyoming; the Montana mining shack, the bleak Maine farm, the plantation in Virginia.

And the man who had so innocently put life into

this monster? A plumpish, kindly-faced man; a be-wildered, gentle, unimaginative and somewhat fright-ened man, fresh-cheeked, eye-glassed. In his suite of offices in the new Administration Building—built two years ago—marble and oak throughout—twelve stories, and we're adding three already; offices all two-toned rugs, and leather upholstery, with dim, rich, brown-toned Dutch masterpieces on the walls, he sat help-less and defenseless while the torrent of millions rushed, and swirled, and foamed about him. I think he had fancied, fifteen years ago, that he would some day be a fairly prosperous man; not rich, as riches are counted nowadays, but with a comfortable number of tens of thousands tucked away. Two or three hun-dred thousand; perhaps five hundred thousand!—per-haps a—but, nonsense! Nonsense!

And then the thing had started. It was as when a man idly throws a pebble into a chasm, or shoves a bit of ice with the toe of his boot, and starts a snow-slide that grows as it goes. He had started this avalanche of money, and now it rushed on of its own momentum, plunging, rolling, leaping, crashing, and as it swept on it gathered rocks, trees, stones, houses, everything that lay in its way. It was beyond the power of human hand to stop this tumbling, roaring slide. In the midst of it sat Nathan Haynes, deafened, stunned, terrified at the immensity of what he had done.

He began giving away huge sums, incredible sums. It piled up faster than he could give it away. And so he sat there in the office hung with the dim old mas-terpieces, and tried to keep simple, tried to keep sane, with that austerity that only mad wealth can afford—or bitter poverty. He caused the land about the plant to be laid out in sunken gardens and baseball fields and tennis courts, so that one approached this monster of commerce through enchanted grounds, glowing with tulips and heady hyacinths in spring, with roses in June, blazing with salvia and golden-glow and asters in autumn. There was something apologetic about these grounds.

This, then, was the environment that Fanny Brandeis had chosen. On the face of things you would have said she had chosen well. The inspiration of the roller skates had not been merely a lucky flash. That idea had been part of the consistent whole. Her mind was her mother's mind raised to the $n$th power, and enhanced by the genius she was trying to crush. Refusing to die, it found expression in a hundred brilliant plans, of which the roller skate idea was only one.

Fanny had reached Chicago on Sunday. She had entered the city as a queen enters her domain, authoritatively, with no fear upon her, no trepidation, no doubts. She had gone at once to the Mendota Hotel, on Michigan Avenue, up-town, away from the roar of the loop. It was a residential hotel, very quiet, decidedly luxurious. She had no idea of making it her home. But she would stay there until she could find an apartment that was small, bright, near the lake, and yet within fairly reasonable transportation facilities for her work. Her room was on the ninth floor, not on the Michigan Avenue side, but east, overlooking the lake. She spent hours at the windows, fascinated by the stone and steel city that lay just below with the incredible blue of the sail-dotted lake beyond, and at night, with the lights spangling the velvety blackness, the flaring blaze of Thirty-first Street's chop-suey restaurants and moving picture houses at the right; and far, far away, the red and white eye of the lighthouse winking, blinking, winking, blinking, the rumble and clank of a flat-wheeled Indiana avenue car, the sound of high laughter and a snatch of song that came faintly up to her from the speeding car of some midnight joy-riders!

But all this had to do with her other side. It had no bearing on Haynes-Cooper, and business. Business! That was it. She had trained herself for it, like an athlete. Eight hours of sleep. A cold plunge on arising. Sane food. Long walks. There was something terrible about her earnestness.

On Monday she presented herself at the Haynes-Cooper plant. Monday and Tuesday were spent in going over the great works. It was an exhausting process, but fascinating beyond belief. It was on Wednesday that she had been summoned for the talk with Michael Fenger. Thursday morning she was at her desk at eight-thirty. It was an obscure desk, in a dingy corner of the infants' wear department, the black sheep section of the great plant. Her very presence in that corner seemed to change it magically. You must remember how young she was, how healthy, how vigorous, with the freshness of the small town still upon her. It was health and youth, and vigor that gave that gloss to her hair (conscientious brushing too, perhaps), that color to her cheeks and lips, that brightness to her eyes. But crafty art and her dramatic instinct were responsible for the tailored severity of her costume, for the whiteness of her blouse, the trim common-sense expensiveness of her shoes and hat and gloves.

Slosson, buyer and head of the department, came in at nine. Fanny rose to greet him. She felt a little sorry for Slosson. In her mind she already knew him for a doomed man.

"Well, well!"—he was the kind of person who would say, well, well!—"You're bright and early, Miss—ah—"

"Brandeis."

"Yes, certainly; Miss Brandeis. Well, nothing like making a good start."

"I wanted to go through the department by myself," said Fanny. "The shelves and bins, and the numbering system. I see that your new maternity dresses have just come in."

"Oh, yes. How do you like them?"

"I think they're unnecessarily hideous, Mr. Slosson."

"My dear young lady, a plain garment is what they want. Unnoticeable."

"Unnoticeable, yes; but becoming. At such a time a woman is at her worst. If she can get it, she at least wants a dress that doesn't add to her unattractiveness."

"Let me see—you are not—ah—married, I believe, Miss Brandeis?"

"No."

"I am. Three children. All girls." He passed a nervous hand over his head, rumpling his hair a little. "An expensive proposition, let me tell you, three girls. But there's very little I don't know about babies, as you may imagine."

But there settled over Fanny Brandeis' face the mask of hardness that was so often to transform it.

The morning mail was in—the day's biggest grist, a deluge of it, a flood. Buyer and assistant buyer never saw the actual letters, or attended to their enclosed orders. It was only the unusual letter, the complaint or protest that reached their desk. Hundreds of hands downstairs sorted, stamped, indexed, filed, after the letter-opening machines had slit the envelopes. Those letter-openers! Fanny had hung over them, enthralled. The unopened envelopes were fed into them. Flip! Zip! Flip! Out! Opened! Faster than eye could follow. It was uncanny. It was, somehow, humorous, like the clever antics of a trained dog. You could not believe that this little machine actually performed what your eyes beheld. Two years later they installed the sand-paper letter-opener, marvel of simplicity. It made the old machine seem cumbersome and slow. Guided by Izzy, the expert, its rough tongue was capable of licking open six hundred and fifty letters a minute.

Ten minutes after the mail came in the orders were being filled; bins, shelves, warehouses, were emptying their contents. Up and down the aisles went the stock clerks; into the conveyors went the bundles, down the great spiral bundle chute, into the shipping room, out by mail, by express, by freight. This leghorn hat for a Nebraska country belle; a tombstone for a rancher's wife; a plow, brave in its red paint; coffee, tea, tinned fruit, bound for Alaska; lace, muslin, sheeting, toweling, all intended for the coarse trousseau of a Georgia bride.

It was not remarkable that Fanny Brandeis fitted into this scheme of things. For years she had ministered to the wants of just this type of person. The letters she saw at Haynes-Cooper's read exactly as customers had worded their wants at Brandeis' Bazaar. The magnitude of the thing thrilled her, the endless possibilities of her own position.

During the first two months of her work there she was as unaggressive as possible. She opened the very pores of her mind and absorbed every detail of her department. But she said little, followed Slosson's instructions in her position as assistant buyer, and suggested no changes. Slosson's wrinkle of anxiety smoothed itself away, and his manner became patronizingly authoritative again. Fanny seemed to have become part of the routine of the place. Fenger did not send for her. June and July were insufferably hot. Fanny seemed to thrive, to expand like a flower in the heat, when others wilted and shriveled. The spring catalogue was to be made up in October, as always, six months in advance. The first week in August Fanny asked for an interview with Fenger.

Slosson was to be there. At ten o'clock she entered Fenger's inner office. He was telephoning—something about dinner at the Union League Club. His voice was suave, his tone well modulated, his accent correct, his English faultless. And yet Fanny Brandeis, studying the etchings on his wall, her back turned to him, smiled to herself. The voice, the tone, the accent, the English, did not ring true. They were acquired graces, exquisite imitations of the real thing. Fanny Brandeis knew. She was playing the same game herself. She understood this man now, after two months in the Haynes-Cooper plant. These marvelous examples of the etcher's art, for example. They were the struggle for expression of a man whose youth had been bare of such things. His love for them was much the same as that which impels the new made millionaire to buy rare pictures, rich hangings, tapestries, rugs, not so much in the desire to impress the world with his wealth as to satisfy the craving for beauty, the longing to possess that which is exquisite, and fine, and almost unobtainable. You have seen how a woman, long denied luxuries, feeds her starved senses on soft silken things, on laces and gleaming jewels, for pure sensuous delight in their feel and look.

Thus Fanny mused as she eyed these treasures— grim, deft, repressed things, done with that economy of line which is the test of the etcher's art.

Fenger hung up the receiver.

"So it's taken you two months, Miss Brandeis. I was awfully afraid, from the start you made, that you'd be back here in a week, bursting with ideas."

Fanny smiled, appreciatively. He had come very near the truth. "I had to use all my self-control, that first week. After that it wasn't so hard."

Fenger's eyes narrowed upon her. "Pretty sure of yourself, aren't you?"

"Yes," said Fanny. She came over to his desk.

" 'Now, Miss Brandeis, what's the trouble with the Haynes-
Cooper infants' wear department?' "

—Page 147

"I wish we needn't have Mr. Slosson here this morning. After all, he's been here for years, and I'm practically an upstart. He's so much older, too. I—I hate to hurt him. I wish you'd—"

But Fenger shook his head. "Slosson's due now. And he has got to take his medicine. This is business, Miss Brandeis. You ought to know what that means. For that matter, it may be that you haven't hit upon an idea. In that case, Slosson would have the laugh, wouldn't he?"

Slosson entered at that moment. And there was a chip on his shoulder. It was evident in the way he bristled, in the way he seated himself. His fingers drummed his knees. He was like a testy, hum-ha stage father dealing with a willful child.

Fenger took out his watch.

"Now, Miss Brandeis."

Fanny took a chair facing the two men, and crossed her trim blue serge knees, and folded her hands in her lap. A deep pink glowed in her cheeks. Her eyes were very bright. All the Molly Brandeis in her was at the surface, sparkling there. And she looked almost insultingly youthful.

"You—you want me to talk?"

"We want you to talk. We have time for just three-quarters of an hour of uninterrupted conversation. If you've got anything to say you ought to say it in that time. Now, Miss Brandeis, what's the trouble with the Haynes-Cooper infants' wear department?"

And Fanny Brandeis took a long breath.

"The trouble with the Haynes-Cooper infants' wear department is that it doesn't understand women. There are millions of babies born every year. An incredible number of them are mail order babies. I mean by that they are born to tired, clumsy-fingered immigrant women, to women in mills and factories, to women on

farms, to women in remote villages. They're the type
who use the mail order method. I've learned this one
thing about that sort of woman: she may not want
that baby, but either before or after it's born she'll
starve, and save, and go without proper clothing, and
even beg, and steal to give it clothes—clothes with lace
on them, with ribbon on them, sheer white things. I
don't know why that's true, but it is. Well, we're not
reaching them. Our goods are unattractive. They're
packed and shipped unattractively. Why, all this department needs is a little psychology—and some lace
that doesn't look as if it had been chopped out with
an ax. It's the little, silly, intimate things that will
reach these women. No, not silly, either. Quite un-
derstandable. She wants fine things for her baby,
just as the silver-spoon mother does. The thing we'll
have to do is to give her silver-spoon models at pewter
prices."

"It can't be done," said Slosson.

"Now, wait a minute, Slosson," Fenger put in,
smoothly. "Miss Brandeis has given us a very fair
general statement. We'll have some facts. Are you
prepared to give us an actual working plan?"

"Yes. At least, it sounds practical to me. And if
it does to you—and to Mr. Slosson—"

"Humph!" snorted that gentleman, in expression of
defiance, unbelief, and a determination not to be impressed.

It acted as a goad to Fanny. She leaned forward
in her chair and talked straight at the big, potent
force that sat regarding her in silent attention.

"I still say that we can copy the high-priced models
in low-priced materials because, in almost every case,
it isn't the material that makes the expensive model;
it's the line, the cut, the little trick that gives it style.
We can get that. We've been giving them stuff that
might have been made by prison labor, for all the dis-

tinction it had. Then I think we ought to make a feature of the sanitary methods used in our infants' department. Every article intended for a baby's use should be wrapped or boxed as it lies in the bin or on the shelf. And those bins ought to be glassed. We would advertise that, and it would advertise itself. Our visitors would talk about it. This department hasn't been getting a square deal in the catalogue. Not enough space. It ought to have not only more catalogue space, but a catalogue all its own—the Baby Book. Full of pictures. Good ones. Illustrations that will make every mother think her baby will look like that baby, once it is wearing our No. 29E798—chubby babies, curly-headed, and dimply. And the feature of that catalogue ought to be, not separate garments, but complete outfits. Outfits boxed, ready for shipping, and ranging in price all the way from twenty-five dollars to three-ninety-eight—"

'It can't be done!" yelled Slosson. "Three-ninety-eight! Outfits!"

"It can be done. I've figured it out, down to a packet of assorted size safety pins. We'll call it our emergency outfit. Thirty pieces. And while we're about it, every outfit over five dollars ought to be packed in a pink or a pale blue pasteboard box. The outfits trimmed in pink, pink boxes; the outfits trimmed in blue, blue boxes. In eight cases out of ten their letters will tell us whether it's a pink or blue baby. And when they get our package, and take out that pink or blue box, they'll be as pleased as if we'd made them a present. It's the personal note—"

"Personal slop!" growled Slosson. "It isn't business. It's sentimental slush!"

"Sentimental, yes," agreed Fanny pleasantly, "but then, we're running the only sentimental department in this business. And we ought to be doing it at the rate of a million and a quarter a year. If you think these last suggestions sentimental, I'm afraid the next one—"

"Let's have it, Miss Brandeis," Fenger encouraged her quietly.

"It's"—she flashed a mischievous smile at Slosson —"it's a mother's guide and helper, and adviser. A woman who'll answer questions, give advice. Some one they'll write to, with a picture in their minds of a large, comfortable, motherly-looking person in gray. You know we get hundreds of letters asking whether they ought to order flannel bands, or the double-knitted kind. That sort of thing. And who's been answering them? Some sixteen-year-old girl in the mailing department who doesn't know a flannel band from a bootee when she sees it. We could call our woman something pleasant and everydayish, like Emily Brand. Easy to remember. And until we can find her, I'll answer those letters myself. They're important to us as well as to the woman who writes them. And now, there's the matter of obstetrical outfits. Three grades, packed ready for shipment, practical, simple, and complete. Our drug section has the separate articles, but we ought to—"

"Oh, lord!" groaned Slosson, and slumped disgustedly in his seat.

But Fenger got up, came over to Fanny, and put a hand on her shoulder for a moment. He looked down at her. "I knew you'd do it." He smiled queerly. "Tell me, where did you learn all this?"

"I don't know," faltered Fanny happily. "Brandeis' Bazaar, perhaps. It's just another case of plush photograph album."

"Plush—?"

Fanny told him that story. Even the discomfited Slosson grinned at it.

But after ten minutes more of general discussion Slosson left. Fenger, without putting it in words, had

conveyed that to him. Fanny stayed. They did things
that way at Haynes-Cooper. No waste. No delay.
That she had accomplished in two months that which
ordinarily takes years was not surprising. They did
things that way, too, at Haynes-Cooper. Take the
case of Nathan Haynes himself. And Michael Fenger too who, not so many years before, had been a
machine-boy in a Racine woolen mill.

For my part, I confess that Fanny Brandeis begins
to lose interest for me. Big Business seems to dwarf
the finer things in her. That red-cheeked, shabby
little schoolgirl, absorbed in Zola and peanut brittle
in the Winnebago library, was infinitely more appealing
than this glib and capable young woman. The spit-
ting wildcat of the street fight so long ago was gentler
by far than this cool person who was so deliberately
taking his job away from Slosson. You, too, feel that
way about her? That is as it should be. It is the
penalty they pay who, given genius, sympathy, and
understanding as their birthright, trade them for the
tawdry trinkets money brings.

Perhaps the last five minutes of that conference between Fanny and Michael Fenger reveals a new side,
and presents something of interest. It was a harrowing and unexpected five minutes.

You may remember how Michael Fenger had a way
of looking at one, silently. It was an intent and concentrated gaze that had the effect of an actual physical hold. Most people squirmed under it. Fanny,
feeling it on her now, frowned and rose to leave.

"Shall you want to talk these things over again?
Of course I've only outlined them, roughly. You gave
me so little time."

Fenger, at his desk, did not answer, or turn away
his gaze. A little blaze of wrath flamed into Fanny's
face.

"General manager or not," she said, very low-voiced,

"I wish you wouldn't sit and glower at me like that. It's rude, and it's disconcerting," which was putting it forthrightly.

"I beg your pardon!" Fenger came swiftly around the desk, and over to her. "I was thinking very hard. Miss Brandeis, will you dine with me somewhere to-night? Then to-morrow night? But I want to talk to you."

"Here I am. Talk."

"But I want to talk to—you."

It was then that Fanny Brandeis saved an ugly situation. For she laughed, a big, wholesome, outdoors sort of laugh. She was honestly amused.

"My dear Mr. Fenger, you've been reading the murky magazines. Very bad for you."

Fenger was unsmiling: "Why won't you dine with me?"

"Because it would be unconventional and foolish. I respect the conventions. They're so sensible. And because it would be unfair to you, and to Mrs. Fenger, and to me."

"Rot! It's you who have the murky magazine viewpoint, as you call it, when you imply—"

"Now, look here, Mr. Fenger," Fanny interrupted, quietly. "Let's be square with each other, even if we're not being square with ourselves. You're the real power in this plant, because you've the brains. You can make any person in this organization, or break them. That sounds melodramatic, but it's true. I've got a definite life plan, and it's as complete and detailed as an engineering blue print. I don't intend to let you spoil it. I've made a real start here. If you want to, I've no doubt you can end it. But before you do, I want to warn you that I'll make a pretty stiff fight for it. I'm no silent sufferer. I'll say things. And people usually believe me when I talk."

Still the silent, concentrated gaze. With a little impatient exclamation Fanny walked toward the door. Fenger, startlingly light and agile for his great height, followed.

"I'm sorry, Miss Brandeis, terribly sorry. You see, you interest me very much. Very much."

"Thanks," dryly.

"Don't go just yet. Please. I'm not a villain. Really. That is, not a deliberate villain. But when I find something very fine, very intricate, very fascinating and complex—like those etchings, for example—I am intrigued. I want it near me. I want to study it."

Fanny said nothing. But she thought, "This is a dangerously clever man. Too clever for you. You know so little about them."

Fenger waited. Most women would have found refuge in words. The wrong words. It is only the strong who can be silent when in doubt.

"Perhaps you will dine with Mrs. Fenger and me at our home some evening? Mrs. Fenger will speak to you about it."

"I'm afraid I'm usually too tired for further effort at the end of the day. I'm sorry——"

"Some Sunday night perhaps, then. Tea."

"Thank you." And so out, past the spare secretary, the anxious-browed stenographer, the academic office boy, to the hallway, the elevator, and finally the refuge of her own orderly desk. Slosson was at lunch in one of the huge restaurants provided for employees in the building across the street. She sat there, very still, for some minutes; for more minutes than she knew. Her hands were clasped tightly on the desk, and her eyes stared ahead in a puzzled, resentful, bewildered way. Something inside her was saying over and over again:

"You lied to him on that very first day. That placed you. That stamped you. Now he thinks you're rotten all the way through. You lied on the very first day."

Ella Monahan poked her head in at the door. The

Gloves were on that floor, at the far end. The two women rarely saw each other, except at lunch time.

"Missed you at lunch," said Ella Monahan. She was a pink-cheeked, bright-eyed woman of forty-one or two, prematurely gray and therefore excessively young in her manner, as women often are who have grown gray before their time.

Fanny stood up, hurriedly. "I was just about to go."

"Try the grape pie, dear. It's delicious." And strolled off down the aisle that seemed to stretch endlessly ahead.

Fanny stood for a moment looking after her, as though meaning to call her back. But she must have changed her mind, because she said, "Oh, nonsense!" aloud. And went across to lunch. And ordered grape pie. And enjoyed it.

## CHAPTER TEN

THE invitation to tea came in due time from Mrs. Fenger. A thin, querulous voice over the telephone prepared one for the thin, querulous Mrs. Fenger herself. A sallow, plaintive woman, with a misbehaving valve. The valve, she confided to Fanny, made any effort dangerous. Also it made her susceptible to draughts. She wore over her shoulders a scarf that was constantly slipping and constantly being retrieved by Michael Fenger. The sight of this man, a physical and mental giant, performing this task ever so gently and patiently, sent a little pang of pity through Fanny, as Michael Fenger knew it would. The Fengers lived in an apartment on the Lake Shore Drive—an apartment such as only Chicago boasts. A view straight across the lake, rooms huge and many-windowed, a glass-enclosed sun-porch gay with chintz and wicker, an incredible number of bathrooms. The guests, besides Fanny, included a young pair, newly married and interested solely in rents, hangings, linen closets, and the superiority of the Florentine over the Jacobean for dining room purposes; and a very scrubbed looking, handsome, spectacled man of thirty-two or three who was a mechanical engineer. Fanny failed to catch his name, though she learned it later. Privately, she dubbed him Fascinating Facts, and he always remained that. His conversation was invariably prefaced with, "Funny thing happened down at the works to-day." The rest of it sounded like something one reads at the foot of each page of a loose-leaf desk calendar.

At tea there was a great deal of silver, and lace, but Fanny thought she could have improved on the chicken à la king. It lacked paprika and personality. Mrs. Fenger was constantly directing one or the other of the neat maids in an irritating aside.

After tea Michael Fenger showed Fanny his pictures, not boastfully, but as one who loves them reveals his treasures to an appreciative friend. He showed her his library, too, and it was the library of a reader. Fanny nibbled at it, hungrily. She pulled out a book here, a book there, read a paragraph, skimmed a page. There was no attempt at classification. Lever rubbed elbows with Spinoza; Mark Twain dug a facetious thumb into Haeckel's ribs. Fanny wanted to sit down on the floor, legs crossed, before the open shelves, and read, and read, and read. Fenger, watching the light in her face, seemed himself to take on a certain glow, as people generally did who found this girl in sympathy with them.

They were deep in book talk when Fascinating Facts strolled in, looking aggrieved, and spoiled it with the thoroughness of one who never reads, and is not ashamed of it.

"My word, I'm having a rotten time, Fenger," he said, plaintively. "They've got a tape-measure out of your wife's sewing basket, those two in there, and they're down on their hands and knees, measuring something. It has to do with their rug, over your rug, or some such rot. And then you take Miss Brandeis and go off into the library."

"Then stay here," said Fanny, "and talk books."

"My book's a blue-print," admitted Fascinating Facts, cheerfully. "I never get time to read. There's enough fiction, and romance, and adventure in my job to give me all the thrill I want. Why, just last Tuesday—no, Thursday it was—down at the works——"

Between Fanny and Fenger there flashed a look made up of dismay, and amusement, and secret sympathy.

It was a look that said, "We both see the humor of this. Most people wouldn't. Our angle is the same." Such a glance jumps the gap between acquaintance and friendship that whole days of spoken conversation cannot cover.

"Cigar?" asked Fenger, hoping to stay the flood.

"No, thanks. Say, Fenger, would there be a row if I smoked my pipe?"

"That black one? With the smell?"

"The black one, yes."

"There would." Fenger glanced in toward his wife, and smiled, dryly.

Fascinating Facts took his hand out of his pocket, regretfully.

"Wouldn't it sour a fellow on marriage! Wouldn't it! First those two in there, with their damned linen closets, and their rugs—I beg your pardon, Miss Brandeis! And now your missus objects to my pipe. You wouldn't treat me like that, would you, Miss Brandeis?"

There was about him something that appealed— something boyish and likeable.

"No, I wouldn't. I'd let you smoke a nargileh, if you wanted to, surrounded by rolls of blue prints."

"I knew it. I'm going to drive you home for that."

And he did, in his trim little roadster. It is a fairy road at night, that lake drive between the north and south sides. Even the Rush street bridge cannot quite spoil it. Fanny sat back luxuriously and let the soft splendor of the late August night enfold her. She was intelligently monosyllabic, while Fascinating Facts talked. At the door of her apartment house (she had left the Mendota weeks before) Fascinating Facts surprised her.

"I—I'd like to see you again, Miss Brandeis. If you'll let me."

"I'm so busy," faltered Fanny. Then it came to her that perhaps he did not know. "I'm with Haynes-

Cooper, you know. Assistant buyer in the infants' wear department."

"Yes, I know. I suppose a girl like you couldn't be interested in seeing a chap like me again, but I thought maybe——"

"But I would," interrupted Fanny, impulsively. "Indeed I would."

"Really! Perhaps you'll drive, some evening. Over to the Bismarck Gardens, or somewhere. It would rest you."

"I'm sure it would. Suppose you telephone me."

That was her honest, forthright, Winnebago Wisconsin self talking. But up in her apartment the other Fanny Brandeis, the calculating, ambitious, determined woman, said: "Now why did I say that! I never want to see the boy again.

"Use him. Experiment with him. Evidently men are going to enter into this thing. Michael Fenger has, already. And now this boy. Why not try certain tests with them as we used to follow certain formulæ in the chemistry laboratory at high school? This compound, that compound, what reaction? Then, when the time comes to apply your knowledge, you'll know."

Which shows how ignorant she was of this dangerous phase of her experiment. If she had not been, she must have known that these were not chemicals, but explosives with which she proposed to play.

The trouble was that Fanny Brandeis, the creative, was not being fed. And the creative fire requires fuel. Fanny Brandeis fed on people, not things. And her work at Haynes-Cooper was all with inanimate objects. The three months since her coming to Chicago had been crowded and eventful. Haynes-Cooper claimed every ounce of her energy, every atom of her wit and resourcefulness. In return it gave—salary. Not too much salary. That would come later, perhaps. Unfortunately, Fanny Brandeis did not thrive on that

kind of fare. She needed people. She craved contact. All these millions whom she served—these unseen,
unheard men and women, and children—she wanted to
see them. She wanted to touch them. She wanted to
talk with them. It was as though a lover of the drama,
eager to see his favorite actress in her greatest part,
were to find himself viewing her in a badly constructed
film play.

So Fanny Brandeis took to prowling. There are
people who have a penchant for cities—more than that,
a talent for them, a gift of sensing them, of feeling their
rhythm and pulse-beats, as others have a highly developed music sense, or color reaction. It is a thing
that cannot be acquired. In Fanny Brandeis there was
this abnormal response to the color and tone of any
city. And Chicago was a huge, polyglot orchestra,
made up of players in every possible sort of bizarre
costume, performing on every known instrument, leader-
less, terrifyingly discordant, yet with an occasional
strain, exquisite and poignant, to be heard through the
clamor and din.

A walk along State street (the wrong side) or Michigan avenue at five, or through one of the city's foreign
quarters, or along the lake front at dusk, stimulated
her like strong wine. She was drunk with it. And all
the time she would say to herself, little blind fool that
she was:

"Don't let it get you. Look at it, but don't think
about it. Don't let the human end of it touch you.
There's nothing in it."

And meanwhile she was feasting on those faces in
the crowds. Those faces in the crowds! They seemed
to leap out at her. They called to her. So she sketched
them, telling herself that she did it by way of relaxation, and diversion. One afternoon she left her desk
early, and perched herself on one of the marble benches
that lined the sunken garden just across from the main

group of Haynes-Cooper buildings. She wanted to see
what happened when those great buildings emptied.
Even her imagination did not meet the actuality. At
5:30 the streets about the plant were empty, except for
an occasional passerby. At 5:31 there trickled down
the broad steps of building after building thin dark
streams of humanity, like the first slow line of lava that
crawls down the side of an erupting volcano. The
trickle broadened into a stream, spread into a flood,
became a torrent that inundated the streets, the sidewalks, filling every nook and crevice, a moving mass.
Ten thousand people! A city! Fanny found herself
shaking with excitement, and something like terror at
the immensity of it. She tried to get a picture of it,
a sketch, with the gleaming windows of the red brick
buildings as a background. Amazingly enough, she
succeeded in doing it. That was because she tried for
broad effects, and relied on one bit of detail for her
story. It was the face of a girl—a very tired and tawdry girl, of sixteen, perhaps. On her face the look that
the day's work had stamped there was being wiped
gently away by another look; a look that said release,
and a sweetheart, and an evening at the movies. Fanny,
in some miraculous way, got it.

She prowled in the Ghetto, and sketched those patient
Jewish faces, often grotesque, sometimes repulsive, always mobile. She wandered down South Clark street,
flaring with purple-white arc-lights, and looked in at
its windows that displayed a pawnbroker's glittering
wares, or, just next door, a flat-topped stove over
which a white-capped magician whose face smacked
of the galley, performed deft tricks with a pancake
turner. "Southern chicken dinner," a lying sign read,
"with waffles and real maple syrup, 35¢." Past these
windows promenaded the Clark street women, hard-
eyed, high-heeled, aigretted; on the street corners loafed
the Clark street men, blue-shaven, wearing checked

suits, soiled faun-topped shoes, and diamond scarf pins.
And even as she watched them, fascinated, they vanished.   Clark street changed overnight, and became a
business thoroughfare, lined with stately office buildings, boasting marble and gold-leaf banks, filled with
hurrying clerks, stenographers, and prosperous bond
salesmen.   It was like a sporting man who, thriving in
middle age, endeavors to live down his shady past.

Fanny discovered Cottage Grove avenue, and Halsted
street, and Jefferson, and South State, where she should
never have walked.   There is an ugliness about Chicago's ugly streets that, for sheer, naked brutality, is
equaled nowhere in the world.   London has its foul
streets, smoke-blackened, sinister.   But they are ugly
as crime is ugly—and as fascinating.   It is like the
ugliness of an old hag who has lived a life, and who
could tell you strange tales, if she would.   Walking
through them you think of Fagin, of Children of the
Ghetto, of Tales of Mean Streets.   Naples is honey-
combed with narrow, teeming alleys, grimed with the
sediment of centuries, colored like old Stilton, and
smelling much worse.   But where is there another Cottage Grove avenue!   Sylvan misnomer!   A hideous
street, and sordid.   A street of flat-wheeled cars, of
delicatessen shops and moving picture houses, of clang-
ing bells, of frowsy women, of men who dart around
corners with pitchers, their coat collars turned up to
hide the absence of linen.   One day Fanny found herself at Fifty-first street, and there before her lay Washington Park, with its gracious meadow, its Italian garden, its rose walk, its lagoon, and drooping willows.
But then, that was Chicago.   All contrast.   The Illinois Central railroad puffed contemptuous cinders into
the great blue lake.   And almost in the shadow of the
City Hall nestled Bath-House John's groggery.

Michigan Avenue fascinated her most.   Here was a
street developing before one's eyes.   To walk on it was

like being present at a birth. It is one of the few
streets in the world. New York has two, Paris a hundred, London none, Vienna one. Berlin, before the war,
knew that no one walked Unter den Linden but American tourists and German shopkeepers from the prov-
inces, with their fat wives. But this Michigan Boulevard, unfinished as Chicago itself, shifting and changing
daily, still manages to take on a certain form and rugged beauty. It has about it a gracious breadth. As you
turn into it from the crash and thunder of Wabash
there comes to you a sense of peace. That's the sweep
of it, and the lake just beyond, for Michigan avenue is
a one-side street. It's west side is a sheer mountain wall
of office buildings, clubs, and hotels, whose ground floors
are fascinating with specialty shops. A milliner tan-
talizes the passer-by with a single hat stuck knowingly on a carved stick. An art store shows two etchings, and a vase. A jeweler's window holds square
blobs of emeralds, on velvet, and perhaps a gold mesh
bag, sprawling limp and invertebrate, or a diamond and
platinum la vallière, chastely barbaric. Past these windows, from Randolph to Twelfth surges the crowd:
matinee girls, all white fox, and giggles and orchids;
wise-eyed saleswomen from the smart specialty shops,
dressed in next week's mode; art students, hugging their
precious flat packages under their arms; immigrants, in
corduroys and shawls, just landed at the Twelfth street
station; sightseeing families, dazed and weary, from
Kansas; tailored and sabled Lake Shore Drive dwellers;
convention delegates spilling out of the Auditorium hotel, red-faced, hoarse, with satin badges pinned on their
coats, and their hats (the wrong kind) stuck far back
on their heads; music students to whom Michigan Avenue means the Fine Arts Building. There you have the
west side. But just across the street the walk is as
deserted as though a pestilence lurked there. Here
the Art Institute rears its smoke-blackened face, and

Grant Park's greenery struggles bravely against the poisonous breath of the Illinois Central engines.

Just below Twelfth street block after block shows the solid plate glass of the automobile shops, their glittering wares displayed against an absurd background of oriental rugs, Tiffany lamps, potted plants, and mahogany. In the windows pose the salesmen, no less sleek and glittering than their wares. Just below these, for a block or two, rows of sinister looking houses, fallen into decay, with slatternly women lolling at their windows, and gas jets flaring blue in dim hallways. Below Eighteenth still another change, where the fat stone mansions of Chicago's old families (save the mark!) hide their diminished heads behind signs that read:

"Marguerite. Robes et Manteaux." And, "Smolkin. Tailor."

Now, you know that women buyers for mail order houses do not spend their Saturday afternoons and Sundays thus, prowling about a city's streets. Fanny Brandeis knew it too, in her heart. She knew that the Ella Monahans of her world spent their holidays in stayless relaxation, manicuring, mending a bit, skimming the Sunday papers, massaging crows'-feet somewhat futilely. She knew that women buyers do not, as a rule, catch their breath with delight at sight of the pock-marked old Field Columbian museum in Jackson Park, softened and beautified by the kindly gray chiffon of the lake mist, and tinted by the rouge of the sunset glow, so that it is a thing of spectral loveliness. Successful mercantile women, seeing the furnace glare of the South Chicago steel mills flaring a sullen red against the lowering sky, do not draw a disquieting mental picture of men toiling there, naked to the waist, and glistening with sweat in the devouring heat of the fires.

I don't know how she tricked herself. I suppose she

said it was the city's appeal to the country dweller, but she lied, and she knew she was lying. She must have known it was the spirit of Molly Brandeis in her, and of Molly Brandeis' mother, and of her mother's mother's mother, down the centuries to Sarah; repressed women, suffering women, troubled, patient, nomadic women, struggling now in her for expression.

And Fanny Brandeis went doggedly on, buying and selling infants' wear, and doing it expertly. Her office desk would have interested you. It was so likely to be littered with the most appealing bits of apparel—a pair of tiny, crocheted bootees, pink and white; a sturdy linen smock; a silken hood so small that one's doubled fist filled it.

The new catalogue was on the presses. Fanny had slaved over it, hampered by Slosson. Fenger had given her practically a free hand. Results would not come in for many days. The Christmas trade would not tell the tale, for that was always a time of abnormal business. The dull season following the holiday rush would show the real returns. Slosson was discouragement itself. His attitude was not resentful; it was pitying, and that frightened Fanny. She wished that he would storm a little. Then she read her department catalogue proof sheets, and these reassured her. They were attractive. And the new baby book had turned out very well, with a colored cover that would appeal to any one who had ever been or seen a baby.

September brought a letter from Theodore. A letter from Theodore meant just one thing. Fanny hesitated a moment before opening it. She always hesitated before opening Theodore's letters. While she hesitated the old struggle would rage in her.

"I don't owe him anything," the thing within her would say. "God knows I don't. What have I done all my life but give, and give, and give to him! I'm a woman. He's a man. Let him work with his hands, as I do. He's had his share. More than his share."

Nevertheless she had sent him one thousand of the six thousand her mother had bequeathed to her. She didn't want to do it. She fought doing it. But she did it.

Now, as she held this last letter in her hands, and stared at the Bavarian stamp, she said to herself:

"He wants something. Money. If I send him some I can't have that new tailor suit, or the furs. And I need them. I'm going to have them."

She tore open the letter.

*"Dear Old Fan:*

"Olga and I are back in Munich, as you see. I think we'll be here all winter, though Olga hates it. She says it isn't *lustig*. Well, it isn't Vienna, but I think there's a chance for a class here of American pupils. Munich's swarming with Americans—whole families who come here to live for a year or two. I think I might get together a very decent class, backed by Auer's recommendations. Teaching! Good God, how I hate it! But Auer is planning a series of twenty concerts for me. They ought to be a success, if slaving can do it. I worked six hours a day all summer. I wanted to spend the summer—most of it, that is—in Holzhausen Am Ammersee, which is a little village, or artist's colony in the valley, an hour's ride from here, and within sight of the Bavarian Alps. We had Kurt Stein's little villa for almost nothing. But Olga was bored, and she wasn't well, poor girl, so we went to Interlaken and it was awful. And that brings me to what I want to tell you.

"There's going to be a baby. No use saying I'm glad, because I'm not, and neither is Olga. About

February, I think. Olga has been simply wretched,
but the doctor says she'll feel better from now on.
The truth of it is she needs a lot of things and I
can't give them to her. I told you I'd been working
on this concerto of mine. Sometimes I think it's the
real thing, if only I could get the leisure and the
peace of mind I need to work on it. You don't know
what it means to be eaten up with ambition and to
be handicapped——"

"Oh, don't I!" said Fanny Brandeis, between her
teeth, and crumpled the letter in her strong fingers.
"Don't I!" She got up from her chair and began to
walk up and down her little office, up and down. A
man often works off his feelings thus; a woman rarely.
Fenger, who had not been twice in her office since her
coming to the Haynes-Cooper plant, chose this moment
to visit her, his hands full of papers, his head full of
plans. He sensed something wrong at once, as a highly
organized human instrument responds to a similarly
constructed one.

"What's wrong, girl?"

"Everything. And don't call me girl."

Fenger saw the letter crushed in her hand.

"Brother?" She had told him about Theodore and
he had been tremendously interested.

"Yes."

"Money again, I suppose?"

"Yes, but——"

"You know your salary's going up, after Christmas."

"Catalogue or no catalogue?"

"Catalogue or no catalogue."

"Why?"

"Because you've earned it."

Fanny faced him squarely. "I know that Haynes-
Cooper isn't exactly a philanthropic institution. A

salary raise here usually means a battle. I've only been here three months."

Fenger seated himself in the chair beside her desk and ran a cool finger through the sheaf of papers in his hand. "My dear girl—I beg your pardon. I forgot. My good woman then—if you like that better—you've transfused red blood into a dying department. It may suffer a relapse after Christmas, but I don't think so. That's why you're getting more money, and not because I happen to be tremendously interested in you, personally."

Fanny's face flamed scarlet. "I didn't mean that."

"Yes you did. Here are those comparative lists you sent me. If I didn't know Slosson to be as honest as Old Dog Tray I'd think he had been selling us to the manufacturers. No wonder this department hasn't paid. He's been giving 'em top prices for shoddy. Now what's this new plan of yours?"

In an instant Fanny forgot about Theodore, the new winter suit and furs, everything but the idea that was clamoring to be born. She sat at her desk, her fingers folding and unfolding a bit of paper, her face all light and animation as she talked.

"My idea is to have a person known as a selector for each important department. It would mean a boiling down of the products of every manufacturer we deal with, and skimming the cream off the top. As it is now a department buyer has to do the selecting and buying too. He can't do both and get results. We ought to set aside an entire floor for the display of manufacturers' samples. The selector would make his choice among these, six months in advance of the season. The selector would go to the eastern markets too, of course. Not to buy. Merely to select. Then, with the line chosen as far as style, quality, and value is concerned, the buyer would be free to deal directly with the manufacturer as to quantity, time, and all that. You know as well as I that that's enough of a job for any one person, with the labor situation what it is. He wouldn't need to bother about styles or colors, or any of that. It would all have been done for him. The selector would have the real responsibility. Don't you see the simplicity of it, and the way it would grease the entire machinery?"

Something very like jealousy came into Michael Fenger's face as he looked at her. But it was gone in an instant. "Gad! You'll have my job away from me in two years. You're a super-woman, do you know that?"

"Super nothing! It's just a perfectly good idea, founded on common sense and economy."

"M-m-m, but that's all Columbus had in mind when he started out to find a short cut to India."

Fanny laughed out at that. "Yes, but see where he landed!"

But Fenger was serious. "We'll have to have a meeting on this. Are you prepared to go into detail on it, before Mr. Haynes and the two Coopers, at a real meeting in a real mahogany directors' room? Wednesday, say?"

"I think so."

Fenger got up. "Look here, Miss Brandeis. You need a day in the country. Why don't you run up to your home town over Sunday? Wisconsin, wasn't it?"

"Oh, no! No. I mean yes it was Wisconsin, but no I don't want to go."

"Then let me send you my car."

"Car! No, thanks. That's not my idea of the country."

"It was just a suggestion. What do you call going to the country, then?"

"Tramping all day, and getting lost, if possible. Lying down under a tree for hours, and letting the ants

amble over you. Dreaming. And coming back tired,
hungry, dusty, and refreshed.''

"It sounds awfully uncomfortable. But I wish you'd
try it, this week.''

"Do I look such a wreck?" Fanny demanded, rather
pettishly.

"You!" Fenger's voice was vibrant. "You're the
most splendidly alive looking woman I ever saw. When
you came into my office that first day you seemed to
spark with health, and repressed energy, and electricity,
so that you radiated them. People who can do that,
stimulate. That's what you are to me—a stimulant.''

What can one do with a man who talks like that?
After all, what he said was harmless enough. His tone
was quietly sincere. One can't resent an expression
of the eyes. Then, too, just as she made up her mind
to be angry she remembered the limp and querulous
Mrs. Fenger, and the valve and the scarf. And her
anger became pity. There flashed back to her the illuminating bit of conversation with which Fascinating
Facts had regaled her on the homeward drive that night
of the tea.

"Nice chap, Fenger. And a wiz in business. Get's
a king's salary. Must be hell for a man to be tied,
hand and foot, the way he is.''

"Tied?''

"Mrs. Fenger's a semi-invalid. At that I don't believe she's as helpless as she seems. I think she just
holds him by that shawl of hers, that's forever slipping.
You know he was a machine boy in her father's woolen
mill. She met him after he'd worked his way up to an
office job. He has forged ahead like a locomotive ever
since.''

That had been their conversation, gossipy, but tremendously enlightening for Fanny. She looked up at
him now.

"Thanks for the vacation suggestion. I may go off

somewhere. Just a last-minute leap. It usually turns out better, that way. I'll be ready for the Wednesday discussion."

She sounded very final and busy. The crumpled letter lay on her desk. She smoothed it out, and the crumple transferred itself to her forehead. Fenger stood a moment, looking down at her. Then he turned, abruptly and left the office. Fanny did not look up.

That was Friday. On Saturday her vacation took a personally conducted turn. She had planned to get away at noon, as most office heads did on Saturday, during the warm weather. When her 'phone rang at eleven she answered it mechanically as does one whose telephone calls mean a row with a tardy manufacturer, an argument with a merchandise man, or a catalogue query from the printer's.

The name that came to her over the telephone conveyed nothing to her.

"Who?" Again the name. "Heyl?" She repeated the name uncertainly. "I'm afraid I—O, of course! Clarence Heyl. Howdy-do."

"I want to see you," said the voice, promptly.

There rose up in Fanny's mind a cruelly clear picture of the little, sallow, sniveling school boy of her girlhood. The little boy with the big glasses and the shiny shoes, and the weak lungs.

"Sorry," she replied, promptly, "but I'm afraid it's impossible. I'm leaving the office early, and I'm swamped." Which was a lie.

"This evening?"

"I rarely plan anything for the evening. Too tired, as a rule."

"Too tired to drive?"

"I'm afraid so."

A brief silence. Then, "I'm coming out there to see you."

"Where? Here? The plant! That's impossible, Mr. Heyl. I'm terribly sorry, but I can't——"

"Yes, I know. Also terribly sure that if I ever get to you it will be over your office boy's dead body. Well, arm him. I'm coming. Good-by."

"Wait a minute! Mr. Heyl! Clarence! Hello! Hello!"

A jiggling of the hook. "Number, please?" droned the voice of the operator.

Fanny jammed the receiver down on the hook and turned to her work, lips compressed, a frown forming a double cleft between her eyes.

Half an hour later he was there. Her office boy brought in his card, as she had rehearsed him to do. Fanny noted that it was the wrong kind of card. She would show him what happened to pushers who pestered business women during office hours.

"Bring him in in twenty minutes," she said, grimly. Her office boy (and slave) always took his cue from her. She hoped he wouldn't be too rude to Heyl, and turned back to her work again. Thirty-nine seconds later Clarence Heyl walked in.

"Hello, Fan!" he said, and had her limp hand in a grip that made her wince.

"But I told——"

"Yes, I know. But he's a crushed and broken office boy by now. I had to be real harsh with him."

Fanny stood up, really angry now. She looked up at Clarence Heyl, and her eyes were flashing. Clarence Heyl looked down at her, and his eyes were the keenest, kindest, most gently humorous eyes she had ever encountered. You know that picture of Lincoln that shows us his eyes with much that expression in them? That's as near as I can come to conveying to you the whimsical pathos in this man. They were the eyes of a lonely little boy grown up. And they had seen much in the process.

Fanny felt her little blaze of anger flicker and die.

"That's the girl," said Heyl, and patted her hand. "You'll like me—presently. After you've forgotten about that sniveling kid you hated." He stepped back a pace and threw back his coat senatorially. "How do I look?" he demanded.

"Look?" repeated Fanny, feebly.

"I've been hours preparing for this. Years! And now something tells me—This tie, for instance."

Fanny bit her lip in a vain effort to retain her solemnity. Then she gave it up and giggled, frankly. "Well, since you ask me, that tie!——"

"What's the matter with it?"

Fanny giggled again. "It's red, that's what."

"Well, what of it! Red's all right. I've always considered red one of our leading colors."

"But you can't wear it."

"Can't! Why can't I?"

"Because you're the brunest kind of brunette. And dark people have a special curse hanging over them that makes them want to wear red. It's fatal. That tie makes you look like a Mafia murderer dressed for business."

"I knew it," groaned Heyl. "Something told me." He sank into a chair at the side of her desk, a picture of mock dejection. "And I chose it. Deliberately. I had black ones, and blue ones, and green ones. And I chose—this." He covered his face with a shaking hand.

Fanny Brandeis leaned back in her chair, and laughed, and laughed, and laughed. Surely she hadn't laughed like that in a year at least.

"You're a madman," she said, finally.

At that Heyl looked up with his singularly winning smile. "But different. Concede that, Fanny. Be fair, now. Refreshingly different."

"Different," said Fanny, "doesn't begin to cover it. Well, now you're here, tell me what you're doing here."

"Seeing you."

"I mean here, in Chicago."

"So do I. I'm on my way from Winnebago to New York, and I'm in Chicago to see Fanny Brandeis."

"Don't expect me to believe that."

Heyl put an arm on Fanny's desk and learned forward, his face very earnest. "I do expect you to believe it. I expect you to believe everything I say to you. Not only that, I expect you not to be surprised at anything I say. I've done such a mass of private thinking about you in the last ten years that I'm likely to forget I've scarcely seen you in that time. Just remember, will you, that like the girl in the sob song, 'You made me what I am to-day?'"

"I! You're being humorous again."

"Never less so in my life. Listen, Fan. That cowardly, sickly little boy you fought for in the street, that day in Winnebago, showed every sign of growing up a cowardly, sickly man. You're the real reason for his not doing so. Now, wait a minute. I was an impressionable little kid, I guess. Sickly ones are apt to be. I worshiped you and hated you from that day. Worshiped you for the blazing, generous, whole-souled little devil of a spitfire that you were. Hated you because—well, what boy wouldn't hate a girl who had to fight for him. Gosh! It makes me sick to think of it, even now. Pasty-faced rat!"

"What nonsense! I'd forgotten all about it."

"No you hadn't. Tell me, what flashed into your mind when you saw me in Temple that night before you left Winnebago? The truth, now."

She learned, later, that people did not lie to him. She tried it now, and found herself saying, rather shamefacedly, "I thought 'Why, it's Clarence Heyl, the Cowardy-Cat!'"

"There! That's why I'm here to-day. I knew you were thinking that. I knew it all the time I was in

Colorado, growing up from a sickly kid, with a bum
lung, to a heap big strong man. It forced me to do
things I was afraid to do. It goaded me on to stunts
at the very thought of which I'd break out in a clammy
sweat. Don't you see how I'll have to turn handsprings
in front of you, like the school-boy in the McCutcheon
cartoon? Don't you see how I'll have to flex my muscles—like this—to show you how strong I am? I may
even have to beat you, eventually. Why, child, I've
chummed with lions, and bears, and wolves, and everything, because of you, you little devil in the red cap!
I've climbed unclimbable mountains. I've frozen my feet
in blizzards. I've wandered for days on a mountain
top, lost, living on dried currants and milk chocolate,—
and Lord! how I hate milk chocolate! I've dodged
snowslides, and slept in trees; I've endured cold, and
hunger and thirst, through you. It took me years to
get used to the idea of passing a timber wolf without
looking around, but I learned to do it—because of you.
You made me. They sent me to Colorado, a lonely kid,
with a pretty fair chance of dying, and I would have,
if it hadn't been for you. There! How's that for a
burst of speech, young woman! And wait a minute.
Remember, too, my name was Clarence. I had that to
live down."

Fanny was staring at him eyes round, lips parted.
"But why?" she said, faintly. "Why?"

Heyl smiled that singularly winning smile of his.
"Since you force me to it, I think I'm in love with that
little, warm-hearted spitfire in the red cap. That's
why."

Fanny sat forward now. She had been leaning back
in her chair, her hands grasping its arms, her face a
lovely, mobile thing, across which laughter, and pity,
and sympathy and surprise rippled and played. It
hardened now, and set. She looked down at her hands,
and clasped them in her lap, then up at him. "In that

case, you can forsake the strenuous life with a free
conscience. You need never climb another mountain,
or wrestle with another—er—hippopotamus. That little girl in the red cap is dead."

"Dead?"

"Yes. She died a year ago. If the one who has
taken her place were to pass you on the street to-
day, and see you beset by forty thieves, she'd not even
stop. Not she. She'd say, 'Let him fight it out alone.
It's none of your business. You've got your own fights
to handle.' "

"Why—Fanny. You don't mean that, do you?
What could have made her like that?"

"She just discovered that fighting for others didn't
pay. She just happened to know some one else who
had done that all her life and—it killed her."

"Her mother?"

"Yes."

A little silence. "Fanny, let's play outdoors to-
morrow, will you? All day."

Involuntarily Fanny glanced around the room. Papers, catalogues, files, desk, chair, typewriter. "I'm
afraid I've forgotten how."

"I'll teach you. You look as if you could stand a
little of it."

"I must be a pretty sight. You're the second man
to tell me that in two days."

Heyl leaned forward a little. "That so? Who's the
other one?"

"Fenger, the General Manager."

"Oh! Paternal old chap, I suppose. No? Well,
anyway, I don't know what he had in mind, but you're
going to spend Sunday at the dunes of Indiana with
me."

"Dunes? Of Indiana?"

"There's nothing like them in the world. Literally.
In September that combination of yellow sand, and

blue lake, and the woods beyond is—well, you'll see what it is. It's only a little more than an hour's ride by train. And it will just wipe that tired look out of your face, Fan." He stood up. "I'll call for you to-morrow morning at eight, or thereabouts. That's early for Sunday, but it's going to be worth it."

"I can't. Really. Besides, I don't think I even want to. I——"

"I promise not to lecture on Nature, if that's what's worrying you." He took her hand in a parting grip. "Bring some sandwiches, will you? Quite a lot of 'em. I'll have some other stuff in my rücksack. And wear some clothes you don't mind wrecking. I suppose you haven't got a red tam o' shanter?"

"Heavens, no!"

"I just thought it might help to keep me humble." He was at the door, and so was she, somehow, her hand still in his. "Eight o'clock. How do you stand it in this place, Fan? Oh, well—I'll find that out to-morrow. Good-by."

Fanny went back to her desk and papers. The room seemed all at once impossibly stuffy, her papers and letters dry, meaningless things. In the next office, separated from her by a partition half glass, half wood, she saw the top of Slosson's bald head as he stood up to shut his old-fashioned roll-top desk. He was leaving. She looked out of the window. Ella Monahan, in hat and suit, passed and came back to poke her head in the door.

"Run along!" she said. "It's Saturday afternoon. You'll work overtime enough when the Christmas rush begins. Come on, child, and call it a day!"

And Fanny gathered papers, figures, catalogue proofs into a glorious heap, thrust them into a drawer, locked the drawer, pushed back her chair, and came.

## CHAPTER ELEVEN

FANNY told herself, before she went to bed Saturday night, that she hoped it would rain Sunday morning from seven to twelve. But when Princess woke her at seven-thirty, as per instructions left in penciled scrawl on the kitchen table, she turned to the window at once, and was glad, somehow, to find it sunflooded. Princess, if you're mystified, was royal in name only—a biscuit-tinted lady, with a very black and no-account husband whose habits made it necessary for Princess to let herself into Fanny's four-room flat at seven every morning, and let herself out at eight every evening. She had an incredibly soft and musical voice, had Princess, and a cooking hand. She kept Fanny mended, fed and comfortable, and her only cross was that Fanny's taste in blouses (ultimately her property) ran to the severe and tailored.

"Mawnin', Miss Fanny. There's a gep'mun waitin' to see yo'."

Fanny choked on a yawn. "A what!"

"Gep'mun. Says yo-all goin' picnickin'. He's in the settin' room, a-lookin' at yo' pictchah papahs. Will Ah fry yo' up a li'l chicken to pack along? San'wiches ain't no eatin' fo' Sunday."

Fanny flung back her covers, swung around to the side of the bed, and stood up, all, seemingly, in one sweeping movement. "Do you mean to tell me he's in there, now?"

From the sitting room. "I think I ought to tell you I can hear everything you're saying. Say, Fanny, these sketches of yours are—— Why, Gee Whiz! I didn't know you did that kind of thing. This one here, with that girl's face in the crowd——"

"For heaven's sake!" Fanny demanded, "what are you doing here at seven-thirty? And I don't allow people to look at those sketches. You said eight-thirty."

"I was afraid you'd change your mind, or something. Besides, it's now twenty-two minutes to eight. And will you tell the lady that's a wonderful idea about the chicken? Only she'd better start now."

Goaded by time bulletins shouted through the closed door, Fanny found herself tubbed, clothed, and ready for breakfast by eight-ten. When she opened the door Clarence was standing in the center of her little sitting room, waiting, a sheaf of loose sketches in his hand.

"Say, look here! These are the real thing. Why, they're great! They get you. This old geezer with the beard, selling fish and looking like one of the Disciples. And this. What the devil are you doing in a mail order house, or whatever it is? Tell me that! When you can draw like this!"

"Good morning," said Fanny, calmly. "And I'll tell you nothing before breakfast. The one thing that interests me this moment is hot coffee. Will you have some breakfast? Oh, well, a second one won't hurt you. You must have got up at three, or thereabouts." She went toward the tiny kitchen. "Never mind, Princess. I'll wait on myself. You go on with that chicken."

Princess was the kind of person who can fry a chicken, wrap it in cool, crisp lettuce leaves, box it, cut sandwiches, and come out of the process with an unruffled temper and an immaculate kitchen. Thanks to her, Fanny and Heyl found themselves on the eight fifty-three train, bound for the dunes.

Clarence swung his rücksack up to the bundle rack. He took off his cap, and stuffed it into his pocket. He was grinning like a schoolboy. Fanny turned from the window and smiled at what she saw in his face. At that he gave an absurd little bounce in his place, like an overgrown child, and reached over and patted her hand.

"I've dreamed of this for years."

"You're just fourteen, going on fifteen," Fanny reproved him.

"I know it. And it's great! Won't you be, too? Forget you're a fair financier, or whatever they call it. Forget you earn more in a month than I do in six. Relax. Unbend. Loosen up. Don't assume that hardshell air with me. Just remember that I knew you when the frill of your panties showed below your skirt."

"Clarence Heyl!"

But he was leaning past her, and pointing out of the window. "See that curtain of smoke off there? That's the South Chicago, and the Hammond and Gary steel mills. Wait till you see those smokestacks against the sky, and the iron scaffoldings that look like giant lacework, and the slag heaps, and the coal piles, and those huge, grim tanks. Gad! It's awful and beautiful. Like the things Pennell does."

"I came out here on the street car one day," said Fanny, quietly. "One Sunday."

"You did!" He stared at her.

"It was hot, and they were all spilling out into the street. You know, the women in wrappers, just blobs of flesh trying to get cool. And the young girls in their pink silk dresses and white shoes, and the boys on the street corners, calling to them. Babies all over the sidewalks and streets, and the men who weren't in the mills—you know how they look in their Sunday shirt-sleeves, with their flat faces, and high cheekbones, and their great brown hands with the broken nails. Hunkies. Well, at five the motor cars began whizzing

by from the country roads back to Chicago. You have
to go back that way. Just then the five o'clock
whistles blew and the day shift came off. There was
a great army of them, clumping down the road the way
they do. Their shoulders were slack, and their lunch
pails dangled, empty, and they were wet and reeking
with sweat. The motor cars were full of wild phlox
and daisies and spiderwort."

Clarence was still turned sideways, looking at her.
"Get a picture of it?"

"Yes. I tried, at least."

"Is that the way you usually spend your Sundays?"

"Well, I—I like snooping about."

"M-m," mused Clarence. Then, "How's business,
Fanny?"

"Business?" You could almost feel her mind jerk
back. "Oh, let's not talk about business on Sunday."

"I thought so," said Clarence, enigmatically. "Now
listen to me, Fanny."

"I'll listen," interrupted she, "if you'll talk about
yourself. I want to know what you're doing, and why
you're going to New York. What business can a naturalist have in New York, anyway?"

"I didn't intend to be a naturalist. You can tell that
by looking at me. But you can't have your very nose
rubbed up against trees, and rocks, and mountains,
and snow for years and years without learning something about 'em. There were whole weeks when I hadn't
anything to chum with but a timber-line pine and an
odd assortment of mountain peaks. We just had to
get acquainted."

"But you're going back, aren't you? Don't they
talk about the spell of the mountains, or some such
thing?"

"They do. And they're right. And I've got to have
them six months in the year, at least. But I'm going
to try spending the other six in the bosom of the hu-

man race. Not only that, I'm going to write about it. Writing's my job, really. At least, it's the thing I like best."

"Nature?"

"Human nature. I went out to Colorado just a lonesome little kid with a bum lung. The lung's all right, but I never did quite get over the other. Two years ago, in the mountains, I met Carl Lasker, who owns the New York *Star*. It's said to be the greatest morning paper in the country. Lasker's a genius. And he fries the best bacon I ever tasted. I took him on a four-weeks' horseback trip through the mountains. We got pretty well acquainted. At the end of it he offered me a job. You see, I'd never seen a chorus girl, or the Woolworth building, or a cabaret, or a broiled lobster, or a subway. But I was interested and curious about all of them. And Lasker said, 'A man who can humanize a rock, or a tree, or a chipmunk ought to be able to make even those things seem human. You've got what they call the fresh viewpoint. New York's full of people with a scum over their eyes, but a lot of them came to New York from Winnebago, or towns just like it, and you'd be surprised at the number of them who still get their home town paper. One day, when I came into Lee Kohl's office, with stars, and leading men, and all that waiting outside to see him, he was sitting with his feet on the desk reading the Sheffield, Illinois, *Gazette*.' You see, the thing he thinks I can do is to give them a picture of New York as they used to see it, before they got color blind. A column or so a day, about anything that hits me. How does that strike you as a job for a naturalist?"

"It's a job for a human naturalist. I think you'll cover it."

If you know the dunes, which you probably don't, you know why they did not get off at Millers, with the crowd, but rode on until they were free of the Sun-

day picnickers. Then they got off, and walked across
the tracks, past saloons, and a few huddled houses,
hideous in yellow paint, and on, and on down a road
that seemed endless. A stretch of cinders, then dust,
a rather stiff little hill, a great length of yellow sand
and—the lake! We say, the lake! like that, with an
exclamation point after it, because it wasn't at all the
Lake Michigan that Chicagoans know. This vast blue
glory bore no relation to the sullen, gray, turbid thing
that the city calls the lake. It was all the blues of
which you've ever heard, and every passing cloud gave
it a new shade. Sapphire. No, cobalt. No, that's
too cold. Mediterranean. Turquoise. And the sand
in golden contrast. Miles of sand along the beach,
and back of that the dunes. Now, any dictionary or
Scotchman will tell you that a dune is a hill of loose
sand. But these dunes are done in American fashion,
lavishly. Mountains of sand, as far as the eye can see,
and on the top of them, incredibly, great pine trees
that clutch at their perilous, shifting foothold with
frantic root-toes. And behind that, still more incredibly, the woods, filled with wild flowers, with strange
growths found nowhere else in the whole land, with
trees, and vines, and brush, and always the pungent
scent of the pines. And there you have the dunes—
blue lake, golden sand-hills, green forest, in one.

Fanny and Clarence stood there on the sand, in
silence, two ridiculously diminutive figures in that great
wilderness of beauty. I wish I could get to you, somehow, the clear sparkle of it, the brilliance of it, and
yet the peace of it. They stood there a long while,
those two, without speaking. Then Fanny shut her
eyes, and I think her lower lip trembled just a little.
And Clarence patted her hand just twice.

"I thank you," he said, "in the name of that much-
abused lady known as Nature."

Said Fanny, "I want to scramble up to the top of

one of those dunes—the high one—and just sit there."

And that is what they did. A poor enough Sunday, I suppose, in the minds of those of you who spend yours golfing at the club, or motoring along grease-soaked roads that lead to a shore dinner and a ukulele band. But it turned Fanny Brandeis back a dozen years or more, so that she was again the little girl whose heart had ached at sight of the pale rose and orange of the Wisconsin winter sunsets. She forgot all about layettes, and obstetrical outfits, and flannel bands, and safety pins; her mind was a blank in the matter of bootees, and catalogues, and our No. 29E8347, and those hungry bins that always yawned for more. She forgot about Michael Fenger, and Theodore, and the new furs. They scrambled up dunes, digging into the treacherous sand with heels, toes, and the side of the foot, and clutching at fickle roots with frantic fingers. Forward a step, and back two—that's dune climbing. A back-breaking business, unless you're young and strong, as were these two. They explored the woods, and Heyl had a fascinating way of talking about stones and shrubs and trees as if they were endowed with human qualities—as indeed they were for him. They found a hill-slope carpeted with dwarf huckleberry plants, still bearing tiny clusters of the blue-black fruit. Fanny's heart was pounding, her lungs ached, her cheeks were scarlet, her eyes shining. Heyl, steel-muscled, took the hills like a chamois. Once they crossed hands atop a dune and literally skated down it, right, left, right, left, shrieking with laughter, and ending in a heap at the bottom.

"In the name of all that's idiotic!" shouted Heyl. "Silk stockings! What in thunder made you wear silk stockings! At the sand dunes! Gosh!"

They ate their dinner in olympic splendor, atop a dune. Heyl produced unexpected things from the rücksack—things that ranged all the way from milk chocolate to literature, and from grape juice to cigarettes. They ate ravenously, but at Heyl's thrifty suggestion they saved a few sandwiches for the late afternoon. It was he, too, who made a little bonfire of papers, crusts, and bones, as is the cleanly habit of your true woodsman. Then they stretched out, full length, in the noon sun, on the warm, clean sand.

"What's your best price on one-sixth doz. flannel vests?" inquired Heyl.

And, "Oh, shut up!" said Fanny, elegantly. Heyl laughed as one who hugs a secret.

"We'll work our way down the beach," he announced, "toward Millers. There'll be northern lights to-night; did you know that? Want to stay and see them?"

"Do I want to! I won't go home till I have."

These were the things they did on that holiday; childish, happy, tiring things, such as people do who love the outdoors.

The charm of Clarence Heyl—for he had charm—is difficult to transmit. His lovableness and appeal lay in his simplicity. It was not so much what he said as in what he didn't say. He was staring unwinkingly now at the sunset that had suddenly burst upon them. His were the eyes of one accustomed to the silent distances.

"Takes your breath away, rather, doesn't it? All that color?" said Fanny, her face toward the blaze.

"Almost too obvious for my taste. I like 'em a little more subdued, myself." They were atop a dune, and he stretched himself flat on the sand, still keeping his bright brown eyes on lake and sky. Then he sat up, excitedly. "Heh, try that! Lie flat. It softens the whole thing. Like this. Now look at it. The lake's like molten copper flowing in. And you can see that silly sun going down in jerks, like a balloon on a string."

They lay there, silent, while the scarlet became orange, the orange faded to rose, the rose to pale pink, to salmon, to mauve, to gray. The first pale star came out, and the brazen lights of Gary, far to the north, defied it.

Fanny sat up with a sigh and a little shiver.

"Fasten up that sweater around your throat," said Heyl. "Got a pin?" They munched their sandwiches, rather soggy by now, and drank the last of the grape juice. "We'll have a bite of hot supper in town, at a restaurant that doesn't mind Sunday trampers. Come on, Fan. We'll start down the beach until the northern lights begin to show."

"It's been the most accommodating day," murmured Fanny. "Sunshine, sunset, northern lights, everything. If we were to demand a rainbow and an eclipse they'd turn those on, too."

They started to walk down the beach in the twilight, keeping close to the water's edge where the sand was moist and firm. It was hard going. They plunged along arm in arm, in silence. Now and again they stopped, with one accord, and looked out over the great gray expanse that lay before them, and then up at the hills and the pines etched in black against the sky. Nothing competitive here, Fanny thought, and took a deep breath. She thought of to-morrow's work, with day after to-morrow's biting and snapping at its heels.

Clarence seemed to sense her thoughts. "Doesn't this make you feel you want to get away from those damned bins that you're forever feeding? I watched those boys for a minute, the other day, outside your office. Jove!"

Fanny dug a heel into the sand, savagely. "Some days I feel that I've got to walk out of the office, and down the street, without a hat, and on, and on, walking and walking, and running now and then, till I come to the horizon. That's how I feel, some days."

"Then some day, Fanny, that feeling will get too strong for you, and you'll do it. Now listen to me. Tuck this away in your subconscious mind, and leave it there until you need it. When that time comes get on a train for Denver. From Denver take another to Estes Park. That's the Rocky Mountains, and they're your destination, because that's where the horizon lives and has its being. When you get there ask for Heyl's place. They'll just hand you from one to the other, gently, until you get there. I may be there, but more likely I shan't. The key's in the mail box, tied to a string. You'll find a fire already laid, in the fireplace, with fat pine knots that will blaze up at the touch of a match. My books are there, along the walls. The bedding's in the cedar chest, and the lamps are filled. There's tinned stuff in the pantry. And the mountains are there, girl, to make you clean and whole again. And the pines that are nature's prophylactic brushes. And the sky. And peace. That sounds like a railway folder, but it's true. I know." They trudged along in silence for a little while. "Got that?"

"M-m," replied Fanny, disinterestedly, without looking at him.

Heyl's jaw set. You could see the muscles show white for an instant. Then he said: "It has been a wonderful day, Fanny, but you haven't told me a thing about yourself. I'd like to know about your work. I'd like to know what you're doing; what your plan is. You looked so darned definite up there in that office. Whom do you play with? And who's this Fenger— wasn't that the name?—who saw that you looked tired?"

"All right, Clancy. I'll tell you all about it," Fanny agreed, briskly.

"All right—who!"

"Well, I can't call you Clarence. It doesn't fit. So just for the rest of the day let's make it Clancy, even

if you do look like one of the minor Hebrew prophets,
minus the beard."

And so she began to tell him of her work and her
aims.  I think that she had been craving just this
chance to talk.  That which she told him was, unconsciously, a confession.  She told him of Theodore and
his marriage; of her mother's death; of her coming to
Haynes-Cooper, and the changes she had brought
about there.  She showed him the infinite possibilities
for advancement there.  Slosson she tossed aside.
Then, rather haltingly, she told him of Fenger, of his
business genius, his magnetic qualities, of his career.
She even sketched a deft word-picture of the limp and
irritating Mrs. Fenger.

"Is this Fenger in love with you?" asked Heyl,
startlingly.

Fanny recoiled at the idea with a primness that did
credit to Winnebago.

"Clancy!  Please!  He's married."

"Now don't sneak, Fanny.  And don't talk like an
ingénue.  So far, you've outlined a life-plan that makes
Becky Sharp look like a cooing dove.  So just answer
this straight, will you?"

"Why, I suppose I attract him, as any man of his
sort, with a wife like that, would be attracted to a
healthily alert woman, whose ideas match his.  And I
wish you wouldn't talk to me like that.  It hurts."

"I'm glad of that.  I was afraid you'd passed that
stage.  Well now, how about those sketches of yours?
I suppose you know that they're as good, in a crude,
effective sort of way, as anything that's being done
to-day."

"Oh, nonsense!"  But then she stopped, suddenly,
and put both hands on his arm, and looked up at him,
her face radiant in the gray twilight.  "Do you really
think they're good!"

"You bet they're good.  There isn't a newspaper

in the country that couldn't use that kind of stuff. And there aren't three people in the country who can do it. It isn't a case of being able to draw. It's being able to see life in a peculiar light, and to throw that light so that others get the glow. Those sketches I saw this morning are life, served up raw. That's your gift, Fanny. Why the devil don't you use it!"

But Fanny had got herself in hand again. "It isn't a gift," she said, lightly. "It's just a little knack that amuses me. There's no money in it. Besides, it's too late now. One's got to do a thing superlatively, nowadays, to be recognized. I don't draw superlatively, but I do handle infants' wear better than any woman I know. In two more years I'll be getting ten thousand a year at Haynes-Cooper. In five years——"

"Then what?"

Fanny's hands became fists, gripping the power she craved. "Then I shall have arrived. I shall be able to see the great and beautiful things of this world, and mingle with the people who possess them."

"When you might be making them yourself, you little fool. Don't glare at me like that. I tell you that those pictures are the real expression of you. That's why you turn to them as relief from the shop grind. You can't help doing them. They're you."

"I can stop if I want to. They amuse me, that's all."

"You can't stop. It's in your blood. It's the Jew in you."

"The—— Here, I'll show you. I won't do another sketch for a year. I'll prove to you that my ancestors' religion doesn't influence my work, or my play."

"Dear, you can't prove that, because the contrary has been proven long ago. You yourself proved it when you did that sketch of the old fish vender in the Ghetto. The one with the beard. It took a thousand years of suffering and persecution and faith to stamp

"Fanny's hands became fists, gripping the power she
craved. 'Then I shall have arrived.' "

—*Page 188*

that look on his face, and it took a thousand years to
breed in you the genius to see it, and put it down on
paper. Fan, did you ever read Fishberg's book?"

"No," said Fanny, low-voiced.

"Sometime, when you can snatch a moment from
the fascinations of the mail order catalogue, read it.
Fishberg says—I wish I could remember his exact
words—'It isn't the body that marks the Jew. It's his
Soul. The type is not anthropological, or physical;
it's social or psychic. It isn't the complexion, the nose,
the lips, the head. It's his Soul which betrays his
faith. Centuries of Ghetto confinement, ostracism,
ceaseless suffering, have produced a psychic type. The
thing that is stamped on the Soul seeps through the
veins and works its way magically to the face——' "

"But I don't want to talk about souls! Please!
You're spoiling a wonderful day."

"And you're spoiling a wonderful life. I don't object to this driving ambition in you. I don't say that
you're wrong in wanting to make a place for yourself
in the world. But don't expect me to stand by and let
you trample over your own immortal soul to get there.
Your head is busy enough on this infants' wear job,
but how about the rest of you—how about You? What
do you suppose all those years of work, and suppression, and self-denial, and beauty-hunger there in Winnebago were meant for! Not to develop the mail order
business. They were given you so that you might recognize hunger, and suppression, and self-denial in
others. The light in the face of that girl in the crowd
pouring out of the plant. What's that but the reflection of the light in you! I tell you, Fanny, we
Jews have got a money-grubbing, loud-talking, dia-
mond-studded, get-there-at-any-price reputation, and
perhaps we deserve it. But every now and then, out of
the mass of us, one lifts his head and stands erect, and
the great white light is in his face. And that person

has suffered, for suffering breeds genius. It expands
the soul just as over-prosperity shrivels it. You see
it all the way from Lew Fields to Sarah Bernhardt;
from Mendelssohn to Irving Berlin; from Mischa Elman to Charlie Chaplin. You were a person set apart
in Winnebago. Instead of thanking your God for that,
you set out to be something you aren't. No, it's worse
than that. You're trying not to be what you are. And
it's going to do for you."

"Stop!" cried Fanny. "My head's whirling. It
sounds like something out of 'Alice in Wonderland.' "

"And you," retorted Heyl, "sound like some one who's
afraid to talk or think about herself. You're suppress-
ing the thing that is you. You're cutting yourself off
from your own people—a dramatic, impulsive, emotional people. By doing those things you're killing the goose
that lays the golden egg. What's that old copy-book
line? 'To thine own self be true,' and the rest of it."

"Yes; like Theodore, for example," sneered Fanny.

At which unpleasant point Nature kindly supplied a
diversion. Across the black sky there shot two
luminous shafts of lights. Northern lights, pale sisters
of the chromatic glory one sees in the far north, but
still weirdly beautiful. Fanny and Heyl stopped short,
faces upturned. The ghostly radiance wavered, ex-
panded, glowed palely, like celestial searchlights. Suddenly, from the tip of each shaft, there burst a cluster
of slender, pin-point lines, like aigrettes set in a band
of silver. Then these slowly wavered, faded, combined
to form a third and fourth slender shaft of light. It
was like the radiance one sees in the old pictures of the
Holy Family. Together Fanny and Heyl watched it
in silence until the last pale glimmer faded and was
gone, and only the brazen lights of Gary, far, far down
the beach, cast a fiery glow against the sky.

They sighed, simultaneously. Then they laughed,
each at the other.

"Curtain," said Fanny. They raced for the station, despite the sand. Their car was filled with pudgy babies lying limp in parental arms; with lunch baskets exuding the sickly scent of bananas; with disheveled vandals whose moist palms grasped bunches of wilted wild flowers. Past the belching chimneys of Gary, through South Chicago, the back yard of a metropolis, past Jackson Park that breathed coolly upon them, and so to the city again. They looked at it with the shock that comes to eyes that have rested for hours on long stretches of sand and sky and water. Monday, that had seemed so far away, became an actuality of to-morrow.

Tired as they were, they stopped at one of those frank little restaurants that brighten Chicago's drab side streets. Its windows were full of pans that held baked beans, all crusty and brown, and falsely tempting, and of baked apples swimming in a pool of syrup. These flanked by ketchup bottles and geometrical pyramids of golden grape-fruit.

Coffee and hot roast beef sandwiches, of course, in a place like that. "And," added Fanny, "one of those baked apples. Just to prove they can't be as good as they look."

They weren't, but she was too hungry to care. Not too hungry, though, to note with quick eye all that the little restaurant held of interest, nor too sleepy to respond to the friendly waitress who, seeing their dusty boots, and the sprig of sumac stuck in Fanny's coat, said, "My, it must have been swell in the country to-day!" as her flapping napkin precipitated crumbs into their laps.

"It was," said Fanny, and smiled up at the girl with her generous, flashing smile. "Here's a bit of it I brought back for you." And she stuck the scarlet sumac sprig into the belt of the white apron.

They finished the day incongruously by taking a

taxi home, Fanny yawning luxuriously all the way.

"Do you know," she said, as they parted, "we've talked about everything from souls to infants' wear. We're talked out. It's a mercy you're going to New York. There won't be a next time."

"Young woman," said Heyl, forcefully, "there will. That young devil in the red tam isn't dead. She's alive. And kicking. There's a kick in every one of those Chicago sketches in your portfolio upstairs. You said she wouldn't fight anybody's battles to-day. You little idiot, she's fighting one in each of those pictures, from the one showing that girl's face in the crowd, to the old chap with the fish-stall. She'll never die—that one. Because she's the spirit. It's the other one who's dead—and she doesn't know it. But some day she'll find herself buried. And I want to be there to shovel on the dirt."

## CHAPTER TWELVE

FROM the first of December the floor of the Haynes-Cooper mail room looked like the New York Stock Exchange, after a panic. The aisles were drifts of paper against which a squad of boys struggled as vainly as a gang of snow-shovelers against a blizzard. The guide talked in terms of tons of mail, instead of thousands. And smacked his lips after it. The Ten Thousand were working at night now, stopping for a hasty bite of supper at six, then back to desk, or bin or shelf until nine, so that Oklahoma and Minnesota might have its Christmas box in time.

Fanny Brandeis, working under the light of her green-shaded desk lamp, wondered, a little bitterly, if Christmas would ever mean anything to her but pressure, weariness, work. She told herself that she would not think of that Christmas of one year ago. One year! As she glanced around the orderly little office, and out to the stock room beyond, then back to her desk again, she had an odd little feeling of unreality. Surely it had been not one year, but many years—a lifetime—since she had elbowed her way up and down those packed aisles of the busy little store in Winnebago—she and that brisk, alert, courageous woman.

"Mrs. Brandeis, lady wants to know if you can't put this blue satin dress on the dark-haired doll, and the pink satin. . . . Well, I did tell her, but she said for me to ask you, anyway."

"Mis' Brandeis, this man says he paid a dollar down on a go-cart last month and he wants to pay the rest and take it home with him."

And then the reassuring, authoritative voice, "Coming! I'll be right there."

"Coming!" That had been her whole life. Service. And now she lay so quietly beneath the snow of the bitter northern winter.

At that point Fanny's fist would come down hard on her desk, and the quick, indrawn breath of mutinous resentment would hiss through her teeth.

She kept away from the downtown shops and their crowds. She scowled at sight of the holly and mistletoe wreaths, with their crimson streamers. There was something almost ludicrous in the way she shut her eyes to the holiday pageant all around her, and doubled and redoubled her work. It seemed that she had a new scheme for her department every other day, and every other one was a good one.

Slosson had long ago abandoned the attempt to keep up with her. He did not even resent her, as he had at first. "I'm a buyer," he said, rather pathetically, "and a pret-ty good one, too. But I'm not a genius, and I never will be. And I guess you've got to be a genius, these days, to keep up. It used to be enough for an infants' wear buyer to know muslins, cottons, woolens, silks, and embroideries. But that's old-fashioned now. These days, when you hire an office boy you don't ask him if he can read and write. You tell him he's got to have personality, magnetism, and imagination. Makes me sick!"

The Baby Book came off the presses and it was good. Even Slosson admitted it, grudgingly. The cover was a sunny, breezy seashore picture, all blue and gold, with plump, dimpled youngsters playing, digging in the sand, romping (and wearing our No. 13E1269, etc., of course). Inside were displayed the complete baby outfits, with a smiling mother, and a chubby, crowing baby as a central picture, and each piece of each outfit separately pictured. Just below this, the outfit number and price, and a list of the pieces that went to make it up. From the emergency outfit at $3.98 to the outfit de luxe (for Haynes-Cooper patrons) at $23.50, each group was comprehensive, practical, complete. In the back of the book was a personal service plea. "Use us," it said. "We are here to assist you, not only in the matter of merchandise, but with information and advice. Mothers in particular are in need of such service. This book will save you weariness and worry. Use us."

Fanny surveyed the book with pardonable pride. But she was not satisfied. "We lack style," she said. "The practical garments are all right. But what we need is a little snap. That means cut and line. And I'm going to New York to get it." That had always been Slosson's work.

She and Ella Monahan were to go to the eastern markets together. Ella Monahan went to New York regularly every three weeks. Fanny had never been east of Chicago. She envied Ella her knowledge of the New York wholesalers and manufacturers. Ella had dropped into Fanny's office for a brief moment. The two women had little in common, except their work, but they got on very well, and each found the other educating.

"Seems to me you're putting an awful lot into this," observed Ella Monahan, her wise eyes on Fanny's rather tense face.

"You've got to," replied Fanny, "to get anything out of it."

"I guess you're right," Ella agreed, and laughed a rueful little laugh. "I know I've given 'em everything I've got—and a few things I didn't know I had. It's a queer game—life. Now if my old father hadn't run a tannery in Racine, and if I hadn't run around there all the day, so that I got so the smell and feel of leather and hides were part of me, why, I'd never be buyer of gloves at Haynes-Cooper. And you———"

"Brandeis' Bazaar." And was going on, when her office boy came in with a name. Ella rose to go, but Fanny stopped her. "Father Fitzpatrick! Bring him right in! Miss Monahan, you've got to meet him. He's"—then, as the great frame of the handsome old priest filled the doorway—"he's just Father Fitzpatrick. Ella Monahan."

The white-haired Irishman, and the white-haired Irish woman clasped hands.

"And who are you, daughter, besides being Ella Monahan?"

"Buyer of gloves at Haynes-Cooper, Father."

"You don't tell me, now!" He turned to Fanny, put his two big hands on her shoulders, and swung her around to face the light. "Hm," he murmured, noncommittally, after that.

"Hm—what?" demanded Fanny. "It sounds unflattering, whatever it means."

"Gloves!" repeated Father Fitzpatrick, unheeding her. "Well, now, what d'you think of that! Millions of dollars' worth, I'll wager, in your time."

"Two million and a half in my department last year," replied Ella, without the least trace of boastfulness. One talked only in terms of millions at Haynes-Cooper's.

"What an age it is! When two slips of women can earn salaries that would make the old kings of Ireland look like beggars." He twinkled upon the older woman. "And what a feeling it must be—independence, and all."

"I've earned my own living since I was seventeen," said Ella Monahan. "I'd hate to tell you how long that is." A murmur from the gallant Irishman. "Thanks, Father, for the compliment I see in your eyes. But what I mean is this: You're right about independence. It is a grand thing. At first. But after a while it begins to pall on you. Don't ask me why. I don't know. I only hope you won't think I'm a wicked woman when I say I could learn to love any man who'd hang a silver fox scarf and a string of pearls around my neck, and ask me if I didn't feel a draft."

"Wicked! Not a bit of it, my girl. It's only natural, and commendable—barrin' the pearls."

"I'd forego them," laughed Ella, and with a parting handshake left the two alone.

Father Fitzpatrick looked after her. "A smart woman, that." He took out his watch, a fat silver one. "It's eleven-thirty. My train leaves at four. Now, Fanny, if you'll get on your hat, and arrange to steal an hour or so from this Brobdingnagian place—a grand word that, my girl, and nearer to swearing than any word I know—I'll take you to the Blackstone, no less, for lunch. How's that for a poor miserable old priest!"

"You dear, I couldn't think of it. Oh, yes, I could get away, but let's lunch right here at the plant, in the grill——"

"Never! I couldn't. Don't ask it of me. This place scares me. I came up in the elevator with a crowd and a guide, and he was juggling millions, that chap, the way a newsboy flips a cent. I'm but a poor parish priest, but I've got my pride. We'll go to the Blackstone, which I've passed, humbly, but never been in, with its rose silk shades and its window boxes. And we'll be waited on by velvet-footed servitors, me girl. Get your hat."

Fanny, protesting, but laughing, too, got it. They took the L. Michigan avenue, as they approached it from Wabash, was wind-swept and bleak as only Michigan avenue can be in December. They entered the warm radiance of the luxurious foyer with a little breathless rush, as wind-blown Chicagoans generally do. The head waiter must have thought Father Fitzpatrick a cardinal, at least, for he seated them at a

window table that looked out upon the icy street, with
Grant Park, crusted with sooty snow, just across the
way, and beyond that the I. C. tracks and the great
gray lake. The splendid room was all color, and perfume, and humming conversation. A fountain tinkled
in the center, and upon its waters there floated lily
pads and blossoms, weirdly rose, and mauve, and laven-
der. The tables were occupied by deliciously slim
young girls and very self-conscious college boys, home
for the holidays, and marcelled matrons, furred and
aigretted. The pink in Fanny's cheeks deepened. She
loved luxury. She smiled and flashed at the handsome
old priest opposite her.

"You're a wastrel," she said, "but isn't it nice!"
And tasted the first delicious sip of soup.

"It is. For a change. Extravagance is good for all
of us, now and then." He glanced leisurely about the
brilliant room, then out to the street, bleakly wind-
swept. He leaned back and drummed a bit with his
fingers on the satin-smooth cloth. "Now and then.
Tell me, Fanny, what would you say, off-hand, was the
most interesting thing you see from here? You used
to have a trick of picking out what they call the human side. Your mother had it, too."

Fanny, smiling, glanced about the room, her eyes
unconsciously following the track his had taken. About
the room, and out, to the icy street. "The most interesting thing?" Back to the flower-scented room,
with its music, and tinkle, and animation. Out again,
to the street. "You see that man, standing at the curb,
across the street. He's sort of crouched against the
lamp post. See him? Yes, there, just this side of
that big gray car? He's all drawn up in a heap. You
can feel him shivering. He looks as if he were trying
to crawl inside himself for warmth. Ever since we came
in I've noticed him staring straight across at these
windows where we're all sitting so grandly, lunching.

I know what he's thinking, don't you? And I wish I didn't feel so uncomfortable, knowing it. I wish we hadn't ordered lobster thermidor. I wish—there! the policeman's moving him on."

Father Fitzpatrick reached over and took her hand, as it lay on the table, in his great grasp. "Fanny, girl, you've told me what I wanted to know. Haynes-Cooper or no Haynes-Cooper, millions or no millions, your ravines aren't choked up with ashes yet, my dear. Thank God."

## CHAPTER THIRTEEN

FROM now on Fanny Brandeis' life became such a swift-moving thing that your trilogist would have regarded her with disgust. Here was no slow unfolding, petal by petal. Here were two processes going on, side by side. Fanny, the woman of business, flourished and throve like a weed, arrogantly flaunting its head above the timid, white flower that lay close to the soil, and crept, and spread, and multiplied. Between the two the fight went on silently.

Fate, or Chance, or whatever it is that directs our movements, was forever throwing tragic or comic little life-groups in her path, and then, pointing an arresting finger at her, implying, "This means you!" Fanny stepped over these obstructions, or walked around them, or stared straight through them.

She had told herself that she would observe the first anniversary of her mother's death with none of those ancient customs by which your pious Jew honors his dead. There would be no *Yahrzeit* light burning for twenty-four hours. She would not go to Temple for Kaddish prayer. But the thing was too strong for her, too anciently inbred. Her ancestors would have lighted a candle, or an oil lamp. Fanny, coming home at six, found herself turning on the shaded electric lamp in her hall. She went through to the kitchen.

"Princess, when you come in to-morrow morning you'll find a light in the hall. Don't turn it off until to-morrow evening at six."

"All day long, Miss Fan! Mah sakes, wa' foh?"

"It's just a religious custom."

"Didn't know yo' had no relijin, Miss Fan. Least-ways, Ah nevah could figgah——"

"I haven't," said Fanny, shortly. "Dinner ready soon, Princess? I'm starved."

She had entered a Jewish house of worship only once in this year. It was the stately, white-columned edifice on Grand Boulevard that housed the congregation presided over by the famous Kirsch. She had heard of him, naturally. She was there out of curiosity, like any other newcomer to Chicago. The beauty of the auditorium enchanted her—a magnificently proportioned room, and restful without being in the least gloomy. Then she had been interested in the congregation as it rustled in. She thought she had never seen so many modishly gowned women in one room in all her life. The men were sleekly broadclothed, but they lacked the well-dressed air, somehow. The women were slimly elegant in tailor suits and furs. They all looked as if they had been turned out by the same tailor. An artist, in his line, but of limited imagination. Dr. Kirsch, sociologist and savant, aquiline, semi-bald, grimly satiric, sat in his splendid, high-backed chair, surveying his silken flock through half-closed lids. He looked tired, and rather ill, Fanny thought, but distinctly a personage. She wondered if he held them or they him. That recalled to her the little Winnebago Temple and Rabbi Thalmann. She remembered the frequent rudeness and open inattention of that congregation. No doubt Mrs. Nathan Pereles had her counterpart here, and the hypocritical Bella Weinberg, too, and the giggling Aarons girls, and old Ben Reitman. Here Dr. Kirsch had risen, and, coming forward, had paused to lean over his desk and, with an awful geniality, had looked down upon two rustling, exquisitely gowned late-comers. They sank into their seats, cowed. Fanny grinned. He began his lecture— something about modern politics. Fanny was fascinated and resentful by turns.  His brilliant satire probed, cut, jabbed like a surgeon's scalpel; or he railed, scolded, snarled, like a dyspeptic schoolmaster. Often he was in wretched taste.  He mimicked, postured, sneered.  But he had this millionaire congregation of his in hand.  Fanny found herself smiling up at him, delightedly.  Perhaps this wasn't religion, as she had been taught to look upon it, but it certainly was tonic.  She told herself that she would have come to the same conclusion if Kirsch had occupied a Methodist pulpit.

There were no Kaddish prayers in Kirsch's Temple. On the Friday following the first anniversary of Molly Brandeis's death Fanny did not go home after working hours, but took a bite of supper in a neighborhood restaurant.  Then she found her way to one of the orthodox Russian Jewish synagogues on the west side. It was a dim, odorous, bare little place, this house of worship.  Fanny had never seen one like it before.  She was herded up in the gallery, where the women sat. And when the patriarchal rabbi began to intone the prayer for the dead Fanny threw the gallery into wild panic by rising for it—a thing that no woman is allowed to do in an orthodox Jewish church.  She stood, calmly, though the beshawled women to right and left of her yanked at her coat.

In January Fanny discovered New York.  She went as selector for her department.  Hereafter Slosson would do only the actual buying.  Styles, prices, and materials would be decided by her.  Ella Monahan accompanied her, it being the time for her monthly trip. Fanny openly envied her her knowledge of New York's wholesale district.  Ella offered to help her.

"No," Fanny had replied, "I think not, thanks. You've your own work.  And besides I know pretty well what I want, and where to go to get it.  It's making them give it to me that will be hard."

They went to the same hotel, and took connecting rooms. Each went her own way, not seeing the other from morning until night, but they often found kimonoed comfort in each other's presence.

Fanny had spent weeks outlining her plan of attack. She had determined to retain the cheap grades, but to add a finer line as well. She recalled those lace-be-decked bundles that the farmer women and mill hands had born so tenderly in their arms. Here was one direction in which they allowed extravagance free rein. As a canny business woman, she would trade on her knowledge of their weakness.

At Haynes-Cooper order is never a thing to be de-spised by a wholesaler. Fanny, knowing this, had made up her mind to go straight to Horn & Udell. Now, Horn & Udell are responsible for the bloomers your small daughter wears under her play frock, in place of the troublesome and extravagant petticoat of the old days. It was they who introduced smocked pina-fores to you; and those modish patent-leather belts for children at which your grandmothers would have raised horrified hands. They taught you that an inch of hand embroidery is worth a yard of cheap lace. And as for style, cut, line—you can tell a Horn & Udell child from among a flock of thirty.

Fanny, entering their office, felt much as Molly Brandeis had felt that January many, many years be-fore, when she had made that first terrifying trip to the Chicago market. The engagement had been made days before. Fanny never knew the shock that her youthfully expectant face gave old Sid Udell. He turned from his desk to greet her, his polite smile of greeting giving way to a look of bewilderment.

"But you are not the buyer, are you, Miss Bran-deis?"

"No, Mr. Slosson buys."

"I thought so."

"But I select for my entire department. I decide on our styles, materials, and prices, six months in advance. Then Mr. Slosson does the actual bulk buying."

"Something new-fangled?" inquired Sid Udell. "Of course, we've never sold much to you people. Our stuff is——"

"Yes, I know. But you'd like to, wouldn't you?"

"Our class of goods isn't exactly suited to your wants."

"Yes, it is. Exactly. That's why I'm here. We'll be doing a business of a million and a quarter in my department in another two years. No firm, not even Horn & Udell, can afford to ignore an account like that."

Sid Udell smiled a little. "You've made up your mind to that million and a quarter, young lady?"

"Yes."

"Well, I've dealt with buyers for a quarter of a century or more. And I'd say that you're going to get it."

Whereupon Fanny began to talk. Ten minutes later Udell interrupted her to summon Horn, whose domain was the factory. Horn came, was introduced, looked doubtful. Fanny had statistics. Fanny had arguments. She had determination. "And what we want," she went on, in her quiet, assured way, "is style. The Horn & Udell clothes have chic. Now, material can't be imitated successfully, but style can. Our goods lack just that. I could copy any model you have, turn the idea over to a cheap manufacturer, and get a million just like it, at one-fifth the price. That isn't a threat. It's just a business statement that you know to be true. I can sketch from memory anything I've seen once. What I want to know is this: Will you make it necessary for me to do that, or will you undertake to furnish us with cheaper copies of your high-priced designs? We could use your entire output. I know the small-town woman of the poorer class, and I know she'll wear a shawl in order to give her child a cloth coat with fancy buttons and a velvet collar."

And Horn & Udell, whose attitude at first had been that of two seasoned business men dealing with a precocious child, found themselves quoting prices to her, shipments, materials, quality, quantities. Then came the question of time.

"We'll get out a special catalogue for the summer," Fanny said. "A small one, to start them our way. Then the big Fall catalogue will contain the entire line."

"That doesn't give us time!" exclaimed both men, in a breath.

"But you must manage, somehow. Can't you speed up the workroom? Put on extra hands? It's worth it."

They might, under normal conditions. But there was this strike-talk, its ugly head bobbing up in a hundred places. And their goods were the kind that required high-class workers. Their girls earned all the way from twelve to twenty-five dollars.

But Fanny knew she had driven home the entering wedge. She left them after making an engagement for the following day. The Horn & Udell factory was in New York's newer loft-building section, around Madison, Fifth avenue, and the Thirties. Her hotel was very near. She walked up Fifth avenue a little way, and as she walked she wondered why she did not feel more elated. Her day's work had exceeded her expectations. It was a brilliant January afternoon, with a snap in the air that was almost western. Fifth avenue flowed up, flowed down, and Fanny fought the impulse to stare after every second or third woman she passed. They were so invariably well-dressed. There was none of the occasional shabbiness or dowdiness of Michigan Avenue. Every woman seemed to have emerged fresh from the hands of masseuse and maid.

Their hair was coiffed to suit the angle of the hat, and the hat had been chosen to enhance the contour of the head, and the head was carried with regard for the dark furs that encircled the throat. They were amazingly well shod. Their white gloves were white. (A fact remarkable to any soot-haunted Chicagoan.) Their coloring rivaled the rose leaf. And nobody's nose was red.

"Goodness knows I've never pretended to be a beauty," Fanny said that evening, in conversation with Ella Monahan. "But I've always thought I had my good points. By the time I'd reached Forty-second street I wouldn't have given two cents for my chances of winning a cave man on a desert island."

She made up her mind that she would go back to the hotel, get a thick coat, and ride outside one of those fascinating Fifth avenue 'buses. It struck her as an ideal way to see this amazing street. She was back at her hotel in ten minutes. Ella had not yet come in. Their rooms were on the tenth floor. Fanny got her coat, peered at her own reflection in the mirror, sighed, shook her head, and was off down the hall toward the elevators. The great hall window looked toward Fifth avenue, but between it and the avenue rose a yellow-brick building that housed tier on tier of manufacturing lofts. Cloaks, suits, blouses, petticoats, hats, dresses—it was just such a building as Fanny had come from when she left the offices of Horn & Udell. It might be their very building, for all she knew. She looked straight into its windows as she stood waiting for the lift. And window after window showed women, sewing. They were sewing at machines, and at handwork, but not as women are accustomed to sew, with leisurely stitches, stopping to pat a seam here, to run a calculating eye along hem or ruffle. It was a dreadful, mechanical motion, that sewing, a machine-like, relentless motion, with no waste in it, no pause. Fanny's mind leaped back to Winnebago, with its pleasant porches on which leisurely women sat stitching peacefully at a fine seam.

What was it she had said to Udell? "Can't you speed up the workroom? It's worth it."

Fanny turned abruptly from the window as the door of the bronze and mirrored lift opened for her. She walked over to Fifth avenue again and up to Forty-fifth street. Then she scrambled up the spiral stairs of a Washington Square 'bus. The air was crisp, clear, intoxicating. To her Chicago eyes the buildings, the streets, the very sky looked startlingly fresh and new-washed. As the 'bus lurched down Fifth avenue she leaned over the railing to stare, fascinated, at the colorful, shifting, brilliant panorama of the most amazing street in the world. Block after block, as far as the eye could see, the gorgeous procession moved up, moved down, and the great, gleaming motor cars crept, and crawled, and writhed in and out, like nothing so much as swollen angle worms in a fishing can, Fanny thought. Her eye was caught by one limousine that stood out, even in that crush of magnificence. It was all black, as though scorning to attract the eye with vulgar color, and it was lined with white. Fanny thought it looked very much like Siegel & Cowan's hearse, back in Winnebago. In it sat a woman, all furs, and orchids, and complexion. She was holding up to the window a little dog with a wrinkled and weary face, like that of an old, old man. He was sticking his little evil, eager red tongue out at the world. And he wore a very smart and woolly white sweater, of the imported kind—with a monogram done in black.

The traffic policeman put up his hand. The 'bus rumbled on down the street. Names that had always been remotely mythical to her now met her eye and became realities. Maillard's. And that great red stone castle was the Waldorf. Almost historic, and it looked newer than the smoke-grimed Blackstone. And straight ahead—why, that must be the Flatiron building! It loomed up like the giant prow of an unimaginable ship. Brentano's. The Holland House. Madison Square. Why there never was anything so terrifying, and beautiful, and palpitating, and exquisite as this Fifth avenue in the late winter afternoon, with the sky ahead a rosy mist, and the golden lights just beginning to spangle the gray. At Madison Square she decided to walk. She negotiated the 'bus steps with surprising skill for a novice, and scurried along the perilous crossing to the opposite side. She entered Madison Square. But why hadn't O. Henry emphasized its beauty, instead of its squalor? It lay, a purple pool of shadow, surrounded by the great, gleaming, many-windowed office buildings, like an amethyst sunk in a circle of diamonds. "It's a fairyland!" Fanny told herself. "Who'd have thought a city could be so beautiful!"

And then, at her elbow, a voice said, "Oh, lady, for the lova God!" She turned with a jerk and looked up into the unshaven face of a great, blue-eyed giant who pulled off his cap and stood twisting it in his swollen blue fingers. "Lady, I'm cold. I'm hungry. I been sittin' here hours."

Fanny clutched her bag a little fearfully. She looked at his huge frame. "Why don't you work?"

"Work!" He laughed. "There ain't any. Looka this!" He turned up his foot, and you saw the bare sole, blackened and horrible, and fringed, comically, by the tattered leather upper.

"Oh—my dear!" said Fanny. And at that the man began to cry, weakly, sickeningly, like a little boy.

"Don't do that! Don't! Here." She was emptying her purse, and something inside her was saying, "You fool, he's only a professional beggar."

And then the man wiped his face with his cap, and

swallowed hard, and said, "I don't want all you got. I ain't holdin' you up. Just gimme that. I been sittin' here, on that bench, lookin' at that sign across the street. Over there. It says, 'EAT.' It goes off an' on. Seemed like it was drivin' me crazy."

Fanny thrust a crumpled five-dollar bill into his hand. And was off. She fairly flew along, so that it was not until she had reached Thirty-third street that she said aloud, as was her way when moved, "I don't care. Don't blame me. It was that miserable little beast of a dog in the white sweater that did it."

It was almost seven when she reached her room. A maid, in neat black and white, was just coming out with an armful of towels.

"I just brought you a couple of extra towels. We were short this morning," she said.

The room was warm, and quiet, and bright. In her bathroom, that glistened with blue and white tiling, were those redundant towels. Fanny stood in the doorway and counted them, whimsically. Four great fuzzy bath towels. Eight glistening hand towels. A blue and white bath rug hung at the side of the tub. Her telephone rang. It was Ella.

"Where in the world have you been, child? I was worried about you. I thought you were lost in the streets of New York."

"I took a 'bus ride," Fanny explained.

"See anything of New York?"

"I saw all of it," replied Fanny. Ella laughed at that, but Fanny's face was serious.

"How did you make out at Horn & Udell's? Never mind, I'm coming in for a minute; can I?"

"Please do. I need you."

A moment later Ella bounced in, fresh as to blouse, pink as to cheeks, her whole appearance a testimony to the revivifying effects of a warm bath, a brief nap, clean clothes.

"Dear child, you look tired. I'm not going to stay. You get dressed and I'll meet you for dinner. Or do you want yours up here?"

"Oh, no!"

" 'Phone me when you're dressed. But tell me, isn't it a wonder, this town? I'll never forget my first trip here. I spent one whole evening standing in front of the mirror trying to make those little spit-curls the women were wearing then. I'd seen 'em on Fifth avenue, and it seemed I'd die if I couldn't have 'em, too. And I dabbed on rouge, and touched up my eyebrows. I don't know. It's a kind of a crazy feeling gets you. The minute I got on the train for Chicago I washed my face and took my hair down and did it plain again."

"Why, that's the way I felt!" laughed Fanny. "I didn't care anything about infants' wear, or Haynes-Cooper, or anything. I just wanted to be beautiful, as they all were."

"Sure! It gets us all!"

Fanny twisted her hair into the relentless knob women assume preparatory to bathing. "It seems to me you have to come from Winnebago, or thereabouts, to get New York—really get it, I mean."

"That's so," agreed Ella. "There's a man on the New York *Star* who writes a column every day that everybody reads. If he isn't a small-town man then we're both wrong."

Fanny, bathward bound, turned to stare at Ella. "A column about what?"

"Oh, everything. New York, mostly. Say, it's the humanest stuff. He says the kind of thing we'd all say, if we knew how. Reading him is like getting a letter from home. I'll bet he went to a country school and wore his mittens sewed to a piece of tape that ran through his coat sleeves."

"You're right," said Fanny; "he did. That man's from Winnebago, Wisconsin."

"No!"

"Yes."

"Do you mean you know him? Honestly? What's he like?"

But Fanny had vanished. "I'm a tired business woman," she called, above the splashing that followed, "and I won't converse until I'm fed."

"But how about Horn & Udell?" demanded Ella, her mouth against the crack.

"Practically mine," boasted Fanny.

"You mean—landed!"

"Well, hooked, at any rate, and putting up a very poor struggle."

"Why, you clever little divil, you! You'll be making me look like a stock girl next."

Fanny did not telephone Heyl until the day she left New York. She had told herself she would not telephone him at all. He had sent her his New York address and telephone number months before, after that Sunday at the dunes. Ella Monahan had finished her work and had gone back to Chicago four days before Fanny was ready to leave. In those four days Fanny had scoured the city from the Palisades to Pell street. I don't know how she found her way about. It was a sort of instinct with her. She seemed to scent the picturesque. She never for a moment neglected her work. But she had found it was often impossible to see these New York business men until ten—sometimes eleven—o'clock. She awoke at seven, a habit formed in her Winnebago days. Eight-thirty one morning found her staring up at the dim vastness of the dome of the cathedral of St. John the Divine. The great gray pile, mountainous, almost ominous, looms up in the midst of the dingy commonplaceness of Amsterdam avenue and 110th street. New Yorkers do not know this, or if they know it, the fact does not interest them. New Yorkers do not go to stare up into the murky shadows

of this glorious edifice. They would if it were situate
in Rome. Bare, crude, unfinished, chaotic, it gives rich
promise of magnificent fulfillment. In an age when
great structures are thrown up to-day, to be torn down
to-morrow, this slow-moving giant is at once a reproach and an example. Twenty-five years in building,
twenty-five more for completion, it has elbowed its way,
stone by stone, into such company as St. Peter's at
Rome, and the marvel at Milan. Fanny found her way
down the crude cinder paths that made an alley-like
approach to the cathedral. She entered at the side
door that one found by following arrows posted on the
rough wooden fence. Once inside she stood a moment,
awed by the immensity of the half-finished nave. As
she stood there, hands clasped, her face turned raptly
up to where the massive granite columns reared their
height to frame the choir, she was, for the moment,
as devout as any Episcopalian whose money had helped
make the great building. Not only devout, but prayerful, ecstatic. That was partly due to the effect of the
pillars, the lights, the tapestries, the great, unfinished
chunks of stone that loomed out from the side walls,
and the purple shadow cast by the window above the
chapels at the far end; and partly to the actress in her
that responded magically to any mood, and always to
surroundings. Later she walked softly down the deserted nave, past the choir, to the cluster of chapels,
set like gems at one end, and running from north to
south, in a semi-circle. A placard outside one said,
"St. Saviour's chapel. For those who wish to rest
and pray." All white marble, this little nook, gleaming softly in the gray half-light. Fanny entered, and
sat down. She was quite alone. The roar and crash
of the Eighth avenue L, the Amsterdam cars, the motors drumming up Morningside hill, were softened here
to a soothing hum.

For those who wish to rest and pray.

Fanny Brandeis had neither rested nor prayed since that hideous day when she had hurled her prayer of defiance at Him. But something within her now began a groping for words; for words that should follow an ancient plea beginning, "O God of my Fathers——" But at that the picture of the room came back to her mental vision—the room so quiet except for the breathing of the woman on the bed; the woman with the tolerant, humorous mouth, and the straight, clever nose, and the softly bright brown eyes, all so strangely pinched and shrunken-looking now——

Fanny got to her feet, with a noisy scraping of the chair on the stone floor. The vague, half-formed prayer died at birth. She found her way out of the dim, quiet little chapel, up the long aisle and out the great door. She shivered a little in the cold of the early January morning as she hurried toward the Broadway subway.

At nine-thirty she was standing at a counter in the infants' wear section at Best's, making mental notes while the unsuspecting saleswoman showed her how the pink ribbon in this year's models was brought under the beading, French fashion, instead of weaving through it, as heretofore. At ten-thirty she was saying to Sid Udell, "I think a written contract is always best. Then we'll all know just where we stand. Mr. Fenger will be on next week to arrange the details, but just now a very brief written understanding to show him on my return would do."

And she got it, and tucked it away in her bag, in triumph.

She tried to leave New York without talking to Heyl, but some quiet, insistent force impelled her to act contrary to her resolution. It was, after all, the urge of the stronger wish against the weaker.

When he heard her voice over the telephone Heyl did not say, "Who is this?" Neither did he put those inevitable questions of the dweller to the transient, "Where are you? How long have you been here?" What he said was, "How're you going to avoid dining with me to-night?"

To which Fanny replied, promptly, "By taking the Twentieth Century back to Chicago to-day."

A little silence. A hurt silence. Then, "When they get the Twentieth Century habit they're as good as lost. How's the infants' wear business, Fanny?"

"Booming, thank you. I want to tell you I've read the column every day. It's wonderful stuff."

"It's a wonderful job. I'm a lucky boy. I'm doing the thing I'd rather do than anything else in the world. There are mighty few who can say that." There was another silence, awkward, heavy. Then, "Fanny, you're not really leaving to-day?"

"I'll be in Chicago to-morrow, barring wrecks."

"You might have let me show you our more or less fair city."

"I've shown it to myself. I've seen Riverside Drive at sunset, and at night. That alone would have been enough. But I've seen Fulton market, too, and the Grand street stalls, and Washington Square, and Central Park, and Lady Duff-Gordon's inner showroom, and the Night Court, and the Grand Central subway horror at six p. m., and the gambling on the Curb, and the bench sleepers in Madison Square—— Oh, Clancy, the misery——"

"Heh, wait a minute! All this, alone?"

"Yes. And one more thing. I've landed Horn & Udell, which means nothing to you, but to me it means that by Spring my department will be a credit to its stepmother; a real success."

"I knew it would be a success. So did you. Anything you might attempt would be successful. You'd have made a successful lawyer, or cook, or actress, or hydraulic engineer, because you couldn't do a thing badly. It isn't in you. You're a superlative sort of person. But that's no reason for being any of those things. If you won't admit a debt to humanity, surely you'll acknowledge you've an obligation to yourself."

"Preaching again. Good-by."

"Fanny, you're afraid to see me."

"Don't be ridiculous. Why should I be?"

"Because I say aloud the things you daren't let yourself think. If I were to promise not to talk about anything but flannel bands——"

"Will you promise?"

"No. But I'm going to meet you at the clock at the Grand Central Station fifteen minutes before train time. I don't care if every infants' wear manufacturer in New York had a prior claim on your time. You may as well be there, because if you're not I'll get on the train and stay on as far as Albany. Take your choice."

He was there before her. Fanny, following the wake of a redcap, picked him at once from among the crowd of clock-waiters. He saw her at the same time, and started forward with that singularly lithe, springy step which was, after all, just the result of perfectly trained muscles in coördination. He was wearing New York clothes—the right kind, Fanny noted.

Their hands met. "How well you look," said Fanny, rather lamely.

"It's the clothes," said Heyl, and began to revolve slowly, coyly, hands out, palms down, eyelids drooping, in delicious imitation of those ladies whose business it is to revolve thus for fashion.

"Clancy, you idiot! All these people! Stop it!"

"But get the grace! Get the easy English hang, at once so loose and so clinging."

Fanny grinned, appreciatively, and led the way through the gate to the train. She was surprisingly glad to be with him again. On discovering that, she began to talk rapidly, and about him.

"Tell me, how do you manage to keep that fresh viewpoint? Everybody else who comes to New York to write loses his identity. The city swallows him up. I mean by that, that things seem to strike you as freshly as they did when you first came. I remember you wrote me an amazing letter."

"For one thing, I'll never be anything but a foreigner in New York. I'll never quite believe Broadway. I'll never cease to marvel at Fifth avenue, and Cooper Union, and the Bronx. The time may come when I can take the subway for granted, but don't ask it of me just yet."

"But the other writers—and all those people who live down in Washington Square?"

"I never see them. It's sure death. Those Greenwichers are always taking out their own feelings and analyzing them, and pawing them over, and passing them around. When they get through with them they're so thumb-marked and greasy that no one else wants them. They don't get enough golf, those Greenwichers. They don't get enough tennis. They don't get enough walking in the open places. Gosh, no! I know better than to fall for that kind of thing. They spend hours talking to each other, in dim-lighted attics, about Souls, and Society, and the Joy of Life, and the Greater Good. And they know all about each other's insides. They talk themselves out, and there's nothing left to write about. A little of that kind of thing purges and cleanses. Too much of it poisons, and clogs. No, ma'am! When I want to talk I go down and chin with the foreman of our composing room. There's a chap that has what I call conversation. A philosopher, and knows everything in the world. Composing room foremen always are and do. Now, that's all of that. How about Fanny Brandeis? Any sketches? Come on. Confess. Grand street, anyway."

"I haven't touched a pencil, except to add up a column of figures or copy an order, since last September, when you were so sure I couldn't stop."

"You've done a thousand in your head. And if you haven't done one on paper so much the better. You'll jam them back, and stifle them, and screw the cover down tight on every natural impulse, and then, some day, the cover will blow off with a loud report. You can't kill that kind of thing, Fanny. It would have to be a wholesale massacre of all the centuries behind you. I don't so much mind your being disloyal to your tribe, or race, or whatever you want to call it. But you've turned your back on yourself; you've got an obligation to humanity, and I'll nag you till you pay it. I don't care if I lose you, so long as you find yourself. The thing you've got isn't merely racial. God, no! It's universal. And you owe it to the world. Pay up, Fanny! Pay up!"

"Look here!" began Fanny, her voice low with anger; "the last time I saw you I said I'd never again put myself in a position to be lectured by you, like a schoolgirl. I mean it, this time. If you have anything else to say to me, say it now. The train leaves"—she glanced at her wrist—"in two minutes, thank Heaven, and this will be your last chance."

"All right," said Heyl. "I have got something to say. Do you wear hatpins?"

"Hatpins!" blankly. "Not with this small hat, but what——"

"That means you're defenseless. If you're going to prowl the streets of Chicago alone get this: If you double your fist this way, and tuck your thumb alongside, like that, and aim for this spot right here, about two inches this side of the chin, bringing your arm back, and up, quickly, like a piston, the person you hit will go down, limp. There's a nerve right here that

communicates with the brain. That blow makes you
see stars, bright lights, and fancy colors. They use
it in the comic papers."

"You *are* crazy," said Fanny, as though at last assured of a long-suspected truth. The train began to
move, almost imperceptibly. "Run!" she cried.

Heyl sped up the aisle. At the door he turned. "It's
called an uppercut," he shouted to the amazement of
the other passengers. And leaped from the train.

Fanny sank into her seat, weakly. Then she began
to laugh, and there was a dash of hysteria in it. He
had left a paper on the car seat. It was the *Star*.
Fanny crumpled it, childishly, and kicked it under the
seat. She took off her hat, arranged her belongings,
and sat back with eyes closed. After a few moments
she opened them, fished about under the seat for the
crumpled copy of the *Star*, and read it, turning at
once to his column. She thought it was a very unpre-
tentious thing, that column, and yet so full of insight,
and sagacity, and whimsical humor. Not a guffaw in
it, but a smile in every fifth line. She wondered if
those years of illness, and loneliness, with weeks of
reading, and tramping, and climbing in the Colorado
mountains had kept him strangely young, or made him
strangely old.

She welcomed the hours that lay between New York
and Chicago. They would give her an opportunity to
digest the events of the past ten days. In her syste-
matic mind she began to range them in the order of
their importance. Horn & Udell came first, of course,
and then the line of maternity dresses she had selected
to take the place of the hideous models carried under
Slosson's régime. And then the slip-over pinafores.
But somehow her thoughts became jumbled here, so
that faces instead of garments filled her mind's eye.
Again and again there swam into her ken the face of
that woman of fifty, in decent widow's weeds, who had

stood there in the Night Court, charged with drunken-ness on the streets. And the man with the frost-bitten fingers in Madison Square. And the dog in the sweater. And the feverish concentration of the piece-work sew-ers in the window of the loft building.

She gave it up, selected a magazine, and decided to go in to lunch.

There was nothing spectacular about the welcome she got on her return to the office after this first trip. A firm that counts its employees by the thousands, and its profits in tens of millions, cannot be expected to draw up formal resolutions of thanks when a hereto-fore flabby department begins to show signs of red blood.

Ella Monahan said, "They'll make light of it—all but Fenger. That's their way."

Slosson drummed with his fingers all the time she was giving him the result of her work in terms of style, material, quantity, time, and price. When she had finished he said, "Well, all I can say is we seem to be going out of the mail order business and into the im-ported novelty line, de luxe. I suppose by next Christ-mas the grocery department will be putting in arti-choke hearts, and truffles and French champagne by the keg for community orders."

To which Fanny had returned, sweetly, "If Oregon and Wyoming show any desire for artichokes and cham-pagne I don't see why we shouldn't."

Fenger, strangely enough, said little. He was apt to be rather curt these days, and almost irritable. Fanny attributed it to the reaction following the strain of the Christmas rush.

One did not approach Fenger's office except by ap-pointment. Fanny sent word to him of her return. For two days she heard nothing from him. Then the voice of the snuff-brown secretary summoned her. She did not have to wait this time, but passed directly

through the big bright outer room into the smaller
room. The Power House, Fanny called it.

Fenger was facing the door. "Missed you," he said.

"You must have," Fanny laughed, "with only nine
thousand nine hundred and ninety-nine to look after."

"You look as if you'd been on a vacation, instead of
a test trip."

"So I have. Why didn't you warn me that business, as transacted in New York, is a series of social
rites? I didn't have enough white kid gloves to go
round. No one will talk business in an office. I don't
see what they use offices for, except as places in which
to receive their mail. You utter the word 'Business,'
and the other person immediately says, 'Lunch.' No
wholesaler seems able to quote you his prices until he
has been sustained by half a dozen Cape Cods. I don't
want to see a restaurant or a rose silk shade for
weeks."

Fenger tapped the little pile of papers on his desk.
"I've read your reports. If you can do that on
lunches, I'd like to see what you could put over in a
series of dinners."

"Heaven forbid," said Fanny, fervently. Then, for
a very concentrated fifteen minutes they went over the
reports together. Fanny's voice grew dry and lifeless
as she went into figures.

"You don't sound particularly enthusiastic," Fenger said, when they had finished, "considering that
you've accomplished what you set out to do."

"That's just it," quickly. "I like the uncertainty.
It was interesting to deal directly with those people,
to stack one's arguments, and personality, and men-
tality and power over theirs, until they had to give
way. But after that! Well, you can't expect me to be
vitally interested in gross lots, and carloads and
dating."

"It's part of business."

"It's the part I hate."

Fenger stacked the papers neatly. "You came in June, didn't you?"

"Yes."

"It has been a remarkable eight-months' record, even at Haynes-Cooper's, where records are the rule. Have you been through the plant since the time you first went through?"

"Through it! Goodness, no! It would take a day."

"Then I wish you'd take it. I like to have the heads of departments go through the plant at least twice a year. You'll find the fourteenth floor has been cleared and is being used entirely by the selectors. The manufacturers' samples are spread on the tables in the various sections. You'll find your place ready for you. You'll be amused at Daly's section. He took your suggestion about trying the blouses on live models instead of selecting them as he used to. You remember you said that one could tell about the lines and style of a dress merely by looking at it, but that a blouse is just a limp rag until it's on."

"It's true of the flimsy Georgette things women want now. They may be lovely in the box and hideously unbecoming when worn. If Daly's going in for the higher grade stuff he can't risk choosing unbecoming models."

"Wait till you see him!" smiled Fenger, "sitting there like a sultan while the pinks and blues, and whites and plaids parade before him." He turned to his desk again. "That's all, Miss Brandeis. Thank you." Then, at a sudden thought. "Do you know that all your suggestions have been human suggestions? I mean they all have had to do with people. Tell me, how do you happen to have learned so much about what people feel and think, in such a short time?"

The thing that Clarence Heyl had said flashed through her mind, and she was startled to find herself quoting it. "It hasn't been a short time," she said.

"It took a thousand years." And left Fenger staring, puzzled.

She took next morning for her tour of the plant as Fenger had suggested. She went through it, not as the startled, wide-eyed girl of eight months before had gone, but critically, and with a little unconscious air of authority. For, this organization, vast though it was, actually showed her imprint. She could have put her finger on this spot, and that, saying, "Here is the mark of my personality." And she thought, as she passed from department to department, "Ten thousand a year, if you keep on as you've started." Up one aisle and down the next. Bundles, bundles, bundles. And everywhere you saw the yellow order-slips. In the hands of the stock boys whizzing by on roller skates; in the filing department; in the traffic department. The very air seemed jaundiced with those clouds of yellow order-slips. She stopped a moment, fascinated as always before the main spiral gravity chute down which the bundles—hundreds of them, thousands of them daily —chased each other to—to what? Fanny asked herself. She knew, vaguely, that hands caught these bundles halfway, and redirected them toward the proper channel, where they were assembled and made ready for shipping or mailing. She turned to a stock boy.

"Where does this empty?" she asked.

"Floor below," said the boy, "on the platform."

Fanny walked down a flight of iron stairs, and around to face the spiral chute again. In front of the chute, and connected with it by a great metal lip, was a platform perhaps twelve feet above the floor and looking very much like the pilot's deck of a ship. A little flight of steps led up to it—very steep steps, that trembled a little under a repetition of shocks that came from above. Fanny climbed them warily, gained the top, and found herself standing next to the girl whose face had gleamed out at her from among those thousands in the crowd pouring out of the plant. The girl glanced up at Fanny for a second—no, for the fraction of a second. Her job was the kind that permitted no more than that. Fanny watched her for one breathless moment. In that moment she understood the look that had been stamped on the girl's face that night; the look that had cried: "Release!" For this platform, shaking under the thud of bundles, bundles, bundles, was the stomach of the Haynes-Cooper plant. Sixty per cent of the forty-five thousand daily orders passed through the hands of this girl and her assistants. Down the chutes swished the bundles, stamped with their section mark, and here they were caught deftly and hurled into one of the dozen conveyers that flowed out from this main stream. The wrong bundle into the wrong conveyer? Confusion in the shipping room. It only took a glance of the eye and a motion of the arms. But that glance and that motion had been boiled down to the very concentrated essence of economy. They seemed to be working with fury, but then, so does a pile-driver until you get the simplicity of it.

Fanny bent over the girl (it was a noisy corner) and put a question. The girl did not pause in her work as she answered it. She caught a bundle with one hand, hurled one into a conveyer with the other.

"Seven a week," she said. And deftly caught the next slithering bundle.

Fanny watched her for another moment. Then she turned and went down the steep stairs.

"None of your business," she said to herself, and continued her tour. "None of your business." She went up to the new selectors' floor, and found the plan running as smoothly as if it had been part of the plant's system for years The elevator whisked her up to the top floor, where she met the plant's latest practical fad, the new textile chemist—a charming youth, disguised in bone-rimmed glasses, who did the honors of his little labratory with all the manner of a Harvard host. This was the fusing oven for silks. Here was the drying oven. This delicate scale weighed every ounce of the cloth swatches that came in for inspection, to get the percentage of wool and cotton. Not a chance for the manufacturer to slip shoddy into his goods, now.

"Mm," said Fanny, politely. She hated complicated processes that had to do with scales, and weights, and pounds, and acids. She crossed over to the Administration Building, and stopped at the door marked, "Mrs. Knowles." If you had been an employee of the Haynes-Cooper company, and had been asked to define Mrs. Knowles's position the chances are that you would have found yourself floundering, wordless. Haynes-Cooper was reluctant to acknowledge the need of Mrs. Knowles. Still, when you employ ten thousand people, and more than half of these are girls, and fifty per cent of these girls are unskilled, ignorant, and terribly human you find that a Mrs. Knowles saves the equivalent of ten times her salary in wear and tear and general prevention. She could have told you tragic stories, could Mrs. Knowles, and sordid stories, and comic too; she knew how to deal with terror, and shame, and stubborn silence, and hopeless misery. Gray-haired and motherly? Not at all. An astonishingly young, pleasingly plumpish woman, with nothing remarkable about her except a certain splendid calm. Four years out of Vassar, and already she had learned that if you fold your hands in your lap and wait, quietly, asking no questions, almost any one will tell you almost anything.

"Hello!" called Fanny. "How are our morals this morning?"

"Going up!" answered Esther Knowles, "considering that it's Tuesday. Come in. How's the infant prodigy? I lunched with Ella Monahan, and she told me your first New York trip was a whirlwind. Congratulations!"

"Thanks. I can't stop. I haven't touched my desk to-day. I just want to ask you if you know the name of that girl who has charge of the main chute in the merchandise building."

"Good Lord, child! There are thousands of girls."

"But this one's rather special. She is awfully pretty, and rather different looking. Exquisite coloring, a discontented expression, and a blouse that's too low in the neck."

"Which might be a description of Fanny Brandeis herself, barring the blouse," laughed Mrs. Knowles. Then, at the startled look in Fanny's face, "Do forgive me. And don't look so horrified. I think I know which one you mean. Her name is Sarah Sapinsky— yes, isn't it a pity!—and it's queer that you should ask me about her because I've been having trouble with that particular girl."

"Trouble?"

"She knows she's pretty, and she knows she's different, and she knows she's handicapped, and that accounts for the discontented expression. That, and some other things. She gets seven a week here, and they take just about all of it at home. She says she's sick of it. She has left home twice. I don't blame the child, but I've always managed to bring her back. Some day there'll be a third time—and I'm afraid of it. She's not bad. She's really rather splendid, and she has a certain dreadful philosophy of her own. Her theory is that there are only two kinds of people in the world. Those that give, and those that take. And she's tired of giving. Sarah didn't put it just that way; but you know what she means, don't you?"

"I know what she means," said Fanny, grimly.

So it was Sarah she saw above all else in her trip through the gigantic plant; Sarah's face shone out

from among the thousands; the thud-thud of Sarah's
bundle-chute beat a dull accompaniment to the hum of
the big hive; above the rustle of those myriad yellow
order-slips, through the buzz of the busy mail room;
beneath the roar of the presses in the printing building, the crash of the dishes in the cafeteria, ran the
leid-motif of Sarah-at-seven-a-week. Back in her office
once more Fanny dictated a brief observation-report
for Fenger's perusal.

"It seems to me there's room for improvement in our
card index file system. It's thorough, but unwieldy.
It isn't a system any more. It's a ceremony. Can't
you get a corps of system sharks to simplify things
there?"

She went into detail and passed on to the next suggestion.

"If the North American Cloak & Suit Company can
sell mail order dresses that are actually smart and in
good taste, I don't see why we have to go on carrying
only the most hideous crudities in our women's dress
department. I know that the majority of our women
customers wouldn't wear a plain, good looking little
blue serge dress with a white collar, and some tailored
buttons. They want cerise satin revers on a plum-
colored foulard, and that's what we've been giving
them. But there are plenty of other women living miles
from anywhere who know what's being worn on Fifth
avenue. I don't know how they know it, but they do.
And they want it. Why can't we reach those women, as
well as their shoddier sisters? The North American
people do it. I'd wear one of their dresses myself. I
wouldn't be found dead in one of ours. Here's a suggestion:

"Why can't we get Camille to design half a dozen
models a season for us? Now don't roar at that. And
don't think that the women on western ranches haven't
heard of Camille. They have. They may know nothing

of Mrs. Pankhurst, and Lillian Russell may be a myth
to them, but I'll swear that every one of them knows
that Camille is a dressmaker who makes super-dresses.
She is as much a household word among them as Roosevelt used to be to their men folks.  And if we can promise them a Camille-designed dress for $7.85 (which we
could) then why don't we?"

At the very end, to her stenographer's mystification,
she added this irrevelant line.

"Seven dollars a week is not a living wage."

The report went to Fenger.  He hurdled lightly over
the first suggestion, knowing that the file system was as
simple as a monster of its bulk could be.  He ignored
the third hint.  The second suggestion amused, then
interested, then convinced him.  Within six months
Camille's name actually appeared in the Haynes-Cooper catalogue.  Not that alone, the Haynes-Cooper
company broke its rule as to outside advertising, and
announced in full-page magazine ads the news of the
$7.85 gowns designed by Camille especially for the
Haynes-Cooper company.  There went up a nation-
wide shout of amusement and unbelief, but the announcement continued.  Camille (herself a frump with
a fringe) whose frocks were worn by queens, and dan-
cers and matrons with millions, and debutantes ; Camille,
who had introduced the slouch, revived the hoop, discovered the sunset chiffon, had actually consented to
design six models every season for the mail order millions of the Haynes-Cooper women's dress department
—at a price that made even Michael Fenger wince.

## CHAPTER FOURTEEN

FANNY BRANDEIS' blouses showed real Cluny
now, and her hats were nothing but line. A scant
two years before she had wondered if she would ever
reach a pinnacle of success lofty enough to enable her to
wear blue tailor suits as smart as the well-cut garments
worn by her mother's friend, Mrs. Emma McChesney.
Mrs. McChesney's trig little suits had cost fifty dollars,
and had looked sixty. Fanny's now cost one hundred
and twenty-five, and looked one hundred and twenty-
five. Her sleeves alone gave it away. If you would test
the soul of a tailor you have only to glance at shoulder-
seam, elbow and wrist. Therein lies the wizardry.
Fanny's sleeve flowed from arm-pit to thumb-bone without a ripple. Also she moved from the South side to
the North side, always a sign of prosperity or social
ambition, in Chicago. Her new apartment was near
the lake, exhilaratingly high, correspondingly expensive. And she was hideously lonely. She was earning
a man-size salary now, and she was working like a man.
A less magnificently healthy woman could not have
stood the strain, for Fanny Brandeis was working with
her head, not her heart. When we say heart we have
come to mean something more than the hollow muscular
structure that propels the blood through the veins.
That, in the dictionary, is the primary definition. The
secondary definition has to do with such words as emotion, sympathy, tenderness, courage, conviction. She
was working, now, as Michael Fenger worked, relentlessly, coldly, indomitably, using all the material at
hand as a means to an end, with never a thought of the

material itself, as a builder reaches for a brick, or stone, and fits it into place, smoothly, almost without actually seeing the brick itself, except as something which will help to make a finished wall. She rarely prowled the city now. She told herself she was too tired at night, and on Sundays and holidays, and I suppose she was. Indeed, she no longer saw things with her former vision. It was as though her soul had shriveled in direct proportion to her salary's expansion. The streets seldom furnished her with a rich mental meal now. When she met a woman with a child, in the park, her keen eye noted the child's dress before it saw the child itself, if, indeed, she noticed the child at all.

Fascinating Facts, the guileless, pink-cheeked youth who had driven her home the night of her first visit to the Fengers, shortly after her coming to Haynes-Cooper's, had proved her faithful slave, and she had not abused his devotion. Indeed, she hardly considered it that. The sex side of her was being repressed with the artist side. Most men found her curt, brisk, businesslike manner a little repellent, though interesting. They never made love to her, in spite of her undeniable attractiveness. Fascinating Facts drove her about in his smart little roadster and one night he established himself in her memory forever as the first man who had ever asked her to marry him. He did it haltingly, painfully, almost grudgingly. Fanny was frankly amazed. She had enjoyed going about with him. He rested and soothed her. He, in turn, had been stimulated by her energy, her humor, her electric force. Nothing was said for a minute after his awkward declaration.

"But," he persisted, "you like me, don't you?"

"Of course I do. Immensely."

"Then why?"

"When a woman of my sort marries it's a miracle. I'm twenty-six, and intelligent and very successful. A frightful combination. Unmarried women of my type aren't content just to feel. They must analyze their feelings. And analysis is death to romance."

"Great Scott! You expect to marry somebody sometime, don't you, Fanny?"

"No one I know now. When I do marry, if I do, it will be with the idea of making a definite gain. I don't mean necessarily worldly gain, though that would be a factor, too."

Fascinating Facts had been staring straight ahead, his hands gripping the wheel with unnecessary rigidity. He relaxed a little now, and even laughed, though not very successfully. Then he said something very wise, for him.

"Listen to me, girl. You'll never get away with that vampire stuff. Talons are things you have to be born with. You'll never learn to grab with these." He reached over, and picked up her left hand lying inertly in her lap, and brought it up to his lips, and kissed it, glove and all. "They're built on the open-face pattern —for giving. You can't fool me. I know."

A year and a half after her coming to Haynes-Cooper Fanny's department was doing a business of a million a year. The need had been there. She had merely given it the impetus. She was working more or less directly with Fenger now, with an eye on every one of the departments that had to do with women's clothing, from shoes to hats. Not that she did any actual buying, or selling in these departments. She still confined her actual selecting of goods to the infants' wear section, but she occupied, unofficially, the position of assistant to the General Merchandise Manager. They worked well together, she and Fenger, their minds often marching along without the necessity of a single spoken word. There was no doubt that Fenger's mind was a marvelous piece of mechanism. Under it the Haynes-Cooper plant functioned with the clockwork regularity of a gigantic automaton. System and Results—these

were his twin gods. With his mind intent on them he
failed to see that new gods, born of spiritual unrest,
were being set up in the temples of Big Business. Their
coming had been rumored for many years. Words
such as Brotherhood, Labor, Rights, Humanity, Hours,
once regarded as the special property of the street
corner ranter, were creeping into our everyday vocabulary. And strangely enough, Nathan Haynes, the gentle, the bewildered, the uninspired, heard them, and listened. Nathan Haynes had begun to accustom himself
to the roar of the flood that had formerly deafened him.
He was no longer stunned by the inrush of his millions.
The report sheet handed him daily had never ceased to
be a wildly unexpected thing, and he still shrank from
it, sometimes. It was so fantastic, so out of all reason.
But he even dared, now and then, to put out a tentative
hand to guide the flood. He began to realize, vaguely,
that Italian Gardens, and marble pools, educational
endowments and pet charities were but poor, ineffectual
barriers of mud and sticks, soon swept away by the
torrent. As he sat there in his great, luxurious office,
with the dim, rich old portraits gleaming down on him
from the walls, he began, gropingly, to evolve a new
plan; a plan by which the golden flood was to be curbed,
divided, and made to form a sub-stream, to be utilized
for the good of the many; for the good of the Ten
Thousand, who were almost Fifteen Thousand now, with
another fifteen thousand in mills and factories at distant points, whose entire output was swallowed up by
the Haynes-Cooper plant. Michael Fenger, Super-
Manager, listened to the plan, smiled tolerantly, and
went on perfecting an already miraculous System.
Sarah Sapinsky, at seven a week, was just so much untrained labor material, easily replaced by material exactly like it. No, Michael Fenger, with his head in the
sand, heard no talk of new gods. He only knew that
the monster plant under his management was yielding

the greatest possible profit under the least possible out-
lay.

In Fanny Brandeis he had found a stimulating, en-
ergizing fellow worker. That had been from the beginning. In the first month or two of her work, when
her keen brain was darting here and there, into forgotten and neglected corners, ferreting out dusty scraps
of business waste and holding them up to the light, disdainfully, Fenger had watched her with a mingling of
amusement and a sort of fond pride, as one would a
precocious child. As the months went on the pride
and amusement welded into something more than admiration, such as one expert feels for a fellow-crafts-
man. Long before the end of the first year he knew
that here was a woman such as he had dreamed of all
his life and never hoped to find. He often found himself sitting at his office desk, or in his library at home,
staring straight ahead for a longer time than he dared
admit, his papers or book forgotten in his hand. His
thoughts applied to her adjectives which proved her a
paradox: Generous, sympathetic, warm-hearted, impulsive, imaginative; cold, indomitable, brilliant, daring, intuitive. He would rouse himself almost angrily
and force himself to concentrate again upon the page
before him. I don't know how he thought it all would
end—he whose life-habit it was to follow out every process to its ultimate step, whether mental or mechanical.
As for Fanny, there was nothing of the intriguant
about her. She was used to admiration. She was accustomed to deference from men. Brandeis' Bazaar
had insured that. All her life men had taken orders
from her, all the way from Aloysius and the blithe traveling men of whom she bought goods, to the salesmen
and importers in the Chicago wholesale houses. If
they had attempted, occasionally, to mingle the social
and personal with the commercial Fanny had not resented their attitude. She had accepted their admira-

tion and refused their invitations with equal good nature, and thus retained their friendship. It is not exaggeration to say that she looked upon Michael Fenger much as she had upon these genial fellow-workers. A woman as straightforward and direct as she has what is known as a single-track mind in such matters. It is your soft and silken mollusc type of woman whose mind pursues a slimy and labyrinthine trail. But it is useless to say that she did not feel something of the intense personal attraction of the man. Often it used to puzzle and annoy her to find that as they sat arguing in the brisk, everyday atmosphere of office or merchandise room the air between them would suddenly become electric, vibrant. They met each other's eyes with effort. When their hands touched, accidentally, over papers or samples they snatched them back. Fanny found herself laughing uncertainly, at nothing, and was furious. When a silence fell between them they would pounce upon it, breathlessly, and smother it with talk.

Do not think that any furtive love-making went on, sandwiched between shop talk. Their conversation might have taken place between two men. Indeed, they often were brutally frank to each other. Fanny had the vision, Fenger the science to apply it. Sometimes her intuition leaped ahead of his reasoning. Then he would say, "I'm not sold on that," which is modern business slang meaning, "You haven't convinced me." She would go back and start afresh, covering the ground more slowly.

Usually her suggestions were practical and what might be termed human. They seemed to be founded on an uncanny knowledge of people's frailties. It was only when she touched upon his beloved System that he was adamant.

"None of that socialistic stuff," he would say. "This isn't a Benevolent Association we're running. It's the biggest mail order business in the world, and its backbone is System. I've been just fifteen years perfecting that System. It's my job. Hands off."

"A fifteen year old system ought to be scrapped," Fanny would retort, boldly. "Anyway, the Simon Legree thing has gone out."

No one in the plant had ever dared to talk to him like that. He would glare down at Fanny for a moment, like a mastiff on a terrier. Fanny, seeing his face rage-red, would flash him a cheerful and impudent smile. The anger, fading slowly, gave way to another look, so that admiration and resentment mingled for a moment.

"Lucky for you you're not a man."

"I wish I were."

"I'm glad you're not."

Not a very thrilling conversation for those of you who are seeking heartthrobs.

In May Fanny made her first trip to Europe for the firm. It was a sudden plan. Instantly Theodore leaped to her mind and she was startled at the tumult she felt at the thought of seeing him and his child. The baby, a girl, was more than a year old. Her business, a matter of two weeks, perhaps, was all in Berlin and Paris, but she cabled Theodore that she would come to them in Munich, if only for a day or two. She had very little curiosity about the woman Theodore had married. The memory of that first photograph of hers, befrizzed, bejeweled, and asmirk, had never effaced itself. It had stamped her indelibly in Fanny's mind.

The day before she left for New York (she sailed from there) she had a letter from Theodore. It was evident at once that he had not received her cable. He was in Russia, giving a series of concerts. Olga and the baby were with him. He would be back in Munich in June. There was some talk of America. When Fanny realized that she was not to see him she experienced a strange feeling that was a mixture of regret and relief. All the family love in her, a racial trait, had been stirred at the thought of again seeing that dear blond brother, the self-centered, willful, gifted boy who had held the little congregation rapt, there in the Jewish house of worship in Winnebago. But she had recoiled a little from the meeting with this other unknown person who gave concerts in Russia, who had adopted Munich as his home, who was the husband of this Olga person, and the father of a ridiculously German looking baby in a very German looking dress, all lace and tucks, and wearing bracelets on its chubby arms, and a locket round its neck. That was what one might expect of Olga's baby. But not of Theodore's. Besides, what business had that boy with a baby, anyway? Himself a baby.

Fenger had arranged for her cabin, and she rather resented its luxury until she learned later, that it is the buyers who always occupy the staterooms de luxe on ocean liners. She learned, too, that the men in yachting caps and white flannels, and the women in the smartest and most subdued of blue serge and furs were not millionaires temporarily deprived of their own private seagoing craft, but buyers like herself, shrewd, aggressive, wise and incredibly endowed with savoir faire. Merely to watch one of them dealing with a deck steward was to know for all time the superiority of mind over matter.

Most incongruously, it was Ella Monahan and Clarence Heyl who waved good-by to her as her ship swung clear of the dock. Ella was in New York on her monthly trip. Heyl had appeared at the hotel as Fanny was adjusting her veil and casting a last rather wild look around the room. Molly Brandeis had been the kind of woman who never misses a train or overlooks a hairpin. Fanny's early training had proved invaluable more than once in the last two years. Nevertheless, she was rather flustered, for her, as the elevator

took her down to the main floor. She told herself it was
not the contemplation of the voyage itself that thrilled
her. It was the fact that here was another step defin-
itely marking her progress.

Heyl, looking incredibly limp, was leaning against a
gaudy marble pillar, his eyes on the downcoming elevators. Fanny saw him just an instant before he saw
her, and in that moment she found herself wondering
why this boy (she felt years older than he) should look
so fantastically out of place in this great, glittering,
feverish hotel lobby. Just a shy, rather swarthy Jewish boy, who wore the right kind of clothes in the wrong
manner—then Heyl saw her and came swiftly toward
her.

"Hello, Fan!"

"Hello, Clancy!" They had not seen each other in
six months.

"Anybody else going down with you?"

"No. Ella Monahan had a last-minute business ap-
pointment, but she promised to be at the dock, somehow, before the boat leaves. I'm going to be grand,
and taxi all the way."

"I've an open car, waiting."

"But I won't have it! I can't let you do that."

"Oh, yes you can. Don't take it so hard. That's the
trouble with you business women. You're killing the
gallantry of a nation. Some day one of you will get
up and give me a seat in a subway——"

"I'll punish you for that, Clancy. If you want the
Jane Austen thing I'll accommodate. I'll drop my
handkerchief, gloves, bag, flowers and fur scarf at intervals of five minutes all the way downtown. Then you
may scramble around on the floor of the cab and feel
like a knight."

Fanny had long ago ceased to try to define the charm
of this man. She always meant to be serenely dignified with him. She always ended by feeling very young,

and, somehow, gloriously carefree and lighthearted. There was about him a naturalness, a simplicity, to which one responded in kind.

Seated beside her he turned and regarded her with disconcerting scrutiny.

"Like it?" demanded Fanny, pertly. And smoothed her veil, consciously.

"No."

"Well, for a man who looks negligée even in evening clothes aren't you overcritical?"

"I'm not criticizing your clothes. Even I can see that that hat and suit have the repressed note that means money. And you're the kind of woman who looks her best in those plain dark things."

"Well, then?"

"You look like a buyer. In two more years your face will have that hard finish that never comes off."

"I am a buyer."

"You're not. You're a creator. Remember, I'm not belittling your job. It's a wonderful job—for Ella Monahan. I wish I had the gift of eloquence. I wish I had the right to spank you. I wish I could prove to you, somehow, that with your gift, and heritage, and racial right it's as criminal for you to be earning your thousands at Haynes-Cooper's as it would have been for a vestal virgin to desert her altar fire to stoke a furnace. Your eyes are bright and hard, instead of tolerant. Your mouth is losing its graciousness. Your whole face is beginning to be stamped with a look that says shrewdness and experience, and success."

"I am successful. Why shouldn't I look it?"

"Because you're a failure. I'm sick, I tell you—sick with disappointment in you. Jane Addams would have been a success in business, too. She was born with a humanity sense, and a value sense, and a something else that can't be acquired. Ida Tarbell could have managed your whole Haynes-Cooper plant, if she'd had to. So could a dozen other women I could name. You don't see any sign of what you call success on Jane Addams's face, do you? You wouldn't say, on seeing her, that here was a woman who looked as if she might afford hundred-dollar tailor suits and a town car. No. All you see in her face is the reflection of the souls of all the men and women she has worked to save. She has covered her job—the job that the Lord intended her to cover. And to me she is the most radiantly beautiful woman I have ever seen."

Fanny sat silent. She was twisting the fingers of one hand in the grip of the other, as she had since childhood, when deeply disturbed. And suddenly she began to cry—silently, harrowingly, as a man cries, her shoulders shaking, her face buried in her furs.

"Fanny! Fanny girl!" He was horribly disturbed and contrite. He patted her arm, awkwardly. She shook free of his hand, childishly. "Don't cry, dear. I'm sorry. It's just that I care so much. It's just——"

She raised an angry, tear-stained face. "It's just that you have an exalted idea of your own perceptions. It's just that you've grown up from what they used to call a bright little boy to a bright young man, and you're just as tiresome now as you were then. I'm happy enough, except when I see you. I'm getting the things I starved for all those years. Why, I'll never get over being thrilled at the idea of being able to go to the theater, or to a concert, whenever I like. Actually whenever I want to. And to be able to buy a jabot, or a smart hat, or a book. You don't know how I wanted things, and how tired I got of never having them. I'm happy! I'm happy! Leave me alone!"

"It's an awful price to pay for a hat, and a jabot, and a book and a theater ticket, Fan."

Ella Monahan had taken the tube, and was standing in the great shed, watching arrivals with interest, long

before they bumped over the cobblestones of Hoboken.
The three descended to Fanny's cabin. Ella had sent
champagne—six cosy pints in a wicker basket.

"They say it's good for seasickness," she announced,
cheerfully, "but it's a lie. Nothing's good for seasickness, except death, or dry land. But even if you do
feel miserable—and you probably will—there's something about being able to lie in your berth and drink
champagne alone, by the spoonful, that's sort of soothing."

Heyl had fallen silent. Fanny was radiant again,
and exclamatory over her books and flowers.

"Of course it's my first trip," she explained, "and
an event in my life, but I didn't suppose that anybody
else would care. What's this? Candy? Glace fruit."
She glanced around the luxurious little cabin, then up
at Heyl, impudently. "I may be a coarse commercial
person, Clancy, but I must say I like this very, very
much. Sorry."

They went up on deck. Ella, a seasoned traveler,
was full of parting instructions. "And be sure to eat
at Kempinski's, in Berlin. Twenty cents for lobster.
And caviar! Big as hen's eggs, and as cheap as cod-
fish. And don't forget to order *mai-bowle*. It tastes
like champagne, but isn't, and it has the most delicious
dwarf strawberries floating on top. This is just the
season for it. You're lucky. If you tip the waiter one
mark he's yours for life. Oh, and remember the plum
*compôte*. You'll be disappointed in their Wertheim's
that they're always bragging about. After all, Field's
makes 'em all look like country stores."

"Wertheim's? Is that something to eat, too?"

"No, idiot. It's their big department store." Ella
turned to Heyl, for whom she felt mingled awe and lik-
ing. "If this trip of hers is successful, the firm will
probably send her over three or four times a year.
It's a wonderful chance for a kid like her."

"Then I hope," said Heyl, quietly, "that this trip may be a failure."

Ella smiled, uncertainly.

"Don't laugh," said Fanny, sharply. "He means it."

Ella, sensing an unpleasant something in which she had no part, covered the situation with another rush of conversation.

"You'll get the jolt of your life when you come to Paris and find that you're expected to pay for the lunches, and all the cab fares, and everything, of those shrimpy little *commissionaires.* Polite little fellows, they are, in frock coats, and mustaches, and they just stand aside, as courtly as you please, while you pay for everything. Their house expects it. I almost passed away, the first time, but you get used to it. Say, imagine one of our traveling men letting you pay for his lunch and taxi."

She rattled on, genially. Heyl listened with unfeigned delight. Ella found herself suddenly abashed before those clear, far-seeing eyes. "You think I'm a gabby old girl, don't you?"

"I think you're a wonderful woman," said Heyl. "Very wise, and very kind."

"Why—thanks," faltered Ella. "Why—thanks."

They said their good-bys. Ella hugged Fanny warm-heartedly. Then she turned away, awkwardly. Heyl put his two hands on Fanny's shoulders and looked down at her. For a breathless second she thought he was about to kiss her. She was amazed to find herself hoping that he would. But he didn't. "Good-by," he said, simply. And took her hand in his steel grip a moment, and dropped it. And turned away. A messenger boy, very much out of breath, came running up to her, a telegram in his hand.

"For me?" Fanny opened it, frowned, smiled. "It's from Mr. Fenger. Good wishes. As if all those flowers weren't enough."

"Mm," said Ella. She and Heyl descended the gang-way, and stood at the dock's edge, looking rather fool-ish and uncertain, as people do at such times. There followed a few moments of scramble, of absurdly shouted last messages, of bells, and frantic waving of handkerchiefs. Fanny, at the rail, found her two among the crowd, and smiled down upon them, mistily. Ella was waving energetically. Heyl was standing quite still, looking up. The ship swung clear, crept away from the dock. The good-bys swelled to a roar. Fanny leaned far over the rail and waved too, a sob in her throat. Then she saw that she was waving with the hand that held the yellow telegram. She crumpled it in the other hand, and substituted her handkerchief. Heyl still stood, hat in hand, motionless.

"Why don't you wave good-by?" she called, though he could not possibly hear. "Wave good-by!" And then the hand with the handkerchief went to her face, and she was weeping. I think it was that old drama-thrill in her, dormant for so long. But at that Heyl swung his hat above his head, three times, like a school-boy, and, grasping Ella's plump and resisting arm, marched abruptly away.

## CHAPTER FIFTEEN

THE first week in June found her back in New York. That month of absence had worked a subtle change. The two weeks spent in crossing and recrossing had provided her with a let-down that had been almost jarring in its completeness. Everything competitive had seemed to fade away with the receding shore, and to loom up again only when the skyline became a thing of smoke-banks, spires, and shafts. She had had only two weeks for the actual transaction of her business. She must have been something of a revelation to those Paris and Berlin manufacturers, accustomed though they were to the brisk and irresistible methods of the American business woman. She was, after all, absurdly young to be talking in terms of millions, and she was amazingly well dressed. This last passed unnoticed, or was taken for granted in Paris, but in Berlin, home of the frump and the flour-sack figure, she was stared at, appreciatively. Her business, except for one or two unimportant side lines, had to do with two factories on whose product the Haynes-Cooper company had long had a covetous eye. Quantity, as usual, was the keynote of their demand, and Fanny's task was that of talking in six-figure terms to these conservative and over-wary foreign manufacturers. That she had successfully accomplished this, and that she had managed to impress them also with the important part that time and promptness in delivery played in a swift-moving machine like the Haynes-Cooper concern, was due to many things beside her natural business ability. Self-confidence was there, and physical vigor, and diplomacy. But above all there was that sheer love of the game; the dramatic sense that enabled her to see herself in the part. That alone precluded the possibility of failure. She knew how youthful she looked, and how glowing. She anticipated the look that came into their faces when she left polite small-talk behind and soared up into the cold, rarefied atmosphere of business. She delighted in seeing the admiring and tolerant smirk vanish and give way to a startled and defensive attentiveness.

It might be mentioned that she managed, somehow, to spend almost half a day in Petticoat Lane, and its squalid surroundings, while in London. She actually prowled, alone, at night, in the evil-smelling, narrow streets of the poorer quarter of Paris, and how she escaped unharmed is a mystery that never bothered her, because she had never known fear of streets. She had always walked on the streets of Winnebago, Wisconsin, alone. It never occurred to her not to do the same in the streets of Chicago, or New York, or London, or Paris. She found Berlin, with its Adlon, its appalling cleanliness, its overfed populace, and its omnipresent Kaiser forever scudding up and down Unter den Linden in his chocolate-colored car, incredibly dull, and unpicturesque. Something she had temporarily lost there in the busy atmosphere of the Haynes-Cooper plant, seemed to have returned, miraculously.

New York, on her return, was something of a shock. She remembered how vividly fresh it had looked to her on the day of that first visit, months before. Now, to eyes fresh from the crisp immaculateness of Paris and Berlin, Fifth avenue looked almost grimy, and certainly shabby in spots.

Ella Monahan, cheerful, congratulatory, beaming, met her at the pier, and Fanny was startled at her own sensation of happiness as she saw that pink, good-natured face looking up at her from the crowd below.

The month that had gone by since last she saw Ella standing just so, seemed to slip away and fade into nothingness.

"I waited over a day," said Ella, "just to see you. My, you look grand! I know where you got that hat. Galeries Lafayette. How much?"

"I don't expect you to believe it. Thirty-five francs. Seven dollars. I couldn't get it for twenty-five here."

They were soon clear of the customs. Ella had engaged a room for her at the hotel they always used. As they rode uptown together, happily, Ella opened her bag and laid a little packet of telegrams and letters in Fanny's lap.

"I guess Fenger's pleased, all right, if telegrams mean anything. Not that I know they're from him. But he said—"

But Fanny was looking up from one of them with a startled expression.

"He's here. Fenger's here."

"In New York?" asked Ella, rather dully.

"Yes." She ripped open another letter. It was from Theodore. He was coming to New York in August. The Russian tour had been a brilliant success. They had arranged a series of concerts for him in the United States. He could give his concerto there. It was impossible in Russia, Munich, even Berlin, because it was distinctly Jewish in theme—as Jewish as the Kol Nidre, and as somber. They would have none of it in Europe. Prejudice was too strong. But in America! He was happier than he had been in years. Olga objected to coming to America, but she would get over that. The little one was well, and she was learning to talk. Actually! They were teaching her to say Tante Fanny.

"Well!" exclaimed Fanny, her eyes shining. She read bits of the letter aloud to Ella. Ella was such a satisfactory sort of person to whom to read a letter aloud. She exclaimed in all the right places. Her face was as radiant as Fanny's. They both had forgotten all about Fenger, their Chief. But they had been in their hotel scarcely a half hour, and Ella had not done exclaiming over the bag that Fanny had brought her from Paris, when his telephone call came.

He wasted very little time on preliminaries.

"I'll call for you at four. We'll drive through the park, and out by the river, and have tea somewhere."

"That would be wonderful. That is, if Ella's free. I'll ask her."

"Ella?"

"Yes. She's right here. Hold the wire, will you?" She turned away from the telephone to face Ella. "It's Mr. Fenger. He wants to take us both driving this afternoon. You can go, can't you?"

"I certainly *can*," replied Miss Monahan, with what might have appeared to be undue force.

Fanny turned back to the telephone. "Yes, thanks. We can both go. We'll be ready at four."

Fanny decided that Fenger's muttered reply couldn't have been what she thought it was.

Ella busied herself with the unpacking of a bag. She showed a disposition to spoil Fanny. "You haven't asked after your friend, Mr. Heyl. My land! If I had a friend like that—"

"Oh, yes," said Fanny, vaguely. "I suppose you and he are great chums by this time. He's a nice boy."

"You don't suppose anything of the kind," Ella retorted, crisply. "That boy, as you call him—and it isn't always the man with the biggest fists that's got the most fight in him—is about as far above me as— as—" she sat down on the floor, ponderously, beside the open bag, and gesticulated with a hairbrush, at loss for a simile—"as an eagle is above a waddling old duck. No, I don't mean that, either, because I never did think much of the eagle, morally. But you get me. Not that he knows it, or shows it. Heyl, I mean. Lord, no! But he's got something—something kind of spiritual in him that makes you that way, too. He doesn't say much, either. That's the funny part of it. I do all the talking, seems, when I'm with him. But I find myself saying things I didn't know I knew. He makes you think about things you're afraid to face by yourself. Big things. Things inside of you." She fell silent a moment, sitting cross-legged before the bag. Then she got up, snapped the bag shut, and bore it across the room to a corner. "You know he's gone, I s'pose."

"Gone?"

"To those mountains, or wherever it is he gets that look in his eyes from. That's my notion of a job. They let him go for the whole summer, roaming around being a naturalist, just so's he'll come back in the winter."

"And the column?" Fanny asked. "Do they let that go, too?"

"I guess he's going to do some writing for them up there. After all, he's the column. It doesn't make much difference where he writes from. Did you know it's being syndicated now, all over the country? Well, it is. That's the secret of its success, I suppose. It isn't only a column written about New York for a New York paper. It's about everything, for anybody. It's the humanest stuff. And he isn't afraid of anything. New York's crazy about him. They say he's getting a salary you wouldn't believe. I'm a tongue-tied old fool when I'm with him, but then, he likes to talk about you, mostly, so it doesn't matter."

Fanny turned swiftly from the dressing-table, where she was taking the pins out of her vigorous, abundant hair.

"What kind of thing does he say about me, Ellen girl. H'm? What kind of thing?"

"Abuse, mostly. I'll be running along to my own room now. I'll be out for lunch, but back at four, for that airing Fenger's so wild to have me take. If I were you I'd lie down for an hour, till you get your land-legs." She poked her head in at the door again. "Not that you look as if you needed it. You've got a different look, somehow. Kind of rested. After all, there's nothing like an ocean voyage."

She was gone. Fanny stood a moment, in the center of the room. There was nothing relaxed or inert about her. Had you seen her standing there, motionless, you would still have got a sense of action from her. She looked so splendidly alive. She walked to the window, now, and stood looking down upon New York in early June. Summer had not yet turned the city into a cauldron of stone and steel. From her height she could glimpse the green of the park, with a glint of silver in its heart, that was the lake. Her mind was milling around, aimlessly, in a manner far removed from its usual orderly functioning. Now she thought of Theodore, her little brother—his promised return. It had been a slow and painful thing, his climb. Perhaps if she had been more ready to help, if she had not always waited until he asked the aid that she might have volunteered—she thrust that thought out of her mind, rudely, and slammed the door on it. . . . Fenger. He had said, "Damn!" when she had told him about Ella. And his voice had been—well—she pushed that thought outside her mind, too. . . . Clarence Heyl. . . . "He makes you think about things you're afraid to face by yourself. Big things. Things inside of you. . . ."

Fanny turned away from the window. She decided she must be tired, after all. Because here she was, with everything to make her happy: Theodore coming home; her foreign trip a success; Ella and Fenger to praise her and make much of her; a drive and tea this afternoon (she wasn't above these creature comforts) —and still she felt unexhilarated, dull. She decided to go down for a bit of lunch, and perhaps a stroll of ten or fifteen minutes, just to see what Fifth avenue was showing. It was half-past one when she reached that ordinarily well-regulated thoroughfare. She found its sidewalks packed solid, up and down, as far as the eye could see, with a quiet, orderly, expectant mass of people. Squads of mounted police clattered up and down, keeping the middle of the street cleared. Whatever it was that had called forth that incredible mass, was scheduled to proceed uptown from far downtown, and that very soon. Heads were turned that way. Fanny, wedged in the crowd, stood a-tiptoe, but she could see nothing. It brought to her mind the Circus Day of her Winnebago childhood, with Elm street packed with townspeople and farmers, all straining their eyes up toward Cherry street, the first turn in the line of march. Then, far away, the blare of a band. "Here they come!" Just then, far down the canyon of Fifth avenue, sounded the cry that had always swayed Elm street, Winnebago. "Here they come!"

"What is it?" Fanny asked a woman against whom she found herself close-packed. "What are they waiting for?"

"It's the suffrage parade," replied the woman. "The big suffrage parade. Don't you know?"

"No. I haven't been here." Fanny was a little disappointed. The crowd had surged forward, so that it was impossible for her to extricate herself. She found herself near the curb. She could see down the broad street now, and below Twenty-third street it was a moving, glittering mass, pennants, banners, streamers flying. The woman next her volunteered additional information.

"The mayor refused permission to let them march.

But they fought it, and they say it's the greatest suffrage parade ever held. I'd march myself, only—"

"Only what?"

"I don't know. I'm scared to, I think. I'm not a New Yorker."

"Neither am I," said Fanny. Fanny always became friendly with the woman next her in a crowd. That was her mother in her. One could hear the music of the band, now. Fanny glanced at her watch. It was not quite two. Oh, well, she would wait and see some of it. Her mind was still too freshly packed with European impressions to receive any real idea of the value of this pageant, she told herself. She knew she did not feel particularly interested. But she waited.

Another surging forward. It was no longer, "Here they come!" but, "Here they are!"

And here they were.

A squad of mounted police, on very prancy horses. The men looked very ruddy, and well set-up and imposing. Fanny had always thrilled to anything in uniform, given sufficient numbers of them. Another police squad. A brass band, on foot. And then, in white, on a snow-white charger, holding a white banner aloft, her eyes looking straight ahead, her face very serious and youthful, the famous beauty and suffrage leader, Mildred Inness. One of the few famous beauties who actually was a beauty. And after that women, women, women! Hundreds of them, thousands of them, a river of them flowing up Fifth avenue to the park. More bands. More horses. Women! Women! They bore banners. This section, that section. Artists. School teachers. Lawyers. Doctors. Writers. Women in college caps and gowns. Women in white, from shoes to hats. Young women. Girls. Gray-haired women. A woman in a wheel chair, smiling. A man next to Fanny began to jeer. He was a red-faced young man, with a coarse, blotchy skin, and thick lips.

He smoked a cigar, and called to the women in a
falsetto voice, "Hello, Sadie!" he called. "Hello, kid!"
And the women marched on, serious-faced, calm-eyed.
There came floats; elaborate affairs, with girls in
Greek robes. Fanny did not care for these. More
solid ranks. And then a strange and pitiful and tragic
and eloquent group. Their banner said, "Garment
Workers. Infants' Wear Section." And at their head
marched a girl, carrying a banner. I don't know how
she attained that honor. I think she must have been
one of those fiery, eloquent leaders in her factory clique.
The banner she carried was a large one, and it flapped
prodigiously in the breeze, and its pole was thick and
heavy. She was a very small girl, even in that group
of pale-faced, under-sized, under-fed girls. A Russian
Jewess, evidently. Her shoes were ludicrous. They
curled up at the toes, and the heels were run down.
Her dress was a sort of parody on the prevailing
fashion. But on her face, as she trudged along, hugging the pole of the great pennant that flapped in the
breeze, was stamped a look!—well, you see that same
look in some pictures of Joan of Arc. It wasn't merely
a look. It was a story. It was tragedy. It was the
history of a people. You saw in it that which told of
centuries of oppression in Russia. You saw eager
groups of student Intellectuals, gathered in secret
places for low-voiced, fiery talk. There was in it the
unspeakable misery of Siberia. It spoke eloquently of
pogroms, of massacres, of Kiev and its sister-horror,
Kishineff. You saw mean and narrow streets, and carefully darkened windows, and, on the other side of those
windows the warm yellow glow of the seven-branched
Shabbos light. Above this there shone the courage of
a race serene in the knowledge that it cannot die. And
illuminating all, so that her pinched face, beneath the
flapping pennant, was the rapt, uplifted countenance
of the Crusader, there blazed the great glow of hope.

This woman movement, spoken of so glibly as Suffrage, was, to the mind of this over-read, under-fed, emotional, dreamy little Russian garment worker the glorious means to a long hoped for end. She had idealized it, with the imagery of her kind. She had endowed it with promise that it would never actually hold for her, perhaps. And so she marched on, down the great, glittering avenue, proudly clutching her unwieldy banner, a stunted, grotesque, magnificent figure. More than a figure. A symbol.

Fanny's eyes followed her until she passed out of sight. She put up her hand to her cheek, and her face was wet. She stood there, and the parade went on, endlessly, it seemed, and she saw it through a haze. Bands. More bands. Pennants. Floats. Women. Women. Women.

"I always cry at parades," said Fanny, to the woman who stood next her—the woman who wanted to march, but was scared to.

"That's all right," said the woman. "That's all right." And she laughed, because she was crying, too. And then she did a surprising thing. She elbowed her way to the edge of the crowd, past the red-faced man with the cigar, out to the street, and fell into line, and marched on up the street, shoulders squared, head high.

Fanny glanced down at her watch. It was quarter after four. With a little gasp she turned to work her way through the close-packed crowd. It was an actual physical struggle, from which she emerged disheveled, breathless, uncomfortably warm, and minus her handkerchief, but she had gained the comparative quiet of the side street, and she made the short distance that lay between the Avenue and her hotel a matter of little more than a minute. In the hotel corridor stood Ella and Fenger, the former looking worried, the latter savage.

"Where in the world—" began Ella.

"Caught in the jam. And I didn't want to get out. It was—it was—glorious!" She was shaking hands with Fenger, and realizing for the first time that she must be looking decidedly sketchy and that she had lost her handkerchief. She fished for it in her bag, hopelessly, when Fenger released her hand. He had not spoken. Now he said:

"What's the matter with your eyes?"

"I've been crying," Fanny confessed cheerfully.

"Crying!"

"The parade. There was a little girl in it—" she stopped. Fenger would not be interested in that little girl. Now Clancy would have—but Ella broke in on that thought.

"I guess you don't realize that out in front of this hotel there's a kind of a glorified taxi waiting, with the top rolled back, and it's been there half an hour. I never expect to see the time when I could enjoy keeping a taxi waiting. It goes against me."

"I'm sorry. Really. Let's go. I'm ready."

"You are not. Your hair's a sight; and those eyes!"

Fenger put a hand on her arm. "Go on up and powder your nose, Miss Brandeis. And don't hurry. I want you to enjoy this drive."

On her way up in the elevator Fanny thought, "He has lost his waistline. Now, that couldn't have happened in a month. Queer I didn't notice it before. And he looks soft. Not enough exercise."

When she rejoined them she was freshly bloused and gloved and all traces of the tell-tale red had vanished from her eyelids. Fifth avenue was impossible. Their car sped up Madison avenue, and made for the Park. The Plaza was a jam of tired marchers. They dispersed from there, but there seemed no end to the line that still flowed up Fifth avenue. Fenger seemed scarcely to see it. He had plunged at once into talk of the European trip. Fanny gave him every detail, omitting nothing. She repeated all that her letters and cables had told. Fenger was more excited than she had ever seen him. He questioned, cross-questioned, criticized, probed, exacted an account of every conversation. Usually it was not method that interested him, but results. Fanny, having accomplished the thing she had set out to do, had lost interest in it now. The actual millions so glibly bandied in the Haynes-Cooper plant had never thrilled her. The methods by which they were made possible had.

Ella had been listening with the shrewd comprehension of one who admires the superior art of a fellow craftsman.

"I'll say this, Mr. Fenger. If I could make you look like that, by going to Europe and putting it over those foreign boys, I'd feel I'd earned a year's salary right there, and quit. Not to speak of the cross-examination you're putting her through."

Fenger laughed, a little self-consciously. "It's just that I want to be sure it's real. I needn't tell you how important this trick is that Miss Brandeis has just turned." He turned to Fanny, with a boyish laugh. "Now don't pose. You know you can't be as bored as you look."

"Anyway," put in Ella, briskly, "I move that the witness step down. She may not be bored, but she certainly must be tired, and she's beginning to look it. Just lean back, Fanny, and let the green of this park soak in. At that, it isn't so awfully green, when you get right close, except that one stretch of meadow. Kind of ugly, Central Park, isn't it? Bare."

Fanny sat forward. There was more sparkle in her face than at any time during the drive. They were skimming along those green-shaded drives that are so sophisticatedly sylvan.

"I used to think it was bare, too, and bony as an old maid, with no soft cuddly places like the parks at home; no gracious green stretches, and no rose gardens. But somehow, it grows on you. The reticence of it. And that stretch of meadow near the Mall, in the late afternoon, with the mist on it, and the sky faintly pink, and that electric sign—Somebody's Tires or other—winking off and on—"

"You're a queer child," interrupted Fenger. "As wooden as an Indian while talking about a million-a-year deal, and lyrical over a combination of electric sign, sunset, and moth-eaten park. Oh, well, perhaps that's what makes you as you are."

Even Ella looked a little startled at that.

They had tea at Claremont, at a table overlooking the river and the Palisades. Fenger was the kind of man to whom waiters always give a table overlooking anything that should be overlooked. After tea they drove out along the river and came back in the cool of the evening. Fanny was very quiet now. Fenger followed her mood. Ella sustained the conversation, somewhat doggedly. It was almost seven when they reached the plaza exit. And there Fanny, sitting forward suddenly, gave a little cry.

"Why—they're marching yet!" she said, and her voice was high with wonder. "They're marching yet! All the time we've been driving and teaing, they've been marching."

And so they had. Thousands upon thousands, they had flowed along as relentlessly, and seemingly as endlessly as a river. They were marching yet. For six hours the thousands had poured up that street, making it a moving mass of white. And the end was not yet. What pen, and tongue, and sense of justice had failed to do, they were doing now by sheer, crude force of numbers. The red-faced hooligan, who had stood next to Fanny in the crowd hours before, had long ago ceased his jibes and slunk away, bored, if not impressed. After all, one might jeer at ten, or fifty, or a hundred women, or even five hundred. But not at forty thousand.

Their car turned down Madison Avenue, and Fenger twisted about for a last look at the throng in the plaza. He was plainly impressed. The magnitude of the thing appealed to him. To a Haynes-Cooper-trained mind, forty thousand women, marching for whatever the cause, must be impressive. Forty thousand of anything had the respect of Michael Fenger. His eyes narrowed, thoughtfully.

"They seem to have put it over," he said. "And yet, what's the idea? Oh, I'm for suffrage, of course. Naturally. And all those thousands of women, in white—still, a thing as huge as this parade has to be reduced to a common denominator, to be really successful. If somebody could take the whole thing, boil it down, and make the country see what this huge demonstration stands for."

Fanny leaned forward suddenly. "Tell the man to stop. I want to get out."

Fenger and Ella stared. "What for?" But Fenger obeyed.

"I want to get something at this stationer's shop." She had jumped down almost before the motor had stopped at the curb.

"But let me get it."

"No. You can't. Wait here." She disappeared within the shop. She was back in five minutes, a flat, loosely wrapped square under her arm. "Cardboard," she explained briefly, in answer to their questions.

Fenger, about to leave them at their hotel, presented his plans for the evening. Fanny, looking up at him, her head full of other plans, thought he looked and sounded very much like Big Business. And, for the moment at least, Fanny Brandeis loathed Big Business, and all that it stood for.

"It's almost seven," Fenger was saying. "We'll be

rubes in New York, this evening. You girls will just have time to freshen up a bit—I suppose you want to —and then we'll have dinner, and go to the theater, and to supper afterward. What do you want to see?"

Ella looked at Fanny. And Fanny shook her head, "Thanks. You're awfully kind. But—no."

"Why not?" demanded Fenger, gruffly.

"Perhaps because I'm tired. And there's something else I must do."

Ella looked relieved. Fenger's eyes bored down upon Fanny, but she seemed not to feel them. She held out her hand.

"You're going back to-morrow?" Fenger asked. "I'm not leaving until Thursday."

"To-morrow, with Ella. Good-by. It's been a glorious drive. I feel quite rested."

"You just said you were tired."

The elevator door clanged, shutting out the sight of Fenger's resentful frown.

"He's as sensitive as a soubrette," said Ella. "I'm glad you decided not to go out. I'm dead, myself. A kimono for the rest of the evening."

Fanny seemed scarcely to hear her. With a nod she left Ella, and entered her own room. There she wasted no time. She threw her hat and coat on the bed. Her suitcase was on the baggage stand. She turned on all the lights, swung the closed suitcase up to the table, shoved the table against the wall, up-ended the suitcase so that its leather side presented a smooth surface, and propped a firm sheet of white cardboard against the impromptu rack. She brought her chair up close, fumbled in her bag for the pens she had just purchased. Her eyes were on the blank white surface of the paper. The table was the kind that has a sub-shelf. It prevented Fanny from crossing her legs under it, and that bothered her. While she fitted her pens, and blocked her paper, she kept on barking her shins in unconscious protest against the uncomfortable conditions under which she must work.

She sat staring at the paper now, after having marked it off into blocks, with a pencil. She got up, and walked across the room, aimlessly, and stood there a moment, and came back. She picked up a thread on the floor. Sat down again. Picked up her pencil, rolled it a moment in her palms, then, catching her toes behind either foreleg of her chair, in an attitude that was as workmanlike as it was ungraceful, she began to draw, nervously, tentatively at first, but gaining in firmness and assurance as she went on.

If you had been standing behind her chair you would have seen, emerging miraculously from the white surface under Fanny's pencil, a thin, undersized little figure in sleazy black and white, whose face, under the cheap hat, was upturned and rapturous. Her skirts were wind-blown, and the wind tugged, too, at the banner whose pole she hugged so tightly in her arms. Dimly you could see the crowds that lined the street on either side. Vaguely, too, you saw the faces and stunted figures of the little group of girls she led. But she, the central figure, stood out among all the rest. Fanny Brandeis, the artist, and Fanny Brandeis, the salesman, combined shrewdly to omit no telling detail. The wrong kind of feet in the wrong kind of shoes; the absurd hat; the shabby skirt—every bit of grotesquerie was there, serving to emphasize the glory of the face. Fanny Brandeis' face, as the figure grew, line by line, was a glorious thing, too.

She was working rapidly. She laid down her pencil, now, and leaned back, squinting her eyes critically. She looked grimly pleased. Her hair was rather rumpled, and her cheeks very pink. She took up her pen, now, and began to ink her drawing with firm black strokes. As she worked a little crow of delight escaped her—the same absurd crow of triumph that had sounded that

day in Winnebago, years and years before, when she, a
school girl in a red tam o' shanter, had caught the
likeness of Schabelitz, the peasant boy, under the exterior of Schabelitz, the famous.

There sounded a smart little double knock at her
door. Fanny did not heed it. She did not hear it. Her
toes were caught behind the chair-legs again. She was
slumped down on the middle of her spine. She had
brought the table, with its ridiculously up-ended suitcase, very near, so that she worked with a minimum of
effort. The door opened. Fanny did not turn her
head. Ella Monahan came in, yawning. She was wearing an expensive looking silk kimono that fell in
straight, simple folds, and gave a certain majesty to
her ample figure.

"Well, what in the world—" she began, and yawned
again, luxuriously. She stopped behind Fanny's chair
and glanced over her shoulder. The yawn died. She
craned her neck a little, and leaned forward. And the
little girl went marching by, in her cheap and crooked
shoes, and her short and sleazy skirt, with the banner
tugging, tugging in the breeze. Fanny Brandeis had
done her with that economy of line, and absence of sentimentality which is the test separating the artist from
the draughtsman.

Silence, except for the scratching of Fanny Brandeis's pen.

"Why—the poor little kike!" said Ella Monahan.
Then, after another moment of silence, "I didn't know
you could draw like that."

Fanny laid down her pen. "Like what?" She pushed
back her chair, and rose, stiffly. The drawing, still wet,
was propped up against the suitcase. Fanny walked
across the room. Ella dropped into her chair, so that
when Fanny came back to the table it was she who
looked over Ella's shoulder. Into Ella's shrewd and
heavy face there had come a certain look.

"They don't get a square deal, do they? They don't get a square deal."

The two looked at the girl a moment longer, in silence. Then Fanny went over to the bed, and picked up her hat and coat. She smoothed her hair, deftly, powdered her nose with care, and adjusted her hat at the smart angle approved by the Galeries Lafayette. She came back to the table, picked up her pen, and beneath the drawing wrote, in large print:

## THE MARCHER.

She picked up the drawing, still wet, opened the door, and with a smile at the bewildered Ella, was gone.

It was after eight o'clock when she reached the *Star* building. She asked for Lasker's office, and sent in her card. Heyl had told her that Lasker was always at his desk at eight. Now, Fanny Brandeis knew that the average young woman, standing outside the office of a man like Lasker, unknown and at the mercy of office boy or secretary, continues to stand outside until she leaves in discouragement. But Fanny knew, too, that she was not an average young woman. She had, on the surface, an air of authority and distinction. She had that quiet assurance of one accustomed to deference. She had youth, and beauty, and charm. She had a hat and suit bought in Paris, France; and a secretary is only human.

Carl Lasker's private office was the bare, bright, newspaper-strewn room of a man who is not only a newspaper proprietor, but a newspaper man. There's a difference. Carl Lasker had sold papers on the street when he was ten. He had slept on burlap sacks, paper stuffed, in the basement of a newspaper office. Ink flowed with the blood in his veins. He could operate a press. He could manipulate a linotype machine (that almost humanly intelligent piece of mechanism). . He

could make up a paper single handed, and had done it.
He knew the newspaper game, did Carl Lasker, from
the composing room to the street, and he was a very
great man in his line. And so he was easy to reach, and
simple to talk to, as are all great men.

A stocky man, decidedly handsome, surprisingly
young, well dressed, smooth shaven, direct.

Fanny entered. Lasker laid down her card. "Brandeis. That's a good name." He extended his hand.
He wore evening clothes, with a white flower in his
buttonhole. He must have just come from a dinner, or
he was to attend a late affair, somewhere. Perhaps
Fanny, taken aback, unconsciously showed her surprise, because Lasker grinned, as he waved her to a
chair. His quick mind had interpreted her thought.

"Sit down, Miss Brandeis. You think I'm gotten up
like the newspaper man in a Richard Harding Davis
short story, don't you? What can I do for you?"

Fanny wasted no words. "I saw the parade this
afternoon. I did a picture. I think it's good. If you
think so too, I wish you'd use it."

She laid it, face up, on Lasker's desk. Lasker picked
it up in his two hands, held it off, and scrutinized it.
All the drama in the world is concentrated in the con-
fines of a newspaper office every day in the year, and
so you hear very few dramatic exclamations in such a
place. Men like Lasker do not show emotion when
impressed. It is too wearing on the mechanism. Besides, they are trained to self-control. So Lasker said,
now:

"Yes, I think it's pretty good, too." Then, raising
his voice to a sudden bellow, "Boy!" He handed the
drawing to a boy, gave a few brief orders, and turned
back to Fanny. "To-morrow morning every other
paper in New York will have pictures showing Mildred
Inness, the beauty, on her snow-white charger, or
Sophronisba A. Bannister, A.B., Ph.D., in her cap and

gown, or Mrs. William Van der Welt as Liberty. We'll
have that little rat with the banner, and it'll get 'em.
They'll talk about it." His eyes narrowed a little.
"Do you always get that angle?"

"Yes."

"There isn't a woman cartoonist in New York who
does that human stuff. Did you know that?"

"Yes."

"Want a job?"

"N-no."

His knowing eye missed no detail of the suit, the hat,
the gloves, the shoes.

"What's your salary now?"

"Ten thousand."

"Satisfied?"

"No."

"You've hit the heart of that parade. I don't know
whether you could do that every day, or not. But if
you struck twelve half the time, it would be enough.
When you want a job, come back."

"Thanks," said Fanny quietly. And held out her
hand.

She returned in the subway. It was a Bronx train,
full of sagging faces, lusterless eyes, grizzled beards; of
heavy, black-eyed girls in soiled white shoes; of stoop-
shouldered men, poring over newspapers in Hebrew
script; of smells and sounds and glaring light.

And though to-morrow would bring its reaction, and
common sense would have her again in its cold grip,
she was radiant to-night and glowing with the exalta-
tion that comes with creation. And over and over a
voice within her was saying:

These are my people! These are my people!

## CHAPTER SIXTEEN

THE ship that brought Theodore Brandeis to America was the last of its kind to leave German ports for years. The day after he sailed from Bremen came the war. Fanny Brandeis was only one of the millions of Americans who refused to accept the idea of war. She took it as a personal affront. It was uncivilized, it was old fashioned, it was inconvenient. Especially inconvenient. She had just come from Europe, where she had negotiated a million-dollar deal. War would mean that she could not get the goods ordered. Consequently there could be no war.

Theodore landed the first week in August. Fanny stole two days from the ravenous bins to meet him in New York. I think she must have been a very love-hungry woman in the years since her mother's death. She had never admitted it. But only emotions denied to the point of starvation could have been so shaken now at the thought of the feast before them. She had trained herself to think of him as Theodore the selfish, Theodore the callous, Theodore the voracious. "An unsuccessful genius," she told herself. "He'll be impossible. They're bad enough when they're successful."

But now her eyes, her thoughts, her longings, her long-pent emotions were straining toward the boat whose great prow was looming toward her, a terrifying bulk. The crowd awaiting the ship was enormous. A dramatic enough scene at any time, the great Hoboken pier this morning was filled with an unrehearsed mob, anxious, thrilled, hysterical. The morning papers had carried wireless news that the ship had been chased by a

French gunboat and had escaped only through the timely warning of the *Dresden,* a German gunboat. That had added the last fillip to an already tense situation. Tears were streaming down half the faces upturned toward the crowded decks. And from every side:

"Do you see her?"

"That's Jessie. There she is! Jessie!"

"Heh! Jim, old boy! Come on down!"

Fanny's eyes were searching the packed rails. "Ted!" she called, and choked back a sob. "Teddy!" Still she did not see him. She was searching, woman-like, for a tall, blondish boy, with a sulky mouth, and humorous eyes, and an unruly lock of hair that would insist on escaping from the rest and straggling down over his forehead. I think she was even looking for a boy with a violin in his arms. A boy in knickers. Women lose all sense of time and proportion at such times. Still she did not see him. The passengers were filing down the gangplank now; rushing down as quickly as the careful hands of the crew would allow them, and hurling themselves into the arms of friends and family crowded below. Fanny strained her eyes toward that narrow passageway, anxious, hopeful, fearful, heartsick. For the moment Olga and the baby did not exist for her. And then she saw him.

She saw him through an unimaginable disguise. She saw him, and knew him in spite of the fact that the fair-haired, sulky, handsome boy had vanished, and in his place walked a man. His hair was close-cropped, German-fashion; his face careworn and older than she had ever thought possible; his bearing, his features, his whole personality stamped with an unmistakable distinction. And his clothes were appallingly, inconceivably German. So she saw him, and he was her brother, and she was his sister, and she stretched out her arms to him.

"Teddy!" She hugged him close, her face buried in his shoulder. "Teddy, you—you *Spitzbube* you!" She laughed at that, a little hysterically. "Not that I know what a *Spitzbube* is, but it's the Germanest word I can think of." That shaven head. Those trousers. That linen. The awful boots. The tie! "Oh, Teddy, and you're the Germanest thing I ever saw." She kissed him again, rapturously.

He kissed her, too, wordlessly at first. They moved aside a little, out of the crowd. Then he spoke for the first time.

"God! I'm glad to see you, Fanny." There was tragedy, not profanation in his voice. His hand gripped hers. He turned, and now, for the first time, Fanny saw that at his elbow stood a buxom, peasant woman, evidently a nurse, and in her arms a child. A child with Molly Brandeis' mouth, and Ferdinand Brandeis' forehead, and Fanny Brandeis' eyes, and Theodore Brandeis' roseleaf skin, and over, and above all these, weaving in and out through the whole, an expression or cast—a vague, undefinable thing which we call a resemblance—that could only have come from the woman of the picture, Theodore Brandeis' wife, Olga.

"Why—it's the baby!" cried Fanny, and swung her out of the nurse's protesting arms. Such a German-looking baby. Such an adorably German-looking baby. "Du kleine, du!" Fanny kissed the roseleaf cheek. "Du süszes—" She turned suddenly to Theodore. "Olga—where's Olga?"

"She did not come."

Fanny tightened her hold of the little squirming bundle in her arms. "Didn't come?"

Theodore shook his head, dumbly. In his eyes was an agony of pain. And suddenly all those inexplicable things in his face were made clear to Fanny. She placed the little Mizzi in the nurse's arms again. "Then we'll go, dear. They won't be a minute over your trunks, I'm sure. Just follow me."

Her arm was linked through Theodore's. Her hand was on his. Her head was up. Her chin was thrust out, and she never knew how startlingly she resembled the Molly Brandeis who used to march so bravely down Norris street on her way to Brandeis' Bazaar. She was facing a situation, and she recognized it. There was about her an assurance, a composure, a blithe capability that imparted itself to the three bewildered and helpless ones in her charge. Theodore felt it, and the strained look in his face began to lift just a little. The heavy-witted peasant woman felt it, and trudged along, cheerfully. The baby in her arms seemed to sense it, and began to converse volubly and unintelligibly with the blue uniformed customs inspector.

They were out of the great shed in an incredibly short time. Fanny seemed equal to every situation. She had taken the tube to Hoboken, but now she found a commodious open car, and drove a shrewd bargain with the chauffeur. She bundled the three into it. Of the three, perhaps Theodore seemed the most bewildered and helpless. He clung to his violin and Fanny.

"I feel like an immigrant," he said. "Fan, you're a wonder. You don't know how much you look and act like mother. I've been watching you. It's startling."

Fanny laughed and took his hand, and held his hand up to her breast, and crushed it there. "And you look like an illustration out of the *Fliegende Blaetter*. It isn't only your clothes. Your face is German. As for Mizzi here—" she gathered the child in her arms again —"you've never explained that name to me. Why, by the way, Mizzi? Of all the names in the world."

Theodore smiled a wry little smile. "Mizzi is named after Olga's chum. You see, in Vienna every other— well, chorus girl I suppose you'd call them—is named

Mizzi. Like all the Gladyses and Flossies here in America. Well, Olga's special friend Mizzi—"

"I see," said Fanny quietly. "Well, anything's better than Fanny. Always did make me think of an old white horse." And at that the small German person in her arms screwed her mouth into a fascinating bunch, and then unscrewed it and, having made these preparations said, "Tante Fanny. Shecago. Tante Fanny."

"Why, Mizzi Brandeis, you darling! Teddy, did you hear that! She said 'Tante Fanny' and 'Chicago' just as plainly!"

"Did I hear it? Have I heard anything else for weeks?"

The plump person on the opposite seat, who had been shaking her head violently all this time here threatened to burst if not encouraged to speak. Fanny nodded to her. Whereupon the flood broke.

"Wunderbar, nicht war! Ich küss' die handt, gnädiges Fraulein." She actually did it, to Fanny's consternation. "Ich hab' ihr das gelernt, Gnädige. Selbst. Ist es nicht ganz entzückend! Tante Fanny. Auch Shecago."

Fanny nodded a number of times, first up and down, signifying assent, then sideways, signifying unbounded wonder and admiration. She made a gigantic effort to summon her forgotten German.

"*Was ist Ihre Name?*" she managed to ask.

"Otti."

"Oh, my!" exclaimed Fanny, weakly. "Mizzi and Otti. It sounds like the first act of the 'Merry Widow.'" She turned to Theodore. "I wish you'd sit back, and relax, and if you must clutch that violin case, do it more comfortably. I don't want you to tell me a thing, now. New York is ghastly in August. We'll get a train out of here to-morrow. My apartment in Chicago is cool, and high, and quiet, and the lake is in the front yard, practically. To-night, perhaps, we'll talk about—things. And, oh, Teddy, how glad I am to see you—to have you—to—" she put out a hand and patted his thin cheek—"to touch you."

And at that the man became a boy again. His face worked a moment, painfully and then his head came down in her lap that held the baby, and so she had them both for a moment, one arm about the child, one hand smoothing the boy's close-cropped hair. And in that moment she was more splendidly maternal than either of the women who had borne these whom she now comforted.

It was Fanny who attended to the hotel rooms, to the baby's comfort, to the railroad tickets, to the ordering of the meals. Theodore was like a stranger in a strange land. Not only that, he seemed dazed.

"We'll have it out to-night," Fanny said to herself. "He'll never get that look off his face until he has told it all. I knew she was a beast."

She made him lie down while she attended to schedules, tickets, berths. She was gone for two hours. When she returned she found him looking amused, terrified and helpless, all at once, while three men reporters and one woman special writer bombarded him with questions. The woman had brought a staff artist with her, and he was now engaged in making a bungling sketch of Theodore's face, with its ludicrous expression.

Fanny sensed the situation and saved it. She hadn't sold goods all these years without learning the value of advertising. She came forward now, graciously (but not too graciously). Theodore looked relieved. Already he had learned that one might lean on this sister who was so capable, so bountifully alive.

"Teddy, you're much too tired to talk. Let me talk for you."

"My sister, Miss Brandeis," said Teddy, and waved a rather feeble hand in an inclusive gesture at the interrogatory five.

Fanny smiled. "Do sit down," she said, "all of you. Tell me, how did you happen to get on my brother's trail?"

One of the men explained. "We had a list of ship's passengers, of course. And we knew that Mr. Brandeis was a German violinist. And then the story of the ship being chased by a French boat. We just missed him down at the pier—"

"But he isn't a German violinist," interrupted Fanny. "Please get that straight. He's American. He is *the* American violinist—or will be, as soon as his concert tour here is well started. It was Schabelitz himself who discovered my brother, and predicted his brilliant career. Here"—she had been glancing over the artist's shoulder—"will you let me make a sketch for you—just for the fun of the thing? I do that kind of thing rather decently. Did you see my picture called 'The Marcher,' in the *Star*, at the time of the suffrage parade in May? Yes, that was mine. Just because he has what we call a butcher haircut, don't think he's German, because he isn't. You wouldn't call Winnebago, Wisconsin, Germany, would you?"

She was sketching him swiftly, daringly, masterfully. She was bringing out the distinction, the suffering, the boyishness in his face, and toning down the queer little foreign air he had. Toning it, but not omitting it altogether. She was too good a showman for that. As she sketched she talked, and as she talked she drew Theodore into the conversation, deftly, and just when he was needed. She gave them what they had come for—a story. And a good one. She brought in Mizzi and Otti, for color, and she saw to it that they spelled those names as they should be spelled. She managed to gloss over the question of Olga. Ill. Detained. Last minute. Too brave to sacrifice her husband's American tour. She finished her sketch and gave it to the woman reporter. It was an amazingly compelling little piece of work—and yet, not so amazing, perhaps, when you consider the thing that Fanny Brandeis had put into it. Then she sent them away, tactfully. They left, knowing all that Fanny Brandeis had wanted them to know; guessing little that she had not wanted them to guess. More than that no human being can accomplish, without the advice of his lawyer.

"Whew!" from Fanny, when the door had closed.

"Gott im Himmel!" from Theodore. "I had forgotten that America was like that."

"But America *is* like that. And Teddy, we're going to make it sit up and take notice."

At that Theodore drooped again. Fanny thought that he looked startlingly as she remembered her father had looked in those days of her childhood, when Brandeis' Bazaar was slithering downhill. The sight of him moved her to a sudden resolve. She crossed swiftly to him, and put one heartening hand on his shoulder.

"Come on, brother. Out with it. Let's have it all now."

He reached up for her hand and held it, desperately. "Oh, Fan!" began Theodore, "Fan, I've been through hell."

Fanny said nothing. She only waited, quietly, encouragingly. She had learned when not to talk. Presently he took up his story, plunging directly into it, as though sensing that she had already divined much.

"She married me for a living. You'll think that's a joke, knowing what I was earning there, in Vienna, and how you and mother were denying yourselves everything to keep me. But in a city that circulates a coin valued at a twentieth of a cent, an American dollar looms up big. Besides, two of the other girls had got married. Good for nothing officers. She was jealous, I suppose. I didn't know any of that. I was flattered to think she'd notice me. She was awfully popular. She has a kind of wit. I suppose you'd call it that.

The other girls were just coarse, and heavy, and—well—animal. You can't know the rottenness of life there in Vienna. Olga could keep a whole supper table laughing all evening. I can see, now, that that isn't difficult when your audience is made up of music hall girls, and stupid, bullet-headed officers, with their damned high collars, and their gold braid, and their silly swords, and their corsets, and their glittering shoes and their miserable petty poverty beneath all the show. I thought I was a lucky boy. I'd have pitied everybody in Winnebago, if I'd ever thought of anybody in Winnebago. I never did, except once in a while of you and mother when I needed money. I kept on with my music. I had sense enough left, for that. Besides, it was a habit, by that time. Well, we were married."

He laughed, an ugly, abrupt little laugh that ended in a moan, and turned his head and buried his face in Fanny's breast. And Fanny's arm was there, about his shoulder. "Fanny, you don't—I can't—" He stopped. Another silence. Fanny's arm tightened its hold. She bent and kissed the top of the stubbly head, bowed so low now. "Fan, do you remember that woman in 'The Three Musketeers'? The hellish woman, that all men loved and loathed? Well, Olga's like that. I'm not whining. I'm not exaggerating. I'm just trying to make you understand. And yet I don't want you to understand. Only you don't know what it means to have you to talk to. To have some one who"—he clutched her hand, fearfully—"You do love me, don't you, Fanny? You do, don't you, Sis?"

"More than any one in the world," Fanny reassured him, quietly. "The way mother would have, if she had lived."

A sigh escaped him, at that, as though a load had lifted from him. He went on, presently. "It would have been all right if I could have earned just a little more money." Fanny shrank at that, and shut her eyes for a sick moment. "But I couldn't. I asked her to be patient. But you don't know the life there. There is no real home life. They live in the cafés. They go there to keep warm, in the winter, and to meet their friends, and gossip, and drink that eternal coffee, and every coffee house—there are thousands—is a rendezvous. We had two rooms, comfortable ones, for Vienna, and I tried to explain to her that if I could work hard, and get into concert, and keep at the composing, we'd be rich some day, and famous, and happy, and she'd have clothes, and jewels. But she was too stupid, or too bored. Olga is the kind of woman who only believes what she sees. Things got worse all the time. She had a temper. So have I—or I used to have. But when hers was aroused it was—horrible. Words that—that —unspeakable words. And one day she taunted me with being a —— with my race. The first time she called me that I felt that I must kill her. That was my mistake. I should have killed her. And I didn't."

"Teddy boy! Don't, brother! You're tired. You're excited and worn out."

"No, I'm not. Just let me talk. I know what I'm saying. There's something clean about killing." He brooded a moment over that thought. Then he went on, doggedly, not raising his voice. His hands were clasped loosely. "You don't know about the intolerance and the anti-Semitism in Prussia, I suppose. All through Germany, for that matter. In Bavaria it's bitter. That's one reason why Olga loathed Munich so. The queer part of it is that all that opposition seemed to fan something in me; something that had been smoldering for a long time." His voice had lost its dull tone now. It had in it a new timbre. And as he talked he began to interlard his English with bits of German, the language to which his tongue had accustomed itself in the past ten years. His sentences, too, took on a German construction, from time to time. He was plainly excited now. "My playing began to improve. There would be a ghastly scene with Olga—sickening— degrading. Then I would go to my work, and I would play, but magnificently! I tell you, it would be playing. I know. To fool myself I know better. One morning, after a dreadful quarrel I got the idea for the concerto, and the psalms. Jewish music. As Jewish as the Kol Nidre. I wanted to express the passion, and fire, and history of a people. My people. Why was that? Tell me. *Selbst, weiss ich nicht.* I felt that if I could put into it just a millionth part of their humiliation, and their glory; their tragedy and their triumph; their sorrow, and their grandeur; their persecution, their *weldtschmerz. Volkschmerz.* That was it. And through it all, weaving in and out, one great underlying motif. Indestructibility. The great cry which says, 'We cannot be destroyed!' "

He stood up, uncertainly. His eyes were blazing. He began to walk up and down the luxurious little room. Fanny's eyes matched his. She was staring at him, fascinated, trembling.

She moistened her lips a little with her tongue. "And you've done it? Teddy! You've done—that!"

Theodore Brandeis stood up, very straight and tall. "Yes," he said, simply. "Yes, I've done that."

She came over to him then, and put her two hands on his shoulders. "Ted—dear—will you ever forgive me? I'll try to make up for it now. I didn't know. I've been blind. Worse than blind. Criminal." She was weeping now, broken-heartedly, and he was patting her with little comforting love pats, and whispering words of tenderness.

"Forgive you? Forgive you what?"

"The years of suffering. The years you've had to spend with her. With that horrible woman—"

"Don't—" He sucked his breath between his teeth. His face had gone haggard again. Fanny, direct as always, made up her mind that she would have it all. And now.

"There's something you haven't told me. Tell me all of it. You're my brother and I'm your sister. We're all we have in the world." And at that, as though timed by some miraculous and supernatural stage manager, there came a cry from the next room; a sleepy, comfortable, imperious little cry. Mizzi had awakened. Fanny made a step in the direction of the door. Then she turned back. "Tell me why Olga didn't come. Why isn't she here with her husband and baby?"

"Because she's with another man."

"Another—"

"It had been going on for a long time. I was the last to know about it. It's that way, always, isn't it? He's an officer. A fool. He'll have to take off his silly corsets now, and his velvet collar, and his shiny boots, and go to war. Damn him! I hope they'll kill him with a hundred bayonets, one by one, and leave him to rot on the field. She had been fooling me all the time, and they had been laughing at me, the two of them. I didn't find it out until just before this American trip. And when I confronted her with it she laughed in my face. She said she hated me. She said she'd rather starve than leave him to come to America with me. She said I was a fiddling fool. She—" he was trembling and sick with the shame of it—"God! I can't tell you the things she said. She wanted to keep Mizzi. Isn't that strange? She loves the baby. She neglects her, and spoils her, and once I saw her beat her, in a rage. But she says she loves my Mizzi, and I believe she does, in her own dreadful way. I promised her, and lied to her, and then I ran away with Mizzi and her nurse."

"Oh, I thank God for that!" Fanny cried. "I thank God for that! And now, Teddy boy, we'll forget all about those miserable years. We'll forget all about her, and the life she led you. You're going to have your chance here. You're going to be repaid for every minute of suffering you've endured. I'll make it up to you. And when you see them applauding you, calling for you, adoring you, all those hideous years will fade from your mind, and you'll be Theodore Brandeis, the successful, Theodore Brandeis, the gifted, Theodore Brandeis, the great! You need never think of her again. You'll never see her again. That beast! That woman!"

And at that Theodore's face became distorted and dreadful with pain. He raised two impotent, shaking arms high above his head. "That's just it! That's just it! You don't know what love is. You don't know what hate is. You don't know how I hate myself. Loathe myself. She's all that's miserable, all that's unspeakable, all that's vile. And if she called me to-day I'd come. That's it." He covered his shamed face with his two hands, so that the words came from him slobberingly, sickeningly. "I hate her! I hate her! And I want her. I want her. I want her!"

## CHAPTER SEVENTEEN

IF Fanny Brandeis, the deliberately selfish, the calculatingly ambitious, was aghast at the trick fate had played her, she kept her thoughts to herself. Knowing her, I think she must have been grimly amused at finding herself saddled with a helpless baby, a bewildered peasant woman, and an artist brother both helpless and bewildered.

It was out of the question to house them in her small apartment. She found a furnished apartment near her own, and installed them there, with a working housekeeper in charge. She had a gift for management, and she arranged all these details with a brisk capability that swept everything before it. A sunny bedroom for Mizzi. But then, a bright living room, too, for Theodore's hours of practice. No noise. Chicago's roar maddened him. Otti shied at every new contrivance that met her eye. She had to be broken in to elevators, electric switches, hot and cold faucets, radiators.

"No apartment ever built could cover all the requirements," Fanny confided to Fenger, after the first harrowing week. "What they really need is a combination palace, houseboat, sanatorium, and crêche."

"Look here," said Fenger. "If I can help, why—" a sudden thought struck him. "Why don't you bring 'em all down to my place in the country? We're not there half the time. It's too cool for my wife in September. Just the thing for the child, and your brother could fiddle his head off."

The Fengers had a roomy, wide-verandaed house

275

near Lake Forest; one of the many places of its kind
that dot the section known as the north shore. Its lawn
sloped gently down to the water's edge. The house was
gay with striped awnings, and scarlet geraniums, and
chintz-covered chairs. The bright, sparkling, luxurious little place seemed to satisfy a certain beauty-sense
in Fenger, as did the etchings on the walls in his office.
Fanny had spent a week-end there in July, with three
or four other guests, including Fascinating Facts. She
had been charmed with it, and had announced that her
energies thereafter would be directed solely toward the
possession of just such a house as this, with a lawn
that was lipped by the lake, awnings and geraniums
to give it a French café air; books and magazines
enough to belie that.

"And I'll always wear white," she promised, gayly,
"and there'll be pitchers on every table, frosty on the
outside, and minty on the inside, and you're all invited."

They had laughed at that, and so had she, but she
had been grimly in earnest just the same.

She shook her head now at Fenger's suggestion.
"Imagine Mrs. Fenger's face at sight of Mizzi, and
Theodore with his violin, and Otti with her shawls and
paraphernalia. Though," she added, seriously, "it's
mighty kind of you, and generous—and just like a
man."

"It isn't kindness nor generosity that makes me want
to do things for you."

"Modest," murmured Fanny, wickedly, "as always."

Fenger bent his look upon her. "Don't try the
ingénue on me, Fanny."

Theodore's manager, Kurt Stein, was to have followed him in ten days. The war changed that. The
war was to change many things. Fanny seemed to
sense the influx of musicians that was to burst upon the
United States following the first few weeks of the catas-
trophe, and she set about forestalling it. Advertising.

That was what Theodore needed. She had faith enough in his genius. But her business sense told her that this genius must be enhanced by the proper setting. She set about creating this setting. She overlooked no chance to fix his personality in the kaleidoscopic mind of the American public—or as much of it as she could reach. His publicity man was a dignified German-American whose methods were legitimate and uninspired. Fanny's enthusiasm and superb confidence in Theodore's genius infected Fenger, Fascinating Facts, even Nathan Haynes himself. Nathan Haynes had never posed as a patron of the arts, in spite of his fantastic millions. But by the middle of September there were few of his friends, or his wife's friends, who had not heard of this Theodore Brandeis. In Chicago, Illinois, no one lives in houses, it is said, except the city's old families, and new millionaires. The rest of the vast population is flat-dwelling. To say that Nathan Haynes' spoken praise reached the city's house-dwellers would carry with it a significance plain to any Chicagoan.

As for Fanny's method; here is a typical example of her somewhat crude effectiveness in showmanship. Otti had brought with her from Vienna her native peasant costume. It is a costume seen daily in the Austrian capital, on the Ring, in the Stadt Park, wherever Viennese nurses convene with their small charges. To the American eye it is a musical comedy costume, picturesque, bouffant, amazing. Your Austrian takes it quite for granted. Regardless of the age of the nurse, the skirt is short, coming a few inches below the knees, and built like a lamp shade, in color usually a bright scarlet, with rows of black velvet ribbon at the bottom. Beneath it are worn skirts and skirts, and skirts, so that the opera-bouffe effect is complete. The bodice is black velvet, laced over a chemise of white. The head-gear a soaring wingèd affair of stiffly starched white, that is a pass between the Breton peasant woman's cap and an aeroplane. Black stockings and slippers finish the costume.

Otti and Mizzi spent the glorious September days in Lincoln park, Otti garbed in staid American stripes and apron, Mizzi resplendent in smartest of children's dresses provided for her lavishly by her aunt. Her fat and dimpled hands smoothed the blue, or pink or white folds with a complacency astonishing in one of her years. "That's her mother in her," Fanny thought.

One rainy autumn day Fanny entered her brother's apartment to find Otti resplendent in her Viennese nurse's costume. Mizzi had been cross and fretful, and the sight of the familiar scarlet and black and white, and the great wingèd cap seemed to soothe her.

"Otti!" Fanny exclaimed. "You gorgeous creature! What is it? A dress rehearsal?" Otti got the import, if not the English.

"So gehen wir im Wien," she explained, and struck a killing pose.

"Everybody? All the nurses? Alle?"

"Aber sure," Otti displayed her half dozen English words whenever possible.

Fanny stared a moment. Her eyes narrowed thoughtfully. "To-morrow's Saturday," she said, in German. "If it's fair and warm you put on that costume and take Mizzi to the park. . . . Certainly the animal cages, if you want to. If any one annoys you, come home. If a policeman asks you why you are dressed that way tell him it is the costume worn by nurses in Vienna. Give him your name. Tell him who your master is. If he doesn't speak German—and he won't, in Chicago—some one will translate for you."

Not a Sunday paper in Chicago that did not carry a startling picture of the resplendent Otti and the dimpled and smiling Mizzi. The omnipresent staff photographer seemed to sniff his victim from afar. He pounced on Theodore Brandeis' baby daughter, accompanied by her Viennese nurse (in costume) and he played her up in a Sunday special that was worth thousands of dollars, Fanny assured the bewildered and resentful Theodore, as he floundered wildly through the billowing waves of the Sunday newspaper flood.

Theodore's first appearance was to be in Chicago as soloist with the Chicago Symphony Orchestra, in the season's opening program in October. Any music-wise Chicagoan will tell you that the Chicago Symphony Orchestra is not only a musical organization functioning marvelously (when playing Beethoven). It is an institution. Its patrons will admit the existence, but not the superiority of similar organizations in Boston, Philadelphia and New York. On Friday afternoons, during the season, Orchestra Hall, situate on Michigan Boulevard, holds more pretty girls and fewer men than one might expect to see at any one gathering other than, perhaps, a wholesale debutante tea crush. A Friday afternoon ticket is as impossible of attainment for one not a subscriber as a seat in heaven for a sinner. Saturday night's audience is staider, more masculine, less staccato. Gallery, balcony, parquet, it represents the city's best. Its men prefer Beethoven to Berlin. Its women could wear pearl necklaces, and don't. Between the audience and the solemn black-and-white rows on the platform there exists an *entente cordiale*. The Konzert-Meister bows to his friend in the third row, as he tucks his violin under his chin. The fifth row, aisle, smiles and nods to the sausage-fingered 'cellist.

"Fritz is playing well to-night."

In a rarefied form, it is the atmosphere that existed between audience and players in the days of the old and famous Daly stock company.

Such was the character of the audience Theodore was to face on his first appearance in America. Fanny explained its nature to him. He shrugged his shoulders in a gesture as German as it was expressive.

Theodore seemed to have become irrevocably German during the years of his absence from America. He had a queer stock of little foreign tricks. He lifted his hat to men acquaintances on the street. He had learned to smack his heels smartly together and to bow stiffly from the waist, and to kiss the hand of the matrons—and they adored him for it. He was quite innocent of pose in these things. He seemed to have imbibed them, together with his queer German haircut, and his incredibly German clothes.

Fanny allowed him to retain the bow, and the courtly hand-kiss, but she insisted that he change the clothes and the haircut.

"You'll have to let it grow, Ted. I don't mean that I want you to have a mane, like Ysaye. But I do think you ought to discard that convict cut. Besides, it isn't becoming. And if you're going to be an American violinist you'll have to look it—with a foreign finish."

He let his hair grow. Fanny watched with interest for the appearance of the unruly lock which had been wont to straggle over his white forehead in his schoolboy days. The new and well-cut American clothes effected surprisingly little change. Fanny, surveying him, shook her head.

"When you stepped off the ship you looked like a German in German clothes. Now you look like a German in American clothes. I don't know—I do believe it's your face, Ted. I wouldn't have thought that ten years or so in any country could change the shape of one's nose, and mouth and cheekbones. Do you suppose it's the umlauts?"

"Cut it out!" laughed Ted, that being his idea of modern American slang. He was fascinated by these crisp phrases, but he was ten years or so behind the times, and he sometimes startled his hearers by an exhibition of slang so old as to be almost new. It was all the more startling in contrast with his conversational English, which was as carefully correct as a born German's.

As for the rest, it was plain that he was interested, but unhappy. He practiced for hours daily. He often took Mizzi to the park and came back storming about the dirt, the noise, the haste, the rudeness, the crowds, the mismanagement of the entire city. *Dummheit*, he called it. They profaned the lake. They allowed the people to trample the grass. They threw papers and banana skins about. And they wasted! His years in Germany had taught him to regard all these things as sacrilege, and the last as downright criminal. He was lonesome for his Germany. That was plain. He hated it, and loved it, much as he hated and loved the woman who had so nearly spoiled his life. The maelstrom known as the southwest corner of State and Madison streets appalled him.

"Gott!" he exclaimed. "Es ist unglaublich! Aber ganz unglaublich! Ich werde bald verückt." He somehow lapsed into German when excited.

Fanny took him to the Haynes-Cooper plant one day, and it left him dazed, and incredulous. She quoted millions at him. He was not interested. He looked at the office workers, the mail-room girls, and shook his head, dumbly. They were using bicycles now, with a bundle rack in the front, in the vast stock rooms, and the roller skates had been discarded as too slow. The stock boys skimmed around corners on these lightweight bicycles, up one aisle, and down the next, snatching bundles out of bins, shooting bundles into bins, as expertly as players in a gymkhana.

Theodore saw the uncanny rapidity with which the letter-opening machines did their work. He watched the great presses that turned out the catalogue—the catalogue whose message meant millions; he sat in Fenger's office and stared at the etchings, and said, "Certainly," with politeness, when Fenger excused himself in the midst of a conversation to pick up the telephone receiver and talk to their shoe factory in Maine. He ended up finally in Fanny's office, no longer a dingy and undesirable corner, but a quietly brisk center that sent out vibrations over the entire plant. Slosson, incidentally, was no longer of the infants' wear. He had been transferred to a subordinate position in the grocery section.

"Well," said Fanny, seating herself at her desk, and smiling radiantly upon her brother. "Well, what do you think of us?"

And then Theodore Brandeis, the careless, the selfish, the blind, said a most amazing thing.

"Fanny, I'll work. I'll soon get some of these millions that are lying about everywhere in this country. And then I'll take you out of this. I promise you."

Fanny stared at him, a picture of ludicrous astonishment.

"Why, you talk as if you were—sorry for me!"

"I am, dear. God knows I am. I'll make it up to you, somehow."

It was the first time in all her dashing and successful career that Fanny Brandeis had felt the sting of pity. She resented it, hotly. And from Theodore, the groper, the— "But at any rate," something within her said, "he has always been true to himself."

Theodore's manager arrived in September, on a Holland boat, on which he had been obliged to share a stuffy inside cabin with three others. Kurt Stein was German born, but American bred, and he had the American love of luxurious travel. He was still testy when he reached Chicago and his charge.

"How goes the work?" he demanded at once, of Theodore. He eyed him sharply. "That's better. You have lost some of the look you had when you left Wien. The ladies would have liked that look, here in America. But it is bad for the work."

He took Fanny aside before he left. His face was serious. It was plain that he was disturbed. "That woman," he began. "Pardon me, Mrs. Brandeis. She came to me. She says she is starving. She is alone there, in Vienna. Her—well, she is alone. The war is everywhere. They say it will last for years. She wept and pleaded with me to take her here."

"No!" cried Fanny. "Don't let him hear it. He mustn't know. He——"

"Yes, I know. She is a paradox, that woman. I tell you, she almost prevailed on me. There is something about her; something that repels and compels." That struck him as being a very fine phrase indeed, and he repeated it appreciatively.

"I'll send her money, somehow," said Fanny.

"Yes. But they say that money is not reaching them over there. I don't know what becomes of it. It vanishes." He turned to leave. "Oh, a message for you. On my boat was Schabelitz. It looks very much as if his great fortune, the accumulation of years, would be swept away by this war. Already they are tramping up and down his lands in Poland. His money—much of it—is invested in great hotels in Poland and Russia, and they are using them for barracks and hospitals."

"Schabelitz! You mean a message for Theodore? From him? That's wonderful."

"For Theodore, and for you, too."

"For me! I made a picture of him once when I was a little girl. I didn't see him again for years. Then I heard him play. It was on his last tour here. I wanted to speak to him. But I was afraid. And my face was red with weeping."

"He remembers you. And he means to see Theodore and you. He can do much for Theodore in this country, and I think he will. His message for you was this: 'Tell her I still have the picture that she made of me, with the jack-in-the-box in my hand, and that look on my face. Tell her I have often wondered about that little girl in the red cap and the black curls. I've wondered if she went on, catching that look back of people's faces. If she did, she should be more famous than her brother.' "

"He said that! About me!"

"I am telling you as nearly as I can. He said, 'Tell her it was a woman who ruined Bauer's career, and caused him to end his days a music teacher in—in— Gott! I can't remember the name of that town——"

"Winnebago."

"Winnebago. That was it. 'Tell her not to let the brother spoil his life that way.' So. That is the message. He said you would understand."

Theodore's face was ominous when she returned to him, after Stein had left.

"I wish you and Stein wouldn't stand out there in the hall whispering about me as if I were an idiot patient. What were you saying?"

"Nothing, Ted. Really."

He brooded a moment. Then his face lighted up with a flash of intuition. He flung an accusing finger at Fanny.

"He has seen her."

"Ted! You promised."

"She's in trouble. This war. And she hasn't any money. I know. Look here. We've got to send her money. Cable it."

"I will. Just leave it all to me."

"If she's here, in this country, and you're lying to me——"

"She isn't. My word of honor, Ted."

He relaxed.

Life was a very complicated thing for Fanny these

days. Ted was leaning on her; Mizzi, Otti, and now
Fenger. Nathan Haynes was poking a disturbing finger into that delicate and complicated mechanism of
System which Fenger had built up in the Haynes-Cooper plant. And Fenger, snarling, was trying to guard
his treasure. He came to Fanny with his grievance.
Fanny had always stimulated him, reassured him, given
him the mental readjustment that he needed.

He strode into her office one morning in late September. Ordinarily he sent for her. He stood by her
desk now, a sheaf of papers in his hand, palpably stage
props, and lifted significant eyebrows in the direction
of the stenographer busy at her typewriter in the corner.

"You may leave that, Miss Mahin," Fanny said.
Miss Mahin, a comprehending young woman, left it,
and the room as well. Fenger sat down. He was under
great excitement, though he was quite controlled.
Fanny, knowing him, waited quietly. His eyes held
hers.

"It's come," Fenger began. "You know that for the
last year Haynes has been milling around with a herd
of sociologists, philanthropists, and students of economics. He had some scheme in the back of his head,
but I thought it was just another of his impractical
ideas. It appears that it wasn't. Between the lot of
them they've evolved a savings and profit-sharing plan
that's founded on a kind of practical universal brotherhood dream. Haynes's millions are bothering him. If
they actually put this thing through I'll get out. It'll
mean that everything I've built up will be torn down.
It will mean that any six-dollar-a-week girl——"

"As I understand it," interrupted Fanny, "it will
mean that there will be no more six-dollar-a-week
girls."

"That's it. And let me tell you, once you get the
ignorant, unskilled type to believing they're actually

capable of earning decent money, actually worth something, they're worse than useless. They're dangerous."

"You don't believe that."

"I do."

"But it's a theory that belongs to the Dark Ages. We've disproved it. We've got beyond that."

"Yes. So was war. We'd got beyond it. But it's here. I tell you, there are only two classes: the governing and the governed. That has always been true. It always will be. Let the Socialists rave. It has never got them anywhere. I know. I come from the mucker class myself. I know what they stand for. Boost them, and they'll turn on you. If there's anything in any of them, he'll pull himself up by his own bootstraps."

"They're not all potential Fengers."

"Then let 'em stay what they are."

Fanny's pencil was tracing and retracing a tortured and meaningless figure on the paper before her. "Tell me, do you remember a girl named Sarah Sapinsky?"

"Never heard of her."

"That's fitting. Sarah Sapinsky was a very pretty, very dissatisfied girl who was a slave to the bundle chute. One day there was a period of two seconds when a bundle didn't pop out at her, and she had time to think. Anyway, she left. I asked about her. She's on the streets."

"Well?"

"Thanks to you and your system."

"Look here, Fanny. I didn't come to you for that kind of talk. Don't, for heaven's sake, give me any sociological drivel to-day. I'm not here just to tell you my troubles. You know what my contract is here with Haynes-Cooper. And you know the amount of stock I hold. If this scheme of Haynes's goes in, I go out. Voluntarily. But at my own price. The

Haynes-Cooper plant is at the height of its efficiency now." He dropped his voice. "But the mail order business is in its infancy. There's no limit to what can be done with it in the next few years. Understand? Do you get what I'm trying to tell you?" He leaned forward, tense and terribly in earnest.

Fanny stared at him. Then her hand went to her head in a gesture of weariness. "Not to-day. Please. And not here. Don't think I'm ungrateful for your confidence. But—this month has been a terrific strain. Just let me pass the fifteenth of October. Let me see Theodore on the way——"

Fenger's fingers closed about her wrist. Fanny got to her feet angrily. They glared at each other a moment. Then the humor of the picture they must be making struck Fanny. She began to laugh. Fenger's glare became a frown. He turned abruptly and left the office. Fanny looked down at her wrist ruefully. Four circlets of red marked its smooth whiteness. She laughed again, a little uncertainly this time.

When she got home that night she found, in her mail, a letter for Theodore, postmarked Vienna, and stamped with the mark of the censor. Theodore had given her his word of honor that he would not write Olga, or give her his address. Olga was risking Fanny's address. She stood looking at the letter now. Theodore was coming in for dinner, as he did five nights out of the week. As she stood in the hallway, she heard the rattle of his key in the lock. She flew down the hall and into her bedroom, her letters in her hand. She opened her dressing table drawer and threw them into it, switched on the light and turned to face Theodore in the doorway.

" 'Lo, Sis."

"Hello, Teddy. Kiss me. Phew! That pipe again. How'd the work go to-day?"

"So—so. Any mail for me?"

"No."

That night, when he had gone, she took out the letter and stood turning it over and over in her hands. She had no thought of reading it. It was its destruction she was contemplating. Finally she tucked it away in her handkerchief box. Perhaps, after the fifteenth of October. Everything depended on that.

And the fifteenth of October came. It had dragged for weeks, and then, at the end, it galloped. By that time Fanny had got used to seeing Theodore's picture and name outside Orchestra Hall, and in the musical columns of the papers. Brandeis. Theodore Brandeis, the violinist. The name sang in her ears. When she walked on Michigan Avenue during that last week she would force herself to march straight on past Orchestra Hall, contenting herself with a furtive and oblique glance at the announcement board. The advance programs hung, a little bundle of them, suspended by a string from a nail on the wall near the box office, so that ticket purchasers might rip one off and peruse the week's musical menu. Fanny longed to hear the comment of the little groups that were constantly forming and dispersing about the box office window. She never dreamed of allowing herself to hover near it. She thought sometimes of the woman in the businesslike gray skirt and the black sateen apron who had drudged so cheerfully in the little shop so that Theodore Brandeis' name might shine now from the very top of the program, in heavy black letters:

### Soloist: MR. THEODORE BRANDEIS, Violin.

The injustice of it. Fanny had never ceased to rage at that.

In the years to come Theodore Brandeis was to have that adulation which the American public, temperamentally so cold, gives its favorite, once the ice of its reserve is thawed. He was to look down on that surging, tempestuous crowd which sometimes packs itself about the foot of the platform in Carnegie Hall, demanding more, more, more, after a generous concert is concluded. He had to learn to protect himself from those hysterical, enraptured, wholly feminine adorers who swarmed about him, scaling the platform itself. But of all this there was nothing on that Friday and Saturday in October. Orchestra Hall audiences are not, as a rule, wildly demonstrative. They were no exception. They listened attentively, appreciatively. They talked, critically and favorably, on the way home. They applauded generously. They behaved as an Orchestra Hall audience always behaves, and would behave, even if it were confronted with a composite Elman-Kreisler-Ysaye soloist. Theodore's playing was, as a whole, perhaps the worst of his career. Not that he did not rise to magnificent heights at times. But it was what is known as uneven playing. He was torn emotionally, nervously, mentally. His playing showed it.

Fanny, seated in the auditorium, her hands clasped tight, her heart hammering, had a sense of unreality as she waited for Theodore to appear from the little door at the left. He was to play after the intermission. Fanny had arrived late, with Theodore, that Friday afternoon. She felt she could not sit through the first part of the program. They waited together in the anteroom. Theodore, looking very slim and boyish in his frock coat, walked up and down, up and down. Fanny wanted to straighten his tie. She wanted to pick an imaginary thread off his lapel. She wanted to adjust the white flower in his buttonhole (he jerked it out presently, because it interfered with his violin, he said). She wanted to do any one of the foolish, futile things that would have served to relieve her own surcharged feelings. But she had learned control in these years. And she yielded to none of them.

The things they said and did were, perhaps, almost ludicrous.

"How do I look?" Theodore demanded, and stood up before her.

"Beautiful!" said Fanny, and meant it.

Theodore passed a hand over his cheek. "Cut myself shaving, damn it!"

"It doesn't show."

He resumed his pacing. Now and then he stopped, and rubbed his hands together with a motion we use in washing. Finally:

"I wish you'd go out front," he said, almost pettishly. Fanny rose, without a word. She looked very handsome. Excitement had given her color. The pupils of her eyes were dilated and they shone brilliantly. She looked at her brother. He stared at her. They swayed together. They kissed, and clung together for a long moment. Then Fanny turned and walked swiftly away, and stumbled a little as she groped for the stairway.

The bell in the foyer rang. The audience strolled to the auditorium. They lagged, Fanny thought. They crawled. She told herself that she must not allow her nerves to tease her like that. She looked about her, with outward calm. Her eyes met Fenger's. He was seated, alone. It was he who had got a subscription seat for her from a friend. She had said she preferred to be alone. She looked at him now and he at her, and they did not nod nor smile. The house settled itself flutteringly.

A man behind Fanny spoke. "Who's this Brandeis?"

"I don't know. A new one. German, I guess. They say he's good. Kreisler's the boy who can play for me, though."

The orchestra was seated now. Stock, the conductor, came out from the little side door. Behind him walked Theodore. There was a little, impersonal burst of applause. Stock mounted his conductor's platform and glanced paternally down at Theodore, who stood at the left, violin and bow in hand, bowing. The audience seemed to warm to his boyishness. They applauded again, and he bowed in a little series of jerky bobs that waggled his coat-tails. Heels close together, knees close together. A German bow. And then a polite series of bobs addressed to Stock and his orchestra. Stock's long, slim hands poised in air. His fingertips seemed to draw from the men before him the first poignant strains of Theodore's concerto. Theodore stood, slim and straight. Fanny's face, lifted toward him, was a prayerful thing. Theodore suddenly jerked back the left lapel of his coat in a little movement Fanny remembered as typical in his boyish days, nuzzled his violin tenderly, and began to play.

It is the most excruciating of instruments, the violin, or the most exquisite. I think Fanny actually heard very little of his playing. Her hands were icy. Her cheeks were hot. The man before her was not Theodore Brandeis, the violinist, but Teddy, the bright-haired, knickered schoolboy who played to those people seated in the yellow wooden pews of the temple in Winnebago. The years seemed to fade away. He crouched over his violin to get the 'cello tones for which he was to become famous, and it was the same hunched, almost awkward pose that the boy had used. Fanny found herself watching his feet as his shifted his position. He was nervous. And he was not taken out of himself. She knew that because she saw the play of his muscles about the jaw-bone. It followed that he was not playing his best. She could not tell that from listening to him. Her music sense was dulled. She got it from these outward signs. The woman next to her was reading a program absorbedly, turning the pages regularly, and with care. Fanny could have killed her with her two hands. She tried to listen detachedly. The music was familiar to her. Theodore had played it for her, again and again. The last movement had never failed to shake her emotionally. It was the glorious and triumphant cry of a people tried and unafraid. She heard it now, unmoved.

And then Theodore was bowing his little jerky bows, and he was shaking hands with Stock, and with the First Violin. He was gone. Fanny sat with her hands in her lap. The applause continued. Theodore appeared again. Bowed. He bent very low now, with his arms hanging straight. There was something gracious and courtly about him. And foreign. He must keep that, Fanny thought. They like it. She saw him off again. More applause. Encores were against the house rules. She knew that. Then it meant they were pleased. He was to play again. A group of Hungarian dances this time. They were wild, gypsy things, rising to frenzy at times. He played them with spirit and poetry. To listen sent the blood singing through the veins. Fanny found herself thinking clearly and exaltedly.

"This is what my mother drudged for, and died for, and it was worth it. And you must do the same, if necessary. Nothing else matters. What he needs now is luxury. He's worn out with fighting. Ease. Peace. Leisure. You've got to give them to him. It's no use, Fanny. You lose."

In that moment she reached a mark in her spiritual career that she was to outdistance but once.

Theodore was bowing again. Fanny had scarcely realized that he had finished. The concert was over.

" . . . the group of dances," the man behind her was saying as he helped the girl next him with her coat, "but I didn't like that first thing. Church music, not concert."

Fanny found her way back to the ante-room. Theodore was talking to the conductor, and one or two others. He looked tired, and his eyes found Fanny's

with appeal and relief in them. She came over to him.
There were introductions, congratulations. Fanny
slipped her hand over his with a firm pressure.

"Come, dear. You must be tired."

At the door they found Fenger waiting. Theodore
received his well-worded congratulations with an ill-
concealed scowl.

"My car's waiting," said Fenger. "Won't you let
me take you home?"

A warning pressure from Theodore. "Thanks, no.
We have a car. Theodore's very tired."

"I can quite believe that."

"Not tired," growled Theodore, like a great boy.
"I'm hungry. Starved. I never eat before playing."

Kurt Stein, Theodore's manager, had been hovering
over him solicitously. "You must remember to-morrow night. I should advise you to rest now, as quickly
as possible." He, too, glared at Fenger.

Fenger fell back, almost humbly. "I've great news
for you. I must see you Sunday. After this is over.
I'll telephone you. Don't try to come to work to-morrow." All this is a hurried aside to Fanny.

Fanny nodded and moved away with Theodore.

Theodore leaned back in the car, but there was no
hint of relaxation. He was as tense and vibrant as one
of his own violin strings.

"It went, didn't it? They're like clods, these American audiences." It was on the tip of Fanny's tongue
to say that he had professed indifference to audiences,
but she wisely refrained. "Gad! I'm hungry. What
makes this Fenger hang around so? I'm going to tell
him to keep away, some day. The way he stares at
you. Let's go somewhere to-night, Fan. Or have
some people in. I can't sit about after I've played.
Olga always used to have a supper party, or something."

"All right, Ted. Would you like the theater?"

For the first time in her life she felt a little whisper of sympathy for the despised Olga. Perhaps, after all, she had not been wholly to blame.

He was to leave Sunday morning for Cleveland, where he would play Monday. He had insisted on taking Mizzi with him, though Fanny had railed and stormed. Theodore had had his way.

"She's used to it. She likes to travel, don't you, Mizzi? You should have seen her in Russia, and all over Germany, and in Sweden. She's a better traveler than her dad."

Saturday morning's papers were kind, but cool. They used words such as promising, uneven, overambitious, gifted. Theodore crumpled the lot into a ball and hurled them across the room, swearing horribly. Then he smoothed them out, clipped them, and saved them carefully. His playing that night was tinged with bravado, and the Saturday evening audience rose to it. There was about his performance a glow, a spirit that had been lacking on the previous day.

Inconsistently enough, he missed the antagonism of the European critics. He was puzzled and resentful.

"They hardly say a word about the meaning of the concerto. They accept it as a piece of music, Jewish in theme. It might as well be entitled Springtime."

"This isn't France or Russia," said Fanny. "Antagonism here isn't religious. It's personal, almost. You've been away so many years you've forgotten. They don't object to us as a sect, or a race, but as a type. That's the trouble, Clarence Heyl says. We're free to build as many synagogues as we like, and worship in them all day, if we want to. But we don't want to. The struggle isn't racial any more, but individual. For some reason or other one flashy, loud-talking Hebrew in a restaurant can cause more ill feeling than ten thousand of them holding a religious mass meeting in Union Square."

Theodore pondered a moment. "Then here each one of us is responsible. Is that it?"

"I suppose so."

"But look here. I've been here ten weeks, and I've met your friends, and not one of them is a Jew. How's that?"

Fanny flushed a little. "Oh, it just worked out that way."

Theodore looked at her hard. "You mean you worked it out that way?"

"Yes."

"Fan, we're a couple of weaklings, both of us, to have sprung from a mother like ours. I don't know which is worse; my selfishness, or yours." Then, at the hurt that showed in her face, he was all contrition. "Forgive me, Sis. You've been so wonderful to me, and to Mizzi, and to all of us. I'm a good-for-nothing fiddler, that's all. You're the strong one."

Fenger had telephoned her on Saturday. He and his wife were at their place in the country. Fanny was to take the train out there Sunday morning. She looked forward to it with a certain relief. The weather had turned unseasonably warm, as Chicago Octobers sometimes do. Up to the last moment she had tried to shake Theodore's determination to take Mizzi and Otti with him. But he was stubborn.

"I've got to have her," he said.

Michael Fenger's voice over the telephone had been as vibrant with suppressed excitement as Michael Fenger's dry, hard tones could be.

"Fanny, it's done—finished," he said. "We had a meeting to-day. This is my last month with Haynes-Cooper."

"But you can't mean it. Why, you *are* Haynes-Cooper. How can they let you go?"

"I can't tell you now. We'll go over it all to-morrow. I've new plans. They've bought me out. D'you see? At a price that—well, I thought I'd got used to juggling millions at Haynes-Cooper. But this surprised even me. Will you come? Early? Take the eight-ten."

"That's too early. I'll get the ten."

The mid-October country was a lovely thing. Fanny, with the strain of Theodore's début and leave-taking behind her, and the prospect of a high-tension business talk with Fenger ahead, drank in the beauty of the wayside woods gratefully.

Fenger met her at the station. She had never seen him so boyish, so exuberant. He almost pranced.

"Hop in," he said. He had driven down in a runabout. "Brother get off all right? Gad! He *can* play. And you've made the whole thing possible." He turned to look at her. "You're a wonder."

"In your present frame of mind and state of being," laughed Fanny, "you'd consider any one a wonder. You're so pleased with yourself you're fairly gummy."

Fenger laughed softly and sped the car on. They turned in at the gate. There was scarlet salvia, now, to take the place of the red geraniums. The gay awnings, too, were gone.

"This is our last week," Fenger explained. "It's too cold out here for Katherine. We're moving into town to-morrow. We're more or less camping out here, with only the Jap to take care of us."

"Don't apologize, please. I'm grateful just to be here, after the week I've had. Let's have the news now."

"We'll have lunch first. I'm afraid you'll have to excuse Katherine. She probably won't be down for lunch." The Jap had spread the luncheon table on the veranda, but a brisk lake breeze had sprung up, and he was busy now transferring his table from the porch to the dining room. "Would you have believed it," said Fenger, "when you left town? Good old lake. Mrs. Fenger coming down?" to the man.

The Jap shook his head. "Nossa."

Their talk at luncheon was all about Theodore and his future. Fenger said that what Theodore needed was a firm and guiding hand. "A sort of combination manager and slave-driver. An ambitious and intelligent wife would do it. That's what we all need. A woman to work for, and to make us work."

Fanny smiled. "Mizzi will have to be woman enough, I'm afraid. Poor Ted."

They rose. "Now for the talk," said Fenger. But the telephone had sounded shrilly a moment before, and the omnipresent little Jap summoned Fenger. He was back in a minute, frowning. "It's Haynes. I'm sorry. I'm afraid it'll take a half hour of telephoning. Don't you want to take a cat-nap? Or a stroll down to the lake?"

"Don't bother about me. I'll probably take a run outdoors."

"Be back in half an hour."

But when she returned he was still at the telephone. She got a book and stretched luxuriously among the cushions of one of the great lounging chairs, and fell asleep. When she awoke Fenger was seated opposite her. He was not reading. He was not smoking. He evidently had been sitting there, looking at her.

"Oh, gracious! Mouth open?"

"No."

Fanny fought down an impulse to look as cross as she felt. "What time? Why didn't you wake me?" The house was very quiet. She patted her hair deftly, straightened her collar. "Where's everybody? Isn't Mrs. Fenger down yet?"

"No. Don't you want to hear about my plans now?"

"Of course I do. That's what I came for. I don't

see why you didn't tell me hours ago. You're as slow in action as a Chinese play. Out with it."

Fenger got up and began to pace the floor, not excitedly, but with an air of repression. He looked very powerful and compelling, there in the low-ceilinged, luxurious room. "I'll make it brief. We met yesterday in Haynes's office. Of course we had discussed the thing before. You know that. Haynes knew that I'd never run the plant under the new conditions. Why, it would kill every efficiency rule I've ever made. Here I had trimmed that enormous plant down to fighting weight. There wasn't a useless inch or ounce about the whole enormous billionaire bulk of it. And then to have Haynes come along, with his burdensome notions, and his socialistic slop. They'd cripple any business, no matter how great a start it had. I told him all that. We didn't waste much time on argument, though. We knew we'd never get together. In half an hour we were talking terms. You know my contract and the amount of stock I hold. Well, we threshed that out, and Haynes is settling for two million and a half."

He came to a stop before Fanny's chair.

"Two million and a half what?" asked Fanny, feebly.

"Dollars." He smiled rather grimly. "In a check."

"One—check?"

"One check."

Fanny digested that in her orderly mind. "I thought I was used to thinking in millions. But this—I'd like to touch the check, just once."

"You shall." He drew up a chair near her. "Now get this, Fanny. There's nothing that you and I can't do with two millions and a half. Nothing. We know this mail order game as no two people in the world know it. And it's in its infancy. I know the technical side of it. You know the human side of it. I tell you that in five years' time you and I can be a national power. Not merely the heads of a prosperous mail order business, but figures in finance. See what's happened to Haynes-Cooper in the last five years! Why, it's incredible. It's grotesque. And it's nothing to what you and I can do, working together. You know people, somehow. You've a genius for sensing their wants, or feelings, or emotions—I don't know just what it is. And I know facts. And we have two million and a half—I can make it nearly three millions—to start with. Haynes, fifteen years ago, had a couple of hundred thousand. In five years we can make the Haynes-Cooper organization look as modern and competent as a cross-roads store. This isn't a dream. These are facts. You know how my mind works. Like a cold chisel. I can see this whole country—and Europe, too, after the war—God, yes!—stretched out before us like a patient before expert surgeons. You to attend to its heart, and I to its bones and ligaments. I can put you where no other woman has ever been. I've a hundred new plans this minute, and a hundred more waiting to be born. So have you. I tell you it's just a matter of buildings. Of bricks and stone, and machinery and people to make the machinery go. Once we get those— and it's only a matter of months—we can accomplish things I daren't even dream of. What was Haynes-Cooper fifteen years ago? What was the North American Cloak and Suit Company? The Peter Johnston Stores, of New York? Wells-Kayser? Nothing. They didn't exist. And this year Haynes-Cooper is declaring a twenty-five per cent dividend. Do you get what that means? But of course you do. That's the wonder of it. I never need explain things to you. You've a genius for understanding."

Fanny had been sitting back in her chair, crouching almost, her eyes fixed upon the man's face, so terrible in its earnestness and indomitable strength. When he stopped talking now, and stood looking down at her, she rose, too, her eyes still on his face. She was twisting the fingers of one hand in the fingers of the other, in a frightened sort of way.

"I'm not really a business woman. I—wait a minute, please—I have a knack of knowing what people are thinking and wanting. But that isn't business."

"It isn't, eh? It's the finest kind of business sense. It's the thing the bugs call psychology, and it's as necessary to-day as capital was yesterday. You can get along without the last. You can't without the first. One can be acquired. The other you've got to be born with."

"But I—you know, of late, it's only the human side of it that has appealed to me. I don't know why. I seem to have lost interest in the actual mechanics of it."

Fenger stood looking at her, his head lowered. A scarlet stripe, that she had never noticed before, seemed to stand out suddenly, like a welt, on his forehead. Then he came toward her. She raised her hand in a little futile gesture. She took an involuntary step backward, encountered the chair she had just left, and sank into it coweringly. She sat there, looking up at him, fascinated. His hand, on the wing of the great chair, was shaking. So, too, was his voice.

"Fanny, Katherine's not here."

Fanny still looked up at him, wordlessly.

"Katherine left here yesterday. She's in town." Then, at the look in her face, "She was here when I telephoned you yesterday. Late yesterday afternoon she had one of her fantastic notions. She insisted that she must go into town. It was too cold for her here. Too damp. Too—well, she went. And I let her go. And I didn't telephone you again. I wanted you to come."

Fanny Brandeis, knowing him, must have felt a great qualm of terror and helplessness. But she was angry,

" 'You nervy little devil, you!' "

—*Page 301*

too, a wholesome ingredient in a situation such as this.
The thing she said and did now was inspired. She
laughed—a little uncertainly, it is true—but still she
laughed. And she said, in a matter-of-fact tone:

"Well, I must say that's a rather shabby trick. Still,
I suppose the tired business man has got to have his
little melodrama. What do I do? H'm? Beat my
breast and howl? Or pound on the door panel?"

Fenger stood looking at her. "Don't laugh at me,
Fanny."

She stood up, still smiling. It was rather a brilliant
piece of work. Fenger, taken out of himself though
he was, still was artist enough to appreciate it.

"Why not laugh," she said, "if I'm amused? And
I am. Come now, Mr. Fenger. Be serious. And let's
get back to the billions. I want to catch the five-fif-
teen."

"I *am* serious."

"Well, if you expect me to play the hunted heroine,.
I'm sorry." She pointed an accusing finger at him.
"I know now. You're quitting Haynes-Cooper for
the movies. And this is a rehearsal for a vampire
film."

"You nervy little devil, you!" He reached out with
one great, irresistible hand and gripped her shoulder.
"You wonderful, glorious girl!" The hand that gripped
her shoulder swung her to him. She saw his face with
veins she had never noticed before standing out, in
knots, on his temples, and his eyes were fixed and queer.
And he was talking, rather incoherently, and rapidly.
He was saying the same thing over and over again:
"I'm crazy about you. I've been looking for a woman
like you—all my life. I'm crazy about you. I'm
crazy——"

And then Fanny's fine composure and self-control
fled, and she thought of her mother. She began to
struggle, too, and to say, like any other girl, "Let me

go! Let me go! You're hurting me. Let me go! You! You!"

And then, quite clearly, from that part of her brain where it had been tucked away until she should need it, came Clarence Heyl's whimsical bit of advice. Her mind released it now, complete.

"If you double your fist this way, and tuck your thumb alongside, like that, and aim for this spot right here, about two inches this side of the chin, bringing your arm back and up quickly, like a piston, the person you hit will go down, limp. There's a nerve right here that communicates with the brain. The blow makes you see stars, and bright lights——"

She went limp in his arms. She shut her eyes, flutteringly. "All men—like you—have a yellow streak," she whispered, and opened her eyes, and looked up at him, smiling a little. He relaxed his hold, in surprise and relief. And with her eyes on that spot barely two inches to the side of the chin she brought her right arm down, slowly, slowly, fist doubled, and then up like a piston—snap! His teeth came together with a sharp little crack. His face, in that second, was a comic mask, surprised, stunned, almost idiotic. Then he went down, as Clarence Heyl had predicted, limp. Not with a crash, but slowly, crumpingly, so that he almost dragged her with him.

Fanny stood looking down at him a moment. Then she wiped her mouth with the back of her hand. She walked out of the room, and down the hall. She saw the little Jap dart suddenly back from a doorway, and she stamped her foot and said, "S-s-cat!" as if he had been a rat. She gathered up her hat and bag from the hall table, and so, out of the door, and down the walk, to the road. And then she began to run. She ran, and ran, and ran. It was a longish stretch to the pretty, vine-covered station. She seemed unconscious of fatigue, or distance. She must have been at least a half hour on the way. When she reached the station the ticket agent told her there was no train until six. So she waited, quietly. She put on her hat (she had carried it in her hand all the way) and patted her hair into place. When the train came she found a seat quite alone, and sank into its corner, and rested her head against her open palm. It was not until then that she felt a stab of pain. She looked at her hand, and saw that the skin of her knuckles was bruised and bleeding.

"Well, if this," she said to herself, "isn't the most idiotic thing that ever happened to a woman outside a near-novel."

She looked at her knuckles, critically, as though the hand belonged to some one else. Then she smiled. And even as she smiled a great lump came into her throat, and the bruise blurred before her eyes, and she was crying rackingly, relievedly, huddled there in her red plush corner.

## CHAPTER EIGHTEEN

I T was eight o'clock when she let herself into her
apartment. She had given the maid a whole holiday. When Fanny had turned on the light in her little
hallway she stood there a moment, against the door,
her hand spread flat against the panel. It was almost
as though she patted it, lovingly, gratefully. Then
she went on into the living room, and stood looking at
its rosy lamplight. Then, still as though seeing it all
for the first time, into her own quiet, cleanly bedroom,
with its cream enamel, and the chaise longue that she
had had cushioned in rose because it contrasted so be-
comingly with her black hair. And there, on her dressing table, propped up against the brushes and bottles,
was the yellow oblong of a telegram. From Theodore
of course. She opened it with a rush of happiness. It
was like a loving hand held out to her in need. It was
a day letter.

> "We sail Monday on the *St. Paul*. Mizzi is with
> me. I broke my word to you. But you lied to me
> about the letters. I found them the week before the
> concert. I shall bring her back with me or stay to
> fight for Germany. Forgive me, dear sister."

Just fifty words. His thrifty German training.
"No!" cried Fanny, aloud. "No! No!" And the
cry quavered and died away, and another took its place,
and it, too, gave way to another, so that she was moan-
ing as she stood there with the telegram in her shaking hand. She read it again, her lips moving, as old

people sometimes read. Then she began to whimper, with her closed fist over her mouth, her whole body shaking. All her fine courage gone now; all her rigid self-discipline; all her iron determination. She was not a tearful woman. And she had wept much on the train. So the thing that wrenched and shook her now was all the more horrible because of its soundlessness. She walked up and down the room, pushing her hair back from her forehead with the flat of her hand. From time to time she smoothed out the crumpled yellow slip of paper and read it again. Her mind, if you could have seen into it, would have presented a confused and motley picture. Something like this: But his concert engagements? . . . That was what had happened to Bauer. . . . How silly he had looked when her fist met his jaw. . . . It had turned cold; why didn't they have steam on? The middle of October. . . . Teddy, how could you do it! How could you do it! . . . Was he still lying in a heap on the floor? But of course the sneaking little Jap had found him. . . . Somebody to talk to. That was what she wanted. Some one to talk to. . . .

Some one to talk to. She stood there, in the middle of her lamp-lighted living room, and she held out her hands in silent appeal. Some one to talk to. In her mind she went over the list of those whose lives had touched hers in the last few crowded years. Fenger, Fascinating Facts, Ella Monahan, Nathan Haynes; all the gay, careless men and women she had met from time to time through Fenger and Fascinating Facts. Not one of them could she turn to now.

Clarence Heyl. She breathed a sigh of relief. Clarence Heyl. He had helped her once, to-day. And now, for the second time, something that he had said long before came from its hiding place in her subconscious mind. She had said:

"Some days I feel I've got to walk out of the office,

and down the street, without a hat, and on and on, walking and walking, and running and running till I come to the horizon."

And Heyl had answered, in his quiet, reassuring way: "Some day that feeling will get too strong for you. When that time comes get on a train marked Denver. From there take another to Estes Park. That's the Rocky Mountains, where the horizon lives and has its being. Ask for Heyl's place. They'll hand you from one to the other. I may be there, but more likely I shan't. The key's in the mail box, tied to a string. You'll find a fire laid with fat pine knots. My books are there. The bedding's in the cedar chest. And the mountains will make you clean and whole again; and the pines . . ."

Fanny went to the telephone. Trains for Denver. She found the road she wanted, and asked for information. She was on her own ground here. All her life she had had to find her own trains, check her own trunks, plan her journeys. Sometimes she had envied the cotton-wool women who had had all these things done for them, always.

One-half of her mind was working clearly and coolly. The other half was numb. There were things to be done. They would take a day. More than a day, but she would neglect most of them. She must notify the office. There were tickets to be got. Reservations. Money at the bank. Packing. When the maid came in at eleven Fanny had suitcases and bags out, and her bedroom was strewn with shoes, skirts, coats.

Late Monday afternoon Fenger telephoned. She did not answer. There came a note from him, then a telegram. She did not read them. Tuesday found her on a train bound for Colorado. She remembered little of the first half of her journey. She had brought with her books and magazines, and she must have read them, but her mind had evidently retained nothing of what she had read. She must have spent hours looking out of the window, for she remembered, long afterward, the endlessness and the monotony of the Kansas prairies. They soothed her. She was glad there were no bits of autumnal woodland, no tantalizing vistas, nothing to break the flat and boundless immensity of it. Here was something big, and bountiful, and real, and primal. Good Kansas dirt. Miles of it. Miles of it. She felt she would like to get out and tramp on it, hard.

"Pretty cold up there in Estes Park," the conductor had said. "Been snowing up in the mountains."

She had arranged to stop in Denver only long enough to change trains. A puffy little branch line was to take her from Denver to Loveland, and there, she had been told, one of the big mountain-road steam automobiles would take her up the mountains to her destination. For one as mentally alert as she normally was, the exact location of that destination was very hazy in her mind. Heyl's place. That was all. Ordinarily she would have found the thought ridiculous. But she concentrated on it now; clung to it.

At the first glimpse of the foot-hills Fanny's listless gaze became interested. If you have ever traveled on the jerky, cleanly, meandering little road that runs between Denver and the Park you know that it winds, and curves, so that the mountains seem to leap about, friskily, first confronting you on one side of the car window, then disappearing and seeming to taunt you from the windows of the opposite side. Fanny laughed aloud. The mountain steam-car was waiting at Loveland. There were few passengers at this time of year. The driver was a great tanned giant, pongee colored from his hair to his puttees and boots. Fanny was to learn, later, that in Estes Park the male tourist was likely to be puny, pallid, and unattractive when compared to the tall, slim, straight, khaki-clad youth, browned by the sun, and the wind, and the dust, who drives his steamer up and down the perilous mountain roads with more dexterity than the charioteering gods ever displayed on Olympus.

Fanny got the seat beside this glorious person. The steamer was a huge vehicle, boasting five rows of seats, and looking very much like a small edition of the sight-seeing cars one finds in tourist-infested cities.

"Heyl's place," said Fanny. Suppose it failed to work!

Said the blond god, "Stopping at the Inn overnight, I s'pose."

"Why—I don't know," faltered Fanny. "Can't I go right on to—to—Heyl's place?"

"Can." Mountain steamer men are not loquacious. "Sure. Better not. You won't get to the Inn till dark. Better stay there over night, and go on up to Heyl's place in the morning."

Then he leaned forward, clawed about expertly among what appeared to Fanny's eyes to be a maze of handles, brakes, valves; and the great car glided smoothly off, without a bump, without a jar. Fanny took a long breath.

There is no describing a mountain. One uses words, and they are futile. And the Colorado Rockies, in October, when the aspens are turning! Well, aspens turn gold in October. People who have seen an aspen grove in October believe in fairies. And such people need no clumsy descriptive passages to aid their fancies. You others who have not seen it? There shall be no poor weaving together of words. There shall be no description of orange and mauve and flame-colored sunsets, no juggling with mists and clouds, and sunrises and purple mountains. Mountain dwellers and mountain lovers are a laconic tribe. They know the futility of words.

But the effect of the mountains on Fanny Brandeis.

That is within our province. In the first place, they
made her hungry. That was the crisp, heady air. The
mountain road, to one who has never traveled it, is a
thing of delicious thrills and near-terror. A narrow,
perilous ribbon of road, cut in the side of the rock itself; a road all horseshoe curves and hairpin twists.
Fanny found herself gasping. But that passed after
a time. Big Thompson canyon leaves no room for petty
terror. And the pongee person was so competent, so
quietly sure, so angularly graceful among his brakes
and levers. Fanny stole a side glance at him now and
then. He looked straight ahead. When you drive a
mountain steamer you do look straight ahead. A
glance to the right or left is so likely to mean death,
or at best a sousing in the Thompson that foams and
rushes below.

Fanny ventured a question. "Do you know Mr.
Heyl?"

"Heyl? Took him down day before yesterday."

"Down?"

"To the village. He's gone back east."

Fanny was not quite sure whether the pang she felt
was relief or consternation.

At Estes village the blond god handed her over to
a twin charioteer who would drive her up the mountain
road to the Inn that nestled in a valley nine thousand
feet up the mountain. It was a drive Fanny never forgot. Fenger, Ted, Haynes-Cooper, her work, her
plans, her ambitions, seemed to dwindle to puny insig-
nificance beside the vast grandeur that unfolded before
her at every fresh turn in the road. Up they went,
and up, and up, and the air was cold, but without a
sting in it. It was dark when the lights of the Inn
twinkled out at them. The door was thrown open as
they swung up the curve to the porch. A great log
fire glowed in the fireplace. The dining room held only
a dozen people, or thereabouts—a dozen weary, healthy

people, in corduroys and sweaters and boots, whose cleanly talk was all about climbing and fishing, and horseback rides and trails. And it was fried chicken night at the Inn. Fanny thought she was too utterly tired to eat, until she began to eat, and then she thought she was too hungry ever to stop. After dinner she sat, for a moment, before the log fire in the low-ceilinged room, with its log walls, its rustic benches, and its soft-toned green and brown cushions. She forgot to be unhappy. She forgot to be anything but deliciously drowsy. And presently she climbed the winding stair whose newel post was a fire-marked tree trunk, richly colored, and curiously twisted. And so to her lamp-lighted room, very small, very clean, very quiet. She opened her window and looked out at the towering mass that was Long's Peak, and at the stars, and she heard the busy little brook that scurries through the Inn yard on its way from the mountain to the valley. She undressed quickly, and crept into bed, meaning to be very, very miserable indeed. And the next thing she knew it was morning. A blue and gold October morning. And the mountains!—but there is no describing a mountain. One uses words, and they are futile. Fanny viewed them again, from her window, between pauses in dressing. And she meant, privately, to be miserable again. But she could only think, somehow, of bacon and eggs, and coffee, and muffins.

## CHAPTER NINETEEN

H EYL'S place. Fanny stood before it, key in hand (she had found it in the mail box, tied to a string), and she had a curious and restful feeling, as if she had come home, after long wanderings. She smiled, whimsically, and repeated her lesson to herself:

"The fire's laid in the fireplace with fat pine knots that will blaze up at the touch of a match. My books are there, along the wall. The bedding's in the cedar chest, and the lamps are filled. There's tinned stuff in the pantry. And the mountains are there, girl, to make you clean and whole again. . . ."

She stepped up to the little log-pillared porch and turned the key in the lock. She opened the door wide, and walked in. And then she shut her eyes for a moment. Because, if it shouldn't be true——

But there was a fire laid with fat pine knots. She walked straight over to it, and took her box of matches from her bag, struck one, and held it to the wood. They blazed like a torch. Books! Along the four walls, books. Fat, comfortable, used-looking books. Hundreds of them. A lamp on the table, and beside it a pipe, blackened from much use. Fanny picked it up, smiling. She held it a moment in her hand, as though she expected to find it still warm.

"It's like one of the fairy tales," she thought, "the kind that repeats and repeats. The kind that says, 'and she went into the next room, and it was as the good fairy had said.'"

There's tinned stuff in the pantry. She went into the tiny kitchen and opened the pantry door cautiously, being wary of mice. But it met her eye in spotless array. Orderly rows of tins. Orderly rows of bottles. Coffee. Condensed milk. Beans. Spaghetti. Flour. Peaches. Pears.

Off the bedroom there was an absurdly adequate little bathroom, with a zinc tub and an elaborate water-heating arrangement.

Fanny threw back her head and laughed as she hadn't laughed in months. "Wild life in the Rockies," she said aloud. She went back to the book-lined living room. The fire was crackling gloriously. It was a many-windowed room, and each window framed an enchanting glimpse of mountain, flaming with aspens up to timber-line, and snow-capped at the top. Fanny decided to wait until the fire had died down to a coalbed. Then she banked it carefully, put on a heavy sweater and a cap, and made for the outdoors. She struck out briskly, tenderfoot that she was. In five minutes she was panting. Her heart was hammering suffocatingly. Her lungs ached. She stopped, trembling. Then she remembered. The altitude, of course. Heyl had boasted that his cabin stood at an altitude of over nine thousand feet. Well, she would have to get used to it. But she was soon striding forward as briskly as before. She was a natural mountain dweller. The air, the altitude, speeded up her heart, her lungs, sent the blood dancing through her veins. Figuratively, she was on tip-toe.

They had warned her, at the Inn, to take it slowly for the first few days. They had asked no questions. Fanny learned to heed their advice. She learned many more things in the next few days. She learned how to entice the chipmunks that crossed her path, streak o' sunshine, streak o' shadow. She learned to broil bacon over a fire, with a forked stick. She learned to ride trail ponies, and to bask in a sun-warmed spot on a wind-swept hill, and to tell time by the sun, and to give

thanks for the beauty of the world about her, and to
leave the wild flowers unpicked, to put out her camp-
fire with scrupulous care, and to destroy all rubbish
(your true woodsman and mountaineer is as painstak-
ingly neat as a French housewife).

She was out of doors all day. At night she read for
a while before the fire, but by nine her eyelids were
heavy. She walked down to the Inn sometimes, but not
often. One memorable night she went, with half a
dozen others from the Inn, to the tiny one-room cabin
of Oscar, the handy man about the Inn, and there she
listened to one of Oscar's far-famed phonograph concerts. Oscar's phonograph had cost twenty-five dollars
in Denver. It stood in one corner of his cabin, and
its base was a tree stump just five hundred years old,
as you could tell for yourself by counting its rings.
His cabin walls were gorgeous with pictures of Maxine
Elliott in her palmy days, and blonde and sophisticated
little girls on vinegar calendars, posing bare-legged
and self-conscious in blue calico and sunbonnets. You
sat in the warm yellow glow of Oscar's lamp and were
regaled with everything from the Swedish National
Anthem to Mischa Elman's tenderest crooning. And
Oscar sat rapt, his weather-beaten face a rich deep
mahogany, his eyes bluer than any eyes could ever be
except in contrast with that ruddy countenance, his
teeth so white that you found yourself watching for his
smile that was so gently sweet and childlike. Oh, when
Oscar put on his black pants and issued invitations for
a musical evening one was sure to find his cabin packed.
Eight did it, with squeezing.

This, then, was the atmosphere in which Fanny Brandeis found herself. As far from Haynes-Cooper as
anything could be. At the end of the first week she
found herself able to think clearly and unemotionally
about Theodore, and about Fenger. She had even
evolved a certain rather crude philosophy out of the

ruins that had tumbled about her ears. It was so
crude, so unformed in her mind that it can hardly be
set down. To justify one's own existence. That was
all that life held or meant. But that included all the
lives that touched on yours. It had nothing to do with
success, as she had counted success heretofore. It was
service, really. It was living as—well, as Molly Brandeis had lived, helpfully, self-effacingly, magnificently.
Fanny gave up trying to form the thing that was growing in her mind. Perhaps, after all, it was too soon to
expect a complete understanding of that which had
worked this change in her from that afternoon in Fenger's library.

After the first few days she found less and less difficulty in climbing. Her astonished heart and lungs
ceased to object so strenuously to the unaccustomed
work. The Cabin Rock trail, for example, whose summit found her panting and exhausted at first, now
seemed a mere stroll. She grew more daring and ambitious. One day she climbed the Long's Peak trail to
timberline, and had tea at Timberline Cabin with Albert Edward Cobbins. Albert Edward Cobbins, Englishman, erstwhile sailor, adventurer and gentleman,
was the keeper of Timberline Cabin, and the loneliest
man in the Rockies. It was his duty to house overnight climbers bound for the Peak, sunrise parties and
sunset parties, all too few now in the chill October
season-end. Fanny was his first visitor in three days.
He was pathetically glad to see her.

"I'll have tea for you," he said, "in a jiffy. And I
baked a pan of French rolls ten minutes ago. I had a
feeling."

A magnificent specimen of a man, over six feet tall,
slim, broad-shouldered, long-headed, and scrubbed-
looking as only an Englishman can be, there was something almost pathetic in the sight of him bustling about
the rickety little kitchen stove.

"To-morrow," said Fanny, over her tea, "I'm going to get an early start, reach here by noon, and go on to Boulder Field and maybe Keyhole."

"Better not, Miss. Not in October, when there's likely to be a snowstorm up there in a minute's notice."

"You'd come and find me, wouldn't you? They always do, in the books."

"Books are all very well, Miss. But I'm not a mountain man. The truth is I don't know my way fifty feet from this cabin. I got the job because I'm used to loneliness, and don't mind it, and because I can cook, d'you see, having shipped as cook for years. But I'm a seafaring man, Miss. I wouldn't advise it, Miss. Another cup of tea?"

But Long's Peak, king of the range, had fascinated her from the first. She knew that the climb to the summit would be impossible for her now, but she had an overwhelming desire to see the terrifying bulk of it from a point midway of the range. It beckoned her and intrigued her, as the difficult always did.

By noon of the following day she had left Albert Edward's cabin (he stood looking after her in the doorway until she disappeared around the bend) and was jauntily following the trail that led to Boulder Field, that sea of jagged rock a mile across. Soon she had left the tortured, wind-twisted timberline trees far behind. How pitiful Cabin Rock and Twin Sisters looked compared to this. She climbed easily and steadily, stopping for brief rests. Early in the week she had ridden down to the village, where she had bought climbing breeches and stout leggings. She laughed at Albert Edward and his fears. By one o'clock she had reached Boulder Field. She found the rocks glazed with ice. Just over Keyhole, that freakish vent in a wall of rock, the blue of the sky had changed to the gray of snow-clouds. Tenderfoot though she was, she knew that the climb over Boulder Field would be perilous, if not impossible. She went on, from rock to rock, for half an hour, then decided to turn back. A clap of thunder, that roared and crashed, and cracked up and down the canyons and over the peaks, hastened her decision. She looked about her. Peak on peak. Purple and black and yellow masses, fantastic in their hugeness. Chasms. Canyons. Pyramids and minarets. And so near. So grim. So ghastly desolate. And yet so threatening. And then Fanny Brandeis was seized with mountain terror. It is a disease recognized by mountain men everywhere, and it is panic, pure and simple. It is fear brought on by the immensity and the silence of the mountains. A great horror of the vastness and ruggedness came upon her. It was colossal, it was crushing, it was nauseating.

She began to run. A mistake, that, when one is following a mountain trail, at best an elusive thing. In five minutes she had lost the trail. She stopped, and scolded herself sternly, and looked about her. She saw the faint trail line again, or thought she saw it, and made toward it, and found it to be no trail at all. She knew that she must be not more than an hour's walk from Timberline Cabin, and Albert Edward, and his biscuits and tea. Why be frightened? It was absurd. But she was frightened, horribly, harrowingly. The great, grim rock masses seemed to be shaking with silent laughter. She began to run again. She was very cold, and a piercing wind had sprung up. She kept on walking, doggedly, reasoning with herself quite calmly, and proud of her calmness. Which proves how terrified she really was. Then the snow came, not slowly, not gradually, but a blanket of it, as it does come in the mountains, shutting off everything. And suddenly Fanny's terror vanished. She felt quite free from weariness. She was alive and tingling to her fingertips. The psychology of fear is a fascinating thing. Fanny had reached the second stage. She was quite taken out of herself. She forgot her stone-bruised feet. She was no longer conscious of cold. She ran now, fleetly, lightly, the ground seeming to spur her on. She had given up the trail completely now. She told herself that if she ran on, down, down, down, she must come to the valley sometime. Unless she was turned about, and headed in the direction of one of those hideous chasms. She stopped a moment, peering through the snow curtain, but she could see nothing. She ran on lightly, laughing a little. Then her feet met a projection, she stumbled, and fell flat over a slab of wood that jutted out of the ground. She lay there a moment, dazed. Then she sat up, and bent down to look at this thing that had tripped her. Probably a tree trunk. Then she must be near timberline. She bent closer. It was a rough wooden slab. Closer still. There were words carved on it. She lay flat and managed to make them out painfully.

"Here lies Sarah Cannon. Lay to rest, and died alone, April 26, 1893."

Fanny had heard the story of Sarah Cannon, a stern spinster who had achieved the climb to the Peak, and who had met with mishap on the down trail. Her guide had left her to go for help. When the relief party returned, hours later, they had found her dead.

Fanny sprang up, filled with a furious energy. She felt strangely light and clear-headed. She ran on, stopped, ran again. Now she was making little short runs here and there. It was snowing furiously, vindictively. It seemed to her that she had been running for hours. It probably was minutes. Suddenly she sank down, got to her feet again, stumbled on perhaps a dozen paces, and sank down again. It was as though her knees had turned liquid. She lay there, with her eyes shut.

"I'm just resting," she told herself. "In a minute I'll go on. In a minute. After I've rested."

"Hallo-o-o-o!" from somewhere on the other side of the snow blanket. "Hallo-o-o-o!"

Fanny sat up, helloing shrilly, hysterically. She got to her feet, staggeringly. And Clarence Heyl walked toward her.

"You ought to be spanked for this," he said.

Fanny began to cry weakly. She felt no curiosity as to his being there. She wasn't at all sure that he actually was there, for that matter. At that thought she dug a frantic hand into his arm. He seemed to understand, for he said, "It's all right. I'm real enough. Can you walk?"

"Yes." But she tried it and found she could not. She decided she was too tired to care. "I stumbled over a thing—a horrible thing—a gravestone. And I must have hurt my leg. I didn't know——"

She leaned against him, a dead weight. "Tell you what," said Heyl, cheerfully. "You wait here. I'll go on down to Timberline Cabin for help, and come back."

"You couldn't manage it—alone? If I tried? If I tried to walk?"

"Oh, impossible." His tone was brisk. "Now you sit right down here." She sank down obediently. She felt a little sorry for herself, and glad, too, and queer, and not at all cold. She looked up at him dumbly. He was smiling. "All right?"

She nodded. He turned abruptly. The snow hid him from sight at once.

"Here lies Sarah Cannon. Lay to rest and died alone, April 26, 1893."

She sank down, and pillowed her head on her arms. She knew that this was the end. She was very drowsy, and not at all sad. Happy, if anything.

"You didn't really think I'd leave you, did you, Fan?"

She opened her eyes. Heyl was there. He reached down, and lifted her lightly to her feet. "Timberline

Cabin's not a hundred yards away. I just did it to try
you."

She had spirit enough left to say, "Beast."

Then he swung her up, and carried her down the
trail. He carried her, not in his arms, as they do it
in books and in the movies. He could not have gone a
hundred feet that way. He carried her over his shoulder, like a sack of meal, by one arm and one leg, I regret to say. Any boy scout knows that trick, and will
tell you what I mean. It is the most effectual carrying
method known, though unromantic.

And so they came to Timberline Cabin, and Albert
Edward Cobbins was in the doorway. Heyl put her
down gently on the bench that ran alongside the table.
The hospitable table that bore two smoking cups of
tea. Fanny's lips were cracked, and the skin was
peeled from her nose, and her hair was straggling and
her eyes red-rimmed. She drank the tea in great
gulps. And then she went into the tiny bunkroom,
and tumbled into one of the shelf-bunks, and slept.

When she awoke she sat up in terror, and bumped
her head against the bunk above, and called, "Clancy!"

"Yep!" from the next room. He came to the door.
The acrid smell of their pipes was incense in her nostrils. "Rested?"

"What time is it?"

"Seven o'clock. Dinner time. Ham and eggs."

She got up stiffly, and bathed her roughened face,
and produced a powder pad (they carry them in the
face of danger, death, and dissolution) and dusted it
over her scaly nose. She did her hair—her vigorous,
abundant hair that shone in the lamplight, pulled down
her blouse, surveyed her torn shoes ruefully, donned
the khaki skirt that Albert Edward had magically produced from somewhere to take the place of her breeches.
She dusted her shoes with a bit of rag, regarded herself
steadily in the wavering mirror, and went in.

The two men were talking quietly. Albert Edward was moving deftly from stove to table. They both looked up as she came in, and she looked at Heyl. Their eyes held.

Albert Edward was as sporting a gentleman as the late dear king whose name he bore. He went out to tend Heyl's horse, he said. It was little he knew of horses, and he rather feared them, as does a sailing man. But he went, nevertheless.

Heyl still looked at Fanny, and Fanny at him.

"It's absurd," said Fanny. "It's the kind of thing that doesn't happen."

"It's simple enough, really," he answered. "I saw Ella Monahan in Chicago, and she told me all she knew, and something of what she had guessed. I waited a few days and came back. I had to." He smiled. "A pretty job you've made of trying to be selfish."

At that she smiled, too, pitifully enough, for her lower lip trembled. She caught it between her teeth in a last sharp effort at self-control. "Don't!" she quavered. And then, in a panic, her two hands came up in a vain effort to hide the tears. She sank down on the rough bench by the table, and the proud head came down on her arms so that there was a little clatter and tinkle among the supper things spread on the table. Then quiet.

Clarence Heyl stared. He stared, helplessly, as does a man who has never, in all his life, been called upon to comfort a woman in tears. Then instinct came to his rescue. He made her side of the table in two strides (your favorite film star couldn't have done it better), put his two hands on her shoulders and neatly shifted the bowed head from the cold, hard surface of the table top to the warm, rough, tobacco-scented comfort of his coat. It rested there quite naturally. Just as naturally Fanny's arm crept up, and about his neck. So they remained for a moment, until he bent so that his lips touched her hair. Her head came up at that, sharply, so that it bumped his chin. They both laughed, looking into each other's eyes, but at what they saw there they stopped laughing and were serious.

"Dear," said Heyl. "Dearest." The lids drooped over Fanny's eyes. "Look at me," said Heyl. So she tried to lift them again, bravely, and could not. At that he bent his head and kissed Fanny Brandeis in the way a woman wants to be kissed for the first time by the man she loves. It hurt her lips, that kiss, and her teeth, and the back of her neck, and it left her breathless, and set things whirling. When she opened her eyes (they shut them at such times) he kissed her again, very tenderly, this time, and lightly, and reassuringly. She returned that kiss, and, strangely enough, it was the one that stayed in her memory long, long after the other had faded.

"Oh, Clancy, I've made such a mess of it all. Such a miserable mess. The little girl in the red tam was worth ten of me. I don't see how you can—care for me."

"You're the most wonderful woman in the world," said Heyl, "and the most beautiful and splendid."

He must have meant it, for he was looking down at her as he said it, and we know that the skin had been peeled off her nose by the mountain winds and sun, that her lips were cracked and her cheeks rough, and that she was red-eyed and worn-looking. And she must have believed him, for she brought his cheek down to hers with such a sigh of content, though she said, "But are we at all suited to each other?"

"Probably not," Heyl answered, briskly. "That's why we're going to be so terrifically happy. Some day I'll be passing the Singer building, and I'll glance up at it and think how pitiful it would look next to Long's Peak. And then I'll be off, probably, to these mountains."

"Or some day," Fanny returned, "we'll be up here, and I'll remember, suddenly, how Fifth Avenue looks on a bright afternoon between four and five. And I'll be off, probably, to the Grand Central station."

And then began one of those beautiful and foolish conversations which all lovers have whose love has been a sure and steady growth. Thus: "When did you first begin to care," etc. And, "That day we spent at the dunes, and you said so and so, did you mean this and that?"

Albert Edward Cobbins announced his approach by terrific stampings and scufflings, ostensibly for the purpose of ridding his boots of snow. He entered looking casual, and very nipped.

"You're here for the night," he said. "A regular blizzard. The greatest piece of luck I've had in a month." He busied himself with the ham and eggs and the teapot. "Hungry?"

"Not a bit," said Fanny and Heyl, together.

"H'm," said Albert Edward, and broke six eggs into the frying pan just the same.

After supper they aided Albert Edward in the process of washing up. When everything was tidy he lighted his most malignant pipe and told them seafaring yarns not necessarily true. Then he knocked the ashes out of his pipe and fell asleep there by the fire, effacing himself as effectually as one of three people can in a single room. They talked; low-toned murmurings that they seemed to find exquisitely meaningful or witty, by turn. Fanny, rubbing a forefinger (his) along her weather-roughened nose, would say, "At least you've seen me at my worst."

Or he, mock serious: "I think I ought to tell you that I'm the kind of man who throws wet towels into the laundry hamper."

But there was no mirth in Fanny's voice when she said, "Dear, do you think Lasker will give me that job?

You know he said, 'When you want a job, come back.'
Do you think he meant it?"

"Lasker always means it."

"But," fearfully, and shyly, too, "you don't think
I may have lost my drawing hand and my seeing eye,
do you? As punishment?"

"I do not. I think you've just found them, for
keeps. There wasn't a woman cartoonist in the country—or man, either, for that matter—could touch you
two years ago. In two more I'll be just Fanny Brandeis' husband, that's all."

They laughed together at that, so that Albert Edward Cobbins awoke with a start and tried to look as if
he had not been asleep, and failing, smiled benignly and
drowsily upon them.

University of Illinois Press
1325 South Oak Street
Champaign, IL 61820-6903
www.press.uillinois.edu